UNCON IN

Nathan Bulley

UNCONQUERED SON
Copyright © Nathan Bulley 2023

All Rights Reserved

No part of this book may be reproduced in any form,
by photocopying or by any electronic or mechanical means,
including information storage or retrieval systems,
without permission in writing from both the copyright
owner and the publisher of this book.

ISBN: 9798871440391

CHAPTER 1: DEPARTURE

LEGION BASES
1- II Parthica
2- XXX Ulpia Victrix
3- I Minervia
4- XXII Primigenia
5- III Italica
6- II Italica
7- X Gemina
8- XIV Gemina
9- I Adiutrix
10- II Adiutrix
11- IV Flavia Felix
12- VII Claudia
13- XIII Gemina
14- V Macedonica
15- I Italica
16- XI Claudia
17- I Parthica
18- III Parthica

For Rachael, Leah, Sarah and Jessica- and their unflagging patience in putting up with my history obsess

I dropped from the small window at the back of the storehouse that doubled as a classroom just as my tutor entered at the other end. All the grammaticus must have seen as he came in was my right leg disappearing behind a large amphora of wine, then the sound as I landed on the ground outside. I heard a loud shout of rage as it dawned on him that I was escaping. I turned and ran through the long grass with a small feeling of guilt: it was not cheap to hire a grammaticus, even given the wealth of my grandfather. And I was at the same time taking advantage of my tutor's limp, sustained, so the man claimed in one of the few stories that could sometimes make spending time with him less painful, in a battle some thirty years ago. His story was that he fought, as a young man, on the side of the divine Valerian when he took the purple in the year of confusion, when four emperors ruled. Of course, I considered as I looked back to see if I was being chased, it did then beg the obvious question: why had this great fighter ended up in a place like Naissus teaching me about the various merits of different forms of poetry?

My justification for flight was easy: it was late spring, and the first unseasonably warm day hinting at the near onset of summer. I had promised myself the week before that I would spend such a day on the riverbank, beneath the hills that served as a backdrop to the town. And neither parental expense nor tutor incapacity was going to stop me. I could not sit in a stuffy dark room studying ancient literature on a day like this! The heavily wooded hills drew steadily nearer and I studied the Haemus mountains, towering in the far distance, as I ran. The river flowed from high in the range and provided cool refreshment in the heat of the day: I could all but feel the cold water pulsing its way down my throat already. Pushing my way through a field planted with corn, panting as I tried to keep up some sort of pace but at least hidden now by the height of the crop, I made my way to a path that had been rarely used since the previous summer. There had been no indication of pursuit other than a few resentful and frustrated yells far behind me, so I slowed further as I climbed through undergrowth that was starting to turn a fresh green. Spring was turning slowly into summer. I ducked under outstretched branches, breaking twigs that stood in my way and sweating from my run in the heat of the day. The wide river opened up before me, sparkling in the sunlight, and I made my way to the gently sloping edge. My race over, I fell to my knees on the sandy bank, thrust my hands into the clear stream and lifted it to my mouth. I gulped down the mountain water, drinking my fill. And then I sank down and lay back, catching my breath properly as I positioned my head on a stone at just the right angle to be able to see around me. I relaxed.

The sun shimmered on the water, sharp flashes of light sparkling across it. Iridescent dragonflies flew all around as they found new lease of life, twirling on a light breeze that blew across the water. They were joined by butterflies, pink, white and red, that pirouetted in and out of the trees, briefly alighting on new shoots before taking up their dance again. The river was so clear that I could even see individual fish plucking unfortunate insects from the surface just a few inches from my feet. Flower-buds were emerging on stems nearby adding to the variety of colours and movement. I sighed with the sheer joy of it. As content as I could be, my attention wandering, I drifted for a bit before willingly dropping into a light slumber. I was so comfortable that I would gladly save the pleasure of a bracing dive into the river for after a midday sleep.

◆◆◆

I was awoken sharply by sounds nearby, sounds that did not fit with the lazy hum of the summer wildlife around me.

I made out words as I emerged, dazed, from my sleep. They slowly took shape as some sense made me aware that they represented a threat. My awareness sharpened as an instinct for self-preservation took hold.

"No sign over here. Aldis- see anything?"

I recognised the voice instantly: Rassogos. He and his family had had to flee their native Dacia five years since. Their fellow tribesmen had revealed their collaboration with the Romans to the Sarmatian chief who had taken over the area and they had had to get out of the former province, abandoned by the empire in a strategic but humiliating retreat, with a warband in close pursuit. They had arrived with nothing; and Rassogos still carried the burden of that humiliation.

And now it was as if he felt he had to prove just how much of a tribesman he was by his hostility to all that was Roman, as if he could earn his way back across the Danube with his aggression. He was cunning rather than violent for the most part, and I had become the obvious target for his devious resentment: the town's best-known bastard, with an immigrant mother, a sycophantic grandfather and an absent father- who was rumoured to have been a noble Roman. I had no idea as to the truth of this myself, but I had heard the whispers; and so had Rassogos. In fact, I thought, as my body tensed in anticipation of the response from Aldis, I would love to know anything about the coward who had run away, leaving me his only legacy: to constantly fight against these Dacians and their bitterness. If this, this… deserter! (I thought with sudden passion and anger) were around, none of this would have happened. I doubted that there could be any nobility to a man who would escape his responsibilities in such a way.

"Nothing here either", came the reply, greeted by me with relief.

Aldis was Rassogos' right-hand. It did not help that they were two years older. It was all very well being twelve- but fourteen year-olds had a significant advantage in height and weight. The only good fortune was that I was tall for my age, and, my grandfather having used me as an additional slave (or so it felt at times) since an early age, I was also strongly built. So I was near to their height and could escape their clutches when dealing with each on his own.

"I swear by all the gods that I saw him running across the field into these woods." Rassogos' tone was excited.

Several other voices chorused varying responses, all indicating a lack of any sighting. Previously relieved, I was alarmed to realise that the whole pack of Dacian immigrants, keen allies of Rassogos and Aldis, was searching the woods for me. I had never before been so vulnerable, and, trying to remain calm and think through my choices, I raised myself to a crouch. I reasoned that, while the sand meant I could move quietly with ease, it also left me exposed as soon as anyone came in sight of the river. On the other hand, the wood, though hiding me, would also mean that noise was unavoidable. My last resort was the river itself. Though shallow, it had some stretches where it had carved out channels during periods of flood. I stepped softly across to the water and saw from its flow that there was a deeper point on the bend. I lowered myself in carefully and crept to a sheltered point, invisible from above, beneath an overhang.

As I hid, growing steadily colder in the mountain run-off, all but my head submerged, I thought about the course of events that had led us to this point. It had not always been like this. The two of us had become friends when Rassogos first arrived, brought together by circumstance and each an outcast in our own way. A few months after his family settled in Naissus, an old retired legionary had beaten out a square just beyond the town walls and invited the parents of local notables to pay him to provide their children with weapons training. I had been keen and eager, especially once I had heard the rumours about my father. I wanted nothing more than to serve in the legions, sure that one day I would find him whether he wished to be found or not. Rassogos, though, was never enthusiastic about such instruction. His father forced him into it, maybe more for honour's sake and possibly to regain his inheritance eventually. Who was I to know his motives? Rassogos' way had always been less in favour of strength and skill and more to do with sly deception and self-interested strategy. A born politician, my grammaticus said.

Either way, Rassogos and I often found ourselves paired together. It had taken place quite naturally and two groups developed, the Dacians and the native Moesians. We Moesians seemed to find that there was always one of us directly opposed to a Dacian whenever practice was called for and an unofficial count began to be kept each week of who was leading. It was the accepted way of things that Rassogos, as their chief, would always beat me, who often took the lead with the Moesians. As long as it remained thus, all was well and Rassogos was willing to treat me in a patronising way as his inferior companion, despite our former friendship.

I laughed quietly to myself: I would never forget the day I bested him. The look of complete surprise, and then shock, on his face when the tip of my wooden blade drew blood on his chest after I broke through his guard. From that day on he never won again. Probably due more to his own fear than my skill, I reflected, as even at my young age I had seen that confidence is a fragile thing, easily shaken and undermined- and more so with some than with others. His reputation and leadership of the Dacians was set back. After this, it was no longer his way to deal with challenges publicly or without certainty of success and I had heard of ambushes of rivals in alleyways with several henchmen to re-establish his authority. He took to moving around the town with Aldis as company, often with others besides, while I made sure to keep out of their way. Of course, I mused wryly, had I adopted the same strategy then I would not be where I was right now. Our friendship, one-sided as it was, had been lost the moment my sword touched him.

Which brought me back to the present. I thanked Sol that these young men were still not yet clever enough to have worked out a methodical way of dividing up their search of the river. Catching me would only have taken time. With so many of them it should have been easy, but each seemed to be going his own way without any organisation from Rassogos. Fools! I condemned them at the same time as praising my god for the fact of their stupidity.

I froze in the water as footsteps crunched gently in the grass and sand of the overhanging bank above.

Aldis' voice was suddenly very near when he spoke loudly from directly over my head. "Rassogos, is it possible that he went further up the river to the gorge? I have heard talk of it as a good place to swim on a hot day."

Time seemed to stand still as I waited for the response, and I felt a chill- beyond the cold of the river- as a cloud chose that moment to move in front of the sun. The temporary shadow gave me a sense of foreboding, every superstitious bone in my body suggesting that Sol Invictus, the Unconquered Sun, was about to allow me to be caught by my pursuers...

But then the cloud passed, the sun flared once again, and the answer came from a distance. "It is possible. I went up there last summer but there was no sign of Constantine. Maybe he's trying it out. With eight of us, we would have caught him quickly were he here."

"Shall we see?" Another response from a different direction. I did not recognise the voice.

"We shall", Rassogos confirmed, his voice drawing nearer. "Tasius, Synges: you stay here for a time. He may appear when we have left, thinking it is safe. We were not quiet in our search! Then come and join us. We will have him. The rest of us", here, raising his voice further to reach the rest of his cronies, "meet back at the path."

A voice came from further away that sounded like Synges, a younger Dacian who had only recently become one of Rassogos' band: "We will wait at the edge of the corn-field. If he is here, we will bring him to the gorge."

Little realising that they had communicated their plans to me, I felt myself relax as I heard Aldis' footsteps turn and fade into the distance. Looking up, it appeared that Aldis would merely have had to look down to see me- he had been that close. Without thinking but sure that I now had the river to myself, I tried to climb up the bank despite the overhang I had been hiding beneath. I slipped and fell, covering my arms and chest in river mud. I eventually clambered out and tried to clean myself- but the combination of water and dirt created more streaks of grime and I gave up.

I crept hastily to the edge of the woods, making sure that I could see the retreating backs of the Dacians as they moved up the path that ran between the woods edging the river and the corn field I had earlier run through with such anticipation. I shrank back quickly, waiting until they were out of sight, and saw the two who had been left behind making themselves comfortable just a few paces further along, nearly hidden in the tall stalks. Fortunately, they had been facing the other way when I had briefly emerged. I made my way silently along the edge of the trees, moving steadily further west until I felt I was far enough away for safety.

◆◆◆

As soon as I came out of the dense treeline, I could see that threatening storm-clouds had gathered over the mountains and I knew it would not remain dry for long. I could already smell the faint metallic scent of coming rain. I had been hidden for longer than I had realised, and the winds were growing stronger. Weary from the anxiety of the last two hours, I could not summon the energy to run any more and so began the tired trudge homewards. My reluctance was added to by the thought of the consequences that would greet my arrival at the villa should my tutor have reported my absence, and I slowed further as a result.

It grew dark with surprising speed, and the lowering clouds were being blown to wisps over the mountains with the fierceness of the gathering winds. A flash of lightning gave the clearest indication of the change in the weather. A clap of thunder warned that the storm was close by, and drops of rain started to fall. The winds tore at small shrubs. Several were uprooted and blown across the path. Trees bowed and waved before the onrush. The hills to the sides of the valley were lit up with bolts of lightning. I sprinted for the main road as the fields of crops had become treacherous to run through, the tall corn in particular whipping in the gusts with a fury that had already left marks on my face and arms. My earlier exhaustion was forgotten. I was determined to make it home before I was too wet, and before my mother could get too worried. If I had been running fast earlier today, Mercury leant wings to my heels now. The menacing sky erupted, the rain coming down so hard it was bouncing off the road.

I reached the edge of town. Due to my avoiding of the Dacians and the impassable fields, my indirect route meant I would have to make my way through Naissus itself. The streets had emptied of people and I slowed, drenched and tiring. I paused briefly in the centre of town, taking shelter to get my breath back in the colonnaded walkway around the forum. Stallholders, exposed to the deluge in the open central market area despite cloth covers above their heads, had already hastily packed up and were crowded in the space with their goods laid out on the ground. I unexpectedly found myself having to step delicately over vegetables, fruit, dried fish and a variety of other wares. Tempers were starting to fray as the stallholders came into conflict with the shopkeepers housed in the colonnade itself as they felt that their trade was being harmed by the obstacles strewn across the covered path. Customers were few, but this seemed to make little difference to the sense of unfairness. When a butcher started to threaten an innocent jeweller with a large cleaver as he claimed a sausage hanging above his counter had gone missing, I decided that it was time to go. Despite my prayers that the rain would ease, the storm had worsened. Eventually I gave up my wait, resigned myself to my fate, and left my refuge.

Naissus was not a large town. It was laid out in the standard grid pattern that was common to most cities of the empire. It made my route home easy to find despite the rain coming down so thickly it was partly blinding me. A few others were also hurrying to their destinations now, having become impatient at the unceasing downpour: mules were being whipped by soaked slaves to move them along faster and ox-drawn wagons fought their way through the small lakes of water building up and not being drained fast enough by the overburdened gutters at the side of the road. I skipped my way nimbly around these, casting a quick spoken prayer as the temple of Jupiter reared up to my right- laughingly asking that he would protect me from the lightning flashing from the black clouds above. His statue just stared back through his beard, thunderbolts in hand, giving the impassive impression that he at least had the benefit of shelter and could make it even worse if he so chose.

Reaching home, I crept around the back of our mansio, recently enlarged yet again, looking for the rear gate to the second courtyard. Although mostly due to the new boundary of the empire being the Danube, and therefore placing Naissus all but on the frontier, the security it brought due to a reinforced legionary presence meant that a real and lasting prosperity had come to my hometown. So my grandfather, Lucius, always having a keen eye to the future- and, more so, to profit- had realised very quickly that there was gold in expanding the villa. A good, albeit sycophantic, relationship with the provincial governor had led to the mansio becoming the sole official waystation in Naissus for the Roman administration, provider of accommodation, supplies, and, not least, of horses, to those on official business. The expansion had been a necessity as Lucius had to provide lodging not only for imperial officials, but also for the staff required to run the establishment. This included two carpenters for repairs, several grooms for the horses, a veterinary surgeon and a number of freedmen and slaves of all ages. But, for my part, I thanked the gods that the size of the buildings and the quantity of people living there made it far easier to get into the house unseen.

I huddled against the wall outside the gate. My mother had taken on the burden of most of the administrative tasks associated with running this enterprise and had little time to watch over me. I was in awe of her ability and was aware that most of what she did, at least in principle, was for my benefit- so I did not hold this lack of attention against her. Rather, I enjoyed the freedom it gave me. Some wise servant had had the foresight to recently light the torches on either side of the back door. They guttered as the last few drops of rain fell, the storm stopping as suddenly as it had started. I tried to tug my tunic back into shape, ran my fingers through my hair in an attempt to tidy it and rubbed at smeared marks on my bare arms in an effort to remove them. Then I crept in through the gate.

It was busy, people flooding out from their shelters as soon as the deluge stopped to complete tasks they had been working on. I stole past the stables, full of horses being fed their grain. Moving further into the courtyard through the bustle of a late afternoon, I grew in confidence as no-one was even looking my way- but remained cautious lest I draw too much attention. There were shadows as the lamps hanging on chains from convenient gable-ends were being used sparingly despite the forbidding weather, and I carefully exploited the darkness. I heard, over the wall in the main courtyard, a sudden eruption of sound- the loud jingling of tack, neighing horses and shouted commands. Little thinking it could affect me, I turned the corner to stroll under the archway from the stables. After all, everyone knew exactly who I was despite being a dishevelled and grimy mess. None would presume to challenge me. So I continued my progress.

Only to have a fully armoured Roman centurion throw reins in my face, grunting, "Sort her out lad- we've come a long way and she's done a good job. Three more to deal with back there."

And he marched off to the main portico. Three more legionaries wordlessly followed suit, leaving their horses standing in front of me.

I stopped still, astonished.

At that point, the centurion, now some distance away, looked back over his shoulder due to a loud comment from one of his comrades. Unfortunately, he saw me doing nothing and assumed the worst. Spinning fully around, he bellowed: "Well boy? Did you hear me? Move!"

He handed his helmet, the yellow feathers of its crest damp and bedraggled after the downpour, to his second in command and uncoiled a whip from around his wrist. Clearly accustomed to instant obedience, he started to move towards me.

I stammered, "But... but..."

This was the worst possible response- I should have seized the reins hanging in front of me and moved to his command.

But it was too late. He moved faster than the lightning flashing across the hills just moments before, lashing the short piece of leather, scarlet in places from frequent use on his horse, across my chest.

The sharp pain startled me and I stared, eyes and mouth wide in amazement.

And then grimacing at the sting that almost instantly turned to agony, I looked down to see the front of my tunic cut open and a welt appeared, tipped with blood. Anger and fear sparked at once and I turned to run. When I thought about it later, I could understand why he would have thought I was a slave. I was dirty from the events of the afternoon- filthy would be a better word. River-mud covered me, sweat and rain had run freely down my face spreading the dirt, my clothes were sodden and red marks dotted my skin from the crops I had run through, the remains of wind-torn corn-stalks in my hair. There was no way a visitor would realise that I was the grandson of the mansio's owner.

He lashed me again, across my back, just as my mother, Helena, stepped out between the portico's columns to welcome her new guests. I stumbled and fell on my front as I heard her cry of alarm, turning over to see the brute towering above me and drawing his arm back for a third swing. I shrieked in panic and my heels scraped the dirt as I scrabbled to get away.

His arm started to descend... and suddenly stopped. The centurion, puzzled, tried to pull it out of the firm grip that stubbornly would not let go. I scrambled back up to my feet and saw that Lucipor, our huge Nubian slave who acted as a personal guard to my mother, had moved with the quickness that always surprised those that did not know him. He was immensely muscled, and the centurion would not be able to move his arm unless he dropped the whip. He did so, was released, and then spun in red-hot fury to deal with this obstacle preventing his rage from fulfilling its mission. When he saw the size of Lucipor, he checked. But his anger reasserted itself, along with the usual Roman arrogance- this was but another slave he saw before him.

He roared, "How dare you touch a Roman officer?"

Lucipor, swift of action but slow of thought, turned to his mistress in mute appeal. Helena replied, with all the substantial dignity and composure of which she was capable: "And how dare you, sir, strike my son, a Roman citizen, and treat him as a common stable-slave?"

She had taken in the situation very quickly and reached the most obvious and reasoned conclusion. Never was I more grateful for her than at that moment. Even a centurion had to pause for thought before responding to this. None of the legionaries were still smiling at the entertainment. The optio, still holding the helmet that had been given to him, stepped forward to his commander.

His whisper, while unheard by my mother, was clear enough to me: "Sir- I beg you: stop and think. We cannot afford to offend this lady. And though you could be forgiven for thinking this young idiot was but a slave it does at least explain his lack of obedience to your command."

The centurion listened carefully, his hostility having been replaced with a stillness that led to a considered response. He nodded and spoke softly, his anger departing as swiftly as it had arrived. "You are right." He walked towards Helena and, a pace in front of her, he stopped and bowed his head. "My lady: please accept my sincere apologies. It has been a long road, an urgent task and a difficult journey. I am not myself. May we have board and lodging for the night, and fresh horses in the morning?"

Helena graciously nodded. Then she beckoned me to her. "Son: what have you been doing to look like this?"

She spoke loudly, and I drew near, bowed over and clutching at my chest while also on the verge of tears due to the agony in my back, unsure of which hurt the most. She leant towards me and said quietly, yet with a fury barely concealed in her tone, "I dare not ask for the truth, and it would not be appropriate here and now." Then, both to conciliate the centurion and to punish me, she ordered, once again raising her voice for effect, "Lucipor, take my son and get his wounds dressed. In the morning, he will prepare the horses for these four servants of the empire and help them on their way."

That was the last she spoke to me that day, sufficient reprimand for my behaviour in itself as we were usually so close. Not a word of sympathy for my pain, nor a moment of care for my injuries. And yet what had I done to warrant this?

◆◆◆

The following morning I rose early. It so happened that the legionaries' journey was urgent and they must be on their way at first light- so it was yet dark. My chest especially pained me a great deal; but, having been sleepless for most of the night as a result, I had had time to consider why my mother did this. Reputation had built our business. To lose it now, while money was short due to the additions to the building, would destroy us. And my grandfather had been to see me while my wounds were being attended to. He had made it clear just how much damage I may have done, and how exactly I could put that right. This centurion was on his way to Salona, taking vital messages to the governor of Dalmatia- I could not have chosen a worse person to disobey. His words were still loud in my ears the next morning. Again, there had been no words of sympathy; though, with my grandfather, I put this down to self-interest for that was often his motivation.

He need not have worried. The image in my mind of that centurion, wrath transforming features that had already seen one blade too many in his decades of soldiering, his experienced whip-arm ready to beat me to a pulp, the stink of his sweat after a long ride almost overpowering in its rancid odour. This was far beyond anything encountered from Rassogos and his band and, despite being so tired from the day I had had, would probably have led to sleeplessness even without my throbbing injuries.

And so it was that I went to the stables with only two slaves to help me; though one was Lucipor, who did the job of at least two in his own right. This was his punishment for having touched a Roman officer- a truly mild one, which was unusual. But it showed my mother's power over others, and her ability to use the charms she had to best effect. As we groomed the horses, I found myself working on the centurion's. I heard the noises of men outside getting their equipment ready and knew it was nearly time for their departure.

As I worked on the horse, any small appreciation of my wrongdoing withered as the frustration of how I had been treated grew. Working with slaves. Whipped like an animal. My own mother all but disowning me. And then my vigorous movements, becoming stronger with my increasing temper, reopened the wound on my chest, and blood seeped through the dressing. As I bent to do up the straps of the horse's harness, I exclaimed at the white-hot stab in my back from the centurion's second lash.

Without thought, acting on instinct, I reached through a crack in the stable wall into the undergrowth. I broke off what felt like a particularly large thorn, and, as Lucipor lifted a large horned saddle on to the horse I was combing, I swiftly put the barb underneath, hiding my movement from him. The horse's hide was tough enough to feel nothing until a heavy weight was placed upon the seat, and there was no reaction. I breathed a sigh of relief. The two slaves led the horses out and I stayed in the stable feeling a great sense of satisfaction that I would be revenged on the brute who had given me such agony. At that moment, my uncle's words meant nothing; his remonstrations were powerless. My own fear of the centurion was as nothing to a burning sense of injustice, in the shape of the fiery blades I could feel scorching themselves across my chest and back, that required some form of repayment. The best intentions of the night before evaporated in the face of this, as did all rational thought.

Which is likely why I then chose to peer out of a window to watch what happened next- foolish though I later realised this was- sufficiently out of sight that I could not be easily seen. There was much milling around outside, the jingling of tack and the grunts of men lifting and placing heavy equipment. I could see my target, the centurion, directing things from the main entrance with vine stick in hand as he pointed and ordered, my mother alongside him. He was no longer in full armour but simply wore a light tunic and dark cloak in preparation for the journey. It sickened me to see my mother laughing and smiling at his asides, though I knew that she charmed him to protect me. She even placed her hand on his arm at what must have been a particularly amusing comment, or merely as flattery. Even I could see that she was a beautiful and attractive woman, and that brought a power all its own that may have been what saved Lucipor from further punishment. Knowing that she had little time for the Roman military (her acidic attacks on them behind closed doors were another cause of my dreams of my father centring on his being a man of authority), it was then that I started to think again.

What had I done? There was little I could do to prevent events taking their course; it was too late. Even if I ran out and removed the thistle, it would be evident that I had sought to injure a Roman officer in the performance of his duty. This could lead to severe consequences. I broke out in a cold sweat, feeling the palms of my hands go clammy at the physical reaction. I consoled myself with the hopeful thought that it might not work. Maybe the spike would break off and not penetrate the horse's skin; perhaps he would decide to walk the horse out; possibly, even if the horse did react, he would not be able to work out what had caused the problem.

I watched as the centurion marched towards his horse. Everything seemed to move slowly, as if in some unstoppable and gradual torture. The dust rose around his feet as each heavy boot met the ground, the horse waiting for him started to jerk at the reigns being held by Lucipor, his fellow soldiers were already up on their steeds and starting to walk them towards the front gate. Even as the centurion's foot rose on to the low wall he would mount the horse from, I could feel my voice starting to rise out of my mouth. As he then lifted himself from the wall into the saddle, Lucipor handed him the reins. I clapped my hand over my mouth to prevent my shouting out a warning. He rose in the air, swung his leg over, then started to drop into the saddle. I looked away, unable to watch.

At that point, everything exploded into chaos. His horse reared with an ear-splitting scream of protest. It landed and kicked out its rear legs, fighting an enemy it could not see. The centurion clung on, every muscle tensed. A laugh escaped from me before I could stop myself. It was not funny; I knew it was not. But at the same time, it was. The horse bucked around the courtyard, having worked out that the pain came from something on its back. It reached the group of soldiers near the entrance, kicking one of their mounts and biting another in its agony, creating even greater pandemonium. Soon there were four horses pounding around the suddenly small courtyard, hooves flying and teeth fierce, accompanied by shouts of warning and noise such as our town rarely heard. Lucipor and the second slave ran for safety in the house while the legionaries tried to get their mounts under control. Three managed it with relative ease, sawing on the bits in the animals' mouths until they responded. But the centurion eventually surrendered as nothing he did had any effect- staying on was a feat in itself. With great agility and assurance he leapt, landing on his shoulder and rolling away from the horse to save himself from harm. The horse started to calm immediately, though it must have still been in some discomfort, and, after some half-hearted kicks, made its way to a clump of grass in a corner of the courtyard where it started grazing as if nothing had happened. A thick rivulet of blood could be seen snaking its way down the dark bay's ribs when I looked closely, hidden from other spectators by the colour and the angle.

The centurion, clearly a man with some affinity for horses, stood, brushed down his tunic and walked over to it, speaking gently, and then started calming it by whispering in its ear and stroking it. Once he thought the horse was fully quietened, he led it back towards his fellow travellers.

"What in Hades was that all about?" said his optio, still regaining his breath from the exertions of the last few moments.

"I have no idea. I think I will need a fresh horse. And possibly even a fresh shoulder", he said, making light of the pain as he massaged the upper arm which had taken the full impact of his tumble. "Let us call on the surgeon. Maybe it will become clear what his difficulty is. Slave", he beckoned to Lucipor who had reappeared from the villa, "remove the saddle."

It was my second slowed instant of the day. Lucipor walked across and took hold of the saddle. The centurion stood to the side with his arms folded, his face in repose like a rocky, time-scarred crag on a mountain-side. And Lucipor lifted. Even from my little window, I could see something on the horse's back and hear as the words that would condemn me were spoken:

"What's this?" The centurion said curiously, his face more animated now, as he leaned over and plucked the object out of the horse's flesh. "A thorn? How could that have arrived there?"

Then, as if a long-embedded battlefield instinct had been triggered, he wheeled around, looking for something. Too late, I realised he was looking for me. Though barely in view, I was visible enough to be easily identified by someone intentionally searching. I could see, or maybe it was my imagination at that distance, last night's fire rekindle in his eyes, make out the lines of his face tautening into a frown, the cords in his neck starting to stand out as he reached down deep for a thunderous bawl that was accustomed to parade-ground communication.

"Come here now, boy!"

Those words reached into my soul and caused my feet to move of their own accord. I walked out of the stable and into what I supposed- had I any sense of independent thought- would be my final moments. There was no consideration of escape, nor of resistance. That voice was such a voice as could not be denied nor contradicted. He knew. And that was a fact. I determined to take my punishment, whatever that may be, like the soldier I aspired to be. Perhaps he would be impressed and not ruin me forever. Possibly he would only beat me as he could have done last night and leave me to die. I might recover. It depended how many strokes he chose to make. In my terror, I started to calculate how many I could survive, based on what I had seen and heard while hanging around the town's retired legionaries as they played their games of dice.

My mother had walked across to join the centurion, and they were having a conversation as I moved across the courtyard to join them.

"That could have killed me. The boy needs to learn his lesson. The whipping did not teach him anything last night." The coldness of command was back in the centurion's voice. "If you cannot control your son…"

With an equal coldness to her, my mother replied: "Do as you will. He is a fool."

My heart turned to hard stone within me as I heard her. My mother, who had told me repeatedly that her life would be worth so much less without me. My mother, who had been willing to sacrifice her own good for my well-being. My mother, who had brought me up alone, nurtured and protected me…

She added, "But know this: his father is Constantius, governor of Dalmatia and former imperial protector. He will make you pay should you touch his son in any way- especially as you say you travel to his palace now. You take the risk as you will. But I will not be held responsible for the consequences."

I was stunned.

What a time to hear this revelation! I was caught between delight at the news of who my father was and terror should the centurion not believe her. So many questions flooded into my mind all at once- how did the two come to meet? Why did he leave? What led to her keeping silent all these years? Why had nobody told me? Why did we live here, in the middle of nowhere, when my father was the governor of an entire province?

And, above all: was she telling the truth?

The centurion spoke, cutting through the questions that engulfed me. I focused on what he was saying, my fear becoming more acute and immediate than my confusion of doubts and joy.

"My lady: this is a crime punishable by death. If he were a slave, I would be executing him right now for his actions. And what do I know of Constantius and his connections to this household? He is known to be unmarried and without children. I hesitate to call you a liar, as our hostess this last night; but I have no proof of what you say."

Though the words in themselves seemed to be pleading, as if the centurion was seeking a way out of this dilemma, there was nothing supplicatory about his tone. He already knew what he was going to do, and no entreaties or arguments would prevent it.

Helena turned and left then, walking back into the villa. Having spoken her piece, she had washed her hands of me and I felt bereft. Truly alone, I was a lamb amongst lions.

The centurion pushed his face into mine- I recoiled, repulsed, at the stink of garlic that hit my face when he opened his mouth to speak. He guffawed in delight at my reaction, none of the regard he had shown my mother now in evidence. "Well, my lad, looks like your mummy's left you to cope by yourself. No apron to run and hide behind any more; no big black beast to stop me giving you your just punishment." He started to uncoil his whip again, at the same time calling to his subordinates, "Right then lads a bit of entertainment for us this fine morning. Get your whips out and let's mark him good and proper. Don't stop till I call it." He looked at me with glee. "We'll try to leave some skin on him." He started to circle me as if trying to find a place to start, then lunged forwards and ripped my tunic down the front to expose my chest, the bandages from last night tearing at the same time and blood starting to ooze afresh from the raw wound beneath. He stood back to gaze at his handiwork with some satisfaction.

Seemingly reluctantly, the three legionaries got off their horses and lifted down a pack each. They appeared to do so slowly, as if they did not really wish to get involved. However, each found his whip soon enough. They moved to surround me, so I was at the centre of their square. One of them spoke up in a voice pitched to carry only to his compatriots and ignoring me completely. "Right then Antius, how do you want to do this? I'm worried that he might be related to Constantius- and we know that he doesn't treat well those who cross him. Could be the end of our careers. Maybe even our lives. If what she says is true."

My mother reappeared at the doorway. I could see she had been rushing, as she was breathing heavily and slightly flushed; but she disguised it so that only those who knew her well would be able to tell. She was carrying a rolled-up object, and as I watched she dramatically threw it into the courtyard in such a way as to open out as it flew. Everyone stopped and watched as the object unravelled, winged its way through the air and landed, throwing up a cloud of dust as it did so. What was revealed to all of those in the courtyard was a scarlet cloak, such as could only be worn by a commander above the rank of centurion, the golden tassels at the edges denoting rank, wealth and power. What landed most heavily, however, and made a solid noise when it hit the ground, was a medallion attached to the cloak.

The legionary closest- the optio- bent down and picked it up. "By all the gods Antius: it's gold, and has the image of

Aurelian on it. I'd recognise him anywhere; saw him in Gaul that time."

I could tell that Antius was thinking fast. "This is no time for you and your memories. So what if it is 'gold and has Aurelian on it'?" This last was mimicked in a child's speech. And then, snarling, his face screwed up: "This is a mansio, Scipio. Where better to find stolen goods, lifted from sleeping Romans who aren't aware enough to keep hold of their possessions. Bet our esteemed hostess here"- his tone had changed, the previous respect lost and mockery taking its place as he sensed the mood of his men changing- "has a thriving trade in black market goods."

Scipio, being Antius' second in command and the best person for the cloak to land beside, was the only person the commander would listen to. "This is not right Antius. You want us to beat this lad, but his mother has shown us a cloak and decoration such as you will not find in any other mansio in the land, despite what you say- not one that is parted from its owner, anyway."

"Then let's take it. It's not hers, it's stolen. So let's take it with us back to Salona and donate it to the legion."

At this point, the other two legionaries chipped in: "Antius", said the first. "We should at least listen to this tale. It seems fanciful, invented, yes; but can we afford to get this wrong?"

"True", said the other legionary. "If we beat this lad to within an inch of his life, and then this lady turns up in Salona petitioning the governor with witnesses that can demonstrate our own thievery alongside the beating of a son that he probably doesn't know he has, he will crucify us. But, I'll tell you lads"- this being said to the others, not to Antius- "that Constantius rewards men who serve him well. I knew a fellow, did him a good turn, got promoted on the spot. If this boy is who his mother says he is…"

Scipio, who, as it later turned out, was the most peaceable of the four, spoke slowly to summarise. "So… we want a suitable punishment for the boy. We don't know if we believe his mother but think it possible she will turn up in Salona sooner or later. So we wish to cover our backs if she tells the truth. Well, assaulting a commander like this boy's done means that we would be justified in taking him there ourselves, seeing as we're going that way- see justice done properly, like. Everyone's happy."

Helena had been silent while the soldiers debated the future of her treasured son. She could not stay quiet for long and this was her opportunity. She spoke calmly, her breath fully restored after running to save me, and with dignity.

"Except me, of course. Losing my only son while you travel away on a journey that will take any amount of time. Who will bring him back to me if he is who I say he is? And Antius cares nothing for him. He would die along the way and no-one would be any the wiser. Buried in an unmarked grave. No: this is not acceptable."

I was impressed with the extent of my mother's imagination- it went far further than mine. But Antius was about to erupt once again due to the offense she had given regarding his sense of honour. Scipio, reacting quickly to pre-empt his centurion, responded with certainty, "So: you come too."

There was no other way out of the situation. Helena informed Lucius that he would be on his own for at least a month. Lucius shouted at me for deliberately causing a situation that he had warned me about the night before (though this held little unease for me given what I had just endured, and the chaotic thoughts spinning around my head regarding what I had heard). And my mother packed our bags, choosing several horses from our stables that were amongst the best we had. Despite my frequent attempts to interrupt and ask questions about my paternity, and especially needing reassurance that none of it was invention, she brushed off my enquiries and eventually told Lucipor to take me away. He was also told that he was coming with us- my mother did not find the prospect of a lengthy journey with four strange men and only a boy to protect her particularly appealing, especially given some of the ground we would be covering.

And so it was that the following morning, with me reeling from the pace of events and the realisation that, perhaps, my mother was telling the truth, we set off for Salona.

CHAPTER 2: JOURNEY

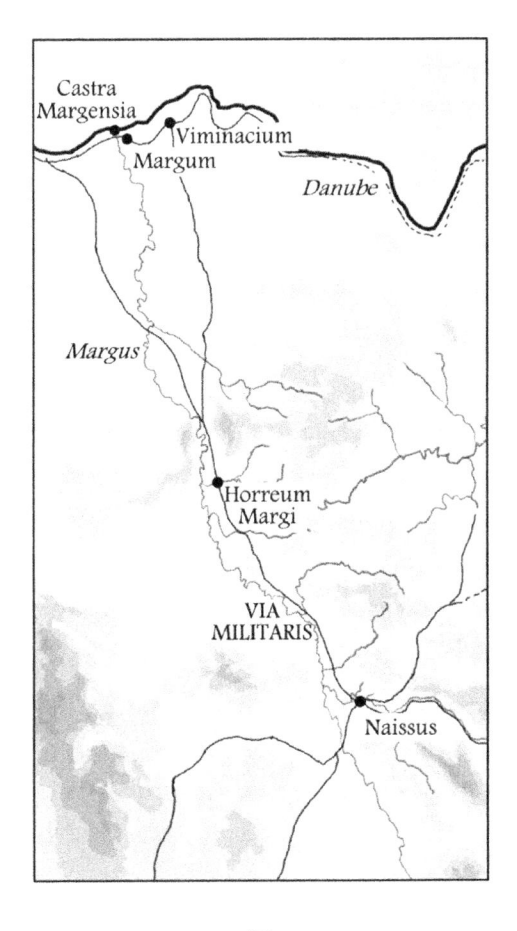

I had much to consider as we set off- and none of it was as might have been expected given my leaving the only home I had ever had, all those I counted as friends and the life I had known so well. My mind was in turmoil. Due to the rush of our getting ready to leave, I had not been able to speak to my mother alone at any point. She must know that the conversation had to be had at some time? Unless she was preparing for the inevitable, thinking about how much she would tell me... But what if our captors were right? What if it was all a wild creation of her imagination, based on a single stolen garment? Where would we be then once we reached Salona? The humiliation of rejection, the dejected return to Naissus, the first meeting with Rassogos on arrival. And this, the best that could possibly happen! It was as if I could see it all- and it scared me. My thoughts had been spinning since the decision to leave was made. One moment: hope and confidence; the next, fear and worry.

For, leaving my anxieties behind, there was a prospect before me such as I had been dreaming of only recently as I hid, cold, wet and dirty, beneath a river bank. Everything had changed so fast. For even I had heard of Constantius. We lived in Moesia Superior and Dalmatia was the neighbouring province. The frequent travellers through Naissus had often spoken of the recent appointment of a new governor the previous year. The talk was of him being a possible future ruler- he had risen to this position swiftly, and was yet young. And the imperial messengers who stayed in our mansio were the most likely to know, for they were the best informed. If it were true, that he really was my father... well, who knew what the future could hold! But... I looked across at my mother as our small band walked the horses down the street outside our villa. She was staring straight ahead, ignoring a pair of neighbours gossiping, even at this early hour, at the side of the road. They turned to stare as we proceeded by, and then fell furiously back to their conversation, now with new fruit for their discussions. As if she could feel my eyes on her, my mother's brow creased slightly. Clearly thinking then, I thought to myself. I would find out the truth. After all, we would have nearly a fortnight on the road together. She could not avoid my eyes or my words for that long.

We were to travel on the Via Militaris. This was the road that had made Naissus so well-known, though in my few years I had rarely set foot on it. This road swept the length of the southern provinces, built to move troops far and fast. It was wide, solidly built and, even at this time of day, would see much traffic. As we were already on the city's outskirts due to the nature of my grandfather's business and its need to be near road-users, the north gates were close by. We passed a few two-storied houses, then the baths and, finally, two minor temples before reaching the walls of my hometown. As one of these temples was to Mercury, god of travellers- and as the sun had not yet risen- I sent up a prayer to him regarding our destiny as we left Naissus, whispering 'Wings to our heels and blessings on our arrival". There was an image of Janus, god of new beginnings, carved into one of the gateposts as we passed through, polished by the hands of many before me. I touched that as well for luck as we left behind my past, for good or ill.

As soon as we approached the heavy, well-polished paving stones of the Via Militaris, Antius called us all to a stop and we gathered around him: my mother and me, Lucipor, Scipio and the two legionaries- who, I quickly found out, were firm friends and did everything together, causing them to be known by their nicknames: Romulus and Remus. No-one could remember their real names, and if they themselves could they were not prepared to reveal them. All four were dressed for travel- armour packed away in their baggage, bucklers covered and hung from their saddles' pommels, swords hidden beneath dark cloaks as if to disguise who they were. This struck me as strange in that moment, but Antius as speaking.

"We will rest tonight at Horreum Margi. You, boy," pointing at me in a forceful fashion, "I don't want any difficulties. You will stay in the centre of the group. You will not wander off at any point, nor will you trouble our horses. You have done more than enough already." He sneered vindictively, "I'd hate anything to happen to you before we reach Salona- I'll be telling the story of your being thrown out on your arse by the governor for years to come. You might find a life in the gutter. You, on the other hand," and here he looked lasciviously at my mother, examining her closely, "I could find a use for you."

She instinctively recoiled from the look in his eyes. The centurion's respect for my mother had evaporated during the last day, and particularly now he had her in his power. Scipio imperceptibly edged his horse slightly in front of my mother's in a protective gesture. A frown started to edge its way over Antius' face as he noticed the movement.

Scipio pre-empted any comment from the centurion: "How far is it to Horreum Margi, sir? It would be good to be there before dark. I've heard stories of the hills- infested with brigands, so they say."

Antius did not want a conflict with his optio and took the opportunity presented, replying, "They used to be. An infantry detachment cleared them out a couple of years back- there's not been any trouble since that vexillation crucified the leaders and sold the rest to the silver mines at

Argentares." Changing the subject, he said, "Let's go then. As Scipio says, a distance to travel today."

He led the way, followed by the three of us from Naissus, with his three legionaries bringing up the rear. The day was uneventful, though I found it fascinating: it was all an adventure. Realising early on that I would not have the chance to speak with my mother due to being in the centre and having no privacy, I resigned myself to that fact and decided to enjoy my new experience. My thoughts being occupied with what I saw would at least keep me distracted from what I really wanted to dwell on but could do nothing about: my own origins.

Though the terrain we travelled was uninteresting, the people we saw were the opposite. From swarthy Anatolian slingers journeying as a band, fast and focused, carrying small round shields and large pouches full of well-chosen stones; to merchants with heavy-laden wagons of varying sizes, weighed down at the axles with everything from Hispanic wines to Samian pottery from Gaul, ready for sale in Naissus. Everyone, I noticed, got off the road very fast for anyone connected with the army. And that was mostly who we saw. The highlight was a quick-marching band of irregular troops, auxiliaries, including some with red hair- red hair! Who would have thought it?- and tattoos in brightly coloured patterns that swirled around upper arms, and even across faces. I soon found that Scipio, who had edged his horse up beside me in a way that made it seem as if he was preventing any escape attempt, was the best possible guide. Noticing how I stared at the vividly coloured hair and the bright blue markings, he leant across.

"Britons. From the end of the world, so I've heard. You've got to go to sea to get to the island. Caesar said in one of his writings that they mostly fight using chariots- but they can't have been that good because they've been part of the empire for centuries."

He guffawed heartily at his own comment.

"How do you fight using a chariot? Doesn't it get in the way? I'd have thought it would be more use for running away from a fight! Maybe that's why they were defeated!"

We started a lively argument about the various merits, or otherwise, of using wheeled vehicles in battle, and this conversation started an unlikely friendship. I both resented and relished this journey due to the anticipation of what the end of it might hold for us. But there was so much of interest that I could not resist discussion. My mother remained silent throughout. Scipio would lean over and reveal a new fact about a recently sighted item of interest, and I could not stop myself asking for more. These scraps of information took my mind off my circumstances and away from the growing pain I was experiencing in riding a horse for longer than I had ever ridden one before. My back in particular was increasingly painful due to the repeated jolting, and my mother, every time we stopped for a rest, would remove my shirt, undo the binding she had placed over it and apply her own special ointment to my injuries. It smelt dreadful, but it partly relieved the pain.

As if sensing that he was building some sort of a relationship with me, Scipio suddenly said, "I've got a son about your age." Startled, I turned to look at his scarred face, encouraging further revelations without intending to do so. "Yes, I have," he said nodding in pleasure at my surprise. "Left him behind in North Africa about eight years ago. I miss him really- he was a good lad. But, you know, when the empire calls..."

Forgetting that my own father had deserted me at even earlier point in my life and seeing some of the attempt to hide regret in his expression, I asked, "Do you ever hear anything of him from his mother?"

"Not really. Don't get me wrong: I think she tries. But it's difficult to find me with any message. The four of us are rarely in one place for long. A letter did catch up with me a while back- maybe three years ago?- and that was good to read. Seems he's growing up."

I lapsed into a pensive quiet, unable to avoid the sense that, whoever my father was, I certainly did not yet know the full story of his absence. It would be harsh to judge him without knowing the facts. Scipio did not seem eager to continue the conversation with further details of his son. After a short while, another thought occurred to me: "What do you mean: 'when the empire calls'?"

He laughed gently, saying kindly, "It's not like we get much choice where we are at any given time Constantine. We are men under orders, and so we have to move when we are told. My legion shipped out of Africa to deal with troubles elsewhere and she could have come too. But it's not an easy life for a soldier's wife. Long absences, delayed pay and a three-year-old to keep up with. We talked about it, and it was easier for her to go back to her family until such a time as I am able to return. I send her some of my pay as often as I can. I'll get back there one day. When I got promoted to this job, it made it even less likely that I'd see her. But it is more money for her…"

There was a sadness in him now. I did not know how to respond. Avoiding his eye, I turned to see my mother's reaction. I had known without looking that she had been listening intently and her face was slightly flushed. She knew why I was asking these questions; Scipio plainly knew too and was trying to help her out in his own way. It just made me even more eager to know my own story.

Each of our party fell silent in their turn, and the novelty of the experience was replaced with the boredom of monotony. I took note of my surroundings. The road itself was a wonder: unlike many of the local streets in Naissus, it was solidly constructed of dressed stones, marked clearly by the passage of time by numerous carts and wagons. It was wide, allowing us to spread out- though, as Scipio had already pointed out, we must make way for any troops travelling on official business. When I suggested we ourselves were on official business of some sort- despite the legionaries' change of clothing- he had moved on quickly, possibly because he could predict that I would ask next what mission the four of them had been on. No-one had been forthcoming about this, and it was still a source of some interest to me. He had hastily followed up by saying that, until not so long ago, use of the roads by anyone other than the military had been heavily restricted; as trade became more important in times of peace, this restriction relaxed and now it was well used by all forms of transport.

Remarkably easy to travel on due to the quality of its construction, not to mention its maintenance, the difficulty was the land the road ran over. Although Naissus itself was in a flat bowl created by the mountains surrounding it to the south and both sides, the road took us out of the bowl to the north-west. It led to steep gorges, sharp climbs and sudden descents. The valley we travelled along was narrow, and we often found ourselves on the sides looking at a drop to one side and a climbing forest on the other.

I was not used to riding on horseback for such a long period of time, and the need to hold on tight made my muscles ache. It was going down the hills that worried me the most. As my strength lessened, I started to worry that I would tumble over my horse's head and humiliate myself in front of the legionaries. Although beautiful and wild to look at, I began to consider the landscape to be more of a nuisance than anything else, another problem for me to overcome. By the time we stopped for lunch at the side of the road around noon, I had enough difficulties of my own to worry about without thinking of how the soldiers would react to evidence of weakness. My head was swimming, my back combining short, sharp stabs of pain with a dull, deep ache. My mother could tell all was not well. As soon as I had dismounted- requiring the help of Scipio to climb down; and receiving a cynical lifted eyebrow from Antius as he watched his optio assisting me- she sat me on a rock and removed my shirt to check how my injuries were progressing. She exclaimed as she lifted my tunic. It had stuck to the fresh blood that had been drawn by the exertions of riding my horse and, no doubt, particularly as I had twisted and turned to get a better view of the red-headed Celts earlier in the day. My desperate attempts to cling on to my horse had also made it worse. She had no choice but to pull my tunic away from the injury and I could not resist a piercing yelp of pain. I heard a sly laugh from Antius, sat a few metres away but watching with interest- "Such a big boy. Crying for his mummy."

I ignored the insult, thinking it made him look more childish than I, and bent forwards so my mother could see the wound clearly. Her gentle, cool and soothing hands went to work, and she murmured endearments to me quietly so that Antius would not hear. I could tell that the injury seemed to have become infected- a rotten, slightly sweet smell came from my mother's hands when she caressed my face after dealing with my back. As a child, I had particularly enjoyed her stroking my face when I could not sleep, and so she did this now to comfort me. I felt better when we re-mounted to continue our journey, though the ache was still there.

My need to focus on staying on my horse and not giving in to the pain meant that Scipio only received grunts in response to his attempts to build further discussion; he soon gave up and went back to his place in our entourage. As the afternoon wore on, I found that the bright late-spring sunlight was beginning to star across my vision. The sparkling chill of the day was the only thing keeping me conscious. I was determined not to complain; so the only indication of my growing fever was an occasional slumping in my seat. My mother's hand would reach across and touch my shoulder, letting me know she was there. When I sometimes took my focus off the road ahead, or from beneath the hooves of my horse, and looked quickly at her, I could see her expression was becoming more and more worried.

The end when it arrived came quickly. She told me afterwards that I blacked out; but I knew nothing of that. One moment I was riding my horse, the next I was strapped on to my saddle by my hands and feet, swaying drunkenly from side to side, with a large bruise on my shoulder darkening and growing steadily more purple. The afternoon then became one long ordeal- made only a little better by the fact that we had now entered the long valley of the river Margus, and the route became flatter and easier to travel. I no longer needed to worry about staying on my horse- but that did not register after a while. My companions told me I was singing, rolling about on the horse in my delirium; then shouting at them to watch out for the ginger-haired barbarians; then in a dark slumber, my chin resting on my chest. As night fell, in one of my rare lucid moments, I caught snatches of a conversation.

"…he's not going to be able to ride tomorrow. We are late enough already- I say we leave the three of them. They can find their own way back…"

This prompted no small panic on my part, even in the midst of my fever. My mother and I would be easy prey for any unscrupulous road-user as we attempted to make our way home. Lucipor could only do so much to ensure our safety.

An appeasing voice spoke up. "I've got an idea, sir. When we get to Horreum Margi, I'll look into it. If it doesn't work out, we may well have no choice but to do exactly as you say."

The instant relief at these words- they must have been those of Scipio- led to me lapsing back into my own world of torment.

◆◆◆

I woke to a slight rocking motion and a harsh smell of some indefinable nature- though very different to that of the corruption in my wounds. It was dark, I seemed to be in a room of some sort, and I could sense another presence. A flame flickered to life in front of me, and I could see an old clay oil lamp lit up in its glow. A face appeared above it- gloomy eyes, a long chin, a puckered scar running from the right temple to the corner of a sad mouth. It came back to me: Scipio.

The face spoke, gently: "We're taking it in turns to watch you. Your mother was exhausted after twenty-four hours of nursing. She's fast asleep in the other cabin. How do you feel?"

"Good. A headache, but that's all." I sat up and reached over my shoulder to touch the top of the whip-mark on my back- it was closed up. I leant towards the lamp and examined my fingertips in the dim light. "No blood." I smelt them. "No infection." I nodded, satisfied. "How long have I been asleep? And where am I? And what, by Mithras, is that reek?" I was particularly proud of my expletive- I had heard the soldiers using it.

Answering my questions in a different order, he said, "You're on a boat. About two days. And the reek is the shields we are carrying- the glue's still drying and the leather's recently tanned. I do not know how much you remember, but after you fell off your horse we had to tie you to the saddle. We thought about strapping you across Lucipor's lap, but there's no way even that hulk could have kept you on, and the weight of the two of you would have been too much for the horse. We realised you wouldn't be able to carry on. We thought seriously about leaving you for dead," here a slight smile crossed his lips as if it were an attempt at humour, "but I thought Helena might miss you." I faintly recalled an overheard discussion along those precise lines and could not find it in myself to see this as amusing- particularly given his informal manner of speaking about my mother. Rather than be offended on either count, I chose to take a different route. "But how did we manage to end up on a boat? I've never even seen the sea!"

This did now make Scipio laugh. "Not at sea. We are on a river boat. I remembered that I'd seen some docked at Horreum Margi last time I passed through. The river is navigable up to here, though not beyond. So as soon as we arrived, I found a local merchant and asked if we could take passage with him to Viminacium. It should be nearly as fast as horseback- which was the only thing that meant Antius would agree to it. And especially when I said I would pay. So here we are. The merchant was sending one of his largest boats downstream with a cargo of shields. It has two cabins, one at either end, this being one of them", he gestured at the walls that were now far clearer due to the oil having fully caught light by this time. "He told me that none of his men ever use the cabins anyway- there's only two of them, and they tend to sleep on deck at this time of year."

"My father will pay," I said confidently, not sure at all if he would pay- or, indeed, if he was even my father. "Can I have a look outside?"

Scipio hesitated. "You can. But it's dawn. Best wait till full light, and then Helena will be awake and I can check with her. She's in the other cabin." Under his breath, he added, "To protect her from Antius, that lecherous old sod."

Fortunately, the words didn't mean a great deal to me- if they had, I would have been far more worried. As it was, I waited with great anticipation for the morning; and was very disappointed when I stepped out to find a narrow but long single-decked wooden structure piled high with round shields made of wooden boards and plain leather that led to it riding low in the water. With little, after all my hopes, to interest me about our transport, I looked out at the river flowing around us smoothly and calmly. It was a far warmer day than yesterday, and the countryside unrolled beside us. It was verging on idyllic, and much to be preferred over riding a horse. I leant at the side, and soon began to feel dizzy again as the wash from other river traffic rocked our boat. I was being watched very closely by both my mother and Scipio and they laid a blanket for me on deck when they saw me start to sway, with a fur-covered wooden block to rest my raised head on in comfort. I lay on it, feeling like royalty as the world passed by under my gaze.

The only sour aspect, other than the foul smell, most of which was fortunately being carried away by the breeze, was Antius, stood close by and looking cynically at me. It was a strange expression: a mixture of antagonism and resentment. It was not helped by his appearance. Eyes that were barely visible slits due to years of riding into wind, rain and sun, combined with a narrow bitter mouth. He was older than the other legionaries by some years- probably not far off his full twenty years' service- and shorter. When I thought about it, and I had plenty of time to think as we drifted gently down that river, I could see why he was as he was. He must have been passed over for promotion numerous times, and this command of three men, though admittedly on special duties, was the most he could hope for. I could guess why he would have been passed over: heavily muscled, but very rough in speech and with a strong accent to his Latin, I suspected that he had risen from the slums of some eastern city with great hopes and ambitions for the future. These would have come to nothing, and he would have been left in no doubt as to the most he could realistically expect of his future, leading to years of frustration. He was not just short- he was squat, and this lack of height must have told against him also. Even these days, there was a certain expectation of what a Roman legionary should look like; and Scipio was made far more in this image despite his scar. Which would probably explain the friction between them.

Scipio saw me staring and came over once Antius had gone to talk to the other two legionaries. He spoke drily, as my expression must have made my thoughts transparent. "He's a great fighter though. You should see him in action. Like a skilled farmhand at his labour during harvest, the way he scythes through the enemy- there's an artistry to it. His size gives him a balance and coordination that few can compete against. That's the real reason he's never been promoted: too good a man to have on the battlefield. Of course, he doesn't see it that way- and he's probably partly right with that too. Though there is far more to him than meets the eye."

"What do you mean by that?" I asked curiously, hoping to find out more of what these four experienced soldiers were about, especially given their recent choice of civilian dress. A hint such as this was my cue.

Scipio once again avoided the subject, as he had on the road previously but in less of an obvious way. "He's clever. Worth getting on the right side of. Worth getting to know in fact."

"I know he hates me. But do you think he would show me how to fight like he does?"

"He might. He loves to show off. But be aware that he doesn't hold back once he starts- for him, there's no such thing as a mock fight. He battles only in earnest."

I left it there. Our journey took another four days and became an opportunity for me to observe new sights in a slower and more relaxed fashion. Through the forests, we caught glimpses of the roads running either side. One, so I was told, took a more direct route to Singidunum, base of the IV Flavia Felix. The other, the route to Viminacium- the road we would have taken if not for my illness, and our eventual destination- we soon lost sight of as Scipio told me it set out to the east on its journey to the city of the VII Claudia. He mentioned that it was also the base of a fleet commander and his squadron. All of these descriptions seemed exotic to me, revealing a world far beyond my previous horizons, and I sat in wonder on the deck in the evenings listening to the men tell tales of distant places and far-flung battles. My mother watched my face and, I suspect, mourned losing me to what a young man saw as glory but she knew to be far less than it seemed. Yet she still refused to fight for me. Our relationship remained distant.

She looked after me, ensured I had all I needed and did all that a mother should; but every attempt to discuss her relationship with my father created an instant tension and her face turned away, her lips remaining firmly sealed on the subject. So I turned ever more to Scipio, as he became a father-figure to me such as I had never had, and our protector against any feared excesses of Antius. Lucius, my grandfather, had never shown any interest in me and I thrived on the male attention I received.

There were some beautiful moments as we travelled: in one small drama we watched, still and hushed, even Antius transfixed, as three orange-chested, blue-headed kingfishers of delicately small size dived together into the river from the reeds on the bank. The boat drifted past them silent and unnoticed. Deer came down to the river to drink, whole herds standing, ready to run at any unexpected movement, as we sailed serenely past. A large eagle descended from high in the sky as we approached the junction with the Danube, its white tail flaring and wingtips rising to arrest its fall, hooked talons emerging and legs swinging forwards to seize a large fish that had been taken unawares near the surface. These incidents were rare, however, as there was much travel taking place on the river itself and this kept the wildlife away. This, though, could often provide its own entertainment. The closer we came to the mouth of the Margus, the busier it became and the more crowded the river. Much outcry ensued from the traders as they attempted to force each other out of the way; but they were for the most part powerless to enforce their enraged shouts unless the wind could be directed more in their favour, or they had sufficient slaves to row them faster than others. Wide, flat grain barges transporting foodstuffs from the Pannonian plan that occupied the fertile land around the river, out of sight beyond the trees, caused the most difficulties for others as they were slow to turn yet took up so much space. Scipio pointed out the wine ships, oared vessels filled with amphorae that looked fragile yet, as he also said, the goods were far more likely to arrive safely than when transported by road- cheaper and faster too. We passed a few boats riding low in the water, single sail spread and thrusting them along slower than most despite their best efforts. When I looked closely, I could observe the ingots of various metals that were showing just above the side despite their cloth covering that attempted to hide them from any excessive interest. It was Antius this time who, looking longingly at the riches passing so closely by, told me of the mining that went on across our area: copper and iron in the main, but there were substantial supplies of gold if you dug in the right place, so he said.

"I'll save spade-work like that for my retirement", he muttered as he watched one ship sail on beyond us as we moored for the night- and then looked sharply at me as if he had unwittingly caught himself in a moment of unexpected familiarity.

As we turned into the main stream of the Danube from the Margus, we saw the town of Margum standing nearby with the small fort of Castra Margensis standing sentry. "Just a few more miles to go, son," Scipio said as he came over and leant on the side of the boat beside me. By this time, my injuries were a fading memory, and they were healing so well that I felt only a slight pull across my chest when I strained forward to look at the town's walls as we passed. "We will have to pull in here at the collecting station to pay our toll on these shields- they will sell well to the legion when we arrive; but the emperor will take his due regardless. Most of these merchants work all but directly for the military, but that makes little difference."

Our riverboat paused to do so, as competing goods transports attempted to get in front of each other and created blockages for everyone else. There was a market in Viminacium the next day, so the officer said as we paid him, and this was always a bad time of the week to try to pass Margum. And then we set off on the last part of the voyage. We arrived in Viminacium the same afternoon. I was awestruck. This was the provincial capital and had been for a long time. I could see, as we came into the docks, piles of wares stacked on the wharves; and we were surrounded by other boats, the largest being cargo ships from as far away as the Black Sea, queueing for space. I overheard, amidst the noise and clatter surrounding us, Scipio talking to my mother further along the rail: "We're lucky. If the squadron were here right now, we'd have to wait for days to find space to unload. We should get priority though- shields are always in great demand and army stores take priority."

A ship bumped into the side of us, almost knocking me off my feet. Antius bellowed as we were shunted aside, "Right lads, give the crew a hand. Hold her steady while they tie us up."

The two crewmen who had accompanied us jumped lightly and easily from the ship's prow and flung a rope around a nearby stanchion. Romulus and Remus took an oar each and we nosed forward next to a stone quay, fending off others competing for our space.

In a week of new and exciting experiences, the rest of this day was the hardest of any to take in. The city was a cacophony of noise- this came as a shock when contrasted with my experience of the peaceful river. I had never heard anything like it. The range of languages being spoken as we made our way through the port area had to be heard to be believed, with foreigners of all shapes and sizes dominating trade- from bearded to shaven, bald-headed to extravagant locks, in clothing that went from exuberant to restrained with everything inbetween, and using words I had never heard before even when those voices were speaking my own tongue. Scipio did his best to tell me where each language came from; but even he was sore pressed for at least half of them. I suspected that his greatest diversion came from inventing nationalities and persuading me to believe they actually existed.

The most striking aspect, however, was the smell. The early summer sun had begun to take effect and to strengthen every odour that existed- or so it seemed. The quayside was a mixture of the pleasant, exotic scents of far eastern spices and the remnants of a substantial population emptying its bowels and bladders into the river. The nearby market selling fish made the stench even worse, taking it far beyond the mere quayside stink. We moved past as swiftly as we could and made our way into the city.

But even there, the contents of the streets led to an equally loud experience. What improved this for me, though, was that I had so much to take in that I, surprisingly, became fast accustomed to it without realising. That was the only way I could imagine anyone continuing to live in such a place. Butchers selling meat from their arcaded stalls; the fragrance of freshly baked bread; the many fruit-sellers marketing their wares from the orchards for which the area was renowned; and the grain merchants having brought the produce of the farms in from the countryside and hawking it in the streets. It was a very busy place. We made our way through the midst of all of this, the three of us from Naissus far more slowly, constantly losing and re-finding our companions due to our gaping at all that was going on. The streets were filled with people going about their business, and, had it not been for the crowds parting before the commanding presence of Antius, we never would have managed to keep up. Wagons were a constant menace, dominating the roadway and forcing us into the gutter; and the beasts pulling them, mainly oxen, repeatedly tangled with each other, or with other teams, in the narrow streets. The noise when this happened as they protested added to the racket. But they were the life-blood of the city.

The other danger was the legionaries that infested the town. The VII Claudia had their barracks just outside, and the soldiers used Viminacium like it was their own personal property. I wondered what happened when the fleet was harboured there in the winter months: the mixing of the two was probably explosive. As it was, they expected the local people to instantly clear the way in front of them. But the locals knew who was an officer and who was not so there was little respect shown for many of those who assumed an authority they did not have. We saw several brawls break out as we walked- very one-sided, as it was still breaking the law to strike a legionary. It usually only took one blow to enforce a physical authority where a moral one did not exist. I had no idea where we were going until we arrived outside an imperial stables, far larger than those my grandfather owned in Naissus due to the size and importance of this city. Antius, once he was sure he had gathered all of those he commanded around him, announced: "We could stay in a hostel here, but I don't very much like the idea of all of these soldiers taking notice of our group, unattached legionaries that we are. It could cause trouble that we do not need. We must be out of the city soon and well on our way by the time the sun sets. We may have to bed down in the open tonight, but that's the way of it. The weather is set fair and should only get better."

I was unsure about this: I very much wanted to explore the city; but on the other hand, there was every possibility that I would fall foul of someone or something due to my ignorance. And there was the reek and noise as well. All in all, I thought I was probably glad to be leaving immediately; a feeling reinforced by the sound as one of the stable's smiths started hammering loudly immediately behind me. There would doubtless be other opportunities in this vast adventure. It even struck me that I had not thought about the questions I was so keen to ask my mother for at least a day.

Antius, needing to demonstrate that we were on imperial business despite our innocuous appearance, set about proving it to the stable-owner by using some form of token hidden secretively in his hand. I tried to see what it was out of curiosity; but he glared when he saw me craning my neck for a better view. His negotiation succeeded, and we mounted our new horses.

Taking up the positions we had been accustomed to on the way to Horreum Margi, we set off once again. As before, and aware of my desire to see and know more of the city, Scipio came up alongside me and pointed out various highlights. The most obvious were the temples, to just about every god that could be imagined. We had these in Naissus, so I was not so surprised; but none of the size that I saw here. They told of the richness and importance of Viminacium. There was a large bath complex as well- I would have very much enjoyed experiencing those, I thought wryly, recognising that I probably smelt as bad to the inhabitants as their city did to me. And, as we came to the edge of the city and just before reaching the gate, an amphitheatre. They were clearly unused that afternoon as the area was silent; however, having experienced a far smaller version in my hometown, I could imagine the volume of sound that would emanate during any games held there. But I saved my awe for the gates when we got to them. Huge, built of massive stone blocks and seeming invincible, they reached as high as I could see when tilting my head back. Antius was waiting for us as we neared the gate, impatient with our slowness and desire to observe every new part of the city we saw.

"Looks like there's a queue. We're going to be a while. Have a look around. And Scipio: hold our place in the line. I'm off for a quick final visit."

He and the twins, as I had dubbed them privately, disappeared, watched by a reproachful optio. "Off for a last drink before the journey. What I'd give for that", he said ruefully.

"I'll save our places if you like?" I said, eager to please.

Scipio smiled, looking over my head at my mother and Lucipor. "Give me a couple of moments. I'd like to ask a guard what's going on. The queue's never usually so long."

He returned soon. "Says there's brigands in the mountains. They're a long way off, but the guards are making sure that they are not going to affect Viminacium. He says to avoid Singidunum if we want a quicker journey. The checks are even tighter. I didn't want to go there anyway- it's faster and more direct to go to the west across the plain, though we will be using tracks rather than roads. With Constantine feeling so much better it should not be difficult. I'll speak to Antius."

We made it to the gates, the rest of our companions rejoining the group suitably refreshed, and were through as soon as the guards saw Antius' token. Scipio smiled at me, whispering, "Yes- we could have moved to the front of the line. But the centurion needed an excuse for a drink."

By nightfall we were well clear of the city and had camped on a comfortable patch of grass next to a stream. As Antius had predicted, the weather was mild, and this led to a pattern for the next few days as we made good progress across easy ground towards a set of hills just visible on the horizon. Even once we passed Singidunum, the smoke of which we could see in the distance rising straight upwards in the still air, we came across no thieves or robbers. My injuries had scabbed over by this time, a ridged pair of hard-edged crusts that would leave permanent scars. Every time I worried at one of them with careful fingers to attempt to pull it off, I reinforced my vow to myself that I would never be treated in such a way ever again. The only way to make this happen was to become well known enough that none would ever assume I was anyone other than myself- no matter how I appeared. I swore this would be the case as soon as it was within my power to achieve it.

CHAPTER 3: HOME

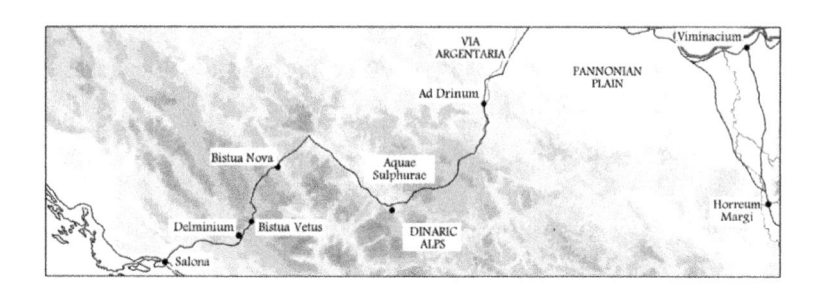

Determined to be able to protect my mother should the worst happen and the three of us be left on our own at the side of the road- which would already have occurred but for Scipio's intervention- I had resolved to speak to Antius about training me in sword-work. That first night out of Viminacium, as we sat wrapped in our cloaks, he stretched his limbs and went about a regular routine with his sword. It whistled through the dusk and cut its own pattern before his face as he strengthened his wrists, stabbed forward in sweeping lunges to break an enemy's guard and then defended with a serious of parries against an opponent's attack. I watched carefully as he suddenly leapt into the air and cut his weapon down fiercely on an imagined foe, the firelight catching the blade's edge and reflecting from the flat. Gathering all of my courage, sacrificing my pride in the interest of my family's protection, I asked in the most subservient yet assured tone I could muster: "Sir, would it be possible for you to teach me your skills?"

"Ha!" He laughed with the pleasure of it. "So the young master seeks to ingratiate himself with his inferior?"

"Not at all, sir. I really do wish to learn the techniques over which you so clearly have mastery." I spoke in as matter-of-fact a tone as I could, so as not to suggest any other motive or imply flattery beyond what was his due.

He paused then, believing the genuine nature of my request and giving it true consideration. "This takes a lifetime boy- it cannot be learnt overnight."

"I know that. But I could make a start. I trained with an old legionary when living in Naissus; but that was as nothing compared with what you have just shown. And I wish my father to be proud of me when I meet him."

He snorted irreverently at the last comment, ignoring the certainty of my words. Refusing to be drawn by my implied confidence as to my mother's claim he went to rummage briefly in his baggage by the fire, eventually pulling out a spare sword. He threw it to me as I stood, unprepared; and a surprised look crossed his face when I dispassionately caught it from the darkness by the hilt.

"Come on then- let us see what you can do," he said, his sword again beginning to inscribe patterns on the night air as he stretched his wrist.

He had, I think, hoped I would fail his first test and clumsily drop the weapon. The rest of the group watched the unexpected entertainment. My mother had a worried look on her face but appeared to decide that I made my own choices now and said nothing. I studied my weapon: a regulation blade, simple and functional. Antius barked his amusement: "It's not what it looks like, boy, it's what you do with it that matters."

And then he attacked, slowly, a blow from the side intended for my left arm- usually an easy strike to block, but not normally for one of my age and with an adult's weapon. My size and strength came into play again, and I stopped him with ease. My wrist was firm as he bore down on his own sword, and it only gave when he began to exert his full weight. He pulled back, a slight indication of respect shown in one faintly raised brow and the lack of comment. More of the same followed, as he tried me out from different angles and with different levels of force. I managed to hold off the edge of his blade for the most part- but struggled far more when he started to use the point of his weapon to break my defence, his footwork making it hard to follow his movement.

We were soon sweating in the warm night, and I was beginning to ache again by the time he stopped. "Not bad at all, lad, not bad at all. You struggle against more skilled use, in common with most soldiers as they train in formation more than as individuals. Same tomorrow night. Oil the blade before sleep."

That was all he said. But my heart leapt within me as I noted my promotion- to be compared with 'most soldiers'! As I made for my bed, Scipio took my arm and whispered, "Well done. He never gives compliments: that was high praise indeed. I'll show you how to look after the sword..."

And from that night on, sword practice was the entertainment of choice for our band.

The other memorable event of that week, though it had little effect on my life in the end despite my anticipation of it, was that I finally accomplished my goal of spending some time alone with my mother. She had been avoiding me. She could not hide forever, however, especially given the limited number of people in our band. As we drew out in a staggered line across the Pannonian plain I detached myself from Scipio, who seemed to have become my constant companion, and cantered my horse forward alongside her.

Choosing the name for her that I had used as a young child I said, "Mama. Can we speak?"

I could see reluctance in every aspect of her movement as she slowly turned her head toward me. In a resigned tone she asked, "Of course. What about?"

"Tell me how the governor came to be my father." I added, in case this should be misinterpreted, "I mean, what was he doing in Naissus? How long did you know him? How is it that he did not marry you?" The questions, once started, poured forth. I was, in my eagerness, at the same time being careful. I did not wish to know too much- though, seeing my mother's brows drawing together, I could tell it was unlikely she would give too much away in any case. I thought I knew all about the performances that women went through with men; you could not be around animals in a rural town like ours for long without seeing for yourself what went on. Nor could you be around other boys, let alone soldiers, without hearing talk of many and varied experiences. I had no desire to imagine my mother in such a situation. Obviously, it must have happened for me to be here. But I did not wish to know details.

She seemed to relax as she realised that I did not wish for specifics and chuckled wryly at the flow of questions. She must have thought long and hard over the last few days regarding how to respond and spoke at last. "My son," she said gently, though with a slight quiver in her voice as she knew the importance of this answer. "I know you have suffered over the years from the jeers of others at your lack of a father. But now you come into your own. There is little to tell. He was passing through. I was an obedient daughter. Your grandfather wished to prove his allegiance to the empire- and, no doubt, for I am under no illusions, to build a future connection of importance. Your father had a look of greatness about him. I have tried to regret the night I spent with him- but how could I? I would not have you were it not for our time together, however fleeting."

"So he did not know of me?"

"He did not", she assured me calmly.

This was a relief. At least he had not left because of me, because he could not endure a squalling child. Nor because of my mother...

"What was he like? What should I expect? And how should I treat him?" As I spoke, I realised with some surprise that there were underlying nerves- even fear- about my eventual first meeting with the man I had dreamed of and longed for. And hated and despised in near-equal measure. I still did not know how I truly felt at the prospect.

She replied simply, "I do not know. It is more than a decade since I last saw him, and then only briefly. He said he was from near Naissus, and that he had risen fast in the army due to a chance friendship with the emperor Aurelian. He looked… well, it's hard to tell, for time mists many things. I remember that he was heavy-set, strong, with a firm and prominent chin- much like yours. But I believe that I am overly influenced by your appearance. You certainly do not take after me in your looks- though you have my height. So you must take after him. It is difficult to distinguish between the two of you in my memory. I knew him but one night only."

"And how should I behave toward him when we arrive in Salona? It can't be more than another fortnight of travel."

"It will come soon enough, true. But he will decide the way of things, and we can only respond to that. It is enough to say that I am sure we will not be 'thrown out' in quite the way that that animal who leads us, Antius, describes." She added this distastefully and with a wrinkling of the nose.

That was as much as she would say. And, while it was a long way from enough as far as I was concerned, I could not draw her out further. I was happy from then on that our relationship appeared to have been restored; and, other than some challenging questioning over my nightly sword-practice with the centurion, she seemed content with this also.

◆◆◆

Days passed. The Pannonian plain, monotonous and flat, ended slowly with the gradual emergence of a series of foothills. In the distance, we could see the sharp, snow-peaked mountains of the Dinaric Alps rising from the land like a series of storm-tossed waves. One evening, round a warming campfire that had been lit on previous nights more for protection from animals than for its heating capabilities, Antius spoke of what was to come next.

He stood, legs apart and hands behind his back, the hard angles of his face defined sharply by the fire's embers. His eyes had a distant look as he imagined what was to come. "We will need to get the extra clothing out of our packs soon. At least a cloak, the leg-wrappings and an additional tunic each. We will mostly be in the valleys for the final part of our journey and so the next week will be the slowest and the coldest- likely the wettest also. My plan is that we will join the Via Argentaria at Ad Drinum. It goes from Sirmium straight to Salona, built to carry the traffic in precious metals- the gold and silver from Moesia that is needed in Italy. It is well travelled as a result, but only at certain times of the year when shipments are sent, usually heavily guarded. But if we do have any trouble on this journey it will be in some little-known pass, likely in the first few days. The road- a generous term, as it is more of a narrow track in places- is also heavily wooded. That is where we could be waylaid by troublemakers. So we will have to travel with weapons easily to hand and remain fully armoured just in case. Not the most comfortable way to go; but certainly the one that gives the greatest chance of survival", he unconsciously touched a gold amulet hanging from a chain around his neck, "Mithras willing."

Adding unnecessary additional drama, he threw another the log on to the fire, causing it to suddenly flare. In the sudden light, I saw his fellow soldiers instinctively and superstitiously touch the item that, for them, represented their faith. Romulus and Remus had rings, each with an image of a bull on the signet; while Scipio reached for a brooch on the cloak he had tightly wrapped himself in. Out of the corner of my eye I saw my mother mutter at length under her breath, having partially turned her face away from the flames. She always wore a headscarf when outside the home; this had slipped, and she raised it back up as her lips moved. It seemed strange to accompany Antius' comment with such actions- but who was I to comment? I supposed, given my strong desire to join a legion when I was old enough, that Mithras, or Sol Invictus- who, from what I had heard, seemed to be one and the same- would be the god I would choose to follow. All gods were equal in my eyes and I would choose the one that did the most for me.

We were all cautious as we climbed higher into the mountains. Our concern seemed to affect the horses, who also became skittish and hard to control at times. We had bought some blankets in Ad Drinum as we passed through, and these served as makeshift tents in combination with cloaks and spears. While legionaries would usually carry leather tents with them, either shared amongst them in their packs or using mules, these men travelled too fast to warrant such luxuries. The wind did not funnel down into the passes too much, and, while we were at no point comfortable, we did at least manage some sleep most nights. It was wet; it was cold; there were occasional flurries of snow, though none lasted long, and we experienced real hardship on this part of our trip as Antius had warned we would. We were at least on a proper road- well constructed, no Via Militaris but with proper planning and reasonably straight. It was not well enough used to justify any sort of way-stations; and so it was that we had to take longer than expected. Our mounts needed more time to recover their energy, and good grazing on the often sparse mountain-side vegetation was hard to find. Encouragement was provided as we gained height by looking back over the plain we had so recently traversed, and seeing how far we had come; though looking forward provided less incentive as the intimidating mountains frowned down on us.

There is little to tell of this time but for one very significant event which changed my view of Antius and gave me my first experience of real fighting. We were travelling through our third or fourth valley- I forget which: they blended into one after a while. It was heavily forested on its steep sides with a stream wandering through the bottom of it, surrounded by narrow meadows of colourful wildflowers. The river paused occasionally, as if taking a breath before its next stretch, gathering in small pools around which the track would run, curving and meandering lazily as directed by the water it followed. The sun glittered exquisitely off the water when its light found a way through the peaks around us, creating a tranquil scene as we travelled. It was an idyllic scene for the most part. But there were also large boulders at regular intervals that at some point in the distant past had come crashing down from the tops of the peaks around us, crushing paths through the trees, though these trails had long ago been grown over.

And it was these rocks that caused our difficulty.

We were halfway through the valley in the late afternoon when Romulus, who had been scouting- not that there was much scouting that could be done given the narrowness of the valley and the lack of alternative roadway- returned.

"Sir", he said to Antius. "I see a problem ahead. The valley narrows even further in about five hundred paces, the woods come right down to our path, and there are two immense boulders from some old landslide positioned, almost as if on purpose, on the track itself. It is only possible for one person at a time to pass through the gap between them; and there is a third boulder a few paces beyond. It is all but perfectly designed for an ambush."

Antius reacted decisively. "Call the others, but quietly. If outlaws are planning something, they will have been watching the entrance to the valley and have a rough idea of how long it takes to get there. Let us talk as we ride- but ride slowly."

We gathered around him, bunching up as if discussing where to stop for our evening meal. I could not understand the concern: everything had gone so smoothly so far, we had experienced no trouble of any kind and had barely seen anyone on the road. Why would anyone waste their time up here waiting for rare travellers rather than the transports carrying precious metals? Of course, I kept my own views quiet rather than make a fool of myself, but I still felt this to be an unnecessary reaction to the distant possibility of attack. A hurried conversation took place, Antius talking through several ways to overcome any opposition. Some of these ideas were far-fetched, such as whether it would be possible to climb one of the two boulders. Others were less imaginative- such as charging straight through without stopping for anyone. A decision was fast reached.

"So. Romulus: you are best with a bow. Give it a moment or two, and then I want you to drop back a bit and shout loudly that you're stopping for a piss. Head for the woods there, tie your horse up once you are beyond the treeline and out of sight, and circle round. You are the only one who has seen these rocks, so you know where you are going. You need to get yourself to a point where you can see all of us once we're past the first gap. If we are stopped by anyone, they will be likely to speak first as they wish to rob and not to kill; it would not do their trade any good in the future to be known for murdering their prey. So when you see me make a cutting motion, like this", he chopped his hand horizontally, "shoot whoever is doing the talking for they will be the leader. Start now."

He continued to look forward as Romulus began to drop back, obeying Antius' direction as commanded and calling out as he did so. The centurion addressed his next comments to the rest of us without turning.

"We'll assume the worst- then we can't be caught out. If there's no danger, we've just wasted a bit of time and provided ourselves with a more interesting day." He grinned. "Bit of practice too."

He seemed to have come alive, as if the prospect of a fight had rejuvenated him, adding vigour to tired bones. His eyes were sparkling with anticipation, and he was a different man with that visible enthusiasm for a fight. I could see why his commanders esteemed him so highly on the field of battle.

"Now Rom's gone, I want us to go through the gap like this. Me first. Then Remus. The woman and the boy in the middle. They'll have someone blocking the escape route, so the slave next and Scipio at the back. Uncover and loosen swords in their scabbards, but try to keep them hidden. Give any spare cloaks to the woman for her and the boy to wear as protection. And don't forget to release your bucklers from your saddles and face them in the direction you're protecting us from." He turned to Lucipor, acknowledging his existence for the first time since our departure. "Of course, your skin will have to be enough. You're big enough for swords to bounce off, I've no doubt." The feeble attempt at humour did at least relieve some of the tension, and there were a couple of chuckles. I noticed that Antius looked confused at this reaction and realised he had not in fact meant it to be amusing. He finished off by saying, "Rom once told me he got lessons off a Persian in firing that bow- and if that's the case we've got nothing to worry about." He said reflectively, "Of course, the Persian might have been a bad shot himself. Anyway, pray to your gods now, whoever and wherever they may be. And… gallop."

We were nearly at the boulders by this point and the last thing any brigands would have expected would be for a slow-moving, exhausted band of travellers to suddenly speed up. We raced through the gap in the order Antius had dictated- and came up short at the sight of tree trunks piled on either side of the third rock. There was brief chaos as we all tried desperately to stop our mounts. Thank Sol, we had not been going too fast due to how close we had been to the rocks on starting to gallop; but several of the horses reared and protested as reins were pulled back sharply and bits caught in mouths. The group milled around in what we now saw was a well-designed killing-ground, completely exposed.

A lithe man swung down athletically from the top of the boulder to land on a smaller rock in front of us that seemed intended to create a small stage. He bowed to us from his perch as we brought our mounts under control, smirking at the success of his ploy. "Welcome to our valley, gentlemen. And- by the gods- a lady and a child! I doubt whether you will be carrying anything of great value given the company you keep. Still, we've started, so we must continue. I am afraid I am duty-bound to relieve you of anything worth something." He spoke in an ironic tone, appearing to perform for the benefit of an invisible audience.

Antius looked around, injecting a note of panic into his voice, "But how can you? We are peaceful travellers." Then, as if noticing for the first time, his voice firming up, "And there's only one of you. There's six of us."

The man, dressed in rough homespun clothing and with matted hair but speaking in a relatively polished tone, frowned slightly at the number, saying under his breath, "I could have sworn...but it was from a distance and you were crowded together...".

But then he shook his head, dismissing his concerns, and whistled. Over the top of the barrier to the right appeared ragged faces all bearing cheerful expressions, presumably due to the success that this ambush had met with. I could see Antius counting, though his face told a story of panic and alarm, and I realised that his response had been but a tactic to get the leader to reveal his men: "No! Will you let us live?" Pleading now, as if in terror for his life. "We'll give you all we have."

The thief shook his head mockingly, "Why would I kill a 'peaceful traveller'? Right lads, move the barriers and take all they've got. Keep your eyes open and your blades ready- just in case." The six men took up positions along their barrier, leaving the left hand one in place, and, grunting, started to apply their weight. They had to put down their weapons at this point despite their leader's admonition in order to use both arms in lifting. As they did so he nodded over our heads to another two men who had appeared with bows at the ready on top of each of the boulders behind us, covering us so that the threat was lessened. As these two settled in good firing positions, relaxing at the apparent lack of threat and a routine they had been through before, the six men moved a trunk each in pairs.

And everything exploded into action.

"Now!" bellowed Antius, chopping his hand laterally. An arrow took the leader in the side of the head. He dropped where he stood, soundlessly, like one of the sacks of sand we had seen being dropped from a dockside crane to ballast barges in Viminacium.

There was a moment of disbelief from the thieves: all the Romans needed. They took advantage, charging their horses at the men carrying the logs. Lucipor jumped to the ground and pulled me from my horse as if I were but a child's toy. My mother leapt down at the same time; and he walled us up in a corner of the killing ground with his body as a physical shield. By this time, the archers behind were sighting along their arrows. The first one shot at the easiest target- Lucipor- and a small shield appeared as if from nowhere, the arrow sinking into it with a dull, solid thump. Scipio, rather than charging the six men, had chosen to protect my mother and me. It was his shield that had appeared. He now turned and threw a knife which seemed to sprout, as if by magic, from the throat of the second bowman. The archer crumpled, hands leaping to this throat as he fell backwards off his rock and out of sight. He had been about to release. Another arrow from Romulus took the first bowman in the upper shoulder as he steadied himself to fire again. He fell from his roost to roll, shouting in pain, on the ground near where we stood.

My attention, for obvious reasons, had been focused completely on these events. But with the immediate danger to us having gone I turned to look at the fight in front. The two legionaries at the barricade were being joined by Scipio, shieldless. Three of the brigands were down and would not be getting up again. The other three were torn- on the verge of flight, but wondering if they could reach their weapons in time and whether, should they flee, they would be ridden down as they did so in any case. The hesitation cost them dearly. One fled; two leapt for their swords, lying at the side of the road where they had dropped them. Antius leapt from his horse, shouting over his shoulder as he did so: "I'll see to these two. Remus- get that other one. Scipio- finish the archer."

And then ensued a fight I would never forget. It was short. It was fast. And it was incredibly skilled. Antius lazily approached the two men, both of whom had reached their swords. They attacked him at once, without saying anything, one from each side. Powerful blows from over their right shoulders, as if that was the only move they knew. Antius leapt back from the first as he swung downwards, and the man staggered as he had expected his blow to connect. Antius ignored the man coming more slowly from the other side and instead jumped forward fast and high, using the point of his sword combined with the attacker's own weight as he stumbled to stab the blade down through his neck. Blood fountained over the centurion as the jugular vein of his opponent was cut. Its pungent metallic scent filled the air. The man died without a sound and slumped to the ground, blood pooling thickly as it continued to pour from his mortal wound. Antius turned, with relish, to deal with the other opponent. The blood dripping now from his face, teeth bared, formed an expression of enjoyment that was terrifying in its appearance. The second fighter had paused his attack and was frozen in the act of striking. Antius had moved so fast that the man's sword would have descended into thin air had he continued, and he now drew back his arm to re-adjust. As he did so, the centurion's sword appeared, penetrating up and out through his shoulder. Antius had, again, approached with such speed that there was no time for his opponent to react. His thrust through the man's armpit had disabled his enemy completely; the commander spun on his heel and with a perfectly timed blow chopped into his neck. The attacker's body went limp and collapsed. Antius, nonchalantly and without taking a breath, leant down to clean his blade on the man's ragged clothes. Seizing some of the poor-quality fabric, he ripped it off and cleaned his face before turning casually back to the rest of us, remnants of blood still untouched in his short hair and in the deep wrinkles around his eyes.

"Well. That was easier than I expected. Any injuries?"

Even Scipio was stunned by the speed with which the end had come. He gathered himself, and then reported, "None sir. There's Remus- looks like he caught the other one." Remus was returning in the distance from the edge of the woods, cleaning his knife as he came. "As for Romulus, here he is."

"Excellent. Who needs gods when I have such fighters- fine shooting Rom. As soon as they put their weapons down I knew we'd win the day without any difficulty." He shook his head in mock disappointment, "A sad lack of training, in my view. I could probably have done something with them if they'd spent a week or so with me. Too late now."

"What should we do with the bodies?"

"Leave 'em. Vultures will settle soon and start their feast. Half-picked bones will be a warning for any other barbarians with ideas; as well as giving confidence to travellers following us."

And the soldiers indifferently set off. I followed, shaking with pent-up nerves. It had happened so fast, was so far beyond any of my previous experience, and was so unexpected given my doubts about whether a threat had really existed at all. I had thought previously that when fighting took place I would have an opportunity to use my new-found skills. The whole thing had happened so swiftly that I had frozen when Antius shouted- and had been terrified. Had Lucipor not acted so quickly I would likely be bent over, up on my mount, with an arrow through my belly. So I knew, really, that I should have been grateful. But as soon as I had the chance, and speaking with righteous indignation, I targeted Scipio in a murmured but incensed tone: "Why was I treated as a child? Even you've said that Antius is impressed with me. I had a part to play!"

Scipio chuckled softly but affectionately and ruffled my hair; I thrust his hand away angrily- which just made him laugh the more. "My young lion. So keen to taste his first kill." He turned serious of a sudden and looked me in the eye, "But could you really kill a man? Especially the one I did away with, finished off when he was only wounded. To slice an undefended man's throat, to see the lifeblood spurt as he breathes his last- could you really do that?"

"But in the heat of battle, I could! Of course!"

"Aye. But even with those men, inexperienced and poor fighters as they were, no doubt starved for lack of food in these mountains, for you can't eat silver- you think you would have stood a second's chance? Did you even know what was going on before Antius finished his second man?"

I paused in my anger. He was right. I had not even reached for my sword, I realised on reflection. And I had never been so scared- not even when Antius whipped me. I lapsed into silent thoughtfulness for the rest of the morning until we stopped to eat at lunchtime. I sidled up to Scipio, said, "Forgive me. I still have a lot to learn."

We did not speak of it again. But I redoubled my evening efforts to improve my skills with Antius.

◆◆◆

The days after the ambush felt dull and slow after the excitement- though I would not repeat those events by choice. Scipio pointed out to me that this was often the nature of warfare: weeks, if not months, of mind-numbing boredom turning to bowel-churning terror in an instant. There was the occasional wild animal to concern myself with: the sound of a boar rooting around in the woods in the darkness as we sat companionably around the fire one evening made me leap up, while the legionaries laughed at my reaction- "He's not interested in you, son. Not enough meat on you to recover from his winter fast!" And we woke one morning as a huge brown bear rambled into our campsite looking for something to eat. A quick scramble into the trees, where Romulus had had the foresight to hang our food in case of such an eventuality, meant an uncomfortable but safe place to wait for him to leave. As we travelled across higher ground in the mountains we were followed by a pack of wolves for several days as well. An uncomfortable experience; but mounting a guard and ensuring the fire was fully ablaze all night kept their threat at bay.

It was on one such night, huddled around the flickering flames and wrapped in our cloaks trying to keep our spirits up, that Scipio told the story of Mithras. The others had heard it many times before; but for me it was the first. He started in a whisper, causing all of us to draw closer to hear- except my mother, who moved away from the fire, rolling herself up in her cloak and closing her eyes as she turned away. His voice took on a dramatic tone, and his hands began to sketch a picture to accompany the words he spoke as if conjuring images out of the cold air. "Many years ago when the world was yet young, the god Mithras was born from a rock. He sprang forth, fully grown, as did Minerva from the brow of her father, Jupiter. In those days, there was a terrible drought and the whole world was at risk of destruction. The cause of this drought was said to be the

Great Bull, which roamed the earth devouring all before it. The task set before Mithras was to hunt the Great Bull, to kill it and to give the world life once again. For many days and nights he searched, following the trail of destruction wrought by the creature. Its tracks were fearsome to behold with hooves larger than an emperor's serving platter, and the damage it caused created a path through the woods and forests that was easier to follow than the road to Rome.

One day, after much hunting, he came across the beast as it lay in a large thicket of thorns. Hiding nearby, he readied his weapons for the battle to follow. He strung his great bow, so powerful that it took two ordinary men to hold it while a third pulled it back. And he checked his sword, sharp enough to slice a feather in two. He strapped his dagger to his side in case the bull managed to get so close he would not be able to use his sword. He wore no armour, for his travels had required fleetness of foot and the weight would have been too much. His blue cloak he swept out of the way so it could not hinder his movements. And then he crept towards the bushes." Here, Scipio's voice went even quieter and slower than before. "And he silently stepped towards the sleeping bull."

And then suddenly louder, so sharp a contrast that I jumped: "And the bull moved! It twitched in its sleep, dreaming of the devastation it would wreak the next day, how it would destroy all that stood in its way. Mithras hid behind a rock and stared in wonder at the bull's horns, as large as a giant's trumpet, and at the muscles that rippled along its sides as it breathed. The legs that pawed the air as it slept were huge and threatening. He drew his bow and placed his first arrow on the string, drawing it back."

And then Scipio leapt up and shouted, his sentences short and fast: "But the mighty string creaked as it was drawn back! The creature awoke. It shook its vast head. It began to get to its legs, alarmed. Mithras scambled to the top of the rock and fired- but his arrow bounced off the fearsome hide of the animal, toughened by age and sun. He threw his bow aside and drew his sword. The bull, now fully alert, charged at where he stood. The first cut drew blood from the animal's shoulder as it swept past, trying to hook him with its magnificent horns, and he jumped on to its back as the bull circled. The creature bellowed in alarm, then ran, trying to shake Mithras off, as he stabbed repeatedly down into the meat of its back. It shook, it rolled, it brushed past rocks and trees, but the god clung on with all of his skill, his arms wrapped tightly around its neck. Some say it ran for days and nights- but he would not let go after his long search.

After much time had passed, and even Mithras' attention and energy were starting to wane, the beast started to tire and he relaxed his grip around the neck. He began instead to ride it, holding just the left horn, using all of his mighty skill. Until at last, the bull surrendered, its front legs collapsing and its jaw ploughing a rut in the ground, the thunder of its fall heard from afar. Mithras leapt from its back. He seized its rear legs and lifted them, such was his great strength, over his shoulders. Dragging the bull behind him he strode to a nearby cave. Once inside, he fixed his knee in the animal's back and forced its head backwards with his left hand. He reached for his dagger, sharp and sure by his side. Taking it, he lunged forwards towards the beast's neck. Searching with the blade in the deep fat under its jaw, he cut the vein. As the bull's lifeblood drained from its throat all creatures came to drink. And Mithras celebrated his victory. From the bull's blood, all life sprang, restoring the world to its former glory, undoing the desolation that the beast had wrought, and bringing the universe into being."

We applauded his storytelling as he ended the tale, and he gave a mock bow in return. His performance showed a side to Scipio that I had been unaware of until now.

I was still curious, however, and as he sat back down I asked, "I have heard from some that Mithras and the Unconquered Sun are the same. Is this true, Scipio?"

The optio thought long and hard about this question before answering. The other legionaries looked interested also, for both gods were popular amongst the army. Eventually, he spoke. "Not the same. The legends as they are told by our priests suggest that they are equals. Some say that that the Sun, who needs the rain also if the world is to live, bowed the knee to Mithras after his victory over the bull as the drought ended and creation was restored. But then the two ate together as Mithras raised him up- sharing the meat of the bull between them."

I thought carefully about this for some time, doubt creeping into my mind. "So Mithras is greater than the Sun?"

"Not so much 'greater than'; the two work in partnership together", was the reply.

I nodded my head, satisfied. And that was the end of the matter- though I did wonder at the Sun's bowing of the knee. This must mean the Sun was conquered, for why else would a god such as he need to be raised up? This would mean Mithras was greater, for he had the power. My faith was shaken a little at this simple theological question. And my mother's strange lack of interest also affected me. Her words to me became even fewer as did her discussions with Scipio. She withdrew further into herself even as I became more familiar with our companions.

◆◆◆

The next day we descended into Aqua Sulphurae from the narrow, craggy gorges and raw windblown passes we had experienced so far. The mountains formed a shallow basin with the town like a gem nestling in the centre. It was well known, as the name suggested, for its hot springs, and that meant many visitors. So we found an inn, determined to enjoy some comfort that would prepare us for the last part of our expedition. We were delighted when we discovered the inn had its own baths, heated by a hypocaust. The innkeeper proudly informed us that the hot mineral springs in the area- hence the name of the town- were such that it was considered to be very healthy. We enjoyed our time there, spending two nights where we originally intended only one; but Antius felt this was justified due to the trials of our journey so far.

Reluctantly, we set off from our temporary respite following a long river that seemed to wander on for far too long. And then over a pass and down to cross a stream before entering Bistua Nova. The landscape was transformed here, the trees on the sides of the valley looking like a deep, soft fabric that you could reach out and touch once you were near enough. There was far less of a threat of wolves and bear as there were many more people; and there was the sight, unusual for us, of flocks of sheep and goats ambling their way around the vegetation followed by bored herders. We ate well for several meals after brief negotiations with those who were eager to take Roman coins without having to drive their stock to market. We followed another river to the entrance to the vale and up another ravine, climbing once again, the bare rock that faced us as we entered its shadow providing a sharp contrast to the fresh green of the hills that preceded it. The track twisted and turned its way up the height, spurs of the mountain obstructing the view but providing shelter for occasional long-forgotten farms and far-flung hamlets. Our climb ended at a saddle in the mountain, the view below us obstructed by a low-lying fog. We crossed swiftly and urgently, the clammy and damp weather lending wings to our heels. We looked ahead, seeing our way blocked again by seemingly impassable mountains- yet they always opened up into previously hidden exits that kept us going.

I asked my mother the reason for this journey- "Surely it would have been easier to travel by the coast-road?"

In a rare, longer answer, she replied, "But further, my son, slower and much more populated. I would agree that going around these mountains would have been much the easier route. I suspect speed and secrecy are important to these men."

Scipio, though more obscure in his response, partly confirmed my mother's view: "We travel fast, for the governor awaits us. We have urgent news."

I realised I may never find out what this cryptic reply really meant but it satisfied my curiosity for the time being.

So it was that we climbed yet another set of bends in the road, clambered through yet another pass, cautioned our mounts as we stepped carefully down yet another mountain- and into yet another valley. The land was starting to change as we drew closer to the coast. By the time we reached Bistua Vetus, it was no longer green and lush but grey and stony. Scrub covered the ground and scree surrounded the sharp peaks, falling down the sides and predominating across the landscape. This was relieved by the stunningly bright sky-blue of the lake that provided a backdrop to the village, but could not take anything away from the stark barrenness of the mountain range that it lay in.

We left the temporary shelter of a fortified waystation situated just off the road itself to scale our final set of summits, the trees that had surrounded the village now fully replaced by the pale and straggling grass that was loosely rooted in the shallow soil. My mood started to fluctuate in sympathy with the surroundings, from eager anticipation of a bright future to a dull resignation to my fate once Antius discovered my mother had lied. This had been forgotten while in the midst of our travels; but now my fears returned with additional force, increasing with every step we took towards our destination.

We descended into our final valley, and the plain surrounding Delminium. We were back in something approaching civilisation, and to see a forum for the first time in several weeks was a pleasure even if the future held uncertainty. It was only a little smaller as a town than Naissus so it felt familiar. But the languages, the clothing and the customs were different enough to make me feel like a foreigner; though it was a reminder of my previous thrill at visiting Viminacium. Despite this, the nights staying in proper accommodation were those I least looked forward to: far more interesting to sit around the campfire once Sol had descended, listening to tales from across the empire. I had no idea whether this was normal for imperial soldiers, but these four had seen sights from the woad-painted barbarians north of what I heard was called the wall of Hadrian in Britannia, to the desert fortifications of Leptis Magna in North Africa, fending off spear-throwing savages with skin not far lighter than that of Lucipor. These stories served to feed my hunger for adventure, and the army seemed the only way to find this. The flames between us highlighted the glint in each man's eye and their tones lowered as they reached the climax of their retelling. The end always came with them leaning closer and suddenly revealing an explosion of glory that glamourised the account even further.

I got to know the men best on these nights and did not look forward to spending time with my mother in more comfortable surroundings. I enjoyed hearing Romulus and Remus tell in their matter-of-fact voices of protecting one another's back as they fought Egyptian city-dwellers desperate from hunger and looking for grain on the docks of Alexandria in an early morning some years ago- how they defended each other, taking only minor injuries as they did so despite being surrounded (here they would show the scar of an old wound standing proud from a calf muscle, or a pierced point on a shoulder long-healed) until the city's procurator arrived with reinforcements. Or hearing Scipio tell of meeting Berber princes in their vast sand-blown tents in Numidia, their source of wealth being their horses; and the size of their herds indicating their greatness. He told also of Mithraic rites. These were meant to be secret; but each legionary was an initiate into the mysteries and assumed without saying so that I would eventually be one of them too. My mother was always sleeping, or pretending to do so, at a short distance when this was spoken of. There was something rousing in the tales of clandestine meetings beneath ground, of banquets of twelve brothers sworn to silence by unbreakable oath.

Most talkative of the four, however, was Antius, most often telling a tale of violence and victory, usually single-handed against numbers of opponents. These were often Gauls, and always given credit for being fierce fighters. Breaking resistance in the breaching of one of their wooden forts, or, occasionally, single combat against a hulking chieftain. Having seen him fight, I could not doubt but that these reports were true. There was no modesty to him; but there was no need for such- he was as good as he claimed to be. It did not occur to me to wonder how it was that these four men, as if by coincidence, had experienced and seen so much- the empire summed up in them, as if chance had brought them together to form this elite band of heroic stature.

Delminium was about two days' journey from Salona, and the final evening, as we descended to the outskirts of that city, was spent by me in a state of complete exhaustion as I imagined every scenario that might occur now that we were near. Only the view was finally able to distract me. For as the sun set we came around the corner of a low hill. Unexpectedly, we were high above the city as it lay clinging to the narrow coastline beneath our range of mountains. The Adriatic was lit up with a wonderful golden glow beneath us, its islands providing a darker counterpoint, and the luminescent wakes of the fishing boats and foreign ships coming from all over the Mediterranean crossed each other in a visible net that, were it not for the wonder of the sight, could have added to my sense of being trapped in a situation not of my own making.

My mother's nerves must have increased as we drew nearer but there was little indication as she was speaking so little already. Engrossed in my own concerns I did not really notice. I saw Scipio speaking to her privately and repeatedly, yet with very little response from her. And it was then that I started to realise some small sense of what she must be feeling. I had not been able to sleep since Delminium due to my excited anticipation, mixed through though it was with trepidation. But as I looked at the darkness below her eyes, and the shadowy emotion at the back of them, as well as the way she had recently started casting them skyward with increasing frequency and visibly muttering, not seeking to hide her divine conversations, I realised the tension she must be experiencing. Without drawing further attention to it, I did my best to be a comfort and a support- without realising that I was, unintentionally, the largest part of the burden she carried.

Descending the hill towards the distant lights, we all jumped at a challenge from the darkness as a legionary suddenly stood up from the roadway, questioning who we were and what was our business. Antius took charge; and it so happened that he was well known to the sentry. Grunting, "Based up there, so he is", Antius pointed out the small guard-fort on a pinnacle of rock above us, silhouetted against a crescent moon, created by a strange outcropping of the stone.

And so it was that in early summer we arrived at Salona through its extensive suburbs just after nightfall and passed through the Porta Caesarea, its main gate. As we entered its mighty lamp-lit buttresses casting deep shadows in corners, bringing its edges into sharper relief, the gate became for me an ending. An ending of the hopes and dreams that had sustained me from a young age. All of my enthusiasm suddenly vanished as I contemplated the prospect of being rejected, thrown out by the governor with my loved mother being revealed as a liar and a thief. This must be why she had become so quiet and reserved, unresponsive and reluctant. She had already seen this future, had never expected that we would be taken all of the way to Salona and her ambitions for me brought to nought. She had gambled and lost- and we would both now pay the price. I started to work out how we would make our way back to Naissus, assuming further punishment did not await us as repayment for her deceit.

CHAPTER 4: DECISIONS

Disguising my many fears so none of my new friends might suspect my dread of what was to come, I peered ahead through the darkness of the late hour. The road stretched dimly before me in the light from the gateway. There was the haunting cry of some lonely gulls in the distance and the harsh salt-smell of the sea was strong in the air. We had talked of Salona as we drew near so I felt I knew something of the place. Usually full of activity due to its being the capital of Dalmatia, humming to the tune of the trade that took place there and full of the roar of business, there was little of it to be seen at this time of night. I was disappointed at the empty streets and the quietness of the town, having expected so much more- and such sights as I had anticipated would have taken my mind away from whatever lay in my future. I urged my horse forward to speak to Scipio. As I did so, a figure emerged confidently on to the main road not far in front of us. Its head turned briefly in our direction, and then the figure pulled its cloak tighter, hooded itself and hurried out of sight, all self-assurance gone. The light thrown by the torches carried by two of our party did not reach far enough to make out any features and they were safe in their anonymity.

"What do we do now, Scipio?" I asked quietly, affected by the muted atmosphere and the scurrying of the distant form.

"We go to the palace and see the governor's chief of staff. He'll get us in to see the governor immediately."

I frowned, confused. "I was sure you said in Viminacium that it was almost impossible to get to see a governor without speaking to the right people, spending a bit of money, and waiting for at least two weeks. So how are we going to get in to see him so quickly?"

Antius, in front of us and listening to what was being said, turned to look at me, our horses moving in rhythm. He finally said, gruffly, and not without rough sympathy, "Come on lad, think it through. You really are an innocent."

I was totally confused. But Scipio put me out of my misery: "We are frumentarii."

I paled and recoiled from him. Three words; but filled with a wealth of deeper meaning. Even I had heard of the frumentarii- imperial spies with the power of life and death, they brought fear and terror wherever they went. I noticed my mother watching me closely with a concerned look in her eye. She spoke quietly, but loud enough for her words to carry to me, "Why do you suppose we approach under cover of night? Why do people flee at the sight of our group entering the city?"

Scipio laughed ironically at her words. He spoke in a low voice, strengthening in power and conviction as he continued. "Not so easy to like us any more, lad? Secret agents for the emperor, no-one is safe from us. Assassins of the law-abiding in their beds, reporters of fictions half-heard in forums across the world. That's what they say isn't it?" He looked at me arrogantly. "Well, that may sometimes be true- but we are so much more. We are a brotherhood who renounce ourselves to maintain a Roman peace that benefits all. What else could take me from my family to share my life with this band of misfits?" He gestured around him at his companions. "You think we wish to be on the road constantly, watching our fellow citizens for a word out of place, expecting to see them disappear if we but give the order? Of course not! But somebody must do such tasks to maintain the peace we all value."

Antius laughed uproariously, the harsh braying sound cracking through the silence of the town. "You really think that Scipio, my friend? I am in awe of your self-sacrifice and generosity of spirit! See those cowards leaping at our shadows?" He gestured in the direction taken by the person we had seen rush away but moments before. "I do it for the respect- nay, fear- that people know when I say that I am one of our band; for the drink and the women it brings with it; and for the extra pay. But you know what I enjoy most of all? The freedom! I go where I like, when I like." He waved the token that had jumped into his hand as if by some magic from inside his tunic, "And this seal is what gives me that power. No-one questions me. I do what I want without answering to anyone. I can be in Lusitania one month, and amongst those dogs the Suebi the next. And I have you motherless sons to protect me and do my will. I love this job. Wouldn't have any other."

This was by far the longest speech I had heard from Antius, and he relapsed into silence with a radiant grin on his face. Our mounts continued to move up the gentle slope, torch flames reflecting off the shaped and dressed stonework of the street ahead as it became better lit by oil lamps outside some of the richer citizens' houses. Columns appeared slowly in the distance, revealed gradually as if a dark cloak were being drawn from across the front of them. Scipio spoke briefly and factually: "The governor's palace."

We stood still for a moment in front of the grand entrance as my mother and I took in the splendour in which my presumed father lived. Then Antius spoke, "Come on then, round to the southern wing at the back. The stores are all sent there so our presence will be less remarked if anyone sees us enter- though that is unlikely. We should get this finished tonight once and for all. Helena: pick your street corner, for it will not be long until you find yourself selling what wares you have there."

The insolent jibe was half-hearted, almost as if being said because it was the expected comment. It drew a barbed response from my mother- "Your mother will no doubt advise me well due to her expertise in that area"- but each was almost performing their antagonism now. I knew that Antius was fond of me. The only way to earn his esteem was with a weapon, and the other three soldiers had all informed me that I was making excellent progress. So that, combined with my mother's spirit, meant that a grudging respect had formed in him.

And, strangely enough, I liked him. His natural talent for killing, combined with the skill of a born tactician, hid under his arrogant attitude a genuine desire for popularity. He was ugly as sin- a chin with a deep cleft in it, above that a small, narrow-lipped and petulant mouth and small eyes, set close together over a large nose, hooked in a way that caused it to dominate his face. Birth had not favoured him. He had but a single scar on his body. It was his proud boast that no man had ever touched him with a blade. The one mark was a severe dagger slash across his stomach, a blow that looked as if it would have gutted any ordinary man. He claimed a warrior princess of Dacia had done it in a fierce battle to the death, single combat in front of his troops on the one side and her massed tribe on the other. But Scipio told me it was a whore from the rough streets of Ostia whom he had refused to pay for what he viewed as a poor quality of work. He had made it back to the camp just in time, holding his intestines in with both hands, and it was Scipio who had taken him to the surgeon. His solid build and the strength of an ox had led to his survival though it had taken a year to get back to full fitness. I had asked what happened to the whore; Scipio turned away and I could just hear him say, in a shamed tone, "Her body was found floating in the harbour a month after he got back on his feet." I did not ask for more. I found that I wanted to like Antius.

We made our way around to a back door, hidden away in an alcove and unnoticeable were it not for Romulus, scouting ahead, standing waiting in the darkness. Antius knocked sharply on it; a small hatch opened and a pair of eyes appeared. He reached up to hand over the seal he had shown us. It disappeared through the narrow gap. And we waited. Waiting was fertile ground for my fears to take flight once again, so I was relieved when, only a short while later, the door was unbolted, the sound of the latches far too loud on this quiet night, and we were surreptitiously beckoned in to follow a guide. He led us a long way. Hard as I tried throughout our walk, I could not see him properly- all that was visible above his shrouding cloak was neatly combed red hair. He led us to a small ante-room, couches set on two sides while a double door occupied the third.

"Sit", ordered Antius, and our guide took him and Scipio through the doors.

Try as I might to get a glimpse through the brief gap before they closed, I could see only more furniture. Romulus and Remus remained standing, as if stationed, unmoving. They appeared to be guarding us, though no-one said anything. I made a sharp movement to test my idea- and both reacted strongly, hands moving to scabbards. As soon as they saw that I was only bending down to re-tie the straps on my sandals they relaxed once more, disguising their movement as either scratching an itch or slapping an insect. My mother knew me well enough to be able to tell what I was doing and made an all but imperceptible downward movement with the flat of her palm: remain calm. Despite the friendship we had built with these men, their duty was everything and our good relations would count for nothing should we be proved to be impostors. The governor would decide our fates; and his soldiers would carry out any sentence without emotion. Lucipor sat stolidly and without expression as expected of a slave. His fate was never his own to choose, whatever should happen here. My mother closed her eyes and her lips started twitching again. As she did so, I could see a renewed confidence enter her. Her back straightened, her seat became more erect and I could see the worry lines on her face smooth away.

We could hear voices beyond the doorway, and suddenly there was a great scraping sound, and then a crash, as a chair hit marble flooring. "What? Claims to be my son! Surely I of all people would know something of this?" We could hear my father shouting, incredulously. "Have you finished telling me what is going on in Dalmatia? And is that the real reason that you have been away so long? Wasting time with some slut from the wheat-fields who's never seen a real soldier before and wants a father for her bastard?"

My mother abruptly rose from where she was sitting, thrusting her cloak to the couch behind her as she did so. Her transformation was nearly complete. With confidence now infusing every movement, she efficiently arranged her hair and set it in place with two silver hairpins, adjusted blue-beaded earrings set in gold that I had never seen before and pushed three silver bracelets on to her wrist. Romulus and Remus clearly did not see her as a threat for they did not move; but they did stare open-mouthed. For, with a startling clarity, I realised that she must have been saving her clothing and jewellery for this occasion. I had last seen her dressed like this several months earlier at a dinner party she threw in Naissus: wearing a grey dress, waistband in turquoise and with a similarly coloured shawl, she looked stunning. She must have put it on that morning, covered by her cloak and the darkness, but it was only slightly creased despite a full day of riding- and it showed how much attention I had been paying her that I had not noticed. She strode forward with assurance, all of her energies being poured into one vital performance. Romulus and Remus were taken completely by surprise as she flung open the double doors, forcefully announcing, "You are a fool."

She did not raise her voice, but the energy in it was so fierce that the man I had not yet been able to see, despite my desperation to do so, went instantly silent. He had probably never been spoken to in such a way. Quieter now, but no less powerful for all that, she repeated: "You are a fool. I bring you the son you never knew of, nor cared about, risking his life and my own to do so, in company with men that no-one trusts, least of all a governor, riding through mud, rain and snow- and this is the welcome you give me? You are a fool."

Struck by her fury, the men were speechless. Even from behind, my mother looked like an avenging deity, reminding mankind of their wrongdoing and the urgency of the need to correct their errors. Her cheeks had spots of red, righteous indignation the prevalent emotion. She turned and motioned me forward urgently, her eyes particularly striking in their kohl-enhanced ferocity. I looked at the twins- both had hands on sword-hilts but were staring at the ceiling. So I moved.

Speaking still in the same tone, she said, "May I present, sir, your son: Flavius Valerius Aurelius Constantinus."

As my mother had put on such a show I must do my best to play my part. So as she stepped to the side, I walked- strutted, more like- into the centre of the doorway, and stopped suddenly. I was told later on by Scipio that, as soon as I appeared, all doubts that he and Antius had as to my paternity were laid to rest. The similarity was striking.

I studied my father; he studied me.

I saw a stocky man, sturdily built, but agile and fit. He was wearing a plain white belted tunic reaching to just above the knee and no adornment other than a large silver signet ring with an image of the sun prominently carved into it. His large, dark eyes were regarding me thoughtfully and steadily despite the high drama of the moment; and I saw that he knew exactly what my mother was doing, that there was a little too much of an emotional drama to her words and actions. His hair was close-cropped over a lined forehead. His face was unusually fair despite the heat of the Dalmatian sun- I had heard our companions describe him as 'the Pale', and that now made more sense.

He, on the other hand, saw a young man, tall for his age and with muscle starting to add itself to his frame, trying to appear sure of himself. No doubt he also, if what Scipio said is to be believed, saw himself. There was a long pause. And then, he spoke.

"Come here… boy," he said, shock at being spoken to as he had been now replaced by curiosity. "Tell me about your life so far."

This question now appears dull and stale considering what he could have said, and the amount I could have told him. But it is burned firmly into my memory- like a scar, but a scar that heals rather than recalls pain. I know now that he wanted to make a judgement, that it would in fact suit him to have an heir, a son, and he did not really mind whether I was or was not truly so. That I turned out to be was an advantage; but an unexpected one initially. All of these thoughts were moving behind his eyes as he lifted his chair, gestured me to one opposite and gave his orders.

He spoke decisively to his procurator, the change in his attitude being immediately apparent. "Felix: prepare a room for the lady. Order three slaves to attend her and have them draw a bath. She has been on the road a while, it would appear. Antius, Scipio- my thanks for your service. You know the way to your rooms. I will see you in the morning."

Our companions walked to the door as I moved towards my seat, Antius astonished at this turn of events. Scipio whispered to me with a grin and a wink, "So your mother can be trusted!"

Antius also dropped a weighty disc with a light thud on the governor's desk as he passed, Constantius casting it a quizzical glance. He raised his eyebrows, his forehead creasing, questioning its presence. My mother had been more reluctant to leave, casting backwards glances over her shoulder as the governor's aide ushered her out- and she saw his expression, saying deferentially: "Your medallion, sire, left in my keeping these last years."

On that note, she left.

Constantius paced the room while I sat, waiting until he was ready to speak. His head was bowed, and he studied the mosaic depicted beneath his feet as he moved, a pair of dolphins leaping through waves, depicted in several distinctive shades of blue and white. He walked over to the desk, picked up the medallion and examined it. I did not risk interrupting his reverie: he clearly had much to think on.

And then, we talked. Or, rather, I talked and he listened. There was the occasional prompt to move me on, but this was my only opportunity to convince and I took it. It was already late, and we talked until the oil lamps started to die. As their light faded, the room grew dark; but I had never had anyone truly listen to me like this and this man had a way with people that meant I kept talking. I told him everything, and he nodded, smiled, spoke only when necessary and usually encouragingly, and by the end of that night he knew all there was to know of my short life.

Time was irrelevant, and my focus was so entirely on the governor that when I finally stopped only one lamp still glowed gently and most of the room was in deep shadow. My eyelids started to droop as the exhaustion of the day's events overtook me. Constantius noticed it as soon as I did, and gently said: "You are in sore need of your bed. I will see you in the afternoon tomorrow, once you have had some sleep and a chance to recover from your journey."

"But," I said, worried and not a little upset, "Do you believe me? Truly believe me? That I am your son? Or will we end up in the gutter like Antius says?"

"You have nothing to be afraid of. I will make sure you are looked after, whatever I decide- but I will not be rushed into any swift decisions. You are a fine young man, one I would be honoured to call my son. But there is only one person can convince me of my responsibilities in that area."

He lifted me from my chair and guided me to a room- I knew not where, as I was all but asleep as I walked. I fell fully clothed on to the bed that appeared in front of me.

◆◆◆

I woke the next day- or was it the same day? I found I had taken my rest in a pleasant room in the palace. There was nothing particularly special about it; but it had a bed, a window, and a gentle breeze blowing through it. The room was painted in a warm cream colour that made me think of a hot day at home in Naissus, and the floor included a brightly-coloured mosaic in shades of red, green and blue showing an underwater scene of fish of various shapes, sizes and colours. I walked to the window and could see out over a wide bay full of shipping. The palace was on a slight rise overlooking both the city and the port attached to it. Coming from Naissus, I had never seen water on this scale before, nor, despite my brief time in Viminacium, so much in the way of water-craft. There was everything from narrow vessels similar to that we had used during my illness to what even from a distance looked like huge long-boats with massed oars down each side of their narrow bodies, curved prows and sterns rearing up in the air as if trying to reach for the sky. There were big, wide ships, fat with large casks weighing them down; boats with sails ten, twenty times larger than any blankets I had ever seen- and all trying to either crowd into the quays below me or escape from the packed harbour without clashing with others. I was far enough away to only hear the noise of it all as a murmur on the scented wind. I watched. It was fascinating and absorbing and I could not take my attention away.

There was a short sharp knock on my door, and then it opened. I turned to see Lucipor standing there, carrying a pile of clothing. "Come with me master. The governor has asked to see you when you wake, but only once you are washed and dressed. He has been waiting- you have slept for a full day and night. Follow me."

I followed obediently. He took me into a courtyard a short distance away down a corridor and revealed a small pool. I could see doors off the courtyard that must lead to the palace's private bath complex.

"Can I try it all?" I asked eagerly.

"Forgive me lord," replied Lucipor impassively. "Your mother has instructed me that you need to see the governor as soon as possible. She is with him at the moment."

Having removed my dirty travelling clothes and dropped them in a heap in front of the slave, I jumped in to the warm water of the first bath we came to and started splashing around with great enthusiasm. My feet could easily touch the bottom so the fact that I was unable to swim made little difference. I stopped abruptly when I noticed that my mother was watching from the colonnade surrounding the courtyard, leaning smiling against one of the columns.

She said, "Come out Constantine. Constantius has a test for you, and you need to be prepared."

I took it as a good sign that she was referring to my father so informally- some progress had been made, though I dared not ask how much. It was not my place. But a test...? What if I failed it? My fears resurfaced, having hoped that all had been resolved.

I climbed out, dried myself and dressed in the simple tunic Lucipor had carried with him. I then followed my mother through the light and airy palace, trying to stop myself marvelling at every new sight that greeted me as I rounded another corner- from statues of past emperors to views from windows that showed Salona to advantage from differing angles. We stopped outside the governor's office doors- I recognised them well from the previous night, having stared at them so intently- and my mother tapped on them gently.

"Come!" came the response. And we walked in to see my father standing in front of a table covered in sand. Water had been poured on it in judicious amounts and it had been moulded into various shapes: a landscape had been re-created before us. To one side of it on the desk was a series of shaped wooden blocks marked with what seemed to be numbers and words.

"Thank you, Helena. You may leave us. Constantine- please break your fast over there." He waved casually at his desk, on which lay a platter of salted bread and some cheese.

I was far too nervous to contemplate eating, so I shook my head and informed him that I was not in need of food. He responded brusquely: "Then you stand on that side; I will stay here. In front of you, you have the scene of a famous battle. It is your job to defeat my troops." He then proceeded to outline the events leading to this battle: "You are Crassus, one of the triumvirate that now rules the empire along with Pompey and Julius Caesar. Do you know these names?"

"Everyone knows who Caesar and Pompey were- even a country boy from the middle of nowhere. But I've not heard of Crassus."

Constantius laughed heartily. "There's a very good reason for that! Anyway, Crassus is not really a general, but he needs to prove himself against a strong opponent if he is to ensure his reputation, so he chooses Parthia- mainly because it is extremely rich. Unfortunately, nobody knew much about the Parthians, but I'm going to tell you enough to give you a chance. Their army's elite troops are cataphracts- armoured cavalry, covered in coats of small metal plates. Even their horses are heavily armoured. They carry heavy, far-reaching lances. Do you have any ideas for how to beat such troops?"

I thought very carefully, knowing that this was the start of my testing. "Well…" I took my time, then decided to say what I was thinking. "Arrows would bounce off them; I suspect spears would too. The only way is to get underneath them with short stabbing swords or spears to attack the horses. The intention would be to either hamstring the horses by slashing as they go past, or to stab at their stomachs. There must be some way that the armour is attached to the animals, and once that's cut then the rider must fall. If the armour is that complete, then it must be very heavy- so once a rider is on the ground they are vulnerable. And if you can get inside their lances there's not much they can do."

My father looked at me approvingly. "Well done. An impressive answer. Bear in mind that there are only limited numbers of them as well due to the expense of equipping them- one thousand at my disposal." Here, he lifted a wooden block and placed it on the sand. "However, supporting them is a much larger force of ten thousand horse archers", taking ten blocks from the desk and placing them next to the first, "armed with short bows that they can fire even when riding away from the enemy." He looked up at me sharply from where he was positioning his men, "Remember that: it's important."

"You, on the other hand, have started off with seven legions of assorted light infantry and cavalry, one thousand Gallic cavalry auxiliaries and you have hired six thousand Arab mercenaries. You have a huge numerical advantage." He placed the rest of the wooden blocks on my side of the sand-pit. Then he continued, with a sidelong grin at me, "However, you have had to garrison several cities as they surrendered during your assault on Parthia," he removed several blocks, much to my annoyance. "Eight thousand troops are occupied with this, leaving you with just under six thousand legionaries. They are armed with heavy javelins and short swords, as well as tall rounded shields. A few are archers. You do still have all of your Gauls, the Arabs and the light support troops. Your move." He stopped, placed his hands behind his back, standing with his legs apart and waited, staring at me innocently.

Ignoring his daunting stance and despite being taken aback by his attitude given our previous friendly discussion, I bought myself time by looking closely at the ground before me. He had placed his men in a block, narrow but deep, towards his side of the sand. The landscape itself was built into a flat plain, with low hills behind his troops and a strip to the left representing what must be a stream, as a long and narrow piece of blue fabric wound its way across the scene. I first positioned my men in a line, legions in the middle in marching order, cavalry outriders surrounding it, with Arabs at the back and my Gauls providing a vanguard. I looked at the formation silently, trying not to look at my father for I felt I had learnt enough of him already to know that he would intentionally remain expressionless. I would drop in his estimation. There was nothing to be gained.

I changed my mind as I looked across at his troops. "Stupid idea," I muttered under my breath. Speaking to myself, I said, "They will get cut apart in no time by horse archers- they will ride around the outside firing, and there is nothing

I can do to stop them. All this does is make it easier to shoot even more of my men."

"But won't your light cavalry be able to catch them?" was the unlooked-for response.

"There are not enough of them, and they will not be skilled enough. You told me about your men being able to fire backwards. No point chasing in that case."

I rearranged my troops into a square, legionaries on the outside, cavalry in the middle. I placed the light infantry in the centre too, while my Gauls formed one side of the square.

"So what do you do now? Just sit there?"

I nodded. "Until I know what you will do," I said, challenging him to his next move.

He chuckled, enjoying the byplay. And then he moved his first few blocks of archers forwards to commence firing at my stationary men.

I scoffed at him. "That's not going to do much."

"You underestimate them. Remember all of your lightly armed troops in the centre- they are at my mercy. Unable to move or to properly defend themselves. Even your legionaries, if they are not careful with their shields, are exposed."

He turned the blocks away down the sides of my square, those moving down the far side turning in behind my troops and riding in almost a full circle to join with those who had been opposite. He left the reunited force tantalisingly a short distance away. "And they start fleeing from your javelins."

Frustrated at his words, I impatiently moved my blocks of covering legionaries apart to release my cavalry so that they could chase the Parthians.

"Haha! Remember what you just said about shooting backwards? Your cavalry are destroyed." He removed the block that was out in the open.

I calmed myself, thought more, then spread my formation out, trying to make it deep but wide with a slight curve to it directed slightly towards the left of the sand. The Gauls were in the centre, supported by the light infantry; the two wings were made up solely of legionaries.

"What are you doing?" he asked curiously.

"Well, I have to trap your cavalry so that I can hit them hard with my infantry. They are too fast to catch in open country, so that stream is my only chance- I have to herd them against it so that they cannot move. Then I can destroy them."

"Brilliant idea! Let us see if it works. You do still have your Arabs, don't forget… Oh- no you do not. They have decided you are going to lose and have ridden off." He gave a deep laugh, throwing his head back in amusement at my expression. "Did I mention that these mercenaries are notoriously unreliable?"

I was getting increasingly frustrated and even irritated at his humour. He could tell, and that just made it worse. I slowly moved my blocks forward at a diagonal as he continued to make sweeping movements with his light archers; it seemed to be working, as the majority of his troops had not engaged mine yet, and the swing of my men was inexorably closing in on them. They would have to move back soon, to where I wanted them. But then my father opened up his formation fully, revealing the cataphracts at the back. He moved them forwards against my centre- which did not have the same strength in depth as my wings due to the lightness of the back rows and the wearing away by the archers that had already particularly affected them due to their lack of armour.

With an extravagant gesture, Constantius blasted through the middle of my men with his heavy armour, knocking my blocks over. Conversationally, he said, "Can you see how they gather speed, and by the time they hit your troops they are unstoppable?" He demonstrated the movement once again, but this time more slowly, having put my soldiers back in their original positions. "There is no chance to attack them from beneath as you suggested: they are through and past before your men can do anything. In the actual battle of Carrhae, the Romans didn't even recognise the cataphracts for what they were until it was too late."

He had left me with just my legionary blocks in two separate squares. "And now there is a hole dividing your force in two which makes it impossible to trap anything; while my archers can stand at a distance and destroy your men with impunity. Once I am ready to send in my cataphracts in rolling charges, I think I have won."

I swept my hand through my two forces, acknowledging the truth in his words, knocking them over. "So: what would you have done?"

He looked me in the eye, suddenly very serious: "I would never have allowed myself to get into that position in the first place. The battle was lost before it began. I would have scouted the enemy, known what their strengths and weaknesses were, chosen my ground and ensured that I took the battle to them. Never react- always initiate. But do it in your own time and when you are ready."

He looked at me piercingly for a moment, brow furrowed as if trying to see into the depths of my soul. "Now, leave me while I think on your future."

◆◆◆

I left the room to be gathered up by my mother, keen to ask me what exactly had passed between us in the governor's office. I spent the next three days unable to settle. I tried to enjoy the palace and all it had to offer, investigating all of its locked rooms and seeing where every stairway led, talking to servants and slaves alike. I tried to go down into Salona several times once the charms of the palace had begun to bore me, but Romulus and Remus, having seemingly been given the task of watching me, prevented my doing so. I instead spent much time in the baths or helping Lucipor with menial tasks he had been given. None of it distracted me from the question that underpinned my restlessness. I was in a shadow-world, unable to do much or go anywhere until my fate had been decided by others. I had no control over this and my frustration grew.

What was my future?

My mind dwelt on this constantly, obsessing me: I had clearly failed the test. But then, he had said I would. So what were his expectations? And did I meet these despite my failure?

I questioned my mother every time I saw her, at every meal time in particular as we ate by ourselves, and she, nervous herself, started to avoid me if she could. I would pester Felix as my father's closest confidant- but he made it very clear that Constantius was keeping his thoughts to himself. Lucipor told me, having heard it in the slaves' quarters, that he had not been seen outside his office for a full day after our battle. And even when he emerged he seemed lost in a world of his own, distracted and wandering into areas of the building where he had never been seen before, then having to ask servants for directions as to how to get back to where he wanted to be. Of course, the whole palace knew what was being considered as it was a tight-knit community- and, from the way that people looked at me, they were sympathetic. I intentionally avoided Antius when I saw him, for his response was the opposite: a sneer, and a sharp reminder that my fate would leave me amongst the many beggars that infested the forum in the town below. I made progress with others, however: by the afternoon of the third day of my wait, the cook in the palace kitchen would smile when she saw me coming and throw me fruit before I had even asked for it. I told myself that Antius was alone in his dislike.

At the end of those three days, without forewarning or preamble, without preparation or negotiation, my father called my mother and me into his office. He married her with five witnesses present- Scipio and Felix being two, and the others being men I had never met before- disregarding his right to a dowry in the process and accepting my mother with only what she had brought with her. Her face lit up as soon as she realised what was happening, and her radiance, in my eyes, made the whole room brighter. I was delighted for her.

To my even greater amazement, he then turned to me and formally adopted me as his son. Unbelievably, incredibly, my new- and old- father was all I had dreamt. My fears had been for nothing, my anxieties not needed. And he was far easier to forgive now that I knew my mother had never informed him of my existence. I went to bed that night and slept like one who knew his future was assured.

CHAPTER 5: TRAINING

My life was transformed from that day on. Constantius was determined that his son should be the best warrior, administrator, strategist and Roman that he could possibly be. He treated my education as though a military operation. Felix was made responsible for spending a day with me each week, ensuring my understanding of the basic logistics of a campaign, feeding and supplying an army on the march, establishing supply routes and storage bases. Scipio remained, probably because I spoke so highly of him to my father, rather than being sent on another mission: he taught me how to gather information and use it to build strategy. My father also hired a tutor- the best that he could find- to spend time with me on Roman history and literature. Coming from a rural Illyrian background himself, he had worked very hard as a young man to improve his own knowledge of these should he ever rise high enough to need to go to Rome, or to spend much time with true-born Romans. Earning respect had been a significant step for him in terms of his acceptance amongst the ruling elite. In fact, his appointment as a governor, though principally due to his military success and his friendships with other Illyrians in high positions, was undoubtedly smoothed by his ability to converse in an educated way with those who considered themselves 'pure' Romans.

The most difficult member of the group tasked with my education was he who had to train me in weapons.

Sitting outside my father's office the day after my adoption, the double doors were suddenly flung backwards with force, slamming into the plaster behind them and raising small clouds of white dust. The figure that thundered out had its head down, an attitude of fury hanging over it like a black storm-cloud, and as it came through it turned to bellow in the familiar parade-ground tones of Antius: "Nursemaid to an infant! Is that all I'm good for now? If you truly wish to retire me, give me my diploma, pay me my money and send me off to some piece of land near a barbarian border. At least they could use me for something better than this!"

An equally stentorian reply came fast on its heels. "You shall do as you are ordered! If I want you to clean my son's shoes, that's what you will do!" The voice followed up more quietly, but very firmly. "And don't you ever speak to me in that way again. I owe you much; but there are limits to my patience."

Still without seeing me, Antius, head yet lower and brows near-joined due to the rage written on his face, stumped off. I liked him more after hearing this exchange, though I knew he had little enough time for me even before being given his new command.

◆◆◆

My training did not begin as I had expected. I was told by Lucipor that I was to be in the central courtyard of the palace at midday, in front of the small temple that Constantius had recently built there to Sol Invictus. It was a large courtyard, and I stood waiting as commanded at the bottom of the steps that led up to the god's worship. I was admiring the recently completed stone carving of a figure surrounded by rays of light next to the doorway when Romulus appeared and handed me a heavy wooden sword. He then pointed silently at a tall post standing in the corner of the grounds and left. I stood looking at the weapon in my hand, thinking that it was so heavy and so blunt that it could only realistically be used as a bludgeon, when a bellow came from a window above me: "Well, what are you waiting for, child?"

Antius was leaning on the sill, biting the remaining pieces of meat off a piece of chicken, "I am having my lunch- attack that pole there. Do it for an hour, then go for a march. I do not wish see you back until you have run around the walls of the city." He casually threw the remnants of his lunch out of the window in my direction and disappeared from view.

I went over to the pole and started hitting it in frustration. Romulus appeared again from behind a column, this time with a grin on his face. "He is going to be a bastard."

"I had noticed!" I hit the pole as hard as I could, which just caused the wood to shudder in my hand and sent a painful tremor through my arm.

"Go with it lad. He is still angry: he will get over it. At least he told you what to do. This is how we all start out, so no harm in it. Let me show you a few strokes to practice: it's all about technique."

And he spent some time going over the standard lunges and strikes that I would need to get used to. I settled into the monotonous repetition and developed my own sequence and rhythm based on what I had been told; by the end of the hour I was practising each thrust and strike without thought. Remus appeared with a heavy pack for me as I worked and instructed me that I was to take it with me on my march. After my sword drill, I marched for an hour in the heat of the day, finishing covered in sweat. Having been trapped in the palace for three days and subject to such tension, I enjoyed the freedom this provided. This was despite the pack, as it happened, being filled with fired clay bricks that weighted it down heavily and left red welts on my shoulders. I saw it as an opportunity to get to know the surrounding area, ending my march next to a sea-inlet. Stripping off my burden, I dropped thankfully into the water and lay for a time in the gently lapping waves to refresh myself before making my way back to my father's palace. I felt that it had been a purposeful afternoon regardless of Antius' intentions. This continued for the next month, and I became a familiar figure to the townspeople and farmers as I made my way around Salona, varying my route for interest's sake and extending it as I grew stronger. However, at the end of that month, Antius emerged into the courtyard for a longer period of time at last. He was short, sharp and to the point: "Show me."

So I showed him. He seemed happy enough. "Right then. You're ready."

"What for?"

"Paired combat."

"Who with?" I replied eagerly.

"Well I haven't been wasting my time in this arse-end of the empire just waiting for you to grow a pair of bollocks. I've been training some of the sons of the other commanders in the city. We've got detachments of the XVIII Gemina, the IV Flavia Felix and the VII Claudia. There's plenty of business. So back here tomorrow as usual, but you'll have some company."

◆◆◆

And that was how I met Hosius. We were wary of each other when we met the next day. He was from Hispania-Baetica to be exact, as he often reminded me. When Antius had all eight of us together in the courtyard- not one daring to be late- he put Hosius and I together because "it would be good to see a short stump of a boy put an arrogant tall lad on his back." As indicated by these words, Hosius was much smaller than me, wiry, with a strength that belied his size. He was fast, so fast. And I could soon tell why Antius had paired us. We were easily the best two fighters of the group, but with very different styles. My reach, strength and height were great advantages; but difficult to use to good effect against speed, quick feet and darting runs. Our battles were interesting enough that, as the days and then weeks passed, the other students would finish their fights and then gather round to watch us. At first, Antius found this infuriating; but he soon turned it to his advantage. He would join them, and offer a commentary on what was happening: "Now the big idiot turns to his right... oh no, too slow, and that's him with a nasty cut on his arm... Ah- but he catches the little gnat and that is a big blow to take: will he get up again after that punch to the belly?... He arises from his slumber!" And more of the same followed.

While at first Hosius and I would compete against each other in the hope of gaining more credit with Antius, we soon realised that this had little point. Our trainer had no favourites. So, on the basis that we hated Antius more than we hated each other, we became fast friends. That friendship caused us to become even more skilful as we would pull our blows so that it hurt less, but made it look to the centurion like we were using as much force as ever. We would laugh together as we swam in the ocean after our training sessions talking about which thrust we had been proudest of in fooling him. It was a risky game to play, baiting Antius in this way; but it served to strengthen our bond. Even when he worked out what we were doing and lashed out with the cane he always carried when training, the comparison of our injuries was another means of tying us together.

So it was that Hosius and I were soon inseparable. He came from a far land and had skin darker than mine; but he rarely spoke of it. I once asked him why not, and he laughed. "I have never been there! My father and mother are both from Hispania and wish me to be proud of this heritage. But it is difficult to be proud of somewhere I've never been." He hastily added: "Though I do know much about it- but secondhand. I was born in Viminacium and coming to Salona is the furthest I have ever travelled."

His father was a cavalry commander- and not just any cavalry commander. He led a vexillation of the Dalmatian Horse, an elite unit formed under the Emperor Gallienus that had contributed to Aurelian's victory over Palmyra a decade before. His unit was attached for the moment to the VII Claudian legion and Hosius was far prouder of that than of any other origins. He was forever talking about the Seventh being the oldest legion in the Empire, founded by Pompey and marching with Julius Caesar. This went as far as sounding as if he had actually been there himself. Despite my irritation, the VII Claudian was known as 'loyal and faithful'- and Hosius took this as his own personal motto. He was a skilled rider, able to build trusting relationships with his horse quickly and easily. It was a particular gift he had, and one I would never master.

Our individual combat was soon of such a high quality that Antius started pitting us as a pair against the other six students. This was often in the form of a stylised combat where he would talk us through each stroke as we made our moves slowly. This was my favourite teaching as it was almost strategic in its intent, using your body and your limbs in a way that created the greatest economy of movement and the highest efficiency of impact. For someone like me, still growing and struggling to coordinate my clumsy muscles, the focus was on control. This was not the way of the traditional Roman army, focused on team and shield work, stabbing out from behind the protection of a limewood wall. Warfare was different these days anyway, and the secret of success- as I was learning from Hosius' fighting technique- was speed in getting to the source of any problems. The cavalry was all important for that. The infantry would follow up and consolidate any victories once the hard work had been done. It was the way of things that most cavalrymen started off as foot-sloggers, so Antius told us early on that it would be a long time until we could actually start learning to fight on horseback. We had not even reached the stage of wearing armour by the end of our first six months, though we were very familiar with the use of shields, javelins, spears and swords.

Tactics were my greatest interest, though. The passion of the fight was only enough for me for a short while; but when I told Scipio a few days after my testing by my father about the battle of Carrhae, he listened closely, taking his role as mentor seriously. We were lounging on a terrace above the city as evening set in. The sun was edging down beyond the mountain escarpment behind the city, and the warm air it left behind created a sense of peace and wellbeing. Even the brickwork we sat on had an afterglow

from the sun's heat during the day. I was still astounded by the size of Salona and this was one of my favourite places to be. Tiled roofs stretched out into the distance in the wooded valley below, lights starting to appear as the wealthier citizens settled in for the night and slaves lit their outside lamps. Across the wide bay below the last ships were coming in to the docks, sailors disembarking and making their way to the taverns while their captains arranged labour for the following day to offload their boats. There was the distant dark outline of Tragurium, a dilapidated poor cousin of Salona further along the coast. Scipio was also gazing out at the islands across the bay and the foaming white wake of a heavy-laden merchant as he came into the harbour. The hiss nearby as a blacksmith put out his fire to finish for the night woke him from his reverie.
"That's what went wrong of course," he said suddenly.
I turned to look at him. "What do you mean?"
"Well, that's the reason Crassus lost at Carrhae: supplies. He was so inexperienced that he sacrificed food and water for speed. He chose to go across the desert, using a trade route- maybe hoping that it would live up to its name- instead of the longer way through the mountains. They would have been protected against cavalry and he would have had easy access to water. Neither of which he got with the route he took. And that's why he ended up in the wrong place at the wrong time. I reckon the Parthians couldn't believe their luck."
"But they were still fighting Romans, and in vast numbers! We had tens of thousands against just over ten thousand. Surely it cannot have been a foregone conclusion?"
"You have a point. I would agree that it wasn't over before it began," he said judiciously. "But they were defending rather than attacking as soon as the Parthians arrived. And

then it was just trying to get out of there without losing too many men. Crassus' Romans were already hot, tired and lacking confidence in their leaders by the time the Parthians came on the scene. It did not help at all that Crassus then formed his infantry into a line: against cavalry and in a desert! I suspect everyone knew what was going to happen, crying to Mars for help as soon as he then tried to re-form into a square- but no god was going to come to rescue them from such stupidity. And when they saw the cataphracts reveal their hidden armour, glaring in the bright sunshine, they must have been asking each other for a coin to give to Charon, ready for when they needed to cross over."

"And that's what happened."

He nodded. "That is what happened. It is a long story- but the Parthians used cavalry charges alongside archers from a distance to slowly destroy the army. Few survived. Some made it to the small town of Carrhae; but there were, once again, too few supplies so they had to leave in a fruitless night-march that brought them back again. Crassus and the remaining commanders were killed in a fight with their own servants. The army surrendered."

"And the Parthians defeated a Roman army four times bigger."

"Exactly." He thought for a second, then asked me directly, "Are you truly interested in strategy, then? Not just to fulfil your father's wishes?"

"Of course! It's decisions and tactics that win the day more than any single skilful fighter. Perhaps it is even possible for a battle to be won through arrangement of troops before any fighting takes place."

"In that case, I will borrow that sandpit from your father with Felix's help and we can go over a few more battles with you. "

◆◆◆

Antius always had us training around midday, when the sun was at its height- though we all cursed him for this, I could appreciate in my milder moments that it was a sound approach. If we could fight in the heat of the noonday sun, with weapons twice the weight of those we would eventually carry, how much easier would battle eventually be for us, in far better conditions?

So before this I would spend the morning testing my mind. After several weeks of working alongside Scipio and Felix- the latter taking great delight in preparing the sand before breakfast, developing imaginative landscapes and formations- I appreciated that I needed someone to fight against to put my knowledge to practical purpose. As Hosius was becoming a fast companion I asked him if he would join us- and that was the start of some of my most enjoyable times in Salona.

The siege of Alesia was Felix's idea. I knew nothing of it except what I had read in Caesar's writings, but I did not recognise the similarities until Felix told us afterwards. Events look very different on papyrus. I took on the role of the Gallic chieftain Vercingetorix without having him named to me. After all, if Scipio had told Hosius that he was Julius Caesar we would all have known the certain outcome immediately! Far better to not foresee ourselves doomed before commencing. Our mentors acted as advisers to each of us. I was trapped in the fortress with eighty thousand infantry and fifteen thousand cavalry, Hosius was outside with seventy thousand troops. However, I also had two hundred thousand tribesmen beyond the Roman line as their army was deep in my territory. The glower on Hosius' face as he studied the situation brought a shadow to the bright sunshine of a glorious morning pouring in through the sea-facing window.

"How can I ever win?" he was soon shouting, accompanied by several expletives.

Felix stood up. "What are your immediate threats?"

"The men inside and the men outside! I am the nut, and they are about to crack me!"

"Ah- but how do they communicate their intentions to each other? And what are your strengths, being Romans? Think hard and long: there is no rush- those men inside are not going anywhere."

Hosius considered these words carefully, staring intently at the landscape in front of him. Eventually, he spoke. "They cannot communicate if I surround the hill. And if I build walls and ditches, I have time to get my men to wherever they are needed. My strengths are organisation- and digging! If there is one thing we are good at, it's digging."

At this point, Felix dramatically drew back a cloth over a table beside him. There were several carefully built models of catapults lying there. "You do also have these, so it does not have to be a solely defensive approach."

Despite all of Hosius' best efforts, though, I eventually overwhelmed him through sheer weight of numbers combined with the attack from in front and behind together that he had predicted. Scipio then took us through Caesar's actual manoeuvres. "You see, lads, he didn't just build a wall to stop the Gauls getting out of Alesia. He built a wall facing the other way as well so that he could stop the relief army getting in. It was a besieging force that was also being besieged. Clever. But even cleverer was to divide and conquer: several local tribes were allied to him so there was no unity. He was getting additional troops and food from nearby Germanic tribes."

"But he's still trapped," piped up Hosius, his voice suddenly squeaking. He was at that stage of his youth where his voice was deepening and it was a never-ending source of hilarity to both of us. He adjusted and repeated, this time in a falsely deeper voice: "But he's still trapped." We were both grinning, and Scipio smiled, waiting patiently for our full attention.

"He is. But it doesn't look like it to the Gauls. His defences are so strong: a wall, two ditches, some flooded and others covered in sharpened stakes, towers at frequent intervals along the line. Vercingetorix does manage to get his cavalry out before the ring closes, but only just. The Romans managed to defeat these and kill many of the relieving force with their heavier horse. But the Gauls trapped inside launch attacks as well. Caesar has Fortuna on his side: for it is only when his legates get reinforcements into position with moments to spare that they cease their fighting- for now."

As he spoke, Scipio was becoming more and more animated, speaking faster, using vigorous hand gestures to demonstrate what happened. It was as if he were living it himself. His voice started to rise as he continued: "The next day the Gauls fight again. Multiple attacks at a range of points. A big battle at one of the Roman forts. Vercingetorix attacks with everything he's got. He wins! The wall is taken. But Caesar commits all his reserves. He gives his legates independence in their commands. The wall is taken back again. The Gauls outside the wall break and run." He lost momentum and his tone slowed, becoming dramatic in its phrasing. "The besieged Gauls are starving and they surrender the next day. Vercingetorix, defeated commander and honourable adversary, emerges from his bolthole and,

in a scene which is talked of across the empire and for centuries to come, lays down his weapons before Caesar."
Felix said gently, "And that, boys, is how you win: strategy, individual courage, clear delegation, and a lot of luck."

◆◆◆

And then there was Actium, a sea battle. Lucipor and several other slaves were in charge of managing our respective fleets in the fountain at the front of the palace. As it was such a hot day none of them seemed sorry to climb into the water and both Hosius and I regretted that we could not join them. Our respective advisers laughingly held us back as we were about to jump in: "No. True commanders do not feel the need to join their troops, though there is always a time and a place to lead by example! Separation and distance are necessary if you wish to be respected by your men." Felix spoke from experience.

For a short while, we did as we were told; but only until Hosius realised that waves could easily be created from the side of the pool without any need to climb in. My wooden models of triple-banked quinqueremes and light, streamlined liburnians were so low to the water that they flooded fast and I soon found myself without a fleet. I grabbed Hosius and managed to tip him into the fountain, to the great amusement of all who were watching. Following after him, we tried to sink each other as effectively as my ships had been sunk. Even Lucipor briefly showed his teeth. Never having seen them before I assumed this was meant to be a smile, but the effect was terrifying in his polished and glistening dome of a head.

In the end, he intervened at a signal from Felix: lifting each of us under an arm, he stepped out of the 'sea' and deposited us firmly on the ground. We were still laughing. Until we saw my father emerge from the main door from which he had been watching. As he approached, the two of us fell silent. But then a faint twinkle in his eye was followed, as he stopped in front of us, by a single comment: "Perhaps the addition of a beautiful woman would have helped the two of you reach a more sensible conclusion." This reference to the role of Cleopatra led to both of us looking disgusted, as women had no interest for either of us as yet- for what would a girl know about fighting and strategy? Constantius pointed to the sun, which was starting to lower over the harbour behind us, and then waved at my soaking clothes. "Time to prepare yourself for dinner, son."

Hosius and I saluted each other then departed to fulfil our respective family duties. To call it a 'duty', I reflected, as I went to my room to change, would be to do my evenings a disservice. After our main meal, my father took the opportunity to tell me stories of his adventures and to question me on what I had been doing. I enjoyed these times more than almost anything else as I had my father to myself with no interruptions. He allowed me to ask anything I wished and I took full advantage of that. Nothing was out of bounds and everything was permissible- because we were in private. When in public, he expected instant obedience and complete submission to his authority. "A man not in control of his family is a man not in control of himself", as he used to say. But behind closed doors, he was a firm believer in passing on the benefit of his experience. Not only this, but he would even ask me for my views on actions taken and decisions made.

As I had no other experience of having a father, I assumed this experience was normal- until Hosius told me of his own family. His father was a distant figure who ran his home as a disciplinarian. Whereas my father would truly consider my answers when he asked my views and would question me further on the consequences of my suggestions, nodding approvingly when he felt I had the right of it. Occasionally, he would describe following events from past choices made and show me how my alternative would have been better. As my judgement was based more on instinct than on rational argument I found that I was learning fast due to his vast expertise.

◆◆◆

That evening, my mother had chosen to remain in the room, reclining on her couch and picking at her embroidery: she was working on a patterned tunic for my father's most important ceremonial occasions. The governor himself seemed content with the meal- the pork had been particularly finely cooked- and was lying back on his seat, belching occasionally and studying the murals on the ceiling.
"Father, will you tell me once more of the war against Zenobia, queen of Palmyra?" The names sounded exotic as they rolled off my tongue.
This request was even better than a good roast to my father- while I had heard this tale twice already and it lived in my dreams. He was also an excellent storyteller which made it doubly enjoyable.
"Where shall I begin?" he ruminated. "Ah yes- Tyana. Where else?"
He began: "We had been very successful so far- Asia Minor had surrendered almost without resistance. The only place that offered anything by way of fighting was Tyana in Cappadocia. They locked the gates and swore they would never surrender. We gave them every opportunity to give up- after all, what possible remaining allegiance could they have to Zenobia? She had proved to be a fickle ally and had left them alone to resist us. This was slowing us down and the campaigning season would soon be over. Aurelian was

very frustrated. I remember it well: standing in his tent, surrounded by his other commanders, when the final reply came back- "Sire, they will not give in." He was furious! The whole thing had been so finely planned and Tyana was as a mosquito on the hide of an elephant- but neither was the emperor willing to pass any bases that could strike him from behind. This must keep all appearances of liberation from the rule of the Palmyrene queen, not a vicious and unprovoked attack on a small kingdom.

"I will not leave even a dog alive when we take this town!" he announced in his anger. We could all appreciate his frustration but this seemed too much. With his usual good fortune, it was solved by a local who volunteered to show us where the walls were vulnerable. We broke through soon after. But it was so easy that Aurelian, with great wisdom and showing his mercy, commanded that there should be no looting and the people living there should be treated with the greatest respect. Of course, he said it was out of respect for their long-dead philosopher who had appeared to him in a dream to appeal for leniency. Much more in keeping with our mission than a massacre of innocent citizens. That didn't go down well at all with the men- they had been expecting gaining much wealth and many slaves. So the night it happened I stood guard with drawn sword outside his quarters. He didn't know I did so but even he had heard the rumours of mutiny.

So the next morning…" my father paused here for dramatic effect. This was one of my favourite parts of the telling and I listened intently. "The next morning, he called everyone together outside the camp." His eyes were closed now as if seeing it all in his vivid memories. "It was beautifully stage-managed, with centurions forewarned and ready to repeat his words to all of those too far away to hear. He declared in front of everyone that he had sworn not to leave even a dog alive in Tyana. Everyone knew this already, as word had gone around and the men had been gleeful at the thought of plunder- everything had been so smooth thus far that no-one had gained anything except their usual pay, which was always late anyway. So, he said," and here my father guffawed , his laughter continuing as he finished: "He said, "I will keep my oath. Kill all of the dogs!" There was a moment as his words made their way out into the crowd of men; then a ripple effect as those at the front, the first to hear, started to chuckle, those further away started to laugh and the entire mood of the army changed in that moment. What a touch that emperor had!

I wandered the camp-fires that night with Aurelian, cloaked and anonymous- I swear not one legionary ate anything other than those poor creatures that night. The humour around the tents was infectious: comments about 'meatballs' being the cleanest of them." He looked quickly at Helena to see her reaction. She ignored the conversation and carried on with her thread. "What a man he was! We had no more rumours of revolt after that. In fact, every city down to Alexandria came over to us with no trouble at all; and the men did very well when they had to march through the mountains to the east of Antioch in order to outflank Zabdas, the Palmyrene general." Warming to his theme, he said, "And let me tell you about that fight too!"

At this point, my mother set down her work and stood up. "I think that's enough for one night, husband. He needs to get to bed." Despite both of our protests, she stood firm and I found myself lying sleeplessly in my room with visions of being an emperor, an army at my feet and the inspiration to solve any obstacles in my path. When I eventually fell asleep, it was to dreams of glory.

◆◆◆

The tone was dramatically different a few nights later. Having just answered some particularly sharp questions regarding Aurelian at the battle of Emesa, and feeling that there would be no better time to ask as I had been congratulated on my insights, I followed up diffidently with a question of my own that had been preying on me for some days. I was aware of the sensitivities surrounding the question I wished to ask.

"Father, I ate at Hosius' house recently. His father was there and silent for most of the meal. Of course, I became very enthusiastic about Aurelian and was repeating some of the stories of his prowess that you have told me. As we moved on to the final course, Hosius' father suddenly looked at me, staring across the room, and asked, "If Aurelian was such an awe-inspiring figure with a record of such unparalleled success, how did it come to pass that he was murdered by his own men?""

My father frowned at this reported question and I reacted to his displeasure, protesting, "He served under Aurelian when he commanded the Dalamatian Horse against the Goths so he must know something of the emperor!"

My father's brow furrowed further. "But his unit was still in northern Italy when Aurelian was killed", he growled. "And only those who were there can possibly know the truth of it." He looked reflective and regretful. "And I was not there- though I do know the truth. I will forever bear the burden of that. I was a protectores who was not there when needed." He stood abruptly, walking to a window and staring silently into the dark outside.

My mother spoke, recognising my father's need for solitude: a rare intervention. "Come with me, Constantine." As we walked along one of the colonnades surrounding the peristyle deep inside our palace, she spoke again. "Do not take it amiss, my son. If he has one regret, it is that he was not where he should have been when he needed to be there. He will talk about it when he is ready. It is less than ten years and the wound is still raw." She spoke, for the first time in my reckoning, as a caring wife rather than as someone fulfilling a legal arrangement.

And he was ready much sooner than expected. To my surprise, Constantius called me to his office in the west wing of the palace. He stood at the wide window that overlooked the sea, the wooden shutters flung wide and the sun beaming in, his hands behind his back and his legs astride, as if a ship's captain on his deck about to face particularly harsh weather.

"Sit there, Constantine." He spoke without turning as he gestured with his hand at the chair before his desk.

I sat. I waited. Eventually, he turned to me. His eyes were red from lack of sleep. He began to pace the room.

He broke the silence. "You must know what took place if you are to be my heir." There was a lengthy pause as he continued to pace, head down.

"It is a simple story, in many ways, quickly enough told. You were right to ask the question, and I have avoided giving an answer." He began without any other preamble, and I leant forward in my seat. "I was not there. As I said last night. I had been sent by the emperor to Nicomedia. Some small task- I suppose it was important enough if we were to invade Persia the following year as Aurelian was so eager to do. So this task assumed a significance that was not warranted. I pleaded with him to keep me near as I had a sense that all was not well. But he insisted- and when the emperor insists, mere mortals must obey. I went. After all, he was the 'Restorer of the World'- what did he have to fear that I would be able to protect him from?"

"Was that why he was moving against Persia? Because he had done all he needed to within the empire?"

"Probably yes. But I don't know for certain. Preparations were being made for an attack on Persia. That is a conversation for another time." He returned to the main subject of our discussion. "I found out what happened from the assassins afterwards. They were tortured and executed." He contemplated this thought for some moments, and I waited patiently. He started again with an unconscious grimace as if from a painful memory. "Some of them were my close friends- or I considered them to be so before the events that followed."

At this point, I recognised a side to my father that I had never before seen, but that helped to explain his rise. I knew of his kindness to those he loved, his courage that inspired his soldiers; but this was accompanied by a ruthlessness that could easily reconcile the end with the means. Given the betrayal and his own sense of guilt over his hero's murder I had little doubt that his personal knowledge of events came directly from brutal interrogations at first-hand. But he was continuing.

"The plan began before them though. It all stemmed from Eros- a small-minded man, one of Aurelian's secretaries. The emperor valued loyalty above all else and Eros had been one of his assistants since the early days of his career. The assassins were used by Eros; and they went to their deaths knowing that they had been manipulated to cause the death of a far better man. When we broke that whining little coward- which, it must be said, took very little effort- he confessed that Aurelian found him going through the drawers of his desk. When the emperor forced him to confess what he was doing, he admitted that he had been copying correspondence and passing it on to Persian contacts. They paid willingly, and high prices, for this sort of information. And the pathetic weasel's reason? He had big gambling debts owed to an Antiochene; and he knew that if we returned to Antioch to launch an invasion of Persia he would probably be dropped off the top of a very high building if he were not able to pay. Eros had become careless as a result of the need for urgency- but there was a lot in it for him, escaping his fate and ending his days a very rich man."

"So how did that lead to the assassination of the emperor?" I was trying not to appear impatient, especially as my father needed to tell the entirety of what happened.

"Aurelian said nothing to us, his bodyguard. He should have done! I would have personally stepped in…" This was the same as a cry of anguish from my father. After a pause accompanied by a near all-consuming anger quickly controlled, he continued. "Aurelian, being the man he was, would have wanted to think long on what action to take- though he had punished many, and publicly, for corruption, this was beyond anything that had gone before. I have no doubt that disappointment would have played a part. But he could not have anticipated what followed."

He took a deep breath, as if the next part of the story would be even more of a trial for him to repeat than what had been related so far.

"You see, Eros felt he had nothing to lose and Aurelian had given him sufficient time to find a solution. He forged death warrants under the emperor's seal for those officers who were closest to the emperor, implicating them in the sale of information to the Persians."

I gasped. It was all clear now- even at my young age, I could see how events would have proceeded from this. But my father forged on regardless and I listened as it poured out.

"Of course, the best lies are based on facts; and when he showed the edicts to those officers his own personal involvement meant that it was extremely convincing. After all, he had the evidence he needed to support the warrants already- but with his own name on them. A general I knew well, one who had risen fast and owed his advancement to the emperor", and here he struck the table hard with his balled fist in anger as he walked past it, the only real sign of his rage, "Mucapor, led the conspiracy to kill the emperor before the emperor could kill them. Aurelian, my mentor, leader and emperor, was stabbed to death one evening in his tent, surrounded by those who had most cause to love and respect him." He turned to me, standing suddenly stock still in the morning glare, silhouetted against its glow, his fury seeming to make him loom even larger in the small room. "And now can you understand how such a great man came to be killed by those so much smaller than him?"

"I can." I left a respectful pause.

My father was staring fiercely at me, willing me to believe in his hero's innocence and the injustice of his brutal murder. "And, son, what shows this best of all? The Emperor Tacitus, chosen to succeed Aurelian, what was his first action? To deify Aurelian!" He declared this triumphantly, as if none could gainsay his implicit verdict. As if to ensure I fully understood, he now made this explicit. "Why would he do that, unless it was to gain the support of the legions who loved the emperor? There was no hint of a general rebellion, no suggestion of anger amongst the men. There was just a little group of fearful and easily-led men who were used by a sly schemer; for they knew they could trust Aurelian- he had proved it time and again."

Unsure how to offer sympathy but wanting to encourage him, I asked simply: "What happened next?"

"After chaos in the empire for a year, with two more wearers of the purple assassinated by the troops, Probus became emperor. That man knew vengeance- though he went the same way himself in the end. We protectores were given permission to question and kill the conspirators. We did this with pleasure. Not that it would bring the emperor back, or make up for our neglect, but revenge can still be enjoyable. Once we knew the full truth from our interrogations, we finished off the remaining conspirators. With my assistance as well as that of the rest of Aurelian's bodyguards, Probus invited all those involved in any way with the murders to a great banquet. He told them it was to thank them for their help in elevating him. But in the middle of the night, when they were all drunk, sated and half asleep, having surrendered their weapons at the gate, we entered the hall where they were being feasted. All of the doors were bolted behind us and then we executed them. It is not something I am proud of as I am sure that there were innocents present too, those Probus found it convenient to dispense with- but it was worth it to ensure that the turmoil came to an end and that justice was done. I believe in order: it is what the empire was built on. And we had chaos." He said this last part almost defiantly, wanting me to think well of him despite the evil of the act.

Seizing the opportunity presented by my father's confession I addressed the issue that had weighed upon me since our first night in Salona. I was convinced that our travel companions' mission was in some way linked to his experiences at that time. I spoke deferentially when I asked, seemingly changing the subject, "And was the mission of the frumentarii somehow connected to the keeping of order in the empire?"

Constantius looked at me sharply. Then, appearing to make a decision, he nodded. "That it was." He sighed. "I might as well tell you, for I will not hide anything from you. You should know already that our emperor Carus was killed by lightning while on campaign against the Sassanid Persians earlier this year. He had been very successful, even capturing their capital, and it seemed most suspicious that he should die in such a way. I sent Antius and his men to find out the truth of what happened. Knowledge is the lifeblood of the empire, and I had to know."

"And did they find the truth?" I asked.

"They did not. But they did hear gossip that Carus had recently been told of his son Carinus, left behind to rule the west in his own absence as a Caesar, a junior emperor, behaving in a way that was unacceptable for any ruler. Carus had only been emperor for months and his son's behaviour was a risk to his continuing in power- particularly given that he was not a young man. Carinus, so they say, and amongst many other crimes, persecutes those in the capital he imagines have slighted him; and he has introduced all kinds of debauchery into the court. The rumours suggest that Carus had decided to replace his son, choosing me as his new heir just before he died."

A modest man, my father shook his head at this as if still surprised that his name would be mentioned in connection with so illustrious a position; maybe even a little embarrassed at repeating this suggestion himself. "So Antius and the other three, taking the initiative, rushed back to inform me as this information will already have been whispered in Carinus' ear. As our new co-emperor with his

brother Numerian since their father's untimely death, my life could be in danger if he sees me as a threat. Your former companions travelled back along the line of the frontier so as to check on the loyalty of the Danubian legions, should civil war break out." He finished in a resigned voice, "Not that this empire of ours needs more instability and chaos."
I asked, alarmed, "Are we at risk then?"
"Not yet," Constantius said. "But when emperors are killed by bolts from the heavens anything may happen next. The one we know little of is Numerian, leading the retreat from Persia at the moment. He was with Carus, his father, when he died so he will know more both of the nature of that death and of his brother's behaviour. He will have his own views on what should be done. But I have heard tell that he is as weak as his brother is forceful. Retreating from his father's conquests would seem to support that. We should not rely on protection from there."
My father sat down sharply behind his desk, sensing that he may have revealed too much for my comfort. I was still but a child, tall and well-built though I was, and the tale of historic troubles accompanied by those more current had cast a pall over the joy of our recent time together. My mother, entering the room with immaculate timing by some unseen prompt, wordlessly held out her hands to me, an invitation for me to leave. As we walked out of the door, I heard my father mutter behind me, his head in his hands, "When will this poor empire of ours know true peace?"

◆◆◆

My mother and I wandered for some time amongst the recently tilled fields surrounding our home. The cool air of autumn, the vibrant colours as leaves descended softly from the trees and the smell of the rich loam being worked by the farmers all brought a sense of normality that I needed after hearing the account of my father's involvement with the emperor Aurelian and the threat of Carinus, son of Carus, and his brother Numerian hanging like the sword of reluctant Damocles above us.

As I talked through this new information with my mother I dwelt on the possibility of our new emperor deciding to take vicious action over any threat to his power. From her responses it became clear that she already knew of my father's worries. More significantly perhaps than any of this, however, I had also come to an understanding of the effect on my father of the past: his deep anger with himself and his wrath at those who easily believed such lies. These emotions disguised what was really an abiding frustration at his own powerlessness. And, in the end, the difficulty Constantius had in forgiving the emperor for having sent him away. I could not see that I would have done any differently to my father- and I hoped he would be able to find some peace when enough time had passed. But these present circumstances- facing a likely threat on his own life from a vengeful grudge-holding emperor so soon after having found such pleasure in building a family for himself- brought back all of his memories of that time of turmoil. I considered this to show the true nature of my father, for his main concern was not himself so much as the empire he served with little thought for personal gain. I admit that I idolized him and gave him far more credit than his motivation probably deserved; but surely he would make a better Caesar than this Carinus?

I considered that day to be the day when my destiny began to reveal itself and I started to become a man. My father never hid anything from me from that time on and discussed every element of his previous experiences with me when they arose. He did so no longer as a story of adventure; but as significant life-changing decisions with potential empire-wide consequences.

CHAPTER 6: CHANGES

Half a year passed from the time of our arrival in Salona. Half a year of establishing our new domestic arrangements. Half a year of building a new family and all that entailed. Half a year of growth in my knowledge and understanding. My training with Antius meant that, as I grew physically, I gained in strength and stamina also. My thinking was tested and developed by Felix and Scipio; while my tutor- not without some resistance from me- ensured that my appreciation of Roman culture, literature and history was as extensive as he was able to make it. We were fortunate, Sol shining on us with all his favour. We knew it. Despite Antius' spies having warned him of the emperor Carinus and a possible attack on my father, all was surprisingly quiet. Alongside this, few demands were made of the empire's governors as the new administrations established themselves- the two sons divided the empire between them as Carus had wished, with Carinus in the West and Numerian in the East. There was a lull in activity which meant little demand on my father and his men. Without external threats, taxes continued to flow and loyalty remained secure. Nothing disrupted our tranquility and the empire seemed to be more stable than it had been for a long time. It appeared that my father's plea for peace was being fulfilled.

This all changed shortly before Saturnalia.

Preparations were being made with just over a week to go until the event itself. Pigs were being slaughtered, gifts bought and the harvest was being transformed into a celebratory banquet. Servants could be seen rushing around purchasing crops from the city market before slaves of other local notables could buy them first. Many were at the docks daily to greet the fishing fleet on their return, attempting to buy the best of the catch for smoking and salting; while ships arriving from other countries on the trade routes were surrounded the instant they arrived. Wagons and carts came in great numbers from the farms along the coast, their wines being a particular focus of attention. The buzz of activity created a sense of excitement that pervaded the city; and the palace was no exception.

Into the midst of these preparations rode an imperial messenger.

As it happened, a fortnight before the eastern empire had changed hands- and we had known nothing of it until now. Our world had turned while we dealt with our own domestic circumstances; and no longer would my horizons be limited to just the governor's palace and Salona.

◆◆◆

"I came as fast as I could", gasped the rider, having leapt from his horse at the main entrance to the palace. Our men had seen him coming from afar and a group of us stood waiting, anticipating news of great significance. It was rare to receive an imperial messenger. The man went down on one knee before my father. Covered in a combination of mud, dust and dirt, his clothes were so filthy as to be a near-uniform brown colour. His face was spattered also, and the horse itself was heaving for breath having been pushed to its limits.

He said simply and briefly, "Lord, it grieves me to inform you of the death of the emperor Numerian; and great joy to tell you of the legions' choice of Diocles as the new emperor."

My father shook his head in wonder and spoke under his breath- so low that it is likely only I could hear him, as the one closest behind. "Diocles…! You old dog." There was a momentary pause as the news was absorbed by all of us, news of empire-changing significance announced so easily.

Then Constantius turned abruptly to those of us standing there: "Follow me to my office. Felix- see to this man's needs and ensure he has a good meal to restore his energy. See that his horse is taken care of. When you have done so, join the rest of us."

He turned sharply and, head bowed in concentration and staring at the floor, he marched swiftly along the marbled corridors until we found ourselves in his room- Antius, Scipio, Helena and me. Turning abruptly to face us, he spoke without hesitation: "Constantine- close those doors. What I am about to tell you all must not be repeated elsewhere. Do you understand me?" I nodded, fully convinced of the gravity of whatever was about to be revealed. The others did the same.

"Felix already knows this so we will not await him." He hesitated, looked to check that I had closed the doors, then launched into what he needed to say. "Diocles is an old friend. As you will all be aware, I was a member of the emperor Aurelian's personal guard; and, as such, I knew most of his generals as both colleagues and friends. Many of these were killed or executed after his death for reasons I will not go into." I exchanged a knowing glance with my mother at this, aware of who had been at least partly responsible for these events. "Diocles was one of the few who proved himself to be entirely and completely trustworthy, an admirer of Aurelian as much as I. He is also an Illyrian and a cavalryman like me, so we have a great deal in common. He told me once that he was even born in this city."

My mother looked at her husband thoughtfully. "So we should expect a visit, and maybe even promotion?"

"We must not interpret portents so optimistically", he replied cautiously. "Numerian's brother, Carinus, is still

Caesar of the western empire as we seem to have so quickly forgotten. He has always been the more dangerous of the brothers. I have no doubt that he will be most unhappy at Diocles' acclamation. Were it not for my comrade's acclamation by his troops, Carinus would have been sole emperor. And, though there was little love between family, Carinus will be anxious to establish the exact circumstances of Numerian's passing- particularly given the suspicious nature of his father's end. We will have to wait and see. This death will undoubtedly be used for political gain. The only question is how."

Scipio spoke up. "I couldn't see that Numerian lasting long. Bit of a wet morning, from what I'm told. Into his books and speech-making. Not really the qualities the legions would want to see in an emperor."

Constantius smiled wryly at this. "Why do you suppose it was that Carinus was given the west while Numerian accompanied his father? Though," he added reflectively, looking to Antius for confirmation, "as we know from our informants in Italy and elsewhere, Carinus is making far more enemies than friends. So he may remain occupied there."

"'Tis true sir", said Antius. "Takes any woman he wants, and especially the married ones. They say he's shagging around like there's no future in celibacy."

Felix entered the room and sputtered involuntarily at this comment, not appreciating the atmosphere in the room. He followed up weakly when he saw he was alone in his humour- "Well, there is no future in it… not really… if you understand my meaning."

My father moved on briskly, ignoring the interruption that was not in keeping with the gravity of the conversation. "So. We will interview this messenger to see what more he can tell us. Then we may be able to make a clearer judgement as to what it is that will be expected, or asked, of us."

The rider was permitted a full night's sleep, particularly when it turned out he had been on his horse for over a week. The next morning we gathered once more in the governor's office to hear of what had taken place. The messenger began by assuring us that what he had to tell had been heard from those who were present as the events to be related took place; but so much was unknown that all would have gaps in their knowledge that must be filled by guesswork. My father impatiently reminded him that we knew there would be many versions but his own was the only one we had for now. The rest could wait until they were available.

"We approached Nicomedia on the line of our withdrawal from fighting the Persians. We know not where the emperor was intending to travel, but it is likely he would want to meet with his brother to confirm arrangements since their father had died."

Antius said, a little too loudly, "Aye. And no doubt to agree which husbands to do away with."

Constantius intervened again. "Ignore him. Continue." He gave Antius a warning glance.

"Well, the emperor Numerian had not been seen for several days and the legion commanders wanted to find out what his orders were as to the direction we were taking. Our retreat had been very slow and the men were becoming impatient. Lucius Aper- you may have heard tell of him, the emperor's father-in-law and Praetorian Prefect- was making the decisions. Nobody knew where Numerian was. But Lucius Aper informed the generals that the litter travelling in the middle of the procession contained Numerian. Said he had an unfortunate eye infection that had been worsened by the unseasonably dry weather increasing the amount of dust being kicked up by the men. They had taken his word for it for several days- despite rumours having been spread around the men that Aper had been involved with Carus' death the previous year. There was much suspicion but nobody was willing to take the risk of challenging his word. But then a Numidian slave, a litter-bearer, approached Diocles as cavalry commander for the imperial bodyguard one evening as we made camp. He said the emperor had not moved nor made a sound for a very long time, even to ask for food or drink."

"That is odd", said my mother. "He was known to be fond of pleasure and would not have enjoyed any discomfort. I am surprised no-one was willing to act before."

The messenger bowed his head in acknowledgement of the comment. "A question, my lady, that remains. However, when Diocles presumed to check, drawing back the linen curtains surrounding the litter, he found a rotting corpse."

Scipio spoke, suddenly and incisively. "When you say that you heard this story from those who were there at the time, who exactly do you mean?"

The messenger looked him in the eye as he replied. "From Diocles himself. He told all of those he was sending out what had happened as he wished it to be known by all just how treacherous Lucius Aper had been."

There were slight movements around the room as all drew their own conclusions from this information. I felt it was my opportunity to ask an obvious question. "Would a 'rotting corpse' not have smelt badly enough to have been noticed by the slaves carrying him?"

My father raised his eyebrows at me appreciatively. "Another good question. But let us assume a degree of licence in the telling of the tale." He turned and spoke pleasantly to our informer. "Please leave us for a moment. If you could wait outside?"

Once the man had left the room, my father turned to us. "We must tread carefully in these circumstances- especially you, Constantine, for that was a naive, if valid, question. I have little doubt that this man will report back on our response. For my part, I am convinced that Diocles, knowing him as I do and much as I would have done in a similar circumstance, orchestrated events to a degree. But his loyalty to a chosen and established emperor is as certain as Sol's light blessing us tomorrow. Despite the questions you must all have as to what really took place, we cannot have Diocles' messenger return with the wrong impression. Our lives and the lives of those we love could be at risk if there is even a hint of distrust- whether he is a friend of mine or not. He cannot afford to take risks. Too many emperors have died at the hands of the army in recent years."

He called the messenger back in, and the man recommenced as if he had never been interrupted.

"The rest of this I saw and heard with my own eyes so I can personally vouch for it. The whole army gathered for the emperor's funeral pyre. As the skies darkened with the smoke from the flames, Diocles raised his sword and swore before the Unconquered Sun that he was not responsible for the death of the emperor. He then ordered Lucius brought forward. He told us all, as we surrounded the small hill on which he stood, that he had arrested Lucius the previous night without warning as he feared the Praetorian Prefect would flee before justice could be done. It was most dramatic, with these men silhouetted against the fire behind them almost as if in the shadow of the murdered emperor, and Diocles ended with a bellow: "Aper: answer for your actions!"

Lucius did his best but the facts were clear. He did appear to lack motive, as he declared that with his son-in-law as emperor and holding the position he had, what reason could he possibly have for the murder? But his worst, and fatal, mistake was when he called Diocles the 'son of a slave' in front of us all. There was no way that any red-blooded soldier was going to tolerate such an accusation, especially in front of a military assembly. I did not hear what Diocles said next. But I did see him take his sword and drive it through Lucius. Even as the Prefect keeled over in his chains, Maximian, one of the legion commanders, was running forward and hailed him as the new Augustus before us all. When Galerius, one of his fellow generals, took up the same cry, the entire army joined in and he was chosen by the legions to be Numerian's successor. He accepted this in all humility."

I looked around the room. A sigh of pent-up breath was released from several of us and all rearranged their seating positions as tension was released. Before anyone could speak and betray any words that might be inappropriate, Constantius bowed his head to the messenger. "My thanks. Your account has been very helpful. What are the emperor's orders now?"

"I am to let you know that the emperor Diocles, or Diocletian as he now wishes to be known, returns to Sirmium forthwith. He will visit you here in Salona once the celebration of Saturnalia is finished; and he requires your support as your new emperor."

My father responded instantly; and I knew he had little other choice. "Of course! He is one of my oldest companions, and we have shared many a meal, and no small number of evenings, together. He has my complete support and my sword, as well as those of any I command, at his disposal. My province is his to order as he wishes and we will welcome him as best we can. Now, Felix, please see to it that this man's horse is ready to depart when he is, and that he has the best of provisions for the journey."

Felix ushered the man out, and those in the room visibly relaxed as the doors closed behind them. My father held his hand up, the palm flat: "I know we all have things we wish to say. I do not want to hear them yet. I will spend some time with Constantine this afternoon"- I was surprised by this but pleased at the consideration, particularly at such a crucial moment- "and we will meet together for the evening meal later today. Helena: please see to the arrangements for this and begin preparations with the kitchens for the arrival of the emperor. And all of us: pray to your gods- or god", he said looking at my mother for some reason, "that this will all work out for our good."

◆◆◆

My father met me that afternoon in the palace baths. His personal guards had cleared the building so we knew that we had absolute privacy. We unclothed ourselves in silence, each alone in his own thoughts. He threw me a towel, and we moved to the steam room. Each of us sat down and neither of us spoke, sitting sweating for some time. It was a cold day outside and the contrast with the heat of the room was even starker than usual. I looked sideways at my father. Rivulets ran down his prominent temples and he sat with his muscles tensed, hands pressed to the seat either side of him, and with his head hunched slightly forward. He must have sensed my stare and turned to gaze at me. Studying me for a brief time, he then said, "What are your thoughts, Constantine?"

This was one of the first times I had noticed him use my name, rather than some other more general designation: he genuinely wished to hear my counsel.

"Well sir, as you say there is no way that Diocles... Diocletian would have killed the emperor...", I began.

He responded before I could continue, recognising the implied question in my tone and hesitation: "There really is no way. He is a believer, as much as I, in duly constituted authority. He was, with me, the principal instigator of the vengeance on imperial assassins years ago. A man does not change such strong beliefs so much in that space of time."

"So Lucius did it?"

"Who knows? All that can be said is that it was definitely not Diocletian."

"But this killing of Aper and the actions of Maximian and Galerius appear a little... coincidental."

He laughed ironically. "They do, don't they? Very convenient. If I know the general- the emperor- he will have prepared very thoroughly, even in a short time. I suspect he was just waiting for Aper to make one false move to justify his killing; and the two commanders will have been made ready for when the time was right."

"Do you know either of them?"

"I don't. But nor do I need to. Who would not wish to take advantage of being on the side of the winner? Lucius in chains and heavily guarded would not stand a chance against him. As soon as the corpse was found, Diocletian was as certain to be the next emperor as..." He searched around for a suitable metaphor, and I jumped in.

"That was good timing as well. As camp was being made, night falling, a slave just happens to approach the chief of the emperor's bodyguards?"

Again, I returned to my theme of whether Diocletian was truly to be trusted. My father looked at me sharply. "Do not doubt me on this. Diocletian will have known that Numerian was dead as soon as the unfortunate event took place; but the timing of the public discovery will have been all important. After all," and he looked around with evidence of some nerves despite knowing we were completely alone, "how does it reflect on him that the emperor in his care was found dead? If anyone had had an opportunity to think longer on this it could well have been him that was executed in front of the troops. Self-preservation meant he had to move quickly, had to manage the situation, and the only escape from his own execution at the command of a newly-chosen emperor would be to take the job himself."

I nodded, dazed. The full ramifications of the murder and the genius of Diocletian's solution were only now becoming clear to me.

My father changed the subject to one of more immediate consequence. "Why do you think he wishes to visit us as one of his first steps to consolidating power?"

I considered this for some time. The room was sweltering and we were both sweating profusely. As I deliberated, Constantius gestured with his hand that we should move through to a nearby room for a massage. One of the strengths of these baths was that, being in a city at the centre of a web of trade and political intrigue, my father had chosen to employ several pairs of deaf and dumb slave masseurs. It was so secure that the governor made it available for others to use- at a price, of course. Business transactions, intelligence gathering and all sorts of other secretive arrangements were made here frequently as complete confidentiality was assured. I suspected my father had some means of knowing what was spoken at those times for he was unusually well informed and these secretive meetings would be too good an opportunity to miss. Even the guards on the main doors were hand-picked by my father from those who had been with him since near the start of his rise and who owed him their personal devotion. We lay down on the slabs in the room and the two large slaves began to pummel us gently and professionally. I closed my eyes and said, "Carinus is still around. And he must know that Diocletian will not be content with merely the slim spoils of the east as a new Augustus. Carinus rules Gaul, Italy, Spain, Britain and Africa. If the brothers had ever met they may even have agreed that Noricum, Pannonia, perhaps even Dalmatia would have been his."

"Maybe, yes. But Carinus has had little do with any of his provinces except a brief foray against the Quadi on the Upper Rhine over a year ago. Since then, it would seem he has been enjoying all of the luxuries and excesses Rome has to offer- even, according to Antius, sending the husbands of attractive women to die in battle."

"But he can still muster a huge army with that number of provinces?"

"He assuredly can", my father replied. "And all Diocletian has is the army he is returning with from Persia- likely the First and Third Parthica in the main, along with a wide selection of specialist units. He will be able to reinforce from Thrace and Moesia on his way through using local recruits, and Antius is convinced that the legion commanders in those provinces will stand by Diocletian. If all are loyal to him he will have vexillations from at least eight legions to call on- perhaps even whole legions- and they will include many auxiliary infantry cohorts and cavalry wings. If Carinus waits long enough, however, he may have a greater number to support his cause- perhaps as many as nine."

"But Diocletian has far more experience in warfare, and of commanding armies?"

"True- but much of his experience is in the east. The choice of eventual battlefield will be vital, as will the loyalty of those who are acquainted with neither Carinus nor Diocletian yet serve within the sphere of one or the other. It will not be a battle between mobile field armies: those are for use in maintaining the integrity of the frontier. This will require legions to choose their side. And that could well be the main strength that Diocletian brings with him. Carinus only became emperor because of his father; Diocletian was chosen by the legions."

"And that sir", I said triumphantly, "is why Diocletian is visiting us."

"What do you mean?"

"You!" I said. "You command a key province. Men of Illyria from both provinces, Dalmatia and Moesia, have led the empire's armies since before Aurelian, several legions have a sense of loyalty to you personally and this is the closest of the provinces Carinus could claim over which Diocletian can have an influence. If you 'change sides'- for that is how it will be seen no matter how negligent Carinus has been in carrying out his duties- then you will carry others with you. It will be common knowledge by now that Carus was considering you to replace his son, and that will carry its own weight with Diocletian also. And if this knowledge is common, then Carinus' revenge on you for it is certain."

"I'm not sure that is all true", he said, considering. "Diocletian was Dux Moesiae, responsible for all armed forces in the area, before he became the commander of the protectores. He has that province's loyalty regardless. As for your point about replacing Carinus with me, assuming of course that the stories regarding Carus' plans were true, his regard for me- and his son's reaction to this- may mean, as you suggest, that our decision is already made for us."

"Aye- but think further sir! What about Pannonia and those provinces with a Danubian frontier? And even Gaul? They know you well from your service with Aurelian. You could be even more of a threat to Carinus and an even greater bonus to Diocletian. Diocletian will also have been present when Carus was deciding what to do about his son and turned to thinking of you as a successor. Perhaps he even whispered your name in the emperor's ear?"

My father was a humble man and this had not occurred to him. He turned his head, resting it on his crossed arms and grunting as his back muscles were gently beaten. He looked at me pensively across the space that separated us. "You may have the right of it."

Both because the masseurs were becoming more vigorous in their attentions and because we had a great deal to think about, we each turned to stare at the wall in front of us, chins resting on our forearms. After what seemed an eternity, my father said without looking my way, "So what do we do?"

Hiding my delight at being included as an advisor, I replied swiftly: "We can choose on the basis either of who will win, or who is the best choice as emperor. These are not necessarily the same; but the ideal situation is one where they are. Self-interest must play its part- and, as you say, it is quite possible that the decision is already made for us. But, assuming that Carinus will be fair to you, who will win?"

In my heart, I felt the decision was already made in reality, the emperor's sense of fairness having been more than called into question through the many tales we had heard. This was but a technical exercise to confirm a decision that had already been made- one that we were forced into through words spoken a world away by a former emperor. But my father ruminated on the choice nonetheless: "There are strengths on both sides. We have spoken of these already. My greatest concern is that Carinus is an not well known as a commander. He has done so little other than on the Rhine against the Quadi- though Tacitus did speak highly of that tribe centuries ago. Carinus may be a military genius. We know too little. Other than that, the two are evenly matched."

"Who will make the best emperor, then?"

"That is clear on the basis of performance thus far: Diocletian. Carinus has been a Caesar for two years, with great responsibilities. But he has done nothing, or near to nothing. He has merely taken advantage of his own power. I know little of the truth of these claims about his affairs; but I know it to be a fact that he has spent huge sums on the games in Rome. His central preoccupation has been ensuring the support of the people of Rome and enjoying his new-found wealth and fame. While Diocletian will bring stability and order to the whole empire, much needed after the constant changes of recent years. I wish for no repeat of the Year of the Six Emperors when the boy-emperor Gordian III eventually took power- the upheaval accompanying that, the confusion, chaos and wars are not worth consideration. Persia may even decide to take advantage after Carus' conquest of their capital in order to get revenge. As it is, by my counting only one emperor in recent years has died of natural causes- and that means over twenty violent deaths."

"There is little debate then father. We support Diocletian, as you have already assured that messenger, and we support his success with our whole-hearted encouragement. You have far more influence than you may think and he will place great value on it. There is also your personal friendship and respect for him. Beyond even that, there is the chance that he can impose some stability on the empire- though that prospect is far distant at the moment, with many obstacles to be overcome before the opportunity will even arise. This is a very astute move by Diocletian: hosting his visit will place a seal on your allegiance and Carinus will treat you as he would a traitor should Diocletian lose. You will be committed whether you choose to be or not."

Constantius spoke carefully, "I know this decision to be the right thing to do even without Diocletian forcing my hand. But it is not just about me. It is about our family, our province and even our empire- particularly if my influence is as great as you claim it to be."

He spoke these last words fondly as the masseurs finished their task and we rose to move back to the caldarium.

◆◆◆

Saturnalia came and went. I had previously been looking forward to it very much as I had only ever experienced it in a backwater like Naissus. However, despite the week-long celebration everyone in the governor's palace was preoccupied and distracted. When Constantius had announced our conclusions to the rest of his advisers they had all accepted them and agreed with the reasoning. I suspected that my father had already made up his mind before speaking to me; but I was flattered at my privileged treatment. Antius had added, based on his network of spies, that my conclusions about the esteem in which my father was held were more accurate than either of us knew.

So gifts were given, the governor went through the formality of our slaves taking the role of the masters and the masters serving them at meal times for one day, and we all wore our freedmen's caps. I was chosen as the master of ceremonies for the week as part of the overturning of the usual state of affairs. I would normally have been flattered by this, enjoyed the opportunity and taken full advantage of the role with the Hosius' connivance; but I could tell that we all felt as if we were waiting for the main event. Despite my leading role in the dinners we gave at the palace and the parties we were invited to, I felt as one playing the part in a shadow. Attention was elsewhere. The emperor's impending visit had been announced to the populace and all knew what this meant for the city, the province and even, likely, the empire. The tension was palpable as we awaited the occasion.

Despite this, the celebration of the birth day of the Unconquered Sun which followed Saturnalia was not allowed to pass in the same manner- not least due to the Emperor Aurelian having been the one to reintroduce this god to the empire. Naturally, my father saw great virtue in this worship; and even more so due to the great changes that were once again taking place in the empire. He saw it as a matter of faith that he celebrate his god and pray for his blessing on our empire at such a troubled time. So the day was treated very seriously due to the help of the Unconquered Sun being needed more than ever.

In the town, the celebrations began with games held in the amphitheatre in honour of Sol Invictus. My father opened these to public acclaim in the morning but only stayed for an hour, until the first few gladiatorial bouts were finished. He slowly led a chariot carrying a statue of the god and drawn by gold-ornamented white horses up the hill to the palace, accompanied by cult priests. Much time was then spent sacrificing in the temple to the sound of music from flutes and drums. We prayed for a good result for the empire as a whole when the clash with Carinus, inevitable as it was, eventually materialized. My mother did not make an appearance; but I saw her leaving the palace with Felix and a small escort in the early afternoon as incense-scented smoke continued to waft from the temple altar in the courtyard. She returned later that evening. My father, having been resentful of her absence earlier in the day, made an abrupt remark as we sat to eat which led to a further family discussion, this time one with my mother at the centre.

"So where does your god stand on this small matter, Helena?"

She tried to ignore him. "I know not. I pray, and he will answer as he chooses."

I was confused by this and looked at the two of them, wondering what was being discussed. Constantius saw this and explained. "Your mother is a Christ-lover. You must have heard of them."

I had. I knew that they had been persecuted under Decius according to my tutor, and then under his successor, Valerian, just three decades ago. But they had been left alone since. Their refusal to sacrifice to our gods made them untrustworthy and disloyal. So this information about my mother, while a revelation to me that explained much that I had noticed previously, was interesting rather than something to be condemned. My response was consequently more curious than judgmental, and based on the few facts I knew about this religion. I also disliked this first indication of conflict between those that I loved and admired the most.

"But father, don't you also believe in one god who is supreme?"

He looked at me, irritation with my mother turning to more of a considered thoughtfulness as he was never one to ignore a reasoned debate. "That I do. But the Unconquered Sun is only the first of many. He is my chosen patron, but I could have chosen from any number of others. I do consider it self-evident that he is the first for we could not live without him. We could live without these others. However, your mother- and Felix", this being said with a tone of mixed anger and sadness, "believe that there is one God alone, no other even existing who could challenge him for supreme authority. All others being a figment of our imaginations, our statues of them being worthless idols…" Here, his voice started to rise as he worked himself up into a froth of indignation at time-honoured traditions being overturned by such polluting ideas.

My mother intervened. "Constantine", she said gently. "It would be best if you left us to our discussion."

"The boy needs to hear this!" My father roared, as if her comment were the last straw.

"Only if you are ready to discuss it reasonably."

At that, Constantius himself left the room, rage written across a face pungently and darkly coloured with its effect, shouting as he left: "I will not be told what to do in my own house!"

The door slammed behind him. I looked at my mother and she looked at me. Neither of us spoke; but I knew this could not be left as it was. It was the only sign of disunity between my parents that I had seen in the six months since they had married. And I know my mother did not wish to sow seeds of discord between me and my new-found father, so she stayed silent.

◆◆◆

It was only two weeks later that the emperor Diocletian arrived. I found it astonishing that a name I had never heard until so recently had come to mean so much to me in such a short time, dominating my waking thoughts. He had requested that we not make too much effort; but it seemed that the people of Salona had other ideas. Antius and Scipio were with me, stood on the walls above the town gates as I had been eager to see my first emperor. The entire city had made an appearance as if it were a public holiday and, along with a great mass of people outside, the roads into and approaching the palace were crowded with members of the local populace. Many had arisen early and travelled in to the city, making a particular effort to see this new emperor who would have such an influence over our lives, for good or ill. Antius, through his paid network, had been keeping us regularly informed as to what people were saying. Much of the excitement stemmed from our hosting Diocletian's visit despite being the capital of one of, at least hypothetically, Carinus' provinces. We were making a clear statement as to who we supported if it should come to a clash. The local people knew that, if this emperor lost, their own futures, if not lives, could be forfeit. Carinus was known for his vengeful nature. But this was Diocletian's hometown and they were not about to turn on one of their own. In fact, their pride in his achievements meant caution was rejected in favour of complete and absolute support: and the whole of Dalamatia wanted him to know it.

We saw the emperor approaching from the hills to the north. Diocletian was in front of his retinue riding a deep black stallion. His choice of dress stood out: he was wearing armour rather than flowing purple cloth, and even I could work out that that meant he intended all to know that his reign would be characterised, at least initially, by warfare. It was a signal that Carinus or he would rule supreme: there would be no co-rulers. The metal shone and glinted in the crisp light of the cold, bright day. Scipio murmured beside me, "And leading from the front. Start as you mean to continue."

His retinue, a small one for an emperor, wound down behind him out of the pass that we had descended the previous year. He did not intend to stay long and Scipio informed me that he would have left the imperial administrators back in Sirmium as they would not need his guidance for the few days he would remain with us. However, as another indication that war lay in the near future, he had included the praetorian guard, evidently seen to be trustworthy now regardless of what had taken place with their previous prefect. This was communicated by their position immediately behind him. They were impressively uniform in their dress and in their movements, and all of a significant height as well as riding identically-coloured horses- Antius leant across and whispered: "Nothing but show troops." He accompanied this comment with a vicious expletive in case I had not fully grasped the depth of his contempt for the praetorians.

Behind these were detachments of different warriors, all mounted for the sake of speed and many brought back from the east by Numerian and now part of this small army belonging to Diocletian. There were Thracian lancers, flying bright pennants from their weapons; mounted Pannonian infantry with swords held aloft as they came in sight to present a sparkling spectacle to the people; and Syrian horse-archers in flowing robes and leather caps. At the back in rolling ox-drawn wagons came the emperor's household, along with their slaves. Felix suddenly appeared beside us, muttering. "And where in the name of God are they all going to stay? We don't have much room at the palace and the camp outside the walls wasn't designed for that number." He walked off distractedly, making his way down from the walls to greet the emperor. I could just hear his final words as he went: "And this is meant to be a negligible number…" I nearly laughed out loud but stopped myself due to my liking for him.

The imperial company approached the Porta Caesarea below us, and, as they did so, the crowd parted. A group made up of the senior town magistrates- duumvirs responsible for justice, aediles for buildings and quaestors for finances- emerged to welcome Diocletian. They were led by my father as governor with Felix at his side as procurator. Priests and augurs of the main gods rushed to join them, delayed through having to make their own religious preparations for the arrival of a new emperor. I watched as that emperor embraced Constantius, a wide smile on each of their faces, and Felix inclined his head, indicating to the emperor that all was ready for him to enter the city. A troop of trumpeters appeared, lining up on each side of the entrance and proudly announcing the emperor's entrance with a serenade. As he drew nearer, Scipio gasped in surprise.

"The emperor's armour: it is battle-armour!"

Confused, I responded by asking, "What else would you expect?" Hosius, on the other side of me, responded more quickly. "You might see an emperor wearing armour on an occasion like this- but it would be ceremonial. Probably gold, heavily decorated. And an ornate helmet with a brightly-coloured plume. You certainly would not expect battle-armour. The emperor is telling us exactly who he is and what happens next."

The crowd were waving banners and the cheering started as Diocletian walked beneath the gate.

Antius, looking down at them, said to me, "You wouldn't believe how much money my men have had to spend on that lot, giving them the flags to wave, getting some of them to start the ovation and applause, even paying some to come out on the streets or get their friends to do so… And Felix thinks it's just about accommodation!" It amused me greatly that an emperor, unheard of and unknown until so recently, should think it was all spontaneous- but until Antius said so it had not occurred to me that it could be anything other. Diocletian waved graciously and accepted the plaudits of the crowd, their performance being adequate enough to at least suggest sincerity. We turned to watch as he continued through the centre of the city, now led by flute-players, incense burning at the brightly garlanded entrances to each temple and creating a haze of scented smoke wafting across the streets. People were hanging out of windows and from balconies, throwing flowers and shouting enthusiastically. The praetorians now had to trot in front of their emperor to clear the way as the narrower road meant many were unintentionally encroaching on ground required for the imperial procession.

"But at least a crowd creates a crowd", Antius followed up reflectively. "I've only paid a tiny number compared with that." He gestured around him, saying cynically, "Maybe some of them even mean it."

Scipio spoke admiringly, "You've done a great job regardless, my friend."

In the spirit of the moment, and in complete contrast to his usual no-nonsense character, Antius bowed dramatically and with a flourish, as if an imperial courtier. "My thanks, sir", he said, at the lowest point in his dip.

Scipio guffawed at this, and then we made our way up to the palace for the formal reception.

◆◆◆

There were moments in the course of the next three days that were particularly significant for me. Diocletian was a military man in every sense: a decision-maker who clearly did not believe in all of the pomp of the imperial court. He himself was an unimpressive man in looks, despite his armour. In fact, his appearance made me realise the need for the court ritual and dress, whether he liked it or not, as without it he would have seemed very ordinary. He was older than I had expected- a few years beyond my father- and was losing his hair. He evidently did his best to brush it forward to disguise this, and his barber, one of the key members of his household who went everywhere with him, met him every morning. At least, so I was told by Lucipor who had heard it in the slaves' gossip. Despite his age and lack of hair, however, he was truly a man of action, fit, keen and fervent. His face was lined with care and with outdoor life as a soldier; but the marks running from beside his nose to the edges of his mouth, and those at the corners of his eyes, were signs of a man with humour who liked to laugh. His eyes were his strongest feature, and it felt at times that he could see through you to the heart of your words, penetrating to your motives and thoughts before you could identify them yourself. It was when he spoke that you realised how deceptive appearances could be, for there was power and authority in every word. But, as I had assumed the new emperor would appear god-like, this was still, overall, a disappointment.

My father included me from the start in every meeting. Despite his words in the bathhouse, Constantius evidently meant far more to Diocletian than maybe even Constantius knew. He saw himself as my father's mentor and their relationship was closer than my father had expressed. This was first obvious when we met in my father's office that evening. The placement of seats had changed to reflect those my father wanted involved, but we were surprised when Diocletian turned up with no companions at all.

When Constantius queried this, he chuckled. "I've been a general for years, and I take advice when I need it. You, my friend," he clapped my father on the shoulder, "have been one of those advisers, and you have never failed me. Why would I need anyone else present for the conversations we are about to have?" His brow darkened. "And, besides anything else, there are spies of Carinus even here with me now in Salona. The fewer know of what we talk the better." My father introduced me, then Felix and Scipio, to the emperor, and we bowed deeply. "Let us sit."

We sat on the hard wooden chairs that Constantius had brought in for this meeting, having thought about what Diocletian would want, and, as we did so, the emperor turned his penetrating eyes on a darker corner of the room. "Have you left someone out my friend? Is that Antius in the shadows?"

The centurion, not usually one to hold himself back, emerged from the darkness. "Lord Emperor," was all he nonchalantly said, along with a nod of the head. There was a degree of familiarity that went beyond the usual approach to the imperial majesty, and I was shocked. There was a pause as we all held our breath.

Diocletian paused… then threw back his head and laughed with gusto. "You haven't changed! I speak of spies, and…" He turned back to my father, "Has he worked well for you?" He nodded. "He has. He is exceptional." Constantius explained to the rest of us. "When Antius and I first met, he was working directly for Diocletian. When Diocletian left Moesia to lead the protectores he transferred Antius' employment to me." He gestured to one of the spare chairs in the circle, "Join us, Antius." He gave the emperor a moment to make himself comfortable before continuing. "So, Diocles- if I may call you that one last time- my congratulations on your rise, my friend."

"My thanks to you. Right place, right time. And Mithras' help."

"What happened, Lord?" Constantius' informality had now gone and been replaced with a more appropriate level of deference. "We heard a version from your messenger but would be grateful if you could tell us more."

"Of course. There may not be much more to add. Lucius Aper, Numerian's uncle, either killed his nephew or had him killed. I found the body and knew I had to be very careful about how the death was revealed. We didn't have time for a lengthy trial, and we know what a travesty justice can be when you have to go through all of the processes. And when he insulted me in front of the entire army… Well, his guilt needed no trial, nor did he deserve the chance to justify himself or deny his actions. So I killed him." He shrugged. "And then the men acclaimed me emperor."

Constantius responded, his tone less barbed due to being accompanied by a conspiratorial smile. "They acclaimed you? Or Maximian and Galerius did so?" He was presuming on their friendship; but the emperor seemed to be open to my father's questions.

Diocletian spread his hands, laughing. "I accept that. It took a little arrangement. But who else was there? We had to have someone take a lead. Might as well be me as any other. And we both knew it would happen eventually."

"Why is that, sir?" I asked politely, a little taken aback at such an astonishing assumption.

My father answered on behalf of the emperor. "We used to joke about it. When Diocles was a young man, a druidess prophesied he would one day become emperor. But she also said he would have to slay a boar first. We used to say that that could mean killing the Emperor Probus- for he could be a real bore at times- or one of the mighty-tusked boars of the Germanian forests. They are truly terrifying and anyone who dared fight one would be justified in claiming the purple!"

Diocletian delightedly finished off the story. "However, it all became clear when I killed Lucius- for 'Aper' means boar! So this was always to be my fate."

After some more conversation regarding family- "How is your daughter, Valeria?" "Very well. Seven years old and already instructing me on what I should do. She rules the empire more than I do."- we moved on.

My father phrased it delicately. "So, sir, what does the future hold for us?"

The smiles disappeared swiftly from all faces at that, for it was the meat of the matter. Diocletian frowned, not as a reaction to Constantius' question so much as to an instinctive dislike of the next word he would say. "Carinus."

Antius spoke up. "My sources tell me that he has declared you to be a 'murderer and usurper'. This must lead to action on his part."

The emperor nodded. "It will. I knew of this already. We have this winter to prepare, and the battle will come in the spring. I wish it to be on ground of my choosing, and when I am ready."

"And can you do that in the next two months?" This was from Felix, our logistician, whose mind, I could tell, was already working through the complications and difficulties. "Carinus has Rome and Italy as well as all of the legions from the western provinces. While you have been making your way back from Nicomedia he has been gathering men. They are fresh, unused except for rare border adventures, and raring for action. Your soldiers need rest."

Diocletian looked at Felix, his frowning brow clearing as he recognized the procurator. "Ah- I remember you now. You were with Constantius during the Palmyran expeditions." Felix nodded confirmation. "You are right. And that is why I need you, your men and Dalmatia, governor."

Without hesitation, my father said, "All are yours to command, myself first and foremost."

"My thanks." Diocletian acknowledged my father's life or death commitment with little drama, despite all those present knowing the great implications of what had just been said. "Then we must plan. I intend to trust you and your men with my destiny in a way I could never do with my imperial court." It was my father's turn to bow his head in appreciation of the praise and faith being given. But the emperor had more to say. "Despite the many challenges facing us it is hardly an easy task for Carinus either. You have heard of the 'Emperor Julian' I assume?"

My father shook his head, managing to somehow combine this with a scowl at Antius for not having provided important information, and Diocletian continued his explanation. "Far simpler for Carinus than it will be defeating us, I can assure you my friend. The administrator of some northern Italian province has rebelled, Julian by name, and seems to have a great deal of influence in Pannonia. It has Carinus worried and is proving to be a rather useful distraction for us. It gives us some breathing space while he deals with the problem that is closest to home- I've even heard rumours that this Julian is so confident and sure of himself that he may well march on Rome itself if Carinus doesn't come out to meet him in battle. Carinus should crush him, of course, but it does give us that all important commodity that is so hard to come by when the empire is in crisis- time."

We took advantage of that the very next day. Diocletian delegated most of the preparation for the war to my father- for the very reasons that we had identified weeks before. However, the additional factor that we had not recognised was that he had already sent out orders to all eastern-based detachments of the Dalmatian Horse to report to Salona. He wanted Constantius to use them to maintain communications across the widely distributed elements of his army- from legions to specialist auxiliary units to cavalry. As my father had already identified, we were preparing for a rare battle for this day and age: speed would not be the key to victory so much as logistics. Ensuring all units arrived together would be crucial. He announced that he would be basing himself at Nicomedia with his two eastern legions. They would make their way through Thrace when the time came. Diocletian needed to ensure their loyalty while they recovered from their exertions in taking Ctesiphon, capital of the Sassanid Persians against whom Carus had been so successful.

In the meantime, planning should be based around peace and unity as the rallying call, the intention being to cause as little blood to be spilt amongst Romans as possible. As the emperor phrased it, far better to butcher Rome's enemies than those who disagreed over who should lead her. Felix was a vital component of this, and we all knew how much we would be relying on him and his abilities to get all of the men he could to a specific place on a given day at a particular time. Antius would also be involved, his men not only bringing back information on Carinus' plans but also doing all they could to sabotage those plans and spread division amongst his allies. Legion commanders could also sometimes be bought if the price was high enough, so this possibility was also a priority for further action.

The next two months went by at the speed of thought. My established routines were completely disrupted. I found myself chasing after Felix, wanting to see how he organised and administered; but more often than not getting under his feet to the extent that he eventually had to ask me to stop following him around. Antius was never in or around the palace any more and my father asked Hosius' father to continue the training of our small group when he was available. This was variable as it depended on when different cavalry vexillations arrived at the barracks, but it did at least mean that we learned to fight on horseback and could practice on our own when needed. As a result of his frequent absences I trained more and more with Hosius, strengthening our friendship further after a week of neglect caused by the imperial visit. Scipio acted as my father's right hand in terms of strategy, scouting and choosing the right ground for a final confrontation, so he was not available either. I was included with some frequency in his meetings with my father, particularly where they were concerned with choosing the most favourable battleground. This would, of course, ultimately be Diocletian's decision; but he did not know whom he could trust amongst his immediate advisers having so recently taken over the court. And he already found it increasingly difficult to make contact with those he used to have confidence in as dux Moesiae. The hidebound tradition in respect of an emperor's behaviour, and the administrators who acted as enforcers of court procedure-as well as his own concerns about being spied upon- meant that he chose to devolve as much as possible to those he could rely on to work in semi-secrecy. The elite riders of the imperial cavalry, along with the Dalmatian Horse, wore the road from Salona to Nicomedia thin with their travels- the Via Flavia leading to the Via Egnatia and ending with the Via Valeria. The journey would take a fortnight by foot, but using the established roads and waystations of the empire reduced that to just over a week.

The other benefit to me, besides spending more time with Hosius, was returning more to my mother's side. We became close once again, and her faith was a regular topic of conversation- particularly its focus on one god. As a philosophical concept I found it fascinating. It was so different to anything I had known, to Roman tradition and to the ancient Greek authors I had been reading. Plato came the closest, as far as I could tell, with his writing of one supreme being. But I found myself unsure as to why anyone would choose to follow a God who took pride in becoming human; who then chose to die; and who not only died, but died in ignominy and shame, crucified like a common criminal. This made no sense to me. It stood in contrast to all that I looked for in a deity worthy of my worship and commitment. My mother had no answer that could satisfy me when I would point this out, other than to say that her faith would be meaningless without that event and her god's rising again three days later- and that it was all somehow based on love. She became particularly upset when I, frustrated with her inability to answer me adequately, suggested that the persecution of Christians under Decius and Valerian was recent enough that I suspected at least half of the empire would relish the return of their policies. Though I knew from my history lessons that the emperor

Gallienus had promoted toleration of her faith it had had little impact on general attitudes from what I had heard. Besides which, it was particularly important at a time like this that our family should choose to follow a being that could give us victory over the enemies we were about to face. Our final conversation ended in her tears when my annoyance led to my implying that she was as a traitor to our family in following such a god- how could Sol Invictus look upon us kindly in fighting Carinus if our own house was divided in who we worshiped? Harmony was all at this moment, as my father prepared for the greatest test of his skills he had yet known; but all she could say was that we should love our enemy. Love the man about to murder us all if the opportunity arose!

In the end, I turned on her bitterly and said: "All very well mother, but you will be relying on father and his legions to protect you from this false emperor's anger! If we do not win, you will pay the price as much as any of us- and let us see you love him when he crucifies you on the nearest tree. At least you will have that in common with your god."

I stalked from our dining room, full of righteous indignation, to prepare myself for the journey back through the mountains from which I had arrived.

For the preferred battleground would be in central Dalmatia, near Viminacium.

CHAPTER 7: ADVENTURES

One early afternoon, roughly four months after Diocletian's visit, Hosius and I crept furtively around the corner of a house on the outskirts of Salona. We were listening as closely as possible as the quartermaster berated the carter on the other side of the building. It was harder to hear due to the noise of the rest of the supply train passing on the main road. But the ferocious sound of a quartermaster furious with an uncooperative handler meant his high-pitched anger could be heard above the low rumble of wagons, the rattling of goods, the shouts of drivers bantering across the street and the occasional snap of whips urging beasts to greater effort. From what we could tell it seemed that the carter had disrupted the traffic due to needing to relieve himself, cutting across others in order to pull to one side of the roadway and out of the main flow. The reason was irrelevant to us, however- we had been watching the supply train for several hours and this was the first opportunity that had presented itself. Hosius whispered from behind me, "Just remind me why we're doing this again?"

I turned to him from peering around the corner. "Don't you at least want to see the battle that will decide our fates?" I hissed.

"Of course I do! But this way...?"

"What other way do we have? Neither of our fathers want us there, each of us has been told we are staying at home with the women, children and greybeards, and yet who will be the first to lose their lives once Carinus has won?"

My mind went back to the night before. It had not been a pleasant evening meal. My father had been giving instructions to my mother as we ate regarding what she should do if the war were lost. It was not a fear he would choose to create, nor intended to imply a lack of faith in our emperor's cause or skill, but my father was ever a careful man and attempted to be prepared for every eventuality. Despite the gold and jewels he had treasured away over the years, and that he was telling Helena to make use of, my mother meekly and gently put it to him: "Where can anyone hide from an emperor? I will accept whatever future my god has for me."

It was at this point that I had spoken up, admittedly not the best choice of moment as he was about to remonstrate with her regarding her apparent acceptance of the inevitable. "Father, I need to tell Lucipor when to be ready tomorrow. What time do we leave?"

He turned to me, taken aback, with a look of blank astonishment on his face, the discussion with my mother forgotten. There was a pause while he struggled to register my words. "We... You... Come with me...?"

I was surprised at his reaction as I could not understand his difficulty. It was a simple enough question. Assuming he had had a little too much of the rich Falernian wine gifted to us by Diocletian during his visit, I repeated patiently, "To fight Carinus? With our Emperor?"

My father regained his composure and said gently but firmly, "Son, I have not just found you only to lose you again so swiftly. I will not risk your life out of choice as I must risk mine out of necessity."

Anger took over instantly as I registered what he was saying, and I protested, to my shame, as petulantly as a child might. "But father! As soon as you told Diocletian we were his to command you risked my life! Aye, and mother's, as she has just said. What greater risk is it for me to come also?"

...I returned to the present, shaking my head with the recent memory. Shocked by his response, my approach had been to attack rather than to reason: I knew him well enough by now to know this would not gain the answer I wanted. My father had become as angry as I, eventually, especially when I resorted to threats of what I would do were I not permitted to join him. I knew his implacable tone already from hearing him dealing with his men; I had not expected to be subject to it myself. Even now, hiding behind this wall, the sense of injustice continued. It leant urgency to our next move.

I stretched to peer out once again from behind our wall. The carter's wagon lay before us, a sudden shaft of sunlight illuminating the hide cover and bringing into relief a gap which lay in shadow, where the material fitted poorly. Thanking Sol for this guidance, as a confirmation that the god blessed our joining the convoy, the two of us ran out quickly and scrambled over the back of the vehicle. I pulled Hosius into the bed of it as the driver was climbing back into his seat. My friend landed heavily with a thud and we waited with bated breath for the sound of the driver deciding to investigate. We heard muttering, then an irritable grunt. The man descended once more. And there was the crunch of footsteps on gravel as he walked around to the back of the vehicle. Both of us shrank back under the cover and I prayed as never before. Then, much to our bewilderment, there was the sound of running water.

I looked at Hosius in confusion, his expression just visible due to a small hole in the cover letting light through. A grin of revelation spread across his face. He whispered, "Taking a piss." He shook with suppressed laughter, "Must have forgotten to go!"

I breathed a very quiet sigh of relief. He had clearly needed to attend to his bodily functions very urgently as it went on for some time. Another shout came from the quartermaster, and we heard him finish swiftly and climb back up. There was the crack of his whip over the backs of the oxen and the cart moved off. We rejoined the flow of transports all heading towards the prospect of a distant battle, following the many troops that had already left earlier that day.

Both Hosius and I had waved our fathers off that morning, me doing my best to give the impression of having resigned myself to my father's verdict. Hosius had not even tried to ask his. I stood by his side as Constantius led the men out of the Porta Caesarea, the two of us naming each part of the army to each other as the various troops went beneath, doing our best to exceed the other in knowledge. We were only truly interested in the supplies, and these came in the middle of the force. They arrived in the form of hundreds of plodding, braying mules; and we looked at each other, shaking our heads hastily at each other as we discounted any potential for hiding away amongst them- neither of us had any desire to smuggle ourselves into that stinking mass of fur and noise.

After this, however, there was a group of two-wheeled wagons, most pulled by oxen. After a quick consultation with each other, we ran to the palace stables and saddled two of the few remaining horses, taking a back route out of the city and choosing a parallel path into the foothills to get ahead of the slow-moving convoy. We had found a convenient small village not far into a wide valley and had jumped off the horses, giving each a smack on the rump to set them running back to their stables. It was our hope that nobody would notice our absence until the next day- if the horses made it back without any problems.

And now we had made it into the caravan.

"I think I'm injured Con", came Hosius' worried voice in the darkness, jolting me out of my delight at our success. "I can feel a lot of blood." He took my hand and guided it towards his arm. It was wet, and my worst fears jumped to the fore. I urgently flipped up the side of the calfskin above us to let in more light so I could see how bad it was. And had to smother my laughter by shoving my hand into my mouth.

"It's wine you idiot!" I whispered, once I had managed to stifle my mirth. There were shards of clay around him. We had climbed into a wagon carrying an officer's provisions. It was not the crack of the driver's whip I had heard, but the amphora breaking as Hosius' elbow came down on it. That did not satisfy my friend.

"And how am I going to dry out now, under this?"

Choosing not to respond immediately, I lifted my head carefully and slowly from underneath the cover. We would be visible to the driver of the next cart in line only if we lifted our heads- fortunately, the early morning start, the slow speed and the warm afternoon had taken effect. He had fallen asleep, a common occurrence when the oxen were ponderously following each other and there was nowhere else to go. I turned my gaze to our own wagon. Our driver was merrily whistling a tune, presumably having thought, like me, that the noise he heard was someone else's whip, and was paying no attention. He would have to stand upright and stare directly at where we were to see us, so I gently drew a section of the hide back so that we could enjoy Sol's rays while the day lasted.

It was very peaceful and Hosius soon dried out, even if his tunic sleeve remained stained a vibrant red, falling asleep in the warmth. The gentle jolting of the cart over the regular ruts in the road created by several thousand men and numerous animals with their loads was soothing, and the train had settled into an easy and slow rhythm. The lowing of the oxen, the occasional neigh of a passing horse, the sun that was bright without being too hot, the only sharp noise being the carters shouting ribald jests at one another; all of this helped to ease our fears. Soon we would likely be discovered, thrown at the feet of my father and sent home to enjoy the company of women and old men while all the excitement happened to others. For now, though, I lay back and decided to worry about such an event when it came to pass. There was little I could do about it from here anyway.

The rest of the day passed and we found it easy enough to stay hidden as the wagoneers made camp and darkness fell. We waited patiently until night-time sounds indicated that the camp was asleep. We climbed out, both to stretch our legs and also to try to find some food- unsurprisingly, not too difficult in a supply convoy. Bread and a lump of hard cheese were sufficient to sustain us, accompanied by a draught from one of the amphorae in the back of our cart. We did make one important decision to help us sleep more easily: as soon as the drivers were asleep, we moved to a wagon carrying fodder for the horses as this made for a far more comfortable bed. We took with us two more amphorae, thinking ahead. "As good as Felix at this supply business", I jokingly said to Hosius. We slept well, despite our having dozed so many times during the day, probably due to the tiring tension of not knowing if we would be caught or not.

We were awakened by the sudden jerk of our new vehicle as it set off. We had intentionally buried ourselves under enough hay that we could not have been spotted, and the day went much as the previous one had- despite the frequent temptation to sneeze due to the straw. That evening, though, as camp was made once more and we waited for darkness and for the site to settle down, a rider arrived. We could tell there was a greater degree of urgency to this one compared with those who had ridden past in a leisurely fashion during the day. The rider came at pace and the horse was panting as it drew up.

"Quick! Another horse. This one is blown, and I must reach the governor quickly."

We had spare steeds for the fast messenger riders attached to the rear of several carts and we could hear one being swiftly found and made ready.

While the cavalryman was waiting he happened to lean against the cart we were in, mainly because it was the closest to the road. Several of the drivers gathered around him, the boredom of the journey making them especially eager for any news. "What's the rush?" was the opening gambit from the self-appointed leader.

The rider, full of his own importance, replied. "It's the governor's son. He's disappeared. His mother thinks he's with the supplies somewhere."

"Ha! Eager to be killed is he? Story doing the rounds says that the false emperor has double our numbers."

"I know nothing of that," retorted the rider. "All I know is that his mother wants to know where he is. And this is not what the governor needs at this time. She took a while to decide to send me because she didn't want him to have any further distractions. But if the child is with you lot..."

I just prevented an indignant snort at being called a child. Could a child have made it this far?

"Is he on his own?"

"We believe so. No other has been reported missing."

I could not see Hosius' expression due to the murk under the hay and the falling dusk, but I could feel his reaction just as easily. I put my hand on his shoulder to remind him to stay quiet.

"Your horse sir."

The sound of hooves leaving was followed by the dispersal of the men around our temporary home. I turned to Hosius before he could say anything. "I'm a child and you're invisible." I grinned. "I'm not sure which is better. But I know we're so much more because we are under here!"

Hosius, to my surprise, showed no sign of resentment at being so overlooked but gazed at me thoughtfully. "Do you feel any guilt? That comment about you being a distraction?"

I considered his question. "Maybe. But if I am to be any kind of a leader then I must be at this battle."

"That answer is about you to the exclusion of all others. But the empire is at stake."

"True. But my father is not the sort of man to be thrown by the disappearance of his son. He knows by now that I am more than capable of looking after myself. He will also be sure that you are with me." I considered it further. "In fact, it would not surprise me if he were secretly proud of me once he knows that I am with the supply train."

"And that is a further aspect to this. Our time with the supplies is not to last too much longer, I suspect."

"Who do you think he will send looking for us?"

"Scipio. He knows us best."

◆◆◆

We had to wait longer than the previous night for the camp to descend into quiet but took advantage once it had to take the supplies we needed.

But Hosius was right. Scipio arrived in the middle of the night. He was not quiet about it. He brought a troop of men with him, all carrying firebrands, and he bellowed as his horse came to a stop, sharply reining in in the middle of our makeshift camp: "Awake, you lazy sods!"

There was a series of bewildered expletives as the men emerged from their slumber. Some staggered out from under their carts where most had bedded down, their bumped heads and loud cursing adding to the noise.

"Let's start with you. We think you have a stowaway with you. Any signs you might have?"

Unfortunately for us, the man chosen happened to be the driver of the wine-cart we had first jumped into. Peering through a knothole in the side of our wagon, I watched anxiously.

Just in time, the carter who had challenged the messenger the night before marched pugnaciously up to Scipio, legs apart and fists on his hips, staring up at the horseman before him: "And who do you think you are to speak to us like that, you jumped-up imperial toady?"

These words, though undoubtedly ill-considered, were probably phrased as they were due to Scipio having been woken from his bed and flinging on his cloak without his usual weapons and armour. He did not look like a man of action.

The carter quickly regretted his assumption. For without a moment's thought, without a shift in his balance or any other indication of what was to follow, Scipio leapt off his horse in one movement. He swept his fist down and across as he did so, his momentum and weight adding even greater force to the blow, and caught his challenger cleanly across the side of his head. The man crashed backwards, landing unconscious and bleeding. All of the assembled drivers took an astonished step back. Having established his credentials in the fastest way possible, Scipio turned to our unwitting former host without referring to the man at his feet. "I will ask one more time: are there any indications of a stowaway in your wagon?"

After some head-scratching time, and repeated assurances that he was very much trying to think, he replied. "Well... Now you mention it. There was a smashed amphora in the back of my cart last night. But I can't see how it happened. It was well packed, and I ain't the sort that loses water to breakages. Twenty years in the business I been."

I turned to Hosius and whispered angrily, "Why didn't we throw the pieces over the side? What idiots!"

He shrugged, resigned. "It's inevitable my friend."

More voices spoke up. "And my bread has been disappearing." "What about my cheese?" "I had some salted beef..."

I looked at Hosius, startled: "Salted beef?"

"Don't ask me. Probably taking advantage."

This was all that Scipio needed. He ordered his men to surround the camp with their torches, then shouted, "Out you come Constantine. And your partner-in-crime too."

Hosius gestured at me, resigned. I was already moving. I had instigated this escapade, and I was not going to let my friend take any of the blame.

I stood up nonchalantly, wisps of hay falling from my clothing as I did so. Adding drama to the moment, the flame of the torch nearest to me guttered and smoke surrounded me as I arose. Determined that I would not cough as I inhaled the fumes, I spoke as casually as I was able, as though I had just come across him on a late night stroll. "Good evening Scipio."

"Down. Now." He spoke with firm authority, ignoring my attempt to retain my pride and avoid the humiliation. The drivers were all wide awake now and grinning at each other. I was not about to provide them with too much of a show so I leapt casually from the back of the cart to stand in front of the fire at the centre of the campsite. "And where there's one there's usually the other. Is the little man with you?" Scipio asked forcefully.

Hosius stood up. He said dryly, "Taller than you right now," before jumping down to join me.

"And whose idea was this ridiculous episode?" asked our captor.

I decided to take charge of the situation, not desiring to see myself humiliated in front of all of these men. "We will discuss it with the governor."

I spoke with a confidence I did not feel. I knew Scipio well enough to be able to tell that he was only just holding his fury in check, and I was relying on his sense of discipline to prevent him hitting me there and then. Even in the firelight I could see his face turn a bright red, his scar a livid purple, before he eventually controlled himself and he looked me up and down appraisingly. He spoke sarcastically, "May I accompany his highness to meet the governor?"

I chose to ignore his insulting tone, feeling that I probably deserved it. "You may."

A cavalryman heeled his horse towards me, leading two other animals by their reins. They halted in front of Hosius and me; Scipio, with a violent but contained gesture, indicated that we should mount. We did so without speaking, whereupon the same soldier took the reins himself and we knew that we were to be led to my father as if children who were unable to control their own horses. My rage grew swiftly but I managed to hold my anger sufficiently to speak curtly but, I felt, respectfully.

"The reins. Now."

The cavalryman looked enquiringly at his commander, and I spoke sharply to forestall any conversation: "I have given you an order. You will obey it."

Scipio looked at me, considering, for long enough that all knew where the true power lay. Then he nodded and the man handed me the reins.

"And Hosius too", I insisted.

As we left the clearing, the wagoneers began to bed down again for the night. There was a faint sense of amusement in the air and the tale would be around the army before sunrise. The carters knew enough to identify me at least, and I could but hope that I had come out of the debacle well enough. Scipio spoke to an optio beside him as we moved on to the main road and I noticed as our formation changed to hem us in on all sides. It was done subtly and without any aggression so I chose not to speak of it.

We rode fast through the vanguard of the encamped army. The supply train we had been part of did not stretch as far as would normally be anticipated in a force of this size, being a fraction of what would usually be needed. But we were in friendly territory and would purchase what we could; and I knew from Felix that the plan was to reprovision from the Danube when we got there, using the naval forces based at Singidunum who had already declared their support for our emperor. Ironically, it was the Pannonian Fleet we would be relying on despite the usurper controlling that province; according to Antius, the Moesian Fleet was also on our side, but navigation through the Danube's 'Iron Gate' series of gorges made their journey unnecessarily risky . As a result, we could save on both time and money by relying on the Pannonian river-sailors for our food and equipment.

Scipio was too angry to speak to me so I let my attention wander as we rode. Due to the low scrub-trees surrounding us, sufficient pathway was left to enable riders to move three abreast so Hosius and I remained confined- not that we would have sought to escape in any case. Scipio was merely sending me a message. We passed the mules first, lying down haphazardly by the side of the road, and reached the cavalry. Men lay where they had sat down when the army halted, their saddles placed on the ground as headrests, their weapons close to hand- javelins, spears and swords wrapped in cloth or sheathed in scabbards. Shields had been left leaning against trees to avoid the morning dew, dim sentries warning of the legionary presence, rolled in cloaks on the ground either side of the road. It was hard to see the differences between one set of soldiers and the next when they were laid on the ground snoring, all colours having been turned to shades of grey. As it was a full moon we could see enough to enable us to trot through them without disturbance. Horses for the auxiliary cavalry scouts had been hobbled and let loose on the few areas of grass that could be found, while those used for the elite forces had been supplied with hay from carts like those we had stowed away in. There were occasional sentries who would quietly acknowledge us as we passed. But there were not many of these, for who would be so foolish as to attack a force of this magnitude? Carinus alone, and he was far distant still.

As a result, though my father was renowned as a general cautious with his men's lives, he had not taken his usual precaution of building a marching camp that was fully secured against the risks of enemy attack. Speed was, at this point, of the essence now that we knew that the 'usurper' (as we all called him; despite the fact that there was in reality little distinction between those acclaimed emperor by their troops, as Diocletian had been, and those who took it as a hereditary succession, as was the case with Carinus) was on his way; and we needed our men as well rested as was possible once they arrived at our intended battle site despite their march through the mountains.

I became more nervous as we moved through the cavalry towards the front of the column. The horses were cropping the grass around us, with occasional grumbling as they sought more from sparse ground. I was not looking forward to the interview with my father. Guilt started to catch up with me. I had such a firm faith in his ability that I had never really thought of the worry my absence might cause; but I could tell that Scipio felt his righteous anger strongly and that was making me re-consider due to my respect for him. Maybe I had been a little selfish. There was also some justified apprehension as my father and I had not yet exchanged a single word spoken in anger, the closest we had come being in the discussion around my joining him for this very expedition. I longed to talk to Scipio about it but knew this would not be well received.

We cantered over the last part of the roadway and into a recently created glade, stumps of fir showing the hard work of the engineers who travelled in front of the main troops. We stopped in front of a large campaign tent. The canvas door swung open and up and my father stepped out. As soon as he saw me relief was written all over his face. An instant pang of shame hit me but I kept my head high as if unconcerned. I was to be a leader of men and, having watched my father over the last six months, felt that I must appear at all times to be convinced that my own decisions had been correct- even if privately uncertain. But it was difficult when proof that my conviction was ill-founded stood before me.

"Son."

There was a wealth of meaning in that one word. He cared, and my disappearance really mattered to him. But there was anger present too, the emotions warring in him. Constantius turned to Scipio. "My thanks. Go and send a messenger to Helena to let her know that our son is found."

"Aye sir. And shall I prepare men to escort the boys home?" My father turned to me, a hard glint in his eye. He looked at me without expression for several moments and asked, "Do you wish to go home?"

"Sir, you know how I feel." I spoke confidently despite my fears, for this was my only opportunity. As the question had been asked I dared to hope. "I wish to stay with you, see my first battle, even wield a weapon in it."

My voice trembled slightly at the end, though it was unlikely any of the surrounding soldiers could identify it for what it was. I was a young boy, doing my best to be an adult, and I had not expected this reaction from my father. I had been sure I would be treated as the child I was, subjected to discipline and returned instantly to my mother's side.

"And you, Hosius? Or have you merely been pulled into this escapade due to Constantine's poor influence?"

Hosius spoke up with false bravado. "I wish to stay too sir." To my immense astonishment, my father- leaving it a few moments while he considered- then replied with, "You may stay." He turned to Scipio- "Send the messenger to Hosius' mother also."

As Scipio saluted and moved off, Constantius turned to me: "You wish to be soldiers in this army: you will be. You will have all you need. You may regret your choice."

He turned his back and moved to the door of the tent behind him as we stood still in amazement at this turn of events. He paused. "Felix! Kit them out", he said without turning, then entered and let the tent flap fall shut behind him.

Felix, lit by a torch and dressed immaculately as always, as if he had just stepped out of his house in Salona, clean shaven and in full uniform despite it being well past the middle of the night, smiled at us grimly. "What did you expect? A 'well done' and a bed in his tent to sleep in? I did not foresee this decision for my part. You may regret it. Come with me."

We walked a short distance to another tent, similar in size to my father's. "Wait here."

We were tired now, and by mutual agreement the two of us sat down on conveniently positioned tree stumps. It was a warm night and that, combined with our tiredness and our youth, meant that it did not take too long for us to stretch out on the ground, propping ourselves against the stumps. We talked quietly as we waited. Felix did not take long, but by the time he came out with our equipment we were both on the verge of sleep. As I drifted off, the last I heard was the rattle of objects being dropped beside me and his voice: "We'll talk in the morning…"

◆◆◆

I woke to a hard boot tapping me firmly and impatiently in the ribs. "On your feet boy."

I clambered, still mostly asleep, to my feet, to be faced with the scarred features and sharply angular profile of a figure that seemed to be indicating that it was my commander. "You're part of my detachment now sonny." He reached behind him and brought out a long sword. "And here's your weapon- if you can carry it." He chuckled. He waved in the direction of what I saw, as I opened my eyes more fully, was a group of dismounted cavalry, the men's horses cropping the grass as the riders themselves lounged on their backs. "Your little friend"- I saw Hosius standing in the midst of the group, evidently the intended object of this man's wave- "he struggled with it. We've decided to call him 'Tiny' from now on. He's sort of like a mascot. He'd get eaten by a legionary in no time- no more than one bite I should think." He sneered at me, waiting for my reaction.

Fully awake now, I grasped firmly the hilt of the sword he was holding out in my direction. Stepping back, I stretched my arms once or twice, then started practicing my sword-strokes to loosen up. After a few swings I looked up at him. "Not bad. Decent balance, if a little overweighted at the tip. Might throw my thrust off."

He looked at me appraisingly. "You might actually know what to do with that thing. But you use it like a footslogger. Remember that you'll be on horseback- strike down, usually on the way past if they are on the ground."

I saluted. "Yes sir."

"You'll do. Mount up."

I climbed on to the horse I was presented with. I had trained a great deal with weaponry of many sorts under Antius' guidance; but he had never enjoyed horse-riding, seeing it as more of a necessary evil that could get him to a fight

177

faster than any other form of transport. Once he was at the fight he would do battle on his own feet. As a result, my abilities in this area were far from exceptional; but I knew the basics. I heeled my steed forward to stand beside Hosius.

"Good morning", he said laconically. "Nice mess we're in now. Thanks for your help." Without further welcome he gestured at the horse, pointing out items he thought it worth me being aware of: "Cloak." He indicated a rolled-up blanket-like object coloured a dull red behind my saddle. "Belt"- he helped me to remove the thick leather object lying across the front of the saddle and attach it around my middle, hooking my sword on to it. "Light spears". These were in a case behind the cloak which I decided I would investigate later.

Our commander was having strong words with a quartermaster- something about insufficient food- so most of the troop were distracted by the entertainment. I leant across to Hosius- "You been awake for long?"

"Long enough. I was a bit readier than you were when Marsallus and his mob turned up. They seem to find me amusing so at least I didn't get kicked."

"Don't they know who we are?"

Hosius looked at me sympathetically. "I think that's the point Con. They're Thracian scouts, and it would seem that Felix has deemed it suitable for us to serve our apprenticeship with the least disciplined and most notorious soldiers he can find. Just look at their uniform- if you can call it that." He gestured at the group. Their appearance suggested men who had picked up whatever clothing they had found in villages they ransacked and put it on. Hosius grimaced. "They know exactly who we are and it doesn't impress them one bit. They laughed when I told them about

my parents; I tried the 'Constantius is his father' line on them, and Marsallus' fake trembling had them all but rolling on the ground. That big lad over there," he pointed at a tall young man with such blonde hair that there was clearly Germanic blood in him, picking his nose absentmindedly as he watched Marsallus take the quartermaster by the throat, "he actually fell off his horse he thought it was so funny."
"What about armour then?"
"Apparently we don't need it as we are scouts- it would just slow us down. They think they're too good for armour anyway: shows they are the best, so they say, rather than idiots likely to be the first killed when the enemy attacks," he said sarcastically. "We can get issued with some when there's a proper fight. Marsallus says that our spies have told us that Carinus is coming towards us desperate for one pitched battle that will settle the whole emperor business once and for all. So we're not in any real danger- yet."
"We really are half-soldiers for now. I wonder if my father will just leave us to fight once we get there."
At that point, our new commander cantered across the clearing towards us. "Here's how it's going to be today. We need to get ahead of the rest of them and see what's out there. New men together." He pointed at me and a giant of a man calmly sitting his horse a few metres away; and then did the same to Hosius and a very tough looking middle-aged soldier nearby. "You've all come in together, so you can all go out together." He grinned at his little joke, then decided to labour the point as no-one was responding. "Go out together? Get it?" He chuckled at his own humour again. "Looks like you've got the short straw with Tiny, my friend." He evidently knew that the impassive men he had paired us with were our bodyguards, though it took me some time to recognise that for myself. This was despite the

fact that the men's scale armour was decorated and polished, while the scouts wore leather protection that had, in several cases, lost the straps that held it together- so it was more 'draped' than 'worn'. The realisation that we had experienced soldiers as support came with a sense of relief as I was grateful that Felix had not left us to fend for ourselves completely.

CHAPTER 8: RISKS

Our small force of scouts moved out of the clearing and the next day was a revelation to me as to what light cavalry did while the army was on the march- and it was not an enjoyable experience. Riding my horse was an increasingly painful exercise. I had not had any breakfast either but was provided with solely by the hard biscuits contained in my baggage, hung around my horse on the saddle horns. I made every effort to strike up a conversation with my companion as we were likely to spend much time together, so it made sense to at least get to know him. He was a taciturn man, however, with little to say- though he did eventually inform me once he had become bored of my constant attempts to strike up a conversation: "Felix posted me here to guard you. That's what I will do. My name is Aemilius. If you need me- that is what you shout."

That ended the conversation. I turned my attention instead to the landscape as it passed by. There were parts I recognised from my previous journey through it. It was a different season, though, the trees and plants flourishing and blooming in the fullness of spring, the cold of the winter now a distant memory, with vivid greens of fresh vegetation surrounding the road. We would occasionally strike off the road at an angle if we saw paths beaten through the undergrowth; but these were always left by wild animals rather than an enemy. It was a startlingly bright day though there was a wind funnelling its way down the valley. That wind came with a sense of freedom to explore: no longer hindered by my age, hiding amongst supplies to make my way to where I wanted to go, nor being constantly under orders- for scouts travelled where they wished as long as it was ahead of the army, expected to use their own initiative to identify danger and communicate it. I was content to make the most of it. Aemilius was happy for me to take the lead for there was little prospect of real danger. All we had received from Marsallus by way of guidance was a point of his index finger in a direction that was halfway up the side of the valley the army was traversing, and a recommendation that he would prefer it if we stayed roughly parallel with the rest of the scouts as we moved forward.

However, due to the thick foliage and shrubbery it was all but impossible to identify where everyone was, so we moved forward as needed, stopping briefly when the horses were distracted and drinking from the refreshingly cold mountain streams. Otherwise, we paused only for my companion, proving himself to be a remarkable shot with the recurved Palmyrene bow he carried behind his saddle, to bring down squirrels as they foraged for food to replenish winter stores. We built ourselves a small fire around midday, when the dust in the valley far behind us settled and we could see that the army had halted its march, and cooked two of the small creatures on spits. I found the taste surprisingly good; but there was little meat on them as yet. My expression of admiration for my companion's archery skills did elicit the first proper response beyond a grunt, and he offered me a quick lesson in the use of his bow.

As I stood there, poised for my fifth attempt with Aemilius stood behind me, his hand on my right arm to guide it, an enormous black bear appeared from a copse beside us. It reared up and roared, only a few metres from me. I was truly terrified; but Aemilius was unmoved. He breathed into my ear, speaking so quietly he could barely be heard, "Do not move. It is running from the noise of the army and it has smelt the cooking squirrel. But it is also very short-sighted. If you stay still it will leave."

I quietly whispered back, my assurance returned after the initial shock, "I have the arrow ready; shall I shoot?"

My eagerness and desire for the glory of the new fur rug I would be able to gift to my father at the camp on our return took over from any rational ability to think.

"Idiot!" The word was spoken as sharply and forcefully as it could be given the beast so close by. "At this range and with your strength it would bounce off. The bear would think a fly had landed and flown away. But your movement would bring it straight to you."

Sufficiently reprimanded, we held our stance- my arms aching as I held the string taut rather than risk the movement and sound caused by releasing it, however gently- for what felt like an eternity. The bear snuffled at the air seeking a scent it could recognise; then it suddenly dropped to its paws and ambled off back into the forest. As I felt the cold wind hit me once again I realised I was sweating heavily.

"That was close!"

I received a grunt in reply.

We returned to camp as the sun started to descend and I slept soundly that night. My next adventure had at last truly begun.

◆◆◆

The next few days, moving from valley to valley, sometimes reaching the occasional peak in order to see what lay ahead, were much the same. I was particularly keen to see a pack of wolves once Marsallus had mentioned them round the fire one night; but had no luck. It was a very different situation to the last time we had come through these mountains, when it had looked at times like there was a pack hunting our small band. Aemelius eventually told me that wolves were so afraid of man that they would be long gone from this area as soon as they scented the massed army approaching.

Four days in, and we were finally given the front position of all of the pairings: the centre of the valley, riding a couple of miles in front of the vanguard. I felt the proudest I ever had though I knew this was also the position of highest risk; but we had been assured that there was nothing to fear. The weather had broken overnight and the late-spring rain was driving hard into our faces. I made sure my chin was held high and my chest puffed out as we passed the rest of the army and moved to our place at its head. Little could dampen my enthusiasm- but several miles in I decided I had had enough. I was wet through and frozen with cold from the chill wind. But then I considered my father's laughter: 'he thought he could stick it! As long as it was nice out- sunshine soldier.' And that kept me going. I was exposed on top of my horse and I quickly learnt that ducking down behind its neck was a slight relief; until, that is, the horse chose to drop its own head as it painstakingly marched into the wind. And then I might as well have been standing in the midst of the storm even though I clutched my thick red cloak tightly around myself and pulled the hood up. It was meant to be water-resistant, but I still could not wait until lunchtime for our first break. We stopped early at my request and huddled behind a boulder next to the route using the sparse vegetation to build ourselves a fire. It took some effort but we eventually got it going. It gave off a lot of smoke and not a great deal of heat but at least it was something to huddle around as we ate the biscuit we carried in our packs.

It was just after lunch that events took a different turn. As the two of us climbed back on to our horses a line of legionaries emerged from around the bend ahead, through the rain and a light mist that had started to descend as the wind had eased while we sheltered. They had not seen us as we hunched behind our rock, and our smoke as we doused the fire mingled with the mist, unintentionally disguising our presence. Unseen as yet, I was able to study them without their knowledge. I was surprised to see that they were not talking, unsmilingly making their focused way along the valley floor in single file despite the path being broad enough to ride two, even three, abreast. A large rocky outcrop temporarily blocked our view of them as they approached. I watched them closely as they emerged from behind the low crags. As I studied the scene it reminded me of the incident we had endured nearly two years before- when mountain bandits had tried to rob us but lost their lives instead. I know not what caused that memory to emerge- perhaps the weather, maybe the suppressed violence that emanated from the group.

Regardless, it was this that made me particularly sensitive to what happened next. The men appeared just like our own soldiers though better uniformed. Even as I thought this, a wry smile unconsciously crossed my face: the comparison was unjust, as I was riding with the worst-dressed men in our force. The scouts, as Aemilius had clarified for me earlier in the day when I raised the subject of the scouts' uniform, tended to have tunics torn from their rough riding through the brush, woollen trousers with holes in unsightly places due to the amount of time they spent ahead of the army, unable to return to fix the damage, and footwear cobbled together from whatever material they could find. Their weapons, however, were always very well kept- swords sharpened every night, bowstrings carefully kept dry, shields repaired after any encounter. So, considering that, these new arrivals were about what might be expected from a normal legionary- I chuckled to myself despite my slight sense of unease.

They paced towards us, looking up as they now saw the two of us standing in the middle of the road.

"Password." Aemilius was always gruff at best and his deep voice was much more authoritative than I could manage.

"Diocletian," replied the leading member of the group.

"Pass, friend."

There were eight men, and, up close as they trotted their horses gently past us, I suddenly noticed how large they were. They had obviously come from a distance as their horses looked tired; but they sat as straight as (I imagined) any of the finest praetorians in Rome itself would sit their steeds- despite the weather they must have come through and that must have affected their mounts. These were no ordinary soldiers, and with my usual curiosity I could not help but be inquisitive. As the fourth man rode past, I spoke up. "Where have you come from?"

Without turning to look at me, or pausing, the warrior alongside said in a strong accent, "Special detachment sent out as pathfinders by Commander Portunus at Singidunum. Wants to do his bit to see your army safe through the mountains."

I managed to keep my expression under control until they were all passed before then turning to Aemilius with a puzzled expression on my face. I looked back to check that they were all out of earshot before speaking to him. "Portunus? Who's he? I thought I'd heard all of the names of the commanders on this side of the Adriatic, but that's a new one. Must be important too if he sent that lot- they don't look like men who'd take orders from just anyone. And what accent was that? I could hardly make out what he said with such a thick way of speaking."

Aemilius looked at me carefully, brows slightly furrowed. "You didn't notice either, but the legionary behind the one you spoke to put his hand on the hilt of his sword and loosened it as you spoke. Might be nothing of course."

He lapsed back into silence.

I shook my head and decided to leave it. It was too little to make a judgement on- and what should I do if I had a suspicion? I was hardly the most reliable witness or the most experienced soldier. We carried on our way down the rock-strewn road. Both of us clearly felt uncomfortable but neither was sure why.

"Didn't they seem a bit tense?" I asked suddenly, thinking I had identified what was making me wary.

"What do you mean?"

"You know… on edge. It doesn't fit really. They were sent to find us, and they had achieved their aim. But there was no pleasure in that fact. Just… tension. No casual conversation with us, no banter about the state of the army today, no complaints about the food. They were very focused. And while we are on that, why, by Jupiter, would we need pathfinders? It's hardly like the road is difficult to find. Look at it." I warmed to my theme as I gesticulated at the route in front of us, my vigorous outflung hand losing something of its force when I observed just how much the mist had started to thicken and obscure the road. "Well, it was easy enough a moment ago… And they were very hung about with weaponry!"

"They were, weren't they," replied my companion. "And big men too. Very experienced- but no military awards on them at all. I'd have expected to see at least some medals- silver discs on their chests or the like- to get respect as they join us." He thought about it. "Reckon that might have been a Hispanic accent, now you mention it. Once served with a bloke from Tarraconensis when I was in Gaul- he sounded a lot like that."

At his comment, I made my decision and spoke urgently: "We're going to collect the rest of them- now! You go north, I'll go south. Meet at the giant elm tree a mile back- the one covered in moss. The main army will not be far short of it by the time we get there. Be fast. If you can't find them quickly, leave them and meet me."

Aemilius obeyed wordlessly despite my lack of authority over him, disappearing to the left in a matter of moments. Neither of us had any idea where our fellow scouts would be, nor could we see much across the fog-bound valley sides; but I knew we had to have more men. If my caution was justified and my instinct correct.

I raced my horse across the uneven ground, swerving around rocks that I knew would injure my horse and throw me painfully to the ground if I did not see them in time, and raising myself off the saddle so that I would not have to endure too much the discomfort that came with my lack of experience with horses.

Suddenly I saw two shapes in the distance, darker than the surrounding fog, one smaller than the other, and I veered to meet them. Panting, I got my breath back after my headlong rush. One was Hosius, the other his bodyguard, Titus- much shorter, more slightly built than the enormous Aemilius, but faster, and capable with any weapon that he was challenged to use. Both had concerned expressions on their faces as my words came in jolts between breaths: "Something not right… men went past… need to catch up…elm tree now."

"We will follow you," Titus said immediately and without question.

I did not seek more scouts but set off, trusting that they would be behind me, and I was soon back on the road. The giant elm loomed at us out of the murk. Aemilius was already there with Marsallus who was his usual brusque self. "What's up lad? Aemilius couldn't tell me much, but I'll listen. If you're playing games I'll have your hide."

"No time sir," I said. "You're just going to have to trust me. It might be nothing- but if it's not, we can't stand around chatting."

I set off again, confident that the four of them would follow and also certain that I had the three best fighters in our band with me. We rode our horses fast and hard, mine starting to falter by the time we reached the first of the outriders immediately in front of the vanguard. The rain was at least now behind our backs, but it was still hard to see what lay ahead. We shouted the password as we rode past, slowing now as our horses began to struggle, the cavalrymen recognising us as having ridden out that morning and so causing us no difficulties. The long column of riders stretched away from us into the mist, the horsemen hunching down behind manes, their red cloaks clinging, sodden, to their miserable frames as the water in the air settled on them. We rode down the flank of the cavalry, slightly off the road to make way for the large force and struggling with deep mud that rose halfway up our horses' hocks and exhausted our beasts further. I shouted to the first commander I saw, signified by a standard bearer riding alongside him, "Where is the governor, Constantius? We must find him urgently."

"Carry on. Just past the last of the vanguard."

My familiarity was either forgiven due to the weather or ignored due to the hurry we were in.

We rode on until, a couple of hundred metres in front, I saw swords drawn in the dim gloom, a sudden glint of sunlight breaking through and illuminating the tip of a silver sword as it rose in the distance. Even from where we were furiously spurring our mounts we could see several of my father's secretaries turning their horses as if to flee, men who were unarmed and without experience in warfare and thus justifiably lacking courage. I thought I could see a series of shocked faces, fearful expressions- or maybe it was my imagination given the lack of light. But then shouts reached our ears and left us in no doubt: "for the only true emperor", "so shall all traitors perish" and more besides. But then there was also a roar of anger the likes of which I had never heard before. And it was followed by a voice like thunder not so much cutting through the air as building into a bass rumble that forced all other sound out of the way. "On me, true men of Rome. Defend your commander!"

In the moments that elapsed next, there was nothing we could do but make as much speed as we could in mud and fog. Gore gouted brightly into the air from a neck wound and I saw one of my father's guards, a man who had often been around our palace in Salona, reel away from a clash, falling from his horse and lying unmoving on the ground. I sent a quick prayer skywards that we would be in time for my father. As we drew nearer, we could see the eight men making quick work of Constantius' defenders.

And then I saw the governor. He was holding off two at once, his blade like lightning in his hand as it flickered from one side to the other. My horse was faster than those of my companions, urged on by my fear for my father, and I was first into the attack. One of the assassins had fallen from his horse but was staggering back to his feet, covered in filth and muck from the muddy, well-trodden road. With a sudden cool detachment I remembered what Marsallus had told me a few days before. I timed my strike as he had instructed. The enemy had not seen me coming, dazed from his fall and his feet not holding him steady; but that almost saved him, as a sudden stumble to his right foot meant I nearly missed. But it ended well. My swift adjustment meant I all but decapitated him. I had been aiming for his shoulder, but the blow took him in the neck. I had been sharpening the sword every night as we sat by the fire and it sliced easily through sinew and muscle. Blood shot from the artery and I dragged my arm back as I worried that I might lose my blade if it stuck. My speed took me past him. I knew that there was no need to concern myself with a second strike.

My horse slid to a stop on the wet ground, a javelin whistling past my ear and taking a second assassin low in his stomach as his blade started to descend above me. It was only the sharp grunt as the javelin struck that warned me that I had been seen and was in mortal danger. At this, I woke up to my surroundings. My attention had been completely focused on my first ever sword stroke that had been truly intended to take life; the routine of weeks of practice now being applied.

Fortunately, no other assassin was near me. The man with the javelin in his stomach was desperately trying to pull it out. I shouted my thanks to Titus. He was the only one looking my way and it must have come from him. He nodded in reply. The soldier managed to withdraw the barb on the spear, widening the wound viciously as he did so. I looked on clinically as time seemed to slow. He should have left it there if he wished to live, even I knew that. The blood now burst from the wound in a vivid spray that exploded across my horse's face. The animal reared in surprise.

The assassin was not finished yet, though- these men were big and tough, and though he knew he was dying he still had a task to complete. His sword swung up once again and as he did so my mount's front feet landed and slipped, saving my life. When the assassin struck it was into thin air, for the poor animal had all but sprawled on the floor and only saved himself with a sudden spring, gathering his legs and shooting up stiff-legged. My opponent lurched forward in his seat, over-extending and exposing his upper arm and head. I took full advantage, my bloodied weapon spraying scarlet as it descended once again. This time I hit where I intended, a vicious cut through his right shoulder and angled down into his chest. He slowly rolled from his horse and landed on his back in the wet mud, the ragged gash of his fatal injury causing his head to loll to the side, the surprised look in his eyes fading as his life pumped slowly out of the wound to soak the already-sodden ground.

I looked up from my second victory, realizing I had been staring while action continued all around, and tried to take it all in once more. I was, oddly, finding that all fear had gone, along with all of my concern for my father, as soon as the fighting started.

The small battleground resolved itself into a clearer picture. Hosius was fighting desperately for his life against a far larger opponent a small distance away. Aemilius was badly injured, his sword held in his left hand, and he had withdrawn to the side of the road bleeding profusely, Marsallus all but carrying him from the battle. There appeared to be only four of the enemy left as my father was now only battling one, the other a trampled, bloodied object lying amongst the hooves of their horses. Titus was swaying and gliding through his fight, his sword licking out to open wounds in exposed flesh. Just as I wished to Sol that Scipio were here, he appeared! As if my wish were not a wish, but an answered prayer, I realised where the fourth assassin had gone: Scipio had isolated him from the rest and his body lay at the side of the track. The fight was moving along the road as more men turned and jostled- either to watch or to draw their weapons.

"Keep back!" came Scipio's voice. "You will only get in the way lads. And the governor has not had a good fight in a while. He needs the practice!"

Even in the midst of a fight we were only just winning this brought shouts of laughter from the men, and I realised how clever a move this was. It made what had initially appeared a desperate last-ditch stand appear to be Constantius and his men toying with a weak and easily defeated enemy.

Hosius was backed up against an obstacle in the middle of the road, fending off battering strokes that drove his shield ever lower. It was a matter of time. I moved to help him and realised the obstacle was those defenceless men murdered when the attack first started. Hosius was trapped, pinned against the barricade of lifeless flesh.

Scipio was taking on the fourth man, the leader of the group who had earlier known the password, and I heard my father say in a deep voice as he traded strokes with his enemy: "Take him alive…Scipio."

And as he spoke the name, his heavy sword struck his opponent's and broke it. The next strike smashed through the man's weakened defence and crushed his chest like a hammer blow, the soldier toppling off his horse to roll on the floor gasping for breath. Several legionaries nearby ran forward and surrounded him, stabbing down into what soon looked like nothing more than a red-sodden bundle of rags.

After this, it was a matter of time before the end came. Titus' sword licked out one more time and a bright bubbling cut appeared across the throat of the man he was fighting. He fell without a sound. By this point, I was trying, and failing, to distract the assassin attacking Hosius. It was only Hosius' skill on horseback that was keeping him clear of more serious injury as the man repeatedly brought his weapon down to batter the small buckler behind which my friend was cowering. I swiftly took in the fact that he was bleeding from several places on his torso as another huge blow shook his defence. And I knew I must do more than merely distract.

I took the javelin from behind my saddle and threw it across the space between us as hard as I could. I know not whether it was luck or judgement but it pierced the enemy high in his back, and my youthful weight and energy meant it went right through. His expression as he stopped mid-stroke to look down at the point that had just appeared from his upper left chest, so Hosius told me later, was one of complete bewilderment. On the verge of victory one second, the next at Hades' gate. I did see his look as he turned to see from where the spear had come; and it gave me some satisfaction to see the pain in his gaze before his eyes swiftly dulled and life fled. He remained sitting upright on his horse, though slightly slumped. If I had not known better I might have thought him to be having a rest after a long day.

There was a sudden quiet, except for the sound of the still pounding rain, as if the world took a deep breath.

Then, "Ha!" My father bellowed. "See that men? Straight through the heart for his final kill. I believe that to be three lives taken by my son this day though he is not even of an age yet. The ease with which we will beat this false emperor will be a wonder to behold." At this, someone- I know not who but I suspect the wounded Aemilius may have started it- began to cheer for me. All seemed to have forgotten the fight still continuing between Scipio and the leader of the assassins, the sound of their weapons dulled by blood and dirt. As the cheer ended, it was as if all remembered- either that, or it was the dull groan of the man as Scipio's sword hilt made hard and forceful contact with his skull, breaking the quiet following the men's shout. He reeled, all but unconscious in the saddle, and was caught roughly as he fell by the footsoldiers who appeared on either side of him.

Scipio ordered without hesitation: "Bind him and throw him in one of the carts. Four guards. Nothing to eat or drink until I require it."

"Good work men," said my father as we gathered round to see how he fared, along with officers who had at last realised something was taking place behind them. They had, amongst them, halted the column.

Felix had arrived nearby and Constantius spoke to him rather than to us. "I am fine, my friend. We will carry on till nightfall; we shall not let a small incident like this interrupt our plans. Bring up a cart and collect the bodies of those killed from our force- we shall give them a suitable burial when we stop. The assassins can be left at the side of the road to be eaten by any beasts as need the sustenance." He nodded to the centurions around us. "We need to be near Viminacium in a week- what are we waiting for?"

They hastily turned their horses and returned to their positions. Soon the column was moving once more, the marching soldiers turning inquisitively to look at the bodies being removed and piled at the side of the road. The blood beneath their boots swiftly turned to a dull brown underfoot then disappeared amongst the muck thrown up as they marched over what had so recently been a killing ground. My father and I stood to one side as Felix moved to act on his commands. I gazed on in wonder, astounded at what had taken place in such a short span of time. No-one would ever hear of this battle- for it was barely even a skirmish- yet I felt somehow forever changed, as if something precious had been taken from me and life would never be the same. I had killed- and, despite the strange feeling of loss, had no regrets nor, and this surprised me, doubts as to the taking of life. It had been kill or be killed; and I had survived.

"Speak quietly, son," my father broke my reverie, speaking out of the corner of his mouth. "Word must not get out of how close this fight was. How did you know to come? We were hard-pressed and would not have survived but for you."

"I was the scout who let them through." I nodded towards Aemilius, sitting on a rock under another elm. "And he said some things that made me suspicious of them. But it was just a feeling really. Nothing more. And surely I of all people could afford to take a risk based on a mere suspicion. There was nothing to lose."

"Just a feeling," he repeated. I gazed at him, his heavy brows knitted over piercing eyes as he squinted through the storm at the work going on around him as the road was fully cleared.

I carefully paraphrased his earlier words. "Father, I have not just found you only to lose you again so swiftly. I will risk my life out of choice as you must risk yours out of necessity."

His head turned slowly towards me as the words registered. I quailed slightly in trepidation as I wondered if I had gone too far in my paraphrasing of his previous rejection; but a smile slowly worked its way across his face, starting with a slight curling of the lips and ending up in a grin as large as a half-moon. "Well said, youngster. You are truly my son."

The feeling of relief and delight at his praise left me caught between tears and hilarity, and we both ended up laughing heartily at the choked sounds that issued from my lips as I tried to speak a response.

"You will march with me from now on, Constantine, though you are clearly one of the best scouts we have!" His look turned more serious, the laughter vanishing as the drips made their way down his face like rivulets of tears as he considered what must happen now. "And I have a hard experience for you tonight when we make camp. You must see these things at some point. Antius is due this afternoon with word from the Emperor, and his timing could not be better."

I looked away in a sudden pang of alarm, my stomach dropping as I considered these words.

◆◆◆

We settled that night within the wooden palisaded walls of a full marching camp, my father having decided when we left the mountains in the early evening that we could no longer, given the events of the day, justify taking any risks.

He took me to his command tent at the centre as soon as it had been finished by his slaves, Lucipor nodding to me as I walked past and in through the door. He took a seat behind his portable desk in a rounded chair, resting his chin on one of his fists as he looked at me sitting opposite, brows furrowed, with regret in his eyes.

The silence grew as we sat there; until it was abruptly broken by him. "Son. There are times in life when you have to do things that you do not wish to do; but it is for a greater good. It is not pleasant or enjoyable, but it needs to be done. This is the price you pay to be a leader and you must know it now."

As if to punctuate the end of his sentence, there was a penetrating scream from somewhere in camp. It was the sound of torment, of pain unending. My father moved uncomfortably when I leapt from my seat.

"By all the gods, what was that?" I swore.

"Sit down son." He spoke quietly. "That was the leader of the assassins- Quintus. He is a praetorian centurion, known to be one of the very best and, some said, a possible future praetorian prefect."

"Do you know him, father?"

"I know of him. That is why my sword was so quickly drawn in the fight. He tried to hide his face from me as I suspect he believed I might be able identify him, so the attack started badly as I moved around to try to see who it was approaching. In fact, I had never met him. But his caution spoilt his first strike at me." Here he paused and sighed, saying softly, "Poor Balius- he would never have hurt any creature willingly; but he died so that I could live."

Balius had been his first secretary, and he had been a silent presence around every meeting I had been a part of over the last few months. Constantius would miss him. I waited for him to continue. "And the weather made it unpredictable. Even with your arrival, we could well have died. But those moments in the first instance were lost because Quintus tried to hide." His head went up as another shriek split the night. "And now he pays the price."

"What do you hope to learn from his interrogation?" I asked, trying my hardest to appear indifferent. But I knew that there must be terrible torture happening nearby and I shivered to my core at the thought of what that might involve. It was one thing killing a man in battle; but I was certain I would not have the stomach to look upon such a sight, let alone administer the pain itself. I had suspected previously that my father had at best sanctioned such actions, at worst been personally involved, once I had heard the tale of vengeance taken after Aurelian's assassination.

As if reading my thoughts, my father sank back in his seat. "We will find out. We go to see soon. Antius has been at work for a while; it is only now that he has allowed the cries to be heard, for the men must know what happens to the enemies of an emperor."

We spoke further, my father drinking a beaker of dark red wine, occasionally stopping to stare into it as if the deep rich colour made it something else altogether. Neither of us could maintain any flow to our discussion and we were both distracted and tense. In the end, we reverted to his old mentoring discourse: "What could have gone wrong in that fight?"

And I fell back into the former way of things. "They could have been armoured?"

"Good point. Why were they not?"

I thought for a second. "They were meant to be pathfinder scouts, fast-riding, fleeing danger before it comes too close as their main duty is to report back. If armour had been worn, that would have told its own tale of deceit. As it was, the quantity of weapons they carried suggested something amiss which was one reason we rode back in such haste."

"You noticed. That was why you were able to cut your enemies so easily- they should have had protection, but there was none."

He lapsed back into silence as the conversation reminded him once again of why we sat here. After a brief moment, he suggested we see what Antius had discovered- more in order to end the uncomfortable situation, disrupted increasingly by weakening screeches of suffering.

I held back as we walked through the darkness, light provided by the burning brands in the right hands of the four guards who escorted us. I was hesitant to cross the threshold of the brightly lit tent that was set back behind the rest of the legionary accommodation; but took a deep breath and stepped over despite my fear of what horrors I might see.

I would never forget the sight before me. Antius was cleaning his hands on a cloth in a satisfied fashion, standing over a figure strapped to a board and propped up against the central pole. The body was slumped forward in its ropes, and as I moved around Antius with a dread fascination, it lifted its head to look at me. I took in the lidless eyes, the strips of bloodied flesh where whole sections of skin had been removed from its face. The flow had stopped; but the streams of blood had coagulated into strange patterns as they ran down while Quintus writhed in his agony. There were but patches of hair left on top of his head, and a strong smell of burning meat was in the air. As he strived to push himself up fully, another scream issued from his mouth as some raw part of him rubbed against the merciless ropes. I did not wish to look further and turned my eyes on Antius with a degree of relief when he spoke, glad that I no longer had to examine the ruined object that tried to stand before me. I was grateful that I had not given way to the sickness that welled up in my stomach, and that I managed to keep my evening meal down. That would have lost all the respect I had previously gained from Antius.

I did see before I turned my eyes away that part of the reason Quintus was struggling to stand was because both of his legs were at strange angles, broken below the knee, and the attempt was making his pain even more agonising. I caught a glimpse of far worse but would not let my mind dwell on what I thought I had seen as I listened to the torturer.

"I think we have everything we need lord", said Antius.

"Let's have it then," Constantius replied brusquely, his ruddy complexion revealing that the wine he had been drinking had fortified him sufficiently for him to be able to view the damage done at his command.

"Well sir: seems there is another band who have been ordered to attempt the assassination of the emperor himself."

"Stop there!" My father turned to one of the guards as Antius waited placidly, and I had the time to notice a fine blood spray covering one side of his face. I stared at it, fixated, as my father spoke. "Fetch our fastest rider and our fleetest horse. I want them ready to leave within the time it takes to saddle and prepare provisions." He turned back to Antius. "Continue."

"Turns out that Carinus defeated that Julian- the Pannonian emperor Diocletian mentioned?- and decided that he couldn't be arsed to carry on to fight you. Wanted to return to his harem in Rome to find more diverting entertainment. So he took the shortcut- sent his best men to get rid of the problems: you and the true emperor. Of course", he ended, "Carinus will have to fight now that his plan has failed. Quintus informs me that he continued marching, should this plan fail."

"Well that should be no surprise to me," my father laughed drily. "He is a man known for shortcuts. And do not be too confident old friend- we have yet to prevent the plot against the true emperor."

Antius acknowledged this point with a nod, then moved on to other matters. "He was supported by his mobile field army, mostly taken from the Second Parthica, from northern Italy in his war against Julian, along with large detachments of the three legions from the northern Rhine. Vexillations of the Second and Third Italica, based in Raetia and Noricum, were involved too- so we know where they stand now, and they will have informed Carinus of our approaching them. And, of course, the most loyal elements of the Praetorian Guard. It appears he may have stripped the Rhine frontier of its cavalry auxiliaries as well- no doubt a mess we will have to tidy up once we have won. This was no doubt a convenient gathering of his troops for the fight with us- by the sound of it, Julian was not expecting this level of response. He only had two legions: the First Adiutrix- not so 'loyal and faithful' any more", he grinned as he mocked the additional name given to the legion for its support of the emperor Trajan as he fought his political battles just under two centuries before, "and the Second of the same name. Seems he had thought the Tenth and Fourteenth Gemina would join him as he marched on northern Italia to attack Carinus. But neither were willing and stayed in Carnuntum and Vindobona- despite being legions that he claimed to have under his authority. I think he got a bit of a shock when he came up against the force Carinus took with him. Quite an easy victory. But Quintus seems to think that Carinus knows our emperor will command at least five legions, maybe more, and against a battle-hardened and very experienced general it would be an altogether different proposition."

I could not help my exclamation: "But what happened to the two legions who fought for Julian once beaten? And what about the two who stayed at home?"

Antius kept his eyes fixed on Constantius, ignoring me. "As I was about to say, sir, the defeated legions were given the choice of joining the false emperor or being disbanded. The men naturally chose to join him- though it must have been through fear, as it is no small thing to abandon your province and your allegiance to the emperor in order to march on Italy as they had done. Their commanders must have been replaced and those men will be as sheep. I doubt they will fight well for anyone now, broken as they must be. Quintus knows nothing of the Tenth and Fourteenth Gemina- though he does say that Carinus sent messengers demanding their presence with his army. They had not responded by the time he left."

My father looked pensively at Antius. "Have we had answers yet?"

"No sir. The messengers have been gone nearly a month. Those who went to Aquincum and Brigetio will obviously never return." As these were the hometowns of the two defeated legions, I realised my father's plans had been far more advanced than I had thought. He had been courting Carinus' supporters long before we set out; and maybe we would see more success than I had initially estimated if these two could join us in time.

Constantius spoke again, his eyes hard. "So. The worst that can happen is that we fight eight legions- albeit with two of them unreliable participants- with four. We can count on the First and Third Parthica. Though the Emperor will want to leave the Arabian legions to cover the border with Persia in case of a counter-attack. And there's the Fourth Flavia Felix and the Seventh Claudia- with, I'm told, Maximian recently appointed as their new commander to keep them in line."

"Aye sir, but we have yet to hear from Novae and Durostorum. And don't forget that there are those two Dacian legions now based in Moesia- the Thirteenth Gemina at Ratiaria and the Fifth Macedonica downstream at Oescus."

My father scoffed. "And how likely is it that we would hear from the first two? Maybe Diocletian should have taken the local auxiliary cohorts from the border to join us after all- if the legions are staying to guard the frontier anyway! The First Italica were never the fastest marchers and the Eleventh Claudia are too far away even should they walk all night and day. As for the Dacian legions, they owe the empire nothing."

"But all are loyal to you and to the emperor, lord, as befits Moesian legions. It is a pity that the Emperor Diocletian was unable to call on the Arabian legions as he came west."

"The empire's defence against the Persians will always take precedence," my father said brusquely. As an afterthought, he added, "And at least two of those you have mentioned are Thracian…"

I interjected brightly but thoughtlessly, "In fact, sir, if the other two commanders do respond and raise their standards for the false emperor, then we could be facing ten legions." I found two pairs of cold eyes turning towards me and regretted my words instantly. Fortunately, before either could speak there was a grunting sound as the captive seemed to be trying to say something. We all turned to listen, expecting something more than Antius had already managed to extract. I could just make out his words through his laboured breathing and the visible effort of raising one last attempt to speak. "And the… rightful emperor shall rule; all false men shall die. I will see you in… Hades."

He coughed and blood spewed from his mouth, his head dropping to his chest as he stared at his life leaving him. Antius, almost absentmindedly, raised his sword from where it stood leaning against the rack to which Quintus was strapped, and chopped down sharply on the bent neck that presented itself. Quintus' head, released from the trunk of his body, rolled to rest against my father's left boot, blood pooling around the remains of the neck. He paled, but only slightly, for he had seen far worse in battle as I knew. It was more the nature of the death that appalled him, for I knew what he was thinking: if Carinus won, both he and I would likely meet our end in a similar fashion. But the pain that we would endure before this would be far worse than Quintus' experiences, for revenge was a greater motivator than mere information-gathering.

At that point, the guard Constantius had sent out returned and said, "Sir. The messenger is ready to travel immediately."

My father responded, "Excellent. The emperor is travelling up the Via Militaris through Thrace as we speak. Tell the messenger to find him and inform him that there are assassins seeking him. They know our passwords but the look of praetorians- though without the uniforms. They may say that they are pathfinder scouts."

"Sir." The guard left the tent.

Constantius turned to the spymaster: "Good work tonight, my friend. You have done well."

◆◆◆

The rest of our journey was dull in comparison to this- not that I would wish similar events on another traitor for the sake of my entertainment- and there were several nights where I lay awake thinking of what I had seen. I eventually found Hosius and told him all that had taken place. He ridiculed me: "What did you expect? That man nearly took all of our lives and would have praised his gods forever for enabling that to happen. And you pity him? Never! It is their lives or ours, and only our gods and the power of our right arms can prevent us being the ones tied to a board and tortured to death ourselves!"

I raised my other question with my father as we marched our final miles across the plain surrounding Singidunum, taking more established routes this time than when we last travelled here. "Father, I am confused. Why is it that each side is able to call the other a usurper? What is the right of it?" I added hastily, "Of course, I know that Diocletian is the legitimate ruler; but how can others think so differently?"

He turned on his horse to stare at me, his right hand resting firmly on his knee as he studied me. "Son, there is no such thing as a 'rightful' emperor." And then the words he said next were so similar to those that Hosius had spoken just the day before that I knew I would not forget them. "All we have is our own strength and that of our closest family and friends, as well as the god above." He pointed upwards in the direction of the Sun. "That is all there is."

I asked, wanting to believe there was something more, "But is there no morality, good and evil, right and wrong?"

"There is; but that is the preserve of those who win. Those who lose do not retain the privilege of making the distinction. When we have won, then we will talk of right and wrong. Remember, my son, your history lessons. When it comes to emperors there has not been an emperor of a so-called legitimate line for over two hundred years, since

Nero committed suicide. And consider these recent events. How did Carus, father of Carinus and Numerian, become emperor? By his troops' acclamation. And not even on the field of battle! He himself- if the stories are to be believed- encouraged the murder of Probus, his predecessor, and did not then ask the Senate of Rome for their approval of his accession. He informed them that he was now emperor. And there was nothing they could do. He tried to set up his own dynasty, as others have tried for short periods since the Julio-Claudians. But who now decides the rightful emperor? The troops." He waved at the column of men ahead and behind us. "This last fifty years has been a period of turmoil as has never before been seen in the empire, starting with the year of the six emperors- only one left alive at the end of that cursed year. I have lost count of the number of men that the Senate has approved as emperor in my lifetime; most of them dead within a brief span. And that does not include those like Julian who merely sought to be emperor and met their end before almost any knew of their claim." He turned to me fiercely, speaking intensely. "We must win this fight, my son, or we will go the same way- and the empire will not last. This is not the end that my god wishes for me."

He spoke no more.

Three days later we met Diocletian; three days after that, we ran from our destiny.

CHAPTER 9: RETREAT

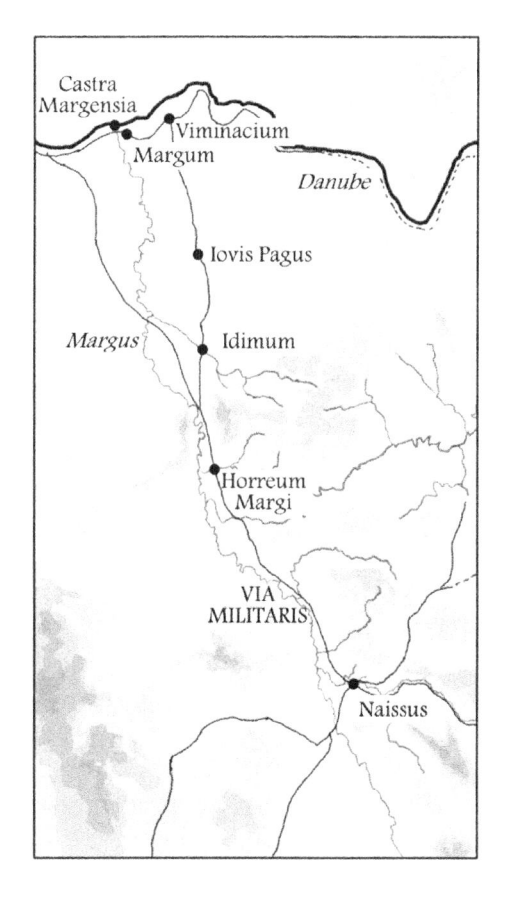

"Of course, they will not cross unless forced to." My father spoke conversationally. We were sitting on the edge of the River Margus near where it joined with the far larger Danube, the walls of the small fortress of Castra Margensia visible behind us, staring across at the enemy on the opposite bank. It was a warm afternoon; having started cold, the light mist covering the river at the start of the day had now burnt off and we were enjoying the sunshine as we moved towards summer.

"Why is that?" I asked.

"Even though we are weaker by far than them, Carinus' generals will have no desire to launch an attack across the river into the face of an entrenched enemy waiting for them on its banks." He gestured expansively to left and right. The three legions with us were rotated on duty, and we could see men from the IV Flavia Felix, usually based in Singidunum, standing ready on either side in full armour and dispersed at intervals down the river bank as far as we could see in each direction. The golden lion that was their symbol stood proud on the shields grounded in front of each soldier, presenting a wall that would have to be broken through if the enemy were to establish themselves on our side of the river. Symbolic rather than truly defensive, it sent a very visible message.

"But you can hear that noise?"

I nodded. It could hardly be missed: sawing and hammering reverberated across the river, along with the regular rhythmic thump of axes. I could see teams of slaves coming down to the opposite bank, collecting water in every conceivable container and taking it back into the darkness of the woods that stood there to provide refreshment for those working so hard.

"They will be keeping busy building pontoons to cross with."

"But you said they had no intention of doing so?"

"Certainly not now- though it ensures we remain prepared. I am sure the Fourth would much rather be relaxing with their fellow legionaries than be stood on duty till sunset. The constant noise will wear away at their nerves as well. But eventually the enemy will have to cross if they wish to bring this war to an end- unless we go to them. It also keeps Carinus' men active and purposeful."

"So what will we do now? Neither side can move or act, and we can't all remain here forever!"

My father turned his attention fully upon me. "I would not be eager too soon to see battle, my son. You will see your fair share before victory is ours. Someone will take the initiative."

We both fell silent, contemplating what that could mean for each side in this civil war. Before long I returned to his initial comment: "What could force Carinus to cross?"

"Disease, rumours of mutiny, further rebellions- we still do not know for sure what the two northern Danubian legions have chosen to do. The other two sided with that usurper, Julian. If what Antius' spies tell us is true, though, one of them may well have deserted last night. It is hard to tell with those trees in the way. But they claim that the I Adiutrix was set up as the rearguard; so the legion took its chance, they left their fires burning and made a run for it back up to Brigetio, refusing to take sides and determined to sit out the rest of the war in safety."

"What will Carinus do?"

"He does not have much of a choice. He cannot very well leave us sitting here and run off after them. What would he do when he caught up with them? He needs the men on his side willingly for this fight; and decimation as a punishment for mutiny hasn't happened since the III Augusta nearly two and a half centuries ago. He has still got, as far as we know, seven legions along with a number of the praetorian guard with him. It looks like the X and XIV Gemina stayed at home as we thought they might. But if he is unable to beat our three with more than double the number then he does not deserve to be called emperor!"

"I had thought that we had more than a mere three legions able to answer the call to support the emperor? Antius' spies told us that all along the Danube were loyal!"

"Aye. It looked that way- before civil war became a reality. There has been much reluctance to commit. Large detachments of the III Parthica have been sent to our four 'missing' legions to persuade them to join the fight- but we are unlikely to see them before this battle is decided, even should they march. Diocletian decided it was worth the risk despite how much that has weakened our force- there are not many of that legion left in camp. And that will change our strategy here. This is deadlock, which suits us for now; but we must fight sooner or later. Sitting astride the Via Militaris is not going to get us very far if we do nothing. There is a meeting in the early evening tonight in our Emperor's quarters. You will attend on me as my servant. Keep my cup brimming and you will be able to hear everything that passes. Do not interrupt- there are prefects and tribunes present with many years of experience. The emperor will be listening for their advice."

◆◆◆

Later that day, we walked through the large camp towards the centre, Diocletian's enormous imperial tent dominating those around it as each commander, followed by a small entourage, entered. Well-armed guards surrounded the tent to ensure that no-one else could listen in, and even I flinched a little at the intimidating sight as we approached. I carried a burning torch to show the way, while the huge Lucipor followed as an attendant should my father require anything. The interior of the tent was brightly lit and there was much forced humour, the sound of laughter booming in the enclosed and well-furnished space. The principal joker was a large man with a substantial stomach, clearly one for enjoying the comforts of home. As he took his seat and arranged his cloak on it, Constantius leant across to me.

"Gaius Julianus Genaialis, prefect of the Fourth who we saw on duty earlier today. If they are lucky, he is certainly the luckiest. Man's never fought a true campaign as you can see from the look of him. Rumour has it that he had no desire to fight, but his men would have killed him if he had not because of their love for Diocletian. Do not stare! He takes offence easily. Particularly since his namesake set himself up as a rival to both Carinus and Diocletian- that governor with the Pannonian legions was a Julian too. He is very sensitive about it."

I tried to subtly take in each person of importance in the scene before me. I recognised Diocletian of course, sitting quietly at one side of the tent. He would smile at the right times, laugh when needed and speak only as necessary. At first glance, you would not have assumed him to be the ruler of the empire; but after a short while of being in his presence you knew who was in charge. He had started wearing a cloak of purple, I noticed, and his shoes were decorated with many gems. Likely a means of demonstrating his authority in a more tangible way, I thought to myself. Julian was unctuously attempting to assert his closeness to Diocletian; but the emperor saw my father sitting himself by the door and indicated that he should come and sit to Diocletian's right. I could see two other generals turn their heads sharply as a court eunuch inserted a chair close to the emperor. As I gathered my father's cloak and followed him across the floor, I heard the emperor say quietly, "How could I manage without my right hand?"

Our arrival in the camp had been greeted by the emperor with similar pleasure the morning before, my father embraced as he leapt off his horse outside this same tent, greeted with delight by Diocletian. Our messenger sent after Quintus' assassination attempt had arrived just in time, and a similar unit had been dealt with before they could reach the emperor. While we did not bring as many troops as others did- perhaps five hundred with each legion being three times that, the Dalmatian Horse having already gone ahead of us- our troops were mounted, including lancers, horse archers and slingers. This made our detachments particularly important. Infantry would still play the key role in a proper battle; but our men could swing the fight at a crucial point. They were the most experienced fighters as the legions usually took up garrison duties rather than experiencing proper battle; while the cavalry was used across the frontiers for fast deployment to solve problems- of which there had been many in recent times. Besides this, there was Diocletian's evident love for my father. As I stood behind my father's chair, I wondered which two of the gathered men were Galerius and Maximian. As Diocletian and Constantius became engrossed in quiet conversation, Julian turned his attentions to his left: "Jealous, eh Galerius? Not the golden boy any more?"

The thickset man, one of the two who had looked up when my father was given his new seat, his broad face reddened by the sun, small eyes squinting whenever they turned towards the light, allowed a look of irritation to cross his face for a very brief moment. "Not at all Julian, not at all," chuckling as he spoke, though the humour did not reach as far as the crows' feet at the corners of his eyes. He deliberately misinterpreted the prefect's comment. "It is many years since I was a boy." Looking cynically and pointedly at Julian's stomach, he added, "But I feel I have aged well where others have not."

The hearty guffawing that came from Galerius' left in response to the cutting riposte from his comrade could only have come from Diocletian's other favourite, Maximian. Only he would have the confidence and assurance to laugh at another prefect's discomfort. I knew from my father's complimentary words that Maximian was completely loyal to the emperor and appeared to have little ambition of his own. Galerius was compared by Constantius to a snake; he was a talented cavalry general who would turn on the emperor if events took the wrong turn. But Maximian was a legion commander who would remain by the emperor's side regardless of the outcome of the battle. He was older, his lined forehead telling the tale of his experiences on the Rhine, and with that age there seemed to be wisdom- he sat and listened to Julian and Galerius continue their thinly-veiled barbs. He commanded the VII Claudia, from nearby Viminacium, and both my father and Diocletian greatly valued his advice. Maximian had served with them under both Aurelian and Probus but was further travelled- he had even served in Britain, and, so it was said, under Carinus himself in that backwater. It was Maximian and Galerius who had assisted in orchestrating Diocletian's rise to the purple after his execution of Lucius Aper so these men had much influence. Around the sides of the tent were other prefects and tribunes; but it would be these five who would make the final decisions.

Diocletian clapped his hands, making me jump slightly as I poured my father's wine. There was instant silence. "So, my friends, what are our choices?"

The quiet continued. The first to speak, in a jovial tone though all suspected there was too much truth in his response, was Julian: "Run?"

A frown creased Diocletian's face; but my father leapt in with the roar of laughter that such a comment richly deserved. Slowly, it spread around the tent until everyone was joining in. The emperor's expression dissolved into a faint smile. "I think you could be the furthest behind and the first to face Carinus' wrath were we to try it, Julian."

Galerius spoke next, seriously and with gravity, the tone of the discussion changing dramatically as Julian was ignored. "I say we make a fight of it here. They cannot stay there forever. Let us send men across at night to fire those cursed bridges where they lie to provoke them into making the attempt to cross. We would kill many on the way across, and my cataphracts would make short work of any troops emerging from the river. They could not transport any horses across."

My father spoke the obvious, in a voice carefully calculated not to infuriate his fellow officer. "If we burn their bridges, they would not be able to cross. So it would slow them down rather than create a provocation. And no commander worthy of his office- and bear in mind that Carinus had a good record on the Rhine before he became emperor- would attempt to cross in force. It would become a mere skirmish. We need a final, decisive battle; not a series of small fights that would eventually leave us far worse off than him due to our smaller army. He must commit his entire force, including cavalry, if we are to win properly."

The emperor summed up: "So this is not the place to make a stand. It is a stalemate."

The prefect of the I Parthica, a man I had not noticed so far, spoke up. "If we pull back from the river to allow them to cross, then they will come. But it is a risk- we must be sure we can win."

Diocletian spoke clearly. "That is a choice, Gratian, certainly. But it is not one I would be willing to take. Pulling back from the river would leave us exposed on an open plain. Their infantry would push us back by sheer weight of numbers, while their cavalry would roll up our flanks at will. We need ground that restricts the larger force and makes them fight on more even terms due to a narrower front. We cannot surrender our advantage in order to provoke a fight we could not win."

Maximian had been listening thoughtfully. "If the III Parthica are on their way back, as would seem to be the case, they cannot be far off; and, as you say, this is not the ground to fight on. Also, if we wait longer, the X and XIV Gemina may appear and join forces with the false emperor- as there is now no way for them to side with us as his army lies in the way. My suggestion would be to take the army south and attempt to meet up with our fourth legion. That will buy us time and enable us to choose the best ground to fight on. Not only that, but they may have persuaded one or more of the other Danubian legions to join us- the XIII Gemina and the V Macedonica are both close enough to march to support us."

Hosius' father, Antonius, was present. His wing had been attached to the Seventh, and he spoke from the group of men representing that legion assembled together, standing, to the side of the doorway. "But it will have to be a fighting retreat?"

Diocletian turned so he was able to catch the eye of each man there. "Fighting of course; but not a retreat. Never call it that. We are taking the initiative to lure them across the river and win the war. One of us must break this deadlock. We will need to create a gap between us and them- they must cross the Danube so that will give us the opportunity to get well ahead of them." He mused, his head lowered for a second. "Ground of our own choosing, another legion and no doubts as to who will be involved in this fight." Speaking loudly once again: "My thanks once again to Prefect Maximian for his sound advice. This is what we will do. We will take Galerius' suggestion as to taking the fight to the enemy. If we were to, say, fire his new-built pontoons, my friend, having fought alongside Carinus as you have, what would be his reaction?"

Maximian, the friend referred to, examined the ground in front of his feet; then his head came up sharply, decision made. "He is impetuous. I believe he would react, maybe in a way we would not expect. We must be ready for all eventualities should we attack as you have said, sir. But I would advise that we prepare for the strategic fallback you have also indicated." He bowed his head again, having spoken his piece- and having successfully avoided using the word 'retreat'.

A look of determination crossed the emperor's face as he made his decision and issued his orders. "We will adopt the best of both plans. Galerius, you will lead a night raid on the bridge-building equipment across the river. This will be a distraction, so do not over-commit your men. We do not in fact wish him to respond with a counter immediately. Return across the river as soon as you have created enough of a problem for Carinus. You must buy us time. As you attack, the rest of the army will withdraw. You will need to ensure that your men keep their horses ready in the trees by the river for when they return. How you get across the river is your decision. Constantius: you will take charge of the rearguard. Your troops are ideal for this sort of fight- and you can have all of the Dalmatian Horse to support you. Get your man Felix to organise the transport of our supplies on barges down the river, keeping pace with us. Galerius: your cavalry will be next in the line of march when they rejoin us, ready to assist Constantius when required. Maximian, the Seventh can come next. Julian: the Fourth will be with me as the vanguard, with my protectores." I could not help thinking that this was wise given what my father had told me. He spoke finally to Gratian. "The Thirteenth will be in the centre of the column. The rest of you", his sweeping arm took in the array of junior commanders, "organise yourselves under the prefects. We leave tomorrow night. Set fires on the plain as normal. Do not tell the men- but make them as ready as possible without revealing any plans. We will take the column across to Ad Nonum to join up with the next stage of the Via Militaris. It will be a hard day's march for we will spend the following night at Iovis Pagus."

This group were ushered out of the tent by the imperial eunuch who had earlier placed my father's chair, and who was clearly used to Diocletian's ways; another appeared with a trestle table which was placed in the centre of the remaining men. It was only at this point that Actius emerged from the dark shadows at the back of the tent. Moving to Constantius he whispered briefly in his ear and then walked out into the early dusk with the rest.

Diocletian raised an enquiring eyebrow at my father. He said, "I am told that buying time is of double worth, sir. We have made contact with one of your former proteges in the camp of the enemy."

"Praetorian Guard?" came the reply.

"Yes sir. I would like to keep the name of the soldier concerned to myself for now, until we know for sure what his intentions are."

"Wise. The Guard resented me as the commander of the emperor's protectores, so I think it unlikely many would be keen to support me as emperor- particularly given my execution of Lucius Aper, their former commander. Now, to other matters." He turned his attention to the table at the centre on which a map now lay open occupying the whole surface, with several other documents lying on top of it. He beckoned for everyone to join him around it. The attendants, including me, stayed where we were- but I raised myself up on my toes and stretched my neck forward to see. "These are reports from our scouts to the south." I could tell at this point how well orchestrated the previous meeting had been. Clearly, the course of action had already been decided by Diocletian but Maximian had been his instrument in ensuring the right direction was taken. For why would anyone be scouting to the south when the enemy was to the north? "There is a narrow defile about seventy miles south of here, roughly three days march. I intend for us to make for this point. It spreads into a wide valley, with a small village in the centre and an ancient fortress on the opposite hill. If we position ourselves well we will force the enemy to come at us on a narrow front rather than being able to use the weight of their numbers to overwhelm us, as well as their cavalry to attack our flanks. If we arrive early enough we will have time to organise defences to reduce the numbers facing us even further. Your thoughts, my friends?"

Maximian was nodding: there would be no opposition from that quarter. But then, likely he already knew of the plan. There was only one question- and that more of a comment. Constantius said, "If I am responsible for the rearguard, communication will be vital if we are to avoid my men being trapped behind whatever methods you use to prepare the ground. My mounted troops could be indispensable in the battle against a constrained enemy, and to lose this force would have serious consequences."

"True. We will ensure that our best riders are in constant contact with you. You will know everything." He turned his blue eyes fully on to my father. "But Constantius, I know you. You must keep yourself clear of the fighting. The messages will not be able to reach you if you are in the midst of the enemy."

He nodded. "Sir."

"You have your orders men. Be ready. May Mithras guide our steps."

◆◆◆

The next day was full of frenetic activity, all of it conducted under cover so as to avoid the false emperor being forewarned. My father sent Hosius and me to assist Felix as he obtained transport for the supplies. This was despite my protests, as it seemed a very dull task. Felix spent the day bartering with barges and boats that had pulled in at the toll-station, persuading them for substantial payments to leave their goods piled on the small dock at Castra Margensis so that we could use their boats to carry all we needed down the River Margus. It was a simple solution, but an expensive one.

And a busy one for us, as Hosius and I spent the day running between the boats and a group of slaves and legionaries who were ready to load more goods on board each ship that agreed to take the payment. As the day wore on, Felix found an increasing number of traders were unwilling to leave their goods, particularly as war meant looting was easy and there would be nobody to protect anything left behind. The decision was made to start commandeering boats by force.

This resulted in shouts of dismay, raging anger and furious fist-shaking as our soldiers climbed on board each barge to unceremoniously remove everything and everyone on board. Although Felix would compensate them substantially and apologetically, this was not enough. He assured them that, when we won, their transports would be returned. But there was much cynicism expressed in no uncertain terms as to the likelihood of this outcome. One or two particularly aggressive merchants ended up in the river and came back out more willing to compromise. This at least provided some light entertainment in a day otherwise filled with taut nerves and quick-fire tempers.

That evening, back in camp, I readied myself. My father had ordered me to stay with him, and Hosius had pleaded to be allowed to do so as well. The two of us watched with no small degree of concern as the men of the Seventh gave their shields to the cavalrymen who made up the rearguard. The strategy was for this rearguard to take over what should have been the duty of the Seventh on the river bank. The enemy would be accustomed by now to our rotation, so the shields with their distinctive bull insignia on would trick them into thinking nothing had changed. Looking at Hosius, I could see my worries reflected in his expression. I said to him, "Do you think it will work?"

Hosius answered quickly, as if he had been waiting for me to ask, saying, "I really do not know. This seems like the tactic of a desperate man. Surely we could have waited for more legions to join us at no cost to ourselves?"

Hosius was naturally cautious, so, curious, I said, "But it is in the interests of the false emperor to attack before that could possibly happen. He is arrogant, impulsive and, some say, careless of his men. Would it not be riskier to remain here waiting to be attacked when we least expect it? Surely it is better to dictate the terms of the confrontation ourselves?"

Hosius said nothing but continued to watch the exchange of shields, his brow furrowed with concern. He had a point: even this first roll of the dice, the retreat- for that was what it was, regardless of the emperor's re-wording- was a gamble. Our peculiar mix of Persian horse archers, Balearic slingers and Sarmatian lancers- alongside a far greater number of light cavalry- would not stand up to close inspection. But then, it would not need to. The rotation was always at dusk, and we would not be staying there for long. We would leave at midnight, once the camp was empty and Galerius had started his diversion.

I waited impatiently for that time. There was a sense of anticipation and excitement combined with nerves throughout the camp. I was affected by it more than most, I suspected, having never participated in anything like this before. Jingling bridles were covered in leather to soften the noise, horses' hooves were muffled in pieces of old tunic, and the men were told to march at the side of the road for several miles so that the studs in their sandals would not ring on the hard surface of the road. Meanwhile, Galerius' men gathered near the water and as night fell I saw the dark shadows of several barges, looking like some of those we had borrowed earlier in the day, glide smoothly around the bend from the Margus and move slowly in to the side of the river as if stopping so that the crews could rest for the night. The waiting men climbed quietly aboard and settled down into the hulls. They carried swords only, as they had been ordered to avoid any resistance and to return to the boats as soon as they was any.

The gods favoured us: the moon was hidden in cloud and the night overcast, so they were able to set off swiftly, aiming for a point downstream from the enemy camp so that they would not be seen too soon. I could see them drift with the current, not even using oars so that the noise would be lessened, directed by a steersman angling the rudder at the back. And they disappeared from sight, blending in with the darkness and the trees on the other side.

An hour passed. Campfires were lit as usual and tents left standing around our camp as the men prepared for departure. The signal went around just before midnight to start the march south; and the camp began to empty quickly and efficiently, every unusual noise provoking whispered swearing and curses at the guilty legionary. Due to the lack of moonlight, there was no need to blacken the legions' brightly polished and well-maintained equipment in case a glint should escape to alert the opposition that all was not right. A few men had been left behind to make the sounds of campmates enjoying a peaceful evening with their brothers in arms, and the raucous noise they were making, intended to be as magnified as possible to make up for their small numbers, only served to increase my concern. I sat in silence, knees drawn up to my chest and looking out of the door of my tent. Hosius sat beside me, as deep in silence as I was.

◆◆◆

There was a sudden explosion of noise across the river. We both leapt to our feet and ran to the bank. Flames blossomed on the other side, growing and spreading fast, as cries of alarm rang out. Figures flittered in front of it, silhouetted as they moved furtively to ignite more kindling. The fire appeared at first to be confined to one area of the waterfront, presumably where the pontoons had been arranged prior to putting them into the river. But now trees were catching light and the blaze spread quickly. The screams of those caught in it combined with the bellows of those trying to take control and establish order. There was a crashing of falling trees as a quick-witted commander started ordering his men to cut a break to prevent the fire spreading further. There was a rush of slaves and legionaries to the river, both visible- outlined against the flames; and heard- a great splashing that commenced over the far side of the water. That sound masked the return of our barges, and Hosius and I were taken by surprise as our raiders began to spill out of boats docking next to us. Our attention had been completely focused on events in the enemy camp. All pretence at quiet was gone now in the release of tension, their task completed. They were laughing, congratulating each other on a successful action, admiring from afar the impact of the combustibles they had carried across- until Galerius arrived to remind them all that it was not a success until we had won the war. At his words and reminded of their duty, his men rushed off to find their horses and to catch up with the main body of Diocletian's army. They used their spare horses to take the Seventh's shields back to them.

After that excitement, we experienced the odd feeling of being left behind- like a household after Saturnalia, there was a peculiar unnatural stillness that hung in the air on our side of the water that seemed wrong compared with what had gone before. The commanders across the river got control over the fire and all began to quieten down there, also. In a remarkably short time, all that could be heard was the shouted queries of the camp guards across the other side of the Danube as they made sure that they were not taken by surprise again. Our men attempted to create some small noise in order to show that there was still a military presence- but not so much that it went beyond the sound of a normal night. It was a difficult balance to strike and that, along with the sense of isolation, caused the mood to be further muted and subdued.

As the moon approached its peak I put on my equipment, starting with the new mail shirt that my father had recently given me. An old one of his own, it was too broad across the shoulders and too short to reach far down my thighs, but I was proud of it. The weight was not as great as I expected. My helmet was one from the stores, and I put it on, before moving out into the open with my friend and both of us mounted our horses, ensuring at the same time that all necessary weapons were easily available- swords at our sides, javelins in their case behind our saddles and oval shields strapped to one of the saddle horns. We walked them to where my father stood next to the emperor's tent. Diocletian had left everything, gambling all.

Constantius turned to us with a grin that bared his teeth enough to look dangerous rather than friendly. "So it begins, my boys."

The men of the rearguard were starting to appear from where they had stood guard on the riverbank, mounting the horses held in lines further inland from the camp; and we went over to join them.

◆◆◆

By means of this deception we achieved a head-start over Carinus' forces. We were told later that it was only the following evening that one of his boldest scouts swam the river and discovered that we were gone. Unfortunately for us, Carinus' plans to cross by bridge and boat were further advanced than we had anticipated; and less damage had been done by Galerius' men than we had wanted; so it was not as much of an advantage as we had hoped. What we did gain, however, was a day. And that went at a leisurely pace for our men. We could not overtake the legions as we were guarding their rear; and I realised that we were, quite possibly, the necessary sacrifice for Diocletian's victory. There were many rest breaks, much relaxed conversation and time for my father to spend with the men, riding up and down their ranks as we travelled and eating with them when we stopped, his words to them intended as encouragement and inspiration. Scipio rode with us also, his company a reassuring presence, his solidity a bolster to our confidence. Once we had rejoined the Via Militaris progress was easier and faster for the legions; though it made little difference to the cavalry as their drills involved much practice on rough ground. The river, familiar to me from my earlier travels on it, still ran peacefully to the right of us as we rode- though any wildlife had fled at the noise of the oncoming infantry. On the left the hills started to close in as we aimed for the narrow gap in the hills that the emperor was intending to use as a defensive weapon.

However, the inevitable of course came to pass. Carinus' cavalry rode across the bridge at first light the day after discovering our disappearance and caught us up at noon; though his infantry remained far behind. An imperial scout informed us that our legions would need at least one more full day's march to make it to Horreum Margi- for that was where the emperor intended to make his stand, on the plain that sat after the gorge through which the enemy would have to pass. We were tasked, as we had expected, with slowing down the enemy's cavalry.

◆◆◆

As the first horsemen came into view behind us late that morning, I turned to see them and felt my stomach heave. For this was the first time I would experience a planned fight. All other killing I had been involved in had been spontaneous, reactive and without much forethought. This would be a different matter. I would be fighting with full knowledge of what was to come, knowing I had been lucky in my first real skirmish and that I needed all the fortune I could find. I prayed continually to Sol Invictus for his blessing on my right arm.

The enemy caught up in the early afternoon, coming on without hesitation. We initially stood our ground as a group facing them in the middle of the wide Margus valley- but more as a deterrent than offering a pitched battle. For we needed to see the extent of their forces in order for my father to decide what strategy to adopt. As they approached, they spread out to flank us, slowing slightly in the centre so that the wings could develop. Constantius allowed this to continue for a time until they were fully extended, their dragon standards fully visible and giving an indication of the scale of the task, our men starting to glance at him nervously as they saw how vulnerable we were. Remaining stationary while forces encircled us did not create confidence, and every additional moment my father waited led to greater apprehension.

As the enemy force began to form a crescent around our position, he suddenly wheeled his horse and shouted, "Away! Follow me."

And our irregular force of five hundred, a mix of horse archers, light cavalry with lances and javelins and mounted slingers, turned to obey with relief apparent in their eagerness to follow orders. The Dalmatian Horse were ahead of us, about four wings amounting to two thousand men, as the Emperor had promised.

We appeared to be fleeing; but my father had a plan. The men had practiced it many times, both while waiting by the Danube and previously in Salona, and confidence returned as we took action. We rode our mounts from the main valley into a side route. Climbing a hill to the south of this track we appeared to be making for the mountains. The enemy gave chase, and soon we were being pursued by at least half the enemy force of around five thousand. We could hear the horns blowing urgently from the ranks of their commanders; but, if it was an attempt to call them back, it was in vain. My father knew we could not continue uphill away from the valley for long, as the rest would simply continue along the flat ground straight into the rear of Galerius' cavalry and he would not have held them off as he had been ordered to do.

But his men were well-drilled. As we reached halfway up the slope and the enemy were just starting their ascent, we turned as one at a signal from the trumpeter. And suddenly, Carinus' men found themselves facing an unstoppable careening deluge of soldiers descending on them. They hesitated, a brave few continuing, isolated, to push their horses up towards us. The rest broke as we screamed our war-cry, "For Diocletian!"

They ran. Our men cut them down from behind, destroying in our momentum those few who attempted to stand and fight. The slope and the ground below it was soon littered with dead and dying soldiers, horses struggling to stand again and others running headlong, without rider or direction, into the distance. Our elite cavalry force hunted the enemy in packs, the trail of their flight back to the main force leaving tattered, bloody bodies lying behind in their haste. Trumpets sounded from beside me as Constantius sounded the recall. Their enthusiasm had to be curbed in the midst of success or we would lose men unnecessarily.

My father, keeping clear of the fighting as instructed by Diocletian, then descended the hill more slowly with Scipio, Hosius and me, a satisfied look on his face as his cavalry returned in delight at their easy victory. As we watched, the remnant of those who had attacked us reached the main column that continued down the valley, disrupting its tidy formation. Some of the cavalry stopped there, the column arresting its progress as the commanders halted to accommodate the returning men. They had been able to see all that had taken place; but had been unable to prevent it. Some of those fleeing did not stop and kept running. Constantius looked at us, joy on his face. He said calmly, despite his pleasure, "I would say only about half made it back."

Scipio, known for his eyesight, replied, "I would respectfully suggest fewer than that sir. A very successful first skirmish."

"Taking lessons from Aurelian, sir?" I asked politely, convinced that this was the former emperor's famous retreating trick used to excellent effect.

Constantius looked at me proudly. "You remembered Emesa. Well done. But we cannot use it again. They all saw, and they will not make the same mistake twice. But I doubt they will attack again today after losing that many."

He was correct. We caught up with Galerius' troops that evening, with the enemy following more cautiously behind. They appeared to be satisfied with tracking our progress rather than halting it; and, other than a few very minor skirmishes between small groups of men on the edges of the valley as they occasionally tried to get around us, it was a wary but relatively peaceful truce between the two sets of cavalry.

Half of our rearguard stood lookout on the road that night, ready to prevent attacks, while the other half slept. In contrast to the night we withdrew from the Margus, the moon was sharp and clear and there were no clouds, the gods smiling on us once again, so we were able to see horsemen coming and repulse them with ease each time. There were not many and it became clear what they were doing: they also needed sleep, and they were working in separate groups to rotate their attack. The night passed with few deaths or injuries as they were only attempting to harass us enough to tire us out. They tried in the main to use their javelins so as not to come too close. Our men replied with their own missiles. These included darts collected overnight from the infantry who carried them behind their shields. Our men proved remarkably accurate with these, particularly the slingers, and the enemy's cavalry began to hold back for fear of the damage they were doing. It was, however- and as they intended- a restless night and their aim of keeping us wakeful was achieved. The three legions, having slept far better than we had, formed up and set off at dawn the following morning making for the narrow entry to the plain in which stood Horreum Margi. We needed to hold Carinus back until at least midday to give Diocletian time to establish the army at the exit from the ravine he had identified.

As our men mounted their horses, Constantius communicated several strategies to a large group of prefects and decurions, each of whom led a turma- thirty-two men.

His tactics were of necessity flexible, dependent on what the enemy did; and this moment was the only clear opportunity to communicate the possibilities. He sent them off to their units, saying, "It will be our hardest day yet, of that you may have no doubt. Carinus will not be satisfied with his cohorts holding back. And you will have to work independently to hold the line."

But his words were soon forgotten. For as we emerged from behind a spur of the mountain to confront the enemy once again, much to our horror, we saw in the distance the armour and banners of Carinus' legions. At my father's shouted question, one of Diocletian's passing scouts informed us that they had marched for most of the night while our men had rested, and they were near to catching us up- perhaps half a day behind. This gave the answer as to why the cavalry had not forced the issue sooner- not for fear of our darts and spears; but because the main force was joining them and there was less need to slow us down.

As if to add to our burden, within an hour Antius appeared from the opposite direction. We looked at him suspiciously, for his presence rarely brought good tidings. He saluted my father as he rode up, keeping his words short and to the point.

"Good morning sir. I have new orders for you. My scouts tell me that there are three legions approaching us from Naissus. The III Parthica, as expected, along with the I Italica and the XI Claudia. Although this is far more than expected, they will not be able to join up with us before tomorrow evening at the earliest. In fact, the longer the better. As a result", and here he shook his head regretfully, "I must ask you to hold the enemy up for as long as you can. If those legions can join with us in time we will fight with equal numbers. Your sacrifice will not be in vain."

Scipio snarled at him, knowing what this would mean, "But we were told we must keep them back only until midday- that we can do. Yet now the legions are a mere half a day behind the cavalry you see there! You ask much of us, and late in the day!" He swept his arm to take in the whole of the valley in front of us, a patchwork of small bands of horsemen all probing for weaknesses as my father orchestrated our own troops to prevent any getting past our line.

Constantius put a hand on his arm to still him, saying to Antius simply, "As the emperor commands."

Antius saluted him once again. "It has been an honour sir." He wheeled his horse and rode off. I watched him go with anger and resentment burning a hole in my chest. For Antius had just passed a death sentence on all of us. We had been told to die to the last man to buy time for the army to double its size. It may mean victory for Diocletian; but we would not be there to witness his glory and triumph.

Constantius turned to us, addressing the challenge before us rather than dwelling on the sacrifice we were being asked to make. "It will be harder than even I imagined, for Carinus' cavalry must break our screen today in order to attack Diocletian's rear. Their scouts will likely have informed their commanders of these reinforcements already, and they cannot afford to wait. We, as a result, cannot afford to surrender any ground. They have been husbanding their forces. Today will see all of that strength used- we must be as strong as them."

As inspiration went, it did not go far. But it was the reality spoken sincerely, and we knew we must be equal to the task. And so began our own final battle. For we would not see the confrontation outside the walls of Horreum Margi, only our own fight. This fight would not be spoken of in the adulatory praises of imperial poets, and there would be no glory in our success or failure. Merely hard and bloody death. Constantius gave his orders. Scipio and he would command from the centre. Hosius and I would be his messengers to the prefects and the turmae scattered across the valley in front of us. As the valley narrowed we would be more easily able to communicate and organize. But, until then, we would have to respond instantly to any command, race our horses across uneven ground, speak with authority and clarity to the unit commanders and ensure that everything was done according to the will of the man who bore the burden of slowing the enemy for the next day and a half.

This we did.

But by midday, strategic retreats, careful and tactful though they may have been, had become the nature of the fight as we were forced further and further back. The steady and unrelenting pressure of the greater cavalry force facing us had pushed us nearly to the narrow defile itself that Diocletian had targeted in our camp on the River Margus. Communication with him increased and my father was reassured that he had not forgotten us despite our distance- though we had by now given up all hope of him recalling us to the main force. There was some good news: our scouts had been tracking the enemy legions' progress and were reporting back that, despite their speed in catching us up, they were spread out over a long distance. Some were giving the impression of being reluctant to fight as they were far behind the rest; while exhaustion from the night march was affecting many. It seemed that Carinus, wisely or unwisely, had chosen to place those legions he trusted least to the rear; and so it was that the II Adiutrix were dragging their feet. It was their sister legion that had already retired back to

Brigetio, and they evidently had some sympathy for that position. The Rhenish legions were at the front with Carinus himself, and they were far more eager for battle, the gap between them and their Pannonian comrades growing by the hour.

We rode into the entry to the gorge in the early afternoon. We had eaten a quick meal in the saddle, our eyes turned back over our shoulders. We watched as yet another attack, this time by a group of Carinus' lancers, was turned back by the brave charge of a decurion spearheading his men as their wedge drove into the enemy. Despite this taking place so close to us, my father's thoughts had been elsewhere and he spoke to me grimly. "This could now be a far more even fight than we thought: your ten may now only be six legions, and against our six should we succeed in our attempts to delay. Though Carinus does have the praetorians as well."

Hosius chirped, "But that does not include these Dalmatian detachments here with us, sir."

I resignedly shook my head at this comment: it would seem my friend had not yet recognised our situation for what it was.

Constantius responded graciously, and in a way that did not remove all hope. "It does not, but this rearguard action has reduced our numbers somewhat. Probably by about one hundred killed, injured or out of action. It is hard to tell due to the freedom we have had to give the decurions to respond to attacks. It is not as if they have time to report numbers."

The rest of us knew that our Dalmatians would likely never experience the final clash, nor ever know whether our three legions would be joined by more.

Constantius turned to the trumpeter riding beside him. "Sound the signal for the decurions to hold here. They will screen us from attack while we decide where to take our stand."

I looked ahead. The pathway funnelled into a pass that grew narrower the further I looked into its depths. The sides were steep and heavily wooded, providing cover for an ambush. The river wound through the space, limiting access further. Trotting our horses alongside the river, we reached a particularly narrow point where a spur of rock protruded from the valley wall to create a natural barricade that reached halfway. Without a word, this being the obvious opportunity we had been seeking, we stopped, dismounted and turned to each other. We hesitated for a moment, each of us considering what words should- or could- be said. Even Hosius, sensing the sombre mood, had at last realised what it was we had been asked to do. My father broke the silence first, speaking carefully as he weighed each word for the value these last moments would have. "Constantine. It has been an honour to know you and to serve with you. You are all that I ever wished for in a son. Hosius, you have been a steadfast friend to Constantine when he needed you most. Thank you. Scipio: you have been an unwavering shield-mate and a true servant of both the empire and me. If we die here, at least we know it is in a good cause and we may have won the victory for the emperor."

I could not speak. This moment had never featured in any of my dreams. It had all been a golden adventure so far and I knew Hosius felt the same way. But now my own father was saying this to me there was no chance of survival. All hope was gone. Resignation was the only option; and giving our lives dearly in the knowledge that every moment would count in the fate of the empire- even if we would be the only ones who would ever know of this sacrifice.

But I had little time to dwell on our fate. Carinus' cavalry, wary of ambush, had not shown any desire to enter the gorge until they had gathered their full force; so the rest of the mounted troops joined us now, climbing off their horses and allowing them to crop on the scrub. One turma had been left at the entrance to the gorge to bring word if there was enemy movement.

My father stepped up on to a larger boulder that lay nearby. He waited patiently and calmly, the very figure of a Roman general in complete command of the situation, while the men organised themselves. Constantius spoke.

"My friends. You have fought well and bought much time for the emperor, at the cost of your blood and lives. Our protection for the rest of the army means we have borne the brunt of the enemy's anger. We have frustrated them and prevented any breakthrough. It has been a privilege to fight beside you. Well done!"

There was a spontaneous outburst of cheers at these words. But my father gestured with his hand, palm down, to indicate silence.

"But we are called on to make one more sacrifice."

"Always the way general," shouted an anonymous voice from the back.

The strain created by my father's words was instantly turned to laughter. I turned to see who it was and there was Antius, cloaked and hooded, standing at the back of the crowd. He saw me looking and winked at me, then vanished behind other soldiers. Having waited for the men to quieten, Constantius spoke once more: "The emperor requires of us that we persuade Carinus to further delay their meeting." He paused for effect. "Here we make our stand, and here Carinus learns what a few well-chosen men can do to his plans. If we achieve this one last thing, three more legions will arrive in time for the fight and we know that our emperor will win the battle with ease."

There was a low roar of approval from the assembled men. He moved on to practical considerations, addressing the prefects now. "Send your horses on to Galerius with any wounded men you have; those with axes, cut down those trees on the slope; and the rest of you, drag them down to build a barricade."

We had about fifteen hundred men still, once the remaining scouts and those holding off enemy lancers had come in. In a couple of hours, we had built a serviceable defence across the defile that reached to chest height; and a hastily dug ditch in front with sharpened stakes embedded in it. We had been undisturbed as the enemy were gathering their strength for a final push. We had seen scouts in the distance, even climbing the sides of the ravine to gain a better view, so we knew that they would be aware of what we were doing. The river ran below and to the left of our position, protecting our flank and providing marshy ground, and there were irregular hummocks in the valley behind which we positioned our best slingers and archers as both protection and as vantage point when needed. By the time dusk fell, we could see the false emperor's vanguard, made up entirely of what looked, from the dying glow of the bright red sunset, to be heavily armoured cataphracts, approaching around the edge of the hill. The light cavalry we had been holding off all day had vanished and this was a far more intimidating sight.

I turned to my father as he completed a final check of his forces: "What will they do now?"

"If what I have heard of Carinus is true, that he is a capable commander with troops who trust his instincts, he will attack right away. Better to launch an initial probe before it is too dark; and it prevents your own men having time to while away the night thinking about what might happen to them the next morning. At least they will know what to expect if he attacks now. The infantry also need time to catch up so he will not be eager to destroy us yet."

As predicted, the wave of armour swept relentlessly forward without pausing as the moon slowly ascended in another cloudless night. The nerves in our own men grew into a near tangible thing as my father bellowed at them to hold their fire. Hosius whispered to me out of the corner of his mouth, "What I would give for a few ballistas and scorpions right about now."

And then the ground started to rumble as the horses gathered speed, the sound of their hooves seeming to shake the earth, the flowing plumes of the men's helmets flying out behind them along with their standards. Just when it seemed that nothing could stop them, not even our suddenly insignificant-looking barricade, Constantius shouted "Fire!"

The slingers' leather thongs had been whipping around their heads for some moments already, awaiting the call, their high keening heard even above the pounding of the cataphracts. And now the snap of their weapons crackled through the air, stones whirring out in a flat trajectory. Their ideal targets were small, from eyeslits in helmets to horses' noses projecting beyond the scaled metal that covered them; but they had an astonishing accuracy and power. Even when they missed these areas, the force of their strike often broke bones. The slingers along with the archers halted the first wave, mainly because, as a few horses fell, the lack of manoeuvrability of the rest meant that the next men in line went over them, tumbling as well. Their heavy armour prevented them rising. This gave our skirmishers time to retreat behind the barricade, stabbing down at the enemy's carapaces as they went, testing for vulnerable gaps, their comrades leaning over the barrier to give them a hand and heaving their weight up.

But a few attackers kept coming, and our lancers first threw javelins- ineffective against cataphracts, bouncing off them as they would from a fort's palisade- then used their lances as spears to present the horses with a wall of points as they approached. As the animals saw these and slowed, their riders also saw the stakes in the ditch- and they went no further. The animals could not be forced into these despite the soldiers' best efforts. The few troops milled around uncertainly in front of us, exposing themselves to further fire. And then there was the sound of a trumpet blowing the retreat. They turned and fled from the killing ground. Horses lay on the field in front, many unmoving. Those that were moving were struggling to stand, partly due to their heavy armour but also because of broken legs and other injuries. Their riders, in some cases, limped away, using their spears as crutches to support them. The ground was strewn with bodies, and it was only the darkness that prevented me seeing the impact that the slingers' small stones had had. But I was able to see the arrows that riddled some of the remains.

I had done nothing but watch. I had not been needed. Neither had my father. He stood looking at me, amused, from the hillock that he had been ordering events from, and said, "Your turn will come! Do not worry about that. There is an entire army behind those cataphracts and they are looking forward to the morning."

He turned away to order our men out from behind their shelter to collect their arrows and stones, and there was the unpleasant sight of the soldiers plundering the enemy, their shouts of joy at finding gold or other items being heard clearly on the light wind that was blowing through the gorge. There were more unpleasant sounds as those of the enemy still alive were finished off.

Constantius turned back to say, "Get some sleep you two. You will need it tomorrow."

❖❖❖

Despite a colder wind and the hard ground, both Hosius and I slept well. I awoke early the next morning. Taking the last piece of hard, stale bread out of the supply-bag that I had used as my pillow I scooped some water out of the river to drink. My father's tough, worn face greeted me as I returned to my position behind the wall of trees.

"This is it, son," he said quietly.

And the long day began. Wave after wave came at us, and all our men were needed this time. The footsoldiers had caught up with the vanguard during the night and we no longer saw any cavalry. Our archers fired lethally accurate missiles accompanied by slingers who shot their carefully-chosen stones viciously from snapping leather- both had to expose themselves to shoot, though, and that led to higher casualty rates than we had hoped. Several of Carinus' legionaries managed to get past or over the barricade despite our soldiers' best efforts to keep them away. By mid-morning I had killed two men. One was trying to spit my father on a lance from the top of one of the tree-trunks that lay across the defile when I, not seen by him, stabbed upwards into his leg. As he fell from his perch, the sword went deeper still and fatally cut an artery. Jets of blood shot out as he fell, and I left him lying there in the mud as he tried to stem the fountaining flow.

There was another who came at me after jumping down from the barricade and, fortunately, losing his footing on the boggy ground. Scipio, ever ready, maimed the man's shield-arm as he slipped, while I took advantage and thrust home into his exposed stomach, twisting my sword to release it to the sound of his screams. And those were just the two I knew I had killed. Hosius and I fought side by side, each of us finding in lulls in the fighting that fresh cuts and bruises had appeared. Fewer of the enemy were reaching the top of our barricade as the morning wore on due to the array of bodies in front of it, and the fighting was at arm's length over the top. When men did manage to climb up, either Hosius or I would hack at their legs- they would disappear as they fell down the other side.

By the time the sun was at its peak, we had endured constant and unremitting attacks by a fresh force each time, and our men, fighting on foot rather than what was for many of them their more natural element- horseback- had been whittled down to half their number. We moved the injured out of the front line and did what we could for them given that every man was needed; and in desperation added the dead to the barricade or threw them over it to increase the obstacle as more attackers ran at us. Having failed to climb it, fighters began to tear at the trunks protecting us when they got close enough, pulling them away or cutting into them, and the barrier was less and less of a defense; our men were increasingly exposed as a result. The archers and slingers were fast running out of ammunition, some creeping over the wall during rare breaks in the attack to retrieve arrows- a risky and dangerous act- or scrabbling in the riverbed in an attempt to find stones of any shape or size that could be used as missiles. The enemy had managed to send their own archers up the sides of the defile and these were now shooting down into any visible group of soldiers. They were less accurate against individuals, due to their height and the adjustment needed to their aim; but we knew the fight could not last much longer.

The end, when it came, was from an unexpected quarter. A few remaining slaves had just been around with buckets of water during a brief gap in the fighting, ladling it into our mouths as we lay gasping behind our partial wall. I had asked for bread and been told that there was no food left. I turned to Hosius despairingly and grimaced at him; he said laconically, "The beginning of the end my friend."

I laughed and replied, "The beginning was long ago- I believe this to be the end of the end!"

We chuckled together at this riposte, the gallows humour providing some light relief.

The river had been our ally until this point; and, although several men had been posted to watch anything that might come from it, they had increasingly been needed at the barricade as our only reserve. So it should not have been a surprise that what had formerly been an ally provided the enemy with their solution.

 ...When a century of Batavian tribesmen, renowned since the days of the invasion of Britain for their ability to swim rivers while fully armed and armoured, swept out of the river it was a complete surprise. Our reserves were fully committed at the wall and the water was unwatched. My father turned from the barricade, while trying to simultaneously defend himself against a big Germanic tribesman who had just managed to fling himself over an outstretched branch and through a hole in the increasingly fragile defence. But our men were already streaming away into the distance, accepting that nothing more could be done. Constantius instantly saw the cause as the soaking wet warriors continued to climb from the river. It is one thing fighting an enemy in front of you; another entirely when they come from a completely unexpected direction-particularly when that is behind you.

Roaring "Retreat!", Constantius stabbed his opponent in the groin then turned to run himself.

I was beside him, and Hosius in front of us, being lighter and faster, when my father tripped on a body and fell; I turned to help him up without thinking. And the first tribesman out of the river hit me across my temple with the flat of his blade. I was, humiliatingly, knocked unconscious. And that was the end of my first, and likely last, true battle.

CHAPTER 10: DEFEAT

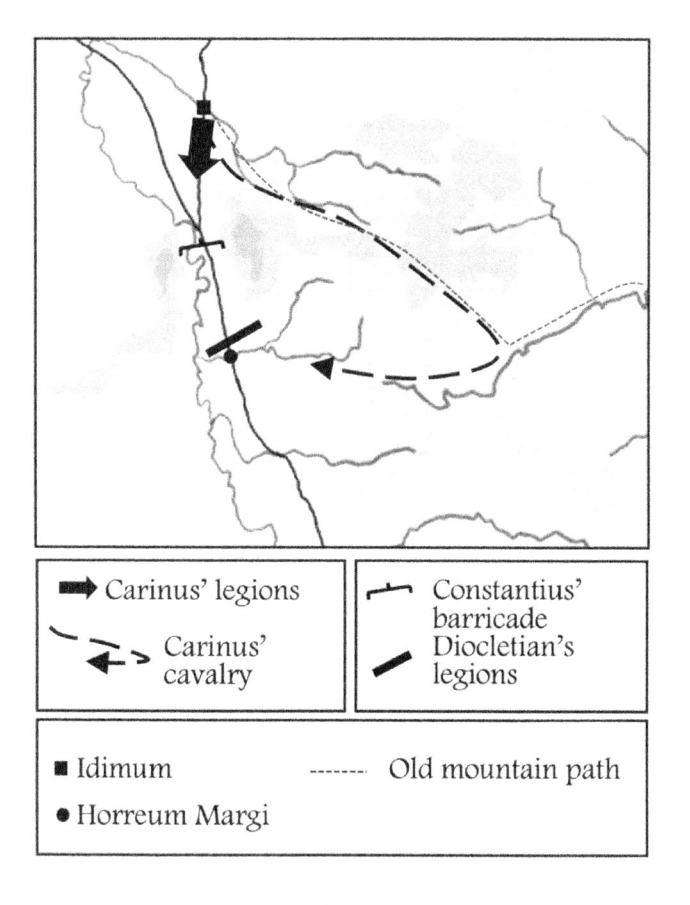

Carinus' legions · **Carinus' cavalry** · **Constantius' barricade** · **Diocletian's legions**

■ Idimum ● Horreum Margi ------- Old mountain path

I groaned and rolled over as I was kicked viciously in the side. A grinning, heavily tanned and weather-worn face glared down at me, then laughed vindictively as I groaned loudly.

"Ha! Lad's awake", he shouted over his shoulder at someone unseen. Turning to me he said with heavy humour, "On your feet. The Emperor has requested the honour of your presence." Ignoring the throbbing in my temple, and the pain in my ribs, I rose unsteadily to my feet, staggering slightly. Looking around, I saw that I was in the midst of a crowd of soldiers, all jovial and smiling. There was a festive atmosphere, and it did occur to me to wonder if I had been unconscious for so long I had missed the battle. Maybe Carinus had won already, and I was to be thrown at his feet as some sort of victory spoil?

"Constantine!" I tried to turn as a voice called to me urgently and received the butt of a spear in my stomach for my efforts.

"Shut that traitor up," snarled my captor, the grin disappearing quickly. I doubled over in pain, but I had at least seen that it was my father, and a sharp sense of relief overrode all other considerations. If he was still alive, there may still be hope.

I was pushed, pulled and prodded into a line with a series of other men, all lacking armour and weaponry, dressed only in their tunics. Our wrists were swiftly tied and we were attached together with ropes. Surrounded by heavily armed legionaries, we were urged forwards with threats and swordpoints. As my dazed head cleared, I managed to take a quick look around me and recognized these as the remnants of the men who had supported my father and I so ably in our final action. A rough estimate, I thought, put the number at over one hundred. Many must have escaped;

or they could be dead. I could not see the smaller figure of Hosius- or the larger one of Scipio- amongst them. I was worried for both but my hope was that they had escaped. Our men did not deserve the vengeance the false emperor was bound to take on them. We were moving through a dense mass of infantry who filled the ravine that had previously contained our barricade. Oddly, there was no cavalry. This surprised me given that they had been following us so closely since midway between Iovis Pagus and Idimum- but then, they had not been used for a long time in the action at the barricade.

We were ignored by many of the enemy we were walking through as they prepared for battle. A few ceased sharpening blades or, in the case of a unit of auxiliaries, checking the fletching on their arrows to spit on us as we stumbled on our way, or to strike us as we passed. Most were smiling and cheerful and ignored our passage. I was left alone, as most were able to see my youth and, I assumed, decided I must have been a boy-slave or a catamite of one of Diocletian's generals, bearing little responsibility for my current situation as a result.

There was a tight cluster of gathered generals ahead as the valley started to widen out, their bright plumes and crests waving gaily in a gentle breeze that funnelled into the ravine, and our line of captives emerged alongside them at the front of the army. We gazed out on to a scene that was strangely tranquil. The sun shone through the clouds overhead though the day was overcast. The river we had been following for what seemed such a long time- and down which I had so peacefully passed when recovering from Antius' whip a matter of months ago- meandered its way through the valley. The grass was a spring green, a few cows and sheep gently making their way across fields in the far distance. A series of low hills could be seen beyond them. Though we ourselves stood in the exit from the steeper defile, the slopes around us swiftly dropped away to create a shallow but wide bowl.

The most striking aspect, however, was the sight of Diocletian's army drawn up just a few hundred metres distant. He had positioned the cavalry on the wings, and the infantry in the centre. A standard formation, I thought, even in my predicament; and one that could potentially crush the force we stood in the middle of if used well. This would even more be the case if, for some inexplicable reason, Carinus had dispensed with his horsemen. The overwhelming weight of his army would be useless if Diocletian could keep it bottled up in the pass and deal with each section of the enemy as it made its way out. As I peered more closely I could see the brave red banners of our three legions, only their familiar emblems of bulls, centaurs and lions visible from this distance. I felt cheered despite my circumstances- and, my head clearing now, I searched for evidence of boars, sea creatures or eagles. None could be seen. And my heart sank again as I came to terms with the fact that our sacrifice had not been enough. None of the other Danubian legions had been in time to join our fight. That would explain the celebrations that had all but started already, for news of their failure to arrive would have made its way swiftly around the assembled troops.

As I thought this, the group of commanders to our right parted and a man I supposed must be Carinus approached us. He was not what I had expected. He wore no armour and clearly intended to take no part in any fighting. He wore the imperial purple as a cloak, and I found myself staring as he drew near, more out of curiosity than anything else.

There was a natural assumption that all others would move aside as he approached, reinforced by several praetorians walking behind him, swords drawn, should there be any doubt as to who he was. He was short and slight, wearing little of the authority that Diocletian carried so easily. I could tell as he drew near that I would be looking down on him if he came close. He would not stand out in a crowd, I thought disdainfully. His guardsmen were far larger. But he was not entirely overshadowed despite such flaws due to a casual arrogance visible in his eyes and petulant lips. His hair was cut close across his scalp and his beard was tightly curled, clinging to his cheeks. As I studied him a boot struck me sharply in my calves in a skilled way, dropping me to my knees instantly. There were grunts as the same happened to the whole row of roped prisoners.

The false emperor stopped. His dark brown eyes studied us without emotion and his words were precisely spoken. He stroked his chin. "Recognise any of them my friend?"

He spoke to the praetorian prefect on his right, one of those carrying a drawn sword. "Constantius Chlorus sir. Served with him years ago."

He pointed behind me, and I succeeded in swinging my head just enough to see my father, his face bleeding and bruised from several blows, four men standing guard around him. "He's the governor of Dalmatia, your father's loyal servant."

This was spoken with heavy sarcasm, and Carinus' face darkened. He responded with anger in his tone. "Soon to be no-one's loyal servant, except perhaps Pluto's."

At least we were in no doubt as to our future, the reference to the god of the underworld ending all of our hopes. The prefect, I noticed, was staring at me. My expression must have given something away, for he said to the soldier who had kicked me, "He looks familiar too. Put him beside the traitor."

I was unceremoniously manhandled into position next to my father. The prefect looked from face to face between the two of us. The resemblance must have been obvious. "See!" the praetorian prefect declared triumphantly. "They are related. I heard a rumour that Constantius had found himself a son from somewhere."

"All the better," Carinus murmured to himself. "Get them ready."

He turned away and walked back to his group of commanders. We were hauled into a line across the front of the army, our knees raw and bloodied by the rough ground as they dragged us into position. I looked around me, taking advantage of my last moments. I tried to take in everything for the final time- the blue of the sky, the shining army opposite in ordered ranks, the sweat-smell of fear from those on their knees, and the sense of excitement emanating from behind. I squinted upwards towards the sun, angry at the divine injustice of that god for not having given me the opportunity to achieve something true and long-lasting now that I had found my father. To have so much, and to have it all taken away so quickly… I did not feel fear, but more a terrible fury at the lost possibilities. The sheer injustice and unfairness of the situation was enough to bring tears to my eyes- not of sadness so much as frustration. My father was beside me and I felt the comfort of that at least.

I turned my face to him, and he spoke softly: "I am sorry, my son, to have brought you to this."

"I made my choices, father, and I regret nothing. I can think of nothing more honourable than to die alongside you."

"Quiet there!" snarled the praetorian prefect who had identified me.

The emperor's head jerked around at the sound; then, acknowledging the influence of this soldier, ordered: "Aristobulus. Remind that slave, Diocles, of who is the rightful emperor."

The praetorian prefect marched through to the front, signalling to those of his guard watching us to take up position behind my compatriots and I. The harsh, grating sound of swords being drawn from scabbards rang out down the line.

Facing the enemy army, Aristobulus bellowed with a parade-ground shout: "Show yourself, usurper!"

I could see Diocletian emerge from the centre of our army, close enough now that I was able to see his tension in the way he moved. Galerius and Maximian accompanied him. They trudged forward, stopping a few metres in front of their troops. Diocletian shouted back, "I am here. My army is here. Let right prevail. Mithras will decide who is the traitor here."

Aristobulus ignored his challenging words, declaring, "You have a final chance to surrender rather than waste the blood of so many good and worthy servants of the empire. Should you choose not to, these men's heads will roll in the dirt of this valley. My emperor's one-time substitute will die first." Here, he turned slightly to sneer at Constantius.

The men of our army standing behind their three commanders raised their weapons and I thought battle would commence instantly; but they began to strike their shields with the swords, slowly at first, then gathering pace and weight until the thunder of their response echoed across the fields and down into the gorge behind us. It was so deeply powerful, it shook the ground and I could see little motes of dust jumping up and down in front of me. The moment that Galerius raised his hand, the dull thudding sound stopped. So suddenly that the faces wincing in anticipation of the next strike took on an unknowing look of surprise.

Far more quietly than Aristobulus' words so far, but loud enough to hear and with all the more dignity as a result, Diocletian responded, "You have our answer."

As his words ended, Aristobulus' hand chopped down sharply. Despite everyone's attention being on my emperor, the praetorian prefect was almost directly in front of me and I saw it. My head spun round sharply. All along the line, swords struck into the necks of my soldier-brothers. Some executioners were not so accurate and screams sounded as blades missed their mark and hacked into soldiers' backs. I could see one man near to me- Cassianus by name, a talented slinger- sobbing as the guardsman sawed back and forth, trying to withdraw his blade and strike again. The kneeling legionary toppled to one side as the only means of avoiding the pain, his hands and legs tied so tight with leather thongs that this was all he could do. The praetorian managed to get the sword out as the man fell and chopped down across the legionary's neck, far more accurately this time. The noise stopped abruptly, the blood from his severed neck spraying upward and outwards and landing near to my left foot. As I watched it land, slow droplets falling to earth in uneven red splashes, it occurred to me that I was still alive to observe these events.

Dazed with the torment of the moment, confusion overcoming me, I twisted my neck around to see my designated killer laughing at my expression. He was cradling his weapon in his arms and clearly had no intention of using it.

My second thought was of my father. Almost as quickly, I snapped my head around in the opposite direction. He was sobbing with impotent fury as he looked past me and down the line of dead and dying men. Relief at his survival combined with rage as he saw the blood and anguish on every side. "Butcher!" he spat out forcefully in the direction of the emperor, who ignored him completely.

Focusing his attention on Diocletian, Carinus ignored him and shouted in a weak, high-pitched voice, very different to that of Aristobulus, "So die traitors! You will join them soon, slave."

It carried well enough, however, and the three generals retired to their line, readying themselves to attack. Their task would be to take the initiative against the force issuing from the gorge, and all they had to do was ensure that they stopped the neck of this bottle.

As for us, we were dragged back to our feet, and I did not have a moment even to thank Sol that I was still alive or feel pity for those who were not. The men lifting us sought to avoid as best they could the rivulets of blood that were now running in streams away from us down the hill, pooling and starting to soak into the dirt, as if it would be unlucky to touch it before risking their own lives in battle. The dead bodies were heaved out of the way, thrown in a large heap to the side of the gorge as the army cleared the ground for their charge at their enemy. As we were pushed back towards the rear of the army, through the crowded masses, there was a roar of triumph that echoed around the canyon. We were being jostled vigorously through the soldiers, and I could see the light of unexpected joy in the eyes of those we passed as they strained to see over the heads of those in front. Many were pointing back over our heads to where we had just come from. They were laughing and gleefully explaining to each other what had happened. My father and

I both jerked around to look, and our captors, equally interested in what was causing such delight, allowed it.

In the distance, over the spears and banners of Diocletian's army, a dust-cloud had appeared. I felt a sinking feeling in the pit of my stomach as I realised immediately what Carinus had done. This could only be the missing cavalry. Why else would his army be cheering? They knew it could not possibly be reinforcements for us, despite the cloud coming from that direction, for even with the fastest marching we all knew the other three legions could not possibly reach Diocletian for several hours more. My father recognised this at the same time. As we were being ignored by the men around us, Constantius leant in close.

"Carinus' cavalry," he grunted, his despair sounding in his voice. His expression showed a defeat that I had not seen in him even as we knelt with swords at the backs of our necks. "He must have sent them down another valley. I thought I saw a rough track off to the east as the road narrowed into the gorge; but we didn't have time to investigate it."

I nodded, resigned. "Not that we could have done much even had we looked into it... This usurper is a true gambler. How did he know that his men would be able to cross from that valley to this? Especially heavy cavalry! I thought our emperor knew this area- Carinus must be well informed."

My father was shouting now, the swelling cheers of Carinus' men echoing in the narrow confines as they realised that it was now all but sealed that they would not die this day. "Aye. And if it had not been possible, he would have been fighting the emperor without any cavalry." His despair was now transparent in his voice, "So near to victory! It would have been the greatest mistake."

At that point, the enemy all around us suddenly quietened, and the now familiar voice of the praetorian prefect could be heard once again, bellowing, "Bring the traitors back."

Our guards turned us sharply and forced us once more back towards the front line. All hope after our reprieve had gone and despair had taken over; I had to be all but carried as I no longer cared what happened to me. This time, none of the enemy legionaries paid us any attention, being too busy slapping one another on the back and congratulating each other on their successful victory. I could see Aristobulus, head bowed, in front of the false emperor, then nodding in seeming delight at whatever was being suggested.

We soon found ourselves back in our previous position, but this time the emperor himself was standing behind us. Before being kicked to our knees once again, we had been able to see from the slight incline on which we stood that the enemy cavalry had drawn up behind Diocletian's forces and halted there. Led by the armoured cataphracts and their powerful horses intended to intimidate with their strength, half of our army were turning to face this new threat with immense precision and organisation, and several cavalry detachments were sent to join them.

Aristobulus once again demanded Diocletian's attention. The emperor came forward more slowly and wearily this time, alone, Galerius and Maximian no doubt sent to make ready elements of our army. For me, this felt like a dream. I was no longer making sense of what was happening for I had no control over my own situation regardless; but the sequence of events, hopes raised and dashed, had left me stunned. Despite my state of misery and shock, I still heard Aristobulus laughing at something the emperor said, and then saying, "Do you wish to kill the cub or the lion? I will take the other."

"I will execute both." The emperor spoke assertively. "The cub first, so the traitor must watch his newfound son die upon my blade- a foretaste of the fate awaiting his family. Then the traitor himself. And so will end all those who oppose me." Surely the voice of this false usurper would not be the last voice I would hear? Sol could not be so unkind!

But Constantius' voice grated beside me, saving me for now from that fate. "You have won. What purpose does this serve? Leave the boy."

Carinus laughed, nearly losing control as the nervous energy of the last few weeks leached away. "Simple revenge! Oh- and I know how much influence you have in these parts Constantius. Assassination by my own troops is the last thing I would choose once your men have sworn allegiance to their true emperor. Your death assures me of my life!"

I could see nothing of him, just hearing his voice, and now he said to me: "Bow your head, child. This will be swift. Aristobulus- a sword." A giggle of delight escaped him.

I heard the weapon being handed to him and bowed my head. My mind had emptied of all but the present, and I had no time for regrets. My father whispered, "Stay strong. Die well. I will see you soon."

As he finished, I heard the movement of the sword behind me through the air…

… and to my astonishment, the emperor Carinus' body thumped to the ground beside me. There was complete silence. The world seemed to still for several moments, suspended as if frozen. Nothing moved. I looked more closely, unable to think any more; but only observe what was before me. The body had landed on its front but, as I continued to watch, it rolled slowly to one side over the slope I knelt on. There was a deep crimson stain across the front of the white tunic, over the upper left chest. The body rolled. The head swung into view. There was a look of complete surprise on the face. As I watched, the last glimmer of light faded from the emperor's eyes. Able to think again my first thought was to bless Sol for yet another reprieve. But what would be next in this upside-down turn-around world?

I remained motionless as a thunderous and by now familiar voice announced, to add to my sense of disbelief, "The false emperor is dead. Long live the Emperor Diocletian!"

The pause was a long one after this, full of suppressed violence and taut as when a bowstring is pulled to its fullest extent and held there. Every man in the valley had to decide what to do, and, though it must have been only a few moments, it felt as an eternity for me as my fate was once again out of my hands. I watched the emperor's life-blood soak into the earth before me and swore to myself and to all of the gods that I would never allow myself to be so fully in someone else's control ever again.

A single plaintive voice from further back in the army could be heard saying "What happened?"

And another spoke, enquiring in a confused tone, "What? Did he mean Carinus?"

And another: "Is Diocletian dead then?"

There was a growing sound of low-spoken questions gathering pace and volume, others turning to explain and exclamations as if the reality of the situation was dawning on an increasing number of legionaries.

Aristobulus' voice exploded from behind me once more, with greater urgency and force, putting doubts to rest with its power, "The false emperor is dead. Long live the Emperor Diocletian!"

And then there were some half-hearted cheers. They gained momentum quickly. I knew, having heard Diocletian's story of his popular acclamation after the death of Lucius Aper, that the praetorian prefect was certain to have seeded his chosen men throughout the army, ready to respond to his cry. The outcome could not have been in doubt, regardless of the slow initial response. Considering this afterwards, it was no wonder that the men joined in. As I had moved through them the second time, back to my death once more, the men had been so certain that they would not die this day. They were sure to have been already thinking of their families, the plunder soon to be theirs, and of returning to their homes. There could be no deaths as Diocletian was sure to surrender due to his hopeless position. And now that it had all changed, and the praetorians, the emperor's own bodyguard, had changed their allegiance. No-one would go against them. Besides which, with Carinus dead, what else was there to fight for?

The roar climaxed behind me as the grinning guardsman from the previous executions came into my line of sight.

"You're alive boy." He laughed at my expression and spat on Carinus' corpse. "Peasant. Didn't deserve to live after what he's done."

He bent down and cut my bonds with the dagger from his belt. I did not think to question his words more, but my father, ever with a cool and collected approach, spoke to Aristobulus as the prefect untied his bonds. "Old friend," and this was spoken with great depth of feeling, "Why did you do this? The risk...!"

He shrugged. "Diocletian's promises." He looked Constantius in the eye. "Your Antius' spies knew who to come to."

"That would not be enough for you. You are," he looked at the body lying in front of us, "were, the emperor's right hand. Surely there is more."

As the men were still cheering around us, and no-one was listening but my father and I, Aristobulus leant in close.

"That filth took my wife. He thought I didn't know, for she killed herself with the shame of it. She couldn't face me. But I knew. I had my own information." He also spat on the corpse, and I watched in fascination as the spittle mingled with the blood. "Only my men know. No-one else. Keep it that way." He paused for a second as if distracted by the memory. He shook his head to remove it. "To business."

He turned around and gestured to the praetorians. The army started to quieten as the guardsman gave orders, gesturing their weighted spears to reinforce their words. Turning, Aristobulus called deferentially in the direction of the army that had been his enemy. "Emperor, these men wish to proclaim you their emperor on this field. Will you accept them?"

Over the heads of Diocletian's army, stood silently still in mute acceptance of whatever the outcome would now be, Carinus' cavalry could be seen milling in confusion. Several small groups broke away and galloped back the way they had come. But the bulk remained.

I could see that Diocletian's energy had returned with the killing of the emperor. He came quickly to the front of his army this time, and, in a display of true courage, walked across the intervening strip of ground between us. Both armies stood and waited as he crossed over, a symbolic transition from death to life both for him and for so many others standing on that ground that day. He took his time, dignified, the full and sole imperial authority descending over him as he walked. He reached Aristobulus and spoke.

We all knew what he would say but waited with apprehension for those two precious words.
"I will."
Two words, but the men alongside me launched into fresh cheers after he said it, acknowledging that the civil war was over and there would be no more bloodshed as their new leader would take no revenge on them, acclaiming Diocletian as their emperor with orchestrated chants of 'Augustus'. He reacted by saluting Aristobulus, then embracing him. The praetorians, spontaneously, reached for him, lifted him to their shoulders and showed him to the army. The roar of approval- "Imperator!"- echoed around the wide valley that could so easily have seen the end of so many lives.

And Diocletian leant down from his praetorian throne, laughing, to touch the hands that were raised to him as if his luck and blessing could pass on to them, and I knew that I would not experience the terror of the recent past again. For my father, tears in his eyes, was hugging me to him and rejoicing. Sol Invictus shone on us once more, unconquered and blessed, two armies ran towards each other to welcome the enemy as friend, and the body of the ruler of most of the known world lay in an unknown valley, reviled, hacked at, and, eventually, after being placed on show in the middle of our camp for several days, thrown into an unmarked grave.

So ended the short-lived dynasty of Carus.

CHAPTER 11: RETURN

"Antius had informed me you swore by Mithras that you would support us, my friend, but I was becoming a bit… concerned… at your timing!" Diocletian clapped Aristobulus on the shoulder, chuckling.

I studied our new ally closely. He had a strong chin, dark eyes and black hair like a raven's wing coming to a widow's peak above a lined forehead. He was imposing in size but spoke little. His lips were narrow and cynical, his face broad, while his expression was guarded. But no wonder, I reflected, if he had been so close to an emperor who had treated him the way Carinus had. Aristobulus would have had to keep quiet and bide his time, waiting for his moment to strike. From what Antius had told me since our victory, the false emperor had been one of the most suspicious men alive after the deaths of several members of his family in the course of the last year.

We were sitting in Carinus' campaign tent, far more lavish and well-furnished than Diocletian's. We met there not only for reasons of comfort, but also as a symbol of the conquest of our foe. It was early evening, and the heightened emotion of the day was still upon all of us. Wine and conversation were flowing, and I was included due to the minor role I had so unintentionally played. Flaming torches and oil lamps added to the mood of celebration. The three legions- most of the Third Parthica, along with the First Italica and the Eleventh Claudia- that we had been so desperately awaiting had arrived an hour earlier, sooner than anticipated, exhausted from forced marches. The latter pair were a surprise, as they were based the furthest west of any. This meant that the two we had expected due to being closest- the Thirteenth Gemina and the Fifth Macedonica- remained missing. Though the three legions were greeted with delight and much mockery due to having missed the action, such as it was, all those men wished to do was to sleep, and there was little disappointment on their part at having not been present for the main event.

"I am sure," said Aristobulus dryly in response to Diocletian's comment. "But I had to have the emperor in a position where he was unguarded by any faithless praetorians who might have protected him. I had sent those I was unsure of with the cavalry; but I could not be certain of all of my men."

The emperor's hard right hand slapped Aristobulus on the back, causing him to splutter a little into his goblet as he took another long draught of the red he was enjoying. "You chose well, then!"

The other men present guffawed at their former enemy's discomfort. "And just soon enough," my father spoke with feeling, having felt the blade at the nape of his neck. "Lord, what are your plans now?"

The emperor turned his gaze on Constantius thoughtfully. "Aye: a time for celebration; but yet a time for planning. I cannot afford to neglect the rest of my new-won empire. I will be travelling immediately to Italy- the Senate and Rome must know of my victory and I should be present in person. That will send a message to one and all as Carus and Carinus cared little for such formalities."

I was sitting on the floor next to the entrance, stroking Diocletian's hounds. Big, bristled Molossians, they had not yet lost their winter coats. Fierce animals, renowned for their power and strength, they served to guard the emperor as much as any legionaries did. Which thought led me back to wondering at Diocletian's choice of action, and Galerius soon echoed my thoughts.

"But sir, is it not worthwhile assuring yourself of the loyalty of those legions in the north of the empire before travelling to Italy? Then at least you are not storing up trouble for yourself."

"True- though most of those legions, other than those in Britain, are represented with us now", the emperor replied. "But once the Senate has accepted my leadership, the rest of the empire will follow. I will be keeping my enemies as close as possible for now. Given the peacefulness of our borders, the Rhine legions and those from the northern Danube will be providing me with an escort as I travel. And I will make sure I always have the Third Parthica to rely on should there be difficulties." He looked directly at my father. "And I will be taking Antius with me also, my friend. I require his services more than you at such a time, particularly with so many vipers in my bosom."

My father bowed his head and accepted his emperor's need as being greater.

◆◆◆

We rested the men for two days in the valley by the Margus, enjoying the lush fields and the plentiful game in the surrounding hills. My father returned to our tent on the second evening with his orders to find me stamping my feet in the chill, moving closer to the large fire.

"We are to stay here," he said straight away, a look of disappointment embedded on his face and outlined in the glow from the flames. "I had hoped we would accompany the emperor to Italy. I have never been to see the wonders of Rome. He is taking Maximian despite his duties with the Seventh."

I could not help but chuckle at his expression. "Your time will come father. Did the emperor say what he wishes you to do instead?"

"He did. Hold the east for the next six months in his absence as dux Moesiae. Obviously, the remit is wider than just the province in the title," he referenced his extensive new power modestly.

I laughed out loud at that. "Hold the east! This is no small role then father. From Dalmatia to Arabia!"

"For but six months", he answered defensively.

"What support do we have?"

"He is sending us with the I Italica and the XI Claudia as they march home, stopping in Naissus on the way to show the imperial banner and make it clear who won the civil war. He wants us to stay there until he returns." It was his turn to grin at me, almost boyish in his enthusiasm. "I will be most interested in meeting my father-in-law once more, and your friends."

I snorted, pretending to ignore his comment but secretly delighted at the opportunity to show off both my father and my new status, the bastard child returning in glory.

Changing the subject, I said: "Do we yet know what happened to the V Macedonica and the XIII Gemina?"

"Ah- and there lies the rest of the tale", Constantius said, with a glower at the thought of those two recalcitrant legions. "This is the other part of the task that we have been given by the emperor. He is ordering the two of them to come to Naissus to meet with me, giving me assurances of their loyalty."

"Why do we not just go to them? Our two legions visiting them in Ratiaria and Oescus would surely send them the same message, and faster?"

"Not quite the same message, son," my father replied gently, correcting me. "In fact, ordering them to come to us makes it clear where the true power lies. And that they are to attend on me, a mere governor and dux, rather than on the emperor himself would also seem to show that they are beneath his notice."

I nodded in agreement, grateful for the explanation. "And what imperial envoy goes chasing after likely traitors to plead with them to rejoin the victors."

"Correct." My father was pleased with my easy understanding of the political manoeuvres taking place. "The emperor has sent the messengers already, acting quickly before they have too much time to think."

I said carefully, "If they come to Naissus as ordered, that will leave you with command of twice as many men as that Julianus had in Pannonia."

He reprimanded me sharply. "Never compare me with that man, especially in public. That is not a comparison I wish anyone else to hear- particularly with a new-made emperor in charge. You should know by now the risk you take with such statements."

◆◆◆

The journey to Naissus was a different experience to my journey away from it, and far more leisurely given that our intention was to show the imperial authority. I remembered little of that, though the stink of the leather tanning at Horreum Margi as we passed through it brought back what felt like distant memories of my journey on the river while my wounds healed. Felix was close by as we entered the village and I recoiled at the sight of children running out behind our horses to collect dung, catching it as it dropped in a race to get there first.

I turned to the procurator in disgust, "What sort of a game is that?"

He grinned at my reaction. "This is how they make their living. The manure is pounded into the skin as part of the tanning process." He gestured to the side of the road, where peculiar small bucket-like objects stood. "Those are for all the urine the inhabitants can offer. It all goes to make our shields. Amazing that the enemy doesn't run as soon as they smell them eh? Today is a festival for their trade, what with so much moving piss and shit wandering through the town."

I laughed.

He warmed to his theme, "And imagine what the feet of the tanners are like! They personally tread the hide into the mixture to make sure it's all pummelled together enough. A truly foul business."

"How do you know all this, Felix?" I asked, interested.

"Constantine, you have to know all sorts in this line of work. I make sure enough shields are where they need to be when they need to be there. So I know what their manufacture involves from start to finish. What other way is there to do it?"

Hosius, still my faithful companion, spoke up. "That is all very well. But your shields aren't much use when the governor is knelt at the feet of some cursed usurping emperor, his sword at Constantine's neck, and our army surrounded and all but defeated."

Hosius had meant my comment in jest; but Felix took it seriously.

"That is true. But some things are beyond our control. I will do all I can to ensure that it never happens that way- but even my power is limited."

I looked up at the summer sun, directly above. "Aye- and thanks be to Sol that he does have power over these matters where we don't."

Felix looked at me thoughtfully. "Either the sun- or the one who created the sun."

I stared back, astonished at his words. Instinctively, I scoffed: "Created the sun? How could that ever be. The sun is all there is! He rises again every morning, invincible."

Hosius said, equally astonished, "And he gives us heat and light. We would not have life at all without him!"

Felix spoke but few words in reply: "All true. However, the sun is but a creation and reflection of the One True God." Unwilling to get deeper into a theological discussion, he trotted off as if no such conversation had taken place. I spoke to Scipio about the brief conversation later that evening and he contemplated my words, taking his time before replying.

"What do you think that was about then?"

I protested, "I have no idea! Surely it is wrong to suggest that anyone could have created the sun?"

"Not wrong, I don't think, but certainly worthy of consideration, wouldn't you say?"

"Stop answering my questions with more questions! Why do you not say what you believe?"

"But Constantine: do you not think that may be the nature of religion? To ask questions?"

Having had my fill of his inadequate responses, I marched off angrily to my tent. Scipio shouted after me, but I ignored him. I would speak to my father about it at a better time; I knew how he felt about what I suspected were the words of a Christ-follower.

However, my father just laughed when I spoke of both conversations with him, saying, "You do know that Felix, like your mother, would call himself a Christian? So his words are no surprise to me. He is far too good at what he does for me to judge him on his choice of faith. And Scipio, I'm afraid, is dabbling in writings about the ancient Greek Pyrrho- fancies himself as something of a philosopher. It's all about scepticism, so he is not intentionally frustrating you. Asking questions is what he does. You are not the only one thinking of cutting his tongue out at the moment, however."

I could not help but burst into laughter myself at this comment, my father's own irritation with his faithful right hand being apparent.

◆◆◆

My mood improved as we neared Naissus. Having had no thought of them for well over a year I found myself struggling to remember the faces of my childhood enemies. Their names eventually came to me. There was Rassogos, with the Dacian heritage and a significant feeling of inferiority, disinherited from his eventual dynastic leadership of his tribe when they discovered his family's collaboration with the occupying Roman forces. And Aldis, another Dacian with his dead and forgotten father, lost in the flight from Apulum in Dacia as he defended their small force from the attacks of vengeful Sarmatians, left with an embittered mother who blamed the empire for all that had taken place. I felt some slight sympathy for them; but this was buried in my desire to enjoy the fulfilment of my dreams of old- but so far beyond my furthest flights of imagination! A father who had supported a powerful emperor, assisted him in gaining an eternal victory, and coming back to my birthplace at the head of two legions- with two more about to come and bow before us as imperial envoys.

We approached the gates of the city, Hosius and I riding behind Constantius. My father had lent me his purebred Arabian white- tall, high-stepping, with a long flowing mane and covered in ceremonial trappings of gold and white. I had had to plead with him the night before to allow me to fully enjoy my status as his son as humility was, for him, the most important trait of a leader. He sought to balance this with his knowledge that there were times when being at the front and taking the glory was part of the role he must play due to his position. He himself rode his warhorse, not built for speed but big, tough and hardy- his role today must be that of the victor, yet needing to ensure order was maintained. It would be a warning to all of the consequences of refusal to accept the emperor.

We rode at the front of three thousand marching men, cavalry ranging on our flanks and trailed by a disorganized horde of camp followers on foot. Messengers sent while we camped at Horreum Margi had ridden fast to give fair warning and prepare the way, albeit that they would provide but a day's notice. It was no small matter to be ready for such a force and Felix had travelled with them to ensure that the local notables appreciated this for themselves. The land was a dusty green around us as summer reached its height and there was a carnival atmosphere as the city's crowds turned out to greet us. The empire had held its breath while the civil war had taken place and nobody had been sure who the victors would be. At least there was now certainty, Constantius' appearance being the first real evidence of that, regardless of personal views as to who had the right of it, and Naissus released its tension all at once. There was music, laughter, plenty of food from sellers taking advantage of events, and impromptu games- one wrestling match of semi-naked young men stopping as we approached the city gates.

Waiting for us, standing in isolation some way outside the gates, was a deputation consisting of the town's four leading magistrates accompanied by my grandfather, Lucius. They wore togas with a purple stripe along the edge, rings and bracelets giving the evidence of their wealth and eminence. They bowed their heads, waiting for my father to speak first, and the multitude looking on went silent also- though I could see Lucius was having to restrain himself. I knew he would not speak, for he would be aware how important his first words to his son-in-law would be.

"Good morning my friends," Constantius said loudly, wishing his words to be heard by as many as possible. "We would ask for your assistance in accommodating our men."

All that could be heard in the pause after this was the sound of distant men repeating what he had said to those further back in the crowd on and under the town walls.

My grandfather spoke then, ingratiatingly, seeing his relationship with my father as giving him a longed-for opportunity to prove his abilities to the rest of the town, the old sycophantic tone so familiar to me. I saw my father wince ever so slightly as well- such a small facial movement that no-one else would notice; but I knew him well enough by now.

"Welcome sir, and willingly. Whatever you require will be yours with but a word."

My father replied, "In that case, Lucius, my son- your grandson- and I will stay at your house with our aides. The rest of you", he turned his gaze on the councillors still standing with heads bowed. "Arrange for the billeting of these troops on the locals. I will hang any man who misbehaves- they know this- so be sure of our goodwill. The First will be marching on to Novae shortly, so the town will not have to endure too long."

Despite his words, I saw two of the magistrates exchange dismayed glances. The cost of accommodating this many men would be exorbitant- and 'shortly' was an open-ended statement. But that was not our concern. I knew Felix would have given fair warning for I could see his familiar red hair beyond the gates, and it was likely that the allocation of billets had already been made. They had probably hoped we would use the ancient auxiliary fort we had just passed; but this was now partly ruined and was not large enough for our numbers. The men had drawn up behind us in parade-ground order, and Constantius knew that he could now leave them to be organised by Felix and the magistrates. He and I, along with our retinue, proceeded under the archway and into Naissus.

I looked around me eagerly, searching for familiar faces. I saw some of my old companions from our fights against the Dacian incomers in training battles, and I waved, doing my best not to appear too excited and over-eager in doing so. I was most keen to identify Rassogos or Aldis, to gloat over them in my new-found position and power, and my eyes searched the crowd. The people were shouting loudly, the street hemmed in by their ranks up to four deep. Many threw fresh-picked flowers from the windows of upper floors and as they fell they created a brightly coloured rain of soft petals in the air (Scipio murmured next to me: "And to think: this is without Antius' efforts at paying for 'spontaneous' celebrations!"). My horse was twitching nervously at the noise and the people, the falling blooms landing gently on him and causing him to jitter. I patted him, and as I did so noticed the face of Rassogos appear from a doorway on my left. I stared him in the eye and gave him a gracious flourish of my hand, my faint smile intended to communicate forgiveness for the beatings and abuse I had endured from him and his friends. This look was evidently not enough, or spoke of some other fate, for a look of terror instantly came over his features as he realised I had not only seen him, but recognised him also. His face went white and he disappeared from view.

I realised that my joy was not as great as I had hoped it would be. This response from Rassogos had not been my intention: I wished to show magnanimity. My father looked at me sternly. He had been paying attention to the byplay, and now he leant across.

"A bit of fear is no bad thing, my son. Respect is all very well but add some fear to the mix and you have security as a leader. Look for followers more than companions, and you will have a future."

◆◆◆

The First left at dawn two days after our arrival, no doubt to the relief of the magistrates. There was no reason for the legion to stay, having had a chance to recover fully from the exertions of their previous forced march. Constantius was determined that the border should be adequately defended given the lack of response so far from the Fifth and the

Thirteenth, and the First could be trusted to do that task well. There had been little made of their departure, though my father and I both rose before first light to see them leave. My father saluted the prefect commanding the legion; and that stalwart saluted in return, saying, "There will be more to come sir, of that I am convinced. No war was ever won with such ease. If we are needed, send the order."

My father answered gravely, "That I will. And for your part, avoid the V Macedonica at Oescus on your way back. We know not what they will do now, and I do not wish you to lose men in an unnecessary battle against fellow Romans." He turned to the legion, drawn up in ranks and prepared to march, and shouted, "Stand tall, I Italica!"

The men cheered at this reference to their origins two centuries before, recruited as men who were all above six feet. The commanders gave the order, and the legion set off on the week-long journey back to their base.

◆◆◆

The town magistrates had formally invited us to a ceremonial feast in our honour that evening and preparations for this event easily overshadowed the legion's departure. It was a public feast, so all citizens were officially invited; though in practice it was attended only by selected local notables. Held in the council chambers at the back of the basilica in the centre of town, it could only accommodate a limited number of people in any case; however, many familiar faces did show themselves there. If they had not turned up then my father, as the representative of the new emperor, would have been suspicious and could well have reached his own conclusions as to the level of loyalty exhibited in his son's hometown. It was a substantial body of men- probably about one hundred- but even in a city like this the politics were very soon clear. Each sat with his own faction.

Despite the darkness of the room providing many shadows in which private conversations were taking place, I soon identified the Dacian group. Rassogos' father, Dotos, was evidently the leader of this faction and was lounging back while others around him, whom I did not recognise so easily, argued in low but furious whispers. They had managed to seat themselves in a particular set-apart alcove. But their vigorous gestures and serious expressions were what had drawn my eyes, particularly as they kept on looking our way, appearing anxious. As I strained every sinew to hear what they were saying, I was distracted by my father, sat to the right of the two senior magistrates with my grandfather opposite, whispering, "Is my father-in-law only ever going to question me as to how he can get close to the emperor using my connections? He is not even subtle about it!"

I grinned at him. "That's Lucius. Wealth is all he ever thinks about. Might as well get used to it. You're his connection to something far bigger, and my mother was only ever his stepping stone to that. His investment over a decade ago was worth this outcome!"

The other significant distraction was the meal itself. It was undoubtedly the best I had ever eaten, ranging from baked dormice dipped in honey to roast pheasant, accompanied by a fine wine mixed with water and some excellent- if unappreciated- entertainment. The dancers this involved had but a small space to perform in, and thus were limited in their movement; and, in any case, most of the diners were far more interested in local intrigue. Given our arrival so soon after Diocletian's victory no-one had had the opportunity to discuss how this would affect them and their town, so gossip and rumour were more important. I felt a little sorry for the performers, as they danced with less and less enthusiasm as the night progressed. No-one seemed to notice except me when they eventually flounced off in a fit of pique that was lost on their audience. Hosius and I joined in clapping them as they went- but we were alone in our applause.

They were replaced by a flute and a lyre: these musicians were content to play in the background- which seemed much more appropriate to the occasion and made private conversations more possible. I took the opportunity to ask one of our companions to remind me of the names of those in the distant alcove. There was an underlying tension throughout the meal. This would usually be expected in any case given the circumstances; but there was, even based on my very limited experience, an unusual sense of unease and anticipation. Felix arrived mid-festivities. I happened to be looking in Dotos' direction as he entered, and the door slammed shut behind him. The loud noise caused Dotos to leap to his feet in surprise, while the heads of those beside him spun around instantly. Others in the room had reacted also; but none to this degree. Dotos sat back down, embarrassed, looking around him to see if anyone had noticed his movement; and the whispering of his companions recommenced with an added vehemence.

I leant across to my father, interrupting his polite but dull conversation responding to a magistrate's indication of how much his wife would like to meet Diocletian some day. He excused himself with some gratitude at my intervention and turned to me.

"Father, something is amiss. I know not what, but the refugees who used to live in Dacia- do not look: over in that corner- have raised my suspicions. They are very nervous. All is not well."

"Do not worry son. I have posted men on all of the walls. We are ready for any threat, within or without. There is nothing to fear."

"But father, you have always told me it is better to take the initiative. Men on the walls is a defense, but not an advantage. Should we send out fast patrols, just to be sure? And perhaps the prefects of our legions should post men on the street during the night? I feel a sense of... discomfort, as an ill-fitting new shirt. It performs its task, but does not feel right."

He looked at me, considering, for a few moments. The line of his jaw, outlined in the light from the lamps, became more defined as a muscle clenched. His decision was reached. "Your suspicions have saved my life before. What is the harm to be done by this- only a sleepless night for a few cavalrymen and legionaries." He beckoned Felix over though he had just started to eat. "Felix: send out two patrols- one north and one east. I want Scipio leading the latter. And post a sentry on every square or gathering place within the city."

"But sir," Felix protested. "The men are tired. These are the first proper beds they have slept in for weeks, and the best food they have eaten after their rations."

Constantius' voice hardened, brooking no dissent. "Now, my friend. Do not worry about the south. The eastern patrol must travel as far as the river. That is the most likely direction any threat will come from- as we both know of old. Send Scipio to command: he knows the dangers." He smiled at Felix, robbing his words of harshness as they both thought back to their first meeting. I had heard this tale before: Constantius had been but a tribune at the time based temporarily at Viminacium. He had been asked to support an inexperienced cavalry centurion- Felix- patrolling the border. The successful ambush of a Sarmatian raid had sealed their friendship; and also led to my birth, as it was Constantius' search for a trained surgeon to heal a wounded legionary that had brought his vexillation to Naissus.

My sleep was better than it might have been due to knowing the patrols had been sent as I had asked- but it was still restless. We slept in my grandfather's mansio at his insistence and as my father had promised he would, and it may have been that my agitation was due to the memories brought back by being in my old bed. I was not a child any longer, and it felt very strange to be back where my journeys had started. So much had changed. I had changed.

My father slept poorly too, rising with dark marks under his eyes. Without eating anything he went to pace the ramparts, waiting for his patrols to return. He was more concerned than he had suggested the night before; and I suspected the night had enabled him to think through all the possibilities of what might be happening. He was a man who hated not knowing what was taking place around him.

Those sent to the north arrived back at noon, the optio in charge coming on to the walls to report to my father directly. His statement was simply and swiftly delivered, no resentment in his tone at having given up his bed and spending the night outside the safety of the walls. "Nothing out there sir. We went a long way back up the road we marched yesterday and there was little of interest."

"To bed then. Well done."

This should have settled Constantius' nerves a little; but they seemed to become more taut with every passing hour. He kept turning to me, saying, "Where is Scipio?"

I tried to calm him, though I felt the same way. "From what Felix tells me, it is a long distance to the Danube. We should only really expect him back tonight. It can take two days just to reach the river, should he need to go that far. You know Scipio would never let you down, nor cause you undue concern."

Night fell, but my father was not going to return to his quarters until he had heard his patrol's report- and, as the expedition had been my idea, I felt obliged to do the same. It was unlikely I would sleep anyway. He chose to walk the walls instead. We were above the east gate when he turned to me suddenly: "When are the gates shut?"

"At dusk, as far as I am aware."

"Then," he spoke, pointing urgently at the space below us. "Why is that one still open? It is at least an hour since the sun went down." He bellowed at the legionaries accompanying us as a makeshift bodyguard, pointing at one of them: "You, get Felix. And quickly!"

Felix arrived a short time later, my father tapping his foot impatiently as he looked down over the wall to try to discern anything in what was a dark and very much moonless night.

"Sir?"

"Why is that gate open?"

"I have no idea. Possibly for our returning patrol?"

"Something is not right. I want that gate closed immediately and send messengers to each of those men Constantine identifies as belonging to the Dacian faction. I want them to attend on me immediately. If they are reluctant to come you have my authority to use force if needed."

Felix spoke to me and memorised the list of names I gave him, then hurried off to do his commander's bidding. We climbed down the steps to watch as the gates were closed. However, as they were about to put the locking bar across, there was a furious thudding on the other side. There was the usual procedure with passwords, hastily exchanged, and then the gates re-opened just enough to admit an exhausted and bloodied patrol, led by Scipio. They scraped their way in through the gate, my father and I exchanging concerned looks as we studied the group.

"Leave to report, sir", said Scipio, appearing faint with relief at seeing my father standing in front of him.

"Of course."

He cut straight to the issue he knew would be of most concern. "Sir. We reached halfway to the river without seeing much, but as we came through the final major pass on the way to Ratiaria, we saw smoke in the distance and there were burnt-out farms visible from the height we were on. I sent a fast rider to identify when the enemy had passed and, as the embers were still very hot, we knew they had been there but recently." He followed up, almost defensively, "There are many routes through the mountains, and we took the road as it is the fastest and most direct. It would not have been difficult for them to have intentionally gone a different way- even just by avoiding the fort at Timacum Maius in the river valley and going the long way around the mountain. They would have been fools to cross the river near to Ratiaria- we would have heard the news of their coming long before they got here." He added as an aside- "Though this does suggest that the XIII Gemina at Ratiaria have not even been sending out patrols while the war has been going on."

My father ignored the final comment. This was for consideration at another time. "How many?"

Scipio said, "Thousands, sir. A Sarmatian raid- probably the Roxolani tribe- across the river such as not happened for years. We backtracked and quickly picked up their trail.

Hard to be sure as there were so many tracks overlaid on top of one another- we may even have seen signs of the Thirteenth's march here, as ordered. But we know where they are now. All Sarmatian cavalry though, and heavily armed. Their imprints were deep. No siege machinery that we could find tracks of- perhaps saying something of where they are aiming for and what will happen when they arrive there. This is no mere raiding force, sir, nor are they expecting fortified resistance."

"You must have been close enough to be attacked."

My father gestured at a groaning legionary, strapped across the horse of one of his fellows in such a way that it was impossible to identify where his injury lay; and another with a coarse bandage wrapped around his head, the blood seeping through and leaving wine-red stains across his left temple.

"We did. Our final gallop for the town, sir. We thought we must have avoided their main force. The urgent thing to do was to return quickly to give you this news so we did not search for them. But we did not notice several of their scouts hidden in the trees over there." He pointed back behind him. "Acteon was caught by an arrow in the left shoulder- deep barbs on it that we had to leave in the wound. Pelagius, the idiot, tried to duck another arrow and hit his head on a tree branch that was inconveniently hanging in the wrong place."

Constantius turned to the legionaries who had been closing the gates but were now stood open-mouthed and listening intently. Ignoring Scipio's barbed humour, he snarled: "Get those gates closed then, you bunch of lice-ridden hairy dogs." Then, turning back to Scipio: "How long ago?"

"They must have crossed a couple of days ago and hidden up in that forest. We thought we would be too late. We rode as fast as we could. We do not know where the main force is, but they must be close by now. Those Roxolani ride fast."

At that moment, Felix came running up. "Sir. We have only been to two houses so far, checking that Dotos first of all. He is missing- his family say they do not know where he is. Thought you would want to know immediately."

"By all the gods, you are right I'd want to know!" Constantius turned to me. "Your suspicions were right again. That is why there was all that whispering last night. Naissus is the target: has to be. We must have taken the plotters by surprise when we turned up. Bet they thought they had it all planned out nicely: both emperors otherwise occupied in their civil war and local legions ignoring their responsibilities on the frontier. From what you have told me, son, this would gain that Dacian group much goodwill: let a Roxolani raiding party into Naissus and all is forgiven! The whole province could have fallen before we knew it, and all because of an open gate. The attack will be soon, and we must be ready."

The machinery of the army went into action, my father ordering out the full force of the Eleventh, along with any local militiamen or retired legionaries. The walls were manned, weaponry deployed and everyone awake by midnight. The vicus, a settlement that had grown up to the south of the town walls consisting of tradesmen and craftworkers, was emptied and all of the people brought into the city for their protection. There was some resistance as the town had not seen fighting for many years now; but all were eventually gathered in. Fortunately for us the clouds cleared soon after we had completed our preparations, and word came from one of our sentries on the walls that there was movement in the hills. Summer was not advanced enough for there to be dust, so it was only as the mass of the Sarmatian cavalry emerged from a valley to the east that we saw how close and swift they were. These horsemen were renowned for their speed, and Scipio estimated that they had likely travelled from the Danube in just two days- perhaps three if they were being sure not to raise the alarm amongst the Thirteenth at Ratiaria; though Scipio also suspected that the legion may have left days before. They had certainly not seen the flames and smoke from the burning farms near the river border.

"Not that they would have done anything about it even had they seen several thousand horse archers and lance-warriors going past them", he commented cynically.

We rested our elbows on the walls as we watched, the enemy's black silhouette a dirty stain on the lighter night-time colours of the land, spreading, growing and lengthening as they came nearer and more emerged from the hills behind them.

As they flew over the ground before us, expecting their charge to be at the open gates of a vulnerable town, Constantius leant across to me and asked, "What will they do when they get here?"

I continued to study the body of men, able to now hear the rumbling of the massed hooves on the packed earth. Then I said, "Perhaps turn around and go back home?"

He laughed. "You're starting to sound like Julian of the Fourth before the Margus. We can but hope!"

I derisively replied, "He wanted us to run- I'm hoping they will run. But it seems unlikely, I agree." I thought longer and tried to imagine myself in their position. Eventually, I said, "I think it depends on many different considerations. Scipio saw only their scouts and the tracks of a bigger force. If it is cavalry alone attacking us, then they will not last long. If there are footsoldiers also, that is a different matter. They may be able to besiege the town."

"Agreed. Let us watch and wait. The cavalry will be several days ahead of any infantry. And Scipio did not mention any- it may be that we will only enjoy the company of these horsemen for a short time."

The charge to our walls was nearly upon us. The main gate was in such shadow under the archway that the warriors would not be able to tell that it was closed until the last moment. They were so confident that there was no slowing of the pace. Our men were well trained and experienced, not one of them intimidated by the sight. They had been told not to show themselves- the hope being that our sudden appearance would dismay the raiders all the more.

Hosius was at my right, and he laughed along with the rest of us when a big Italian next to us said, "Like to see them knock down this wall with their lances. Looks like they forgot to bring any ladders."

The spearhead formation came directly at the east gate immediately beneath our position on the wall, silent in its urgency, determined to not raise the alarm. When suddenly, about two hundred metres in front and below our position, a figure leapt up from the ground. It had been hidden in the darkness behind a fold in the ground. The figure started shouting, screaming and waving its arms as the leading men bore down on it.

I turned to my father and spoke one word in irritation, for I recognized the voice: "Rassogos!"

The charge pulled up short, the leading men stopping and their horses rearing at the unexpected curb on their momentum. Either side of them, the rest who, had the charge continued into the arch, would have piled up on top of each other, swept by this leading group with great skill and swerved from the walls, sufficiently warned to be cautious, racing parallel to them for some distance before veering away. Our auxiliary archers, ready and waiting, stood up from their hiding places and fired, but mostly in vain due to the speed of the tribesmen. We had intended this to be a trap, the gateway beneath us turned into a killing ground, but Rassogos had ended any prospect of that. I could just see him in the increasing darkness swiftly swept up behind a commander as the leaders followed their men, making sure they remained out of the range of our bows. They stopped at a distance.

They dismounted. We could see the start of a conversation as the Sarmatian chiefs talked to Rassogos. By this time all pretence at surprise had vanished, as had the silence. My father responded swiftly to the change of circumstances, ordering our archers to fire at the group- but it was long range for them, and the arrows fell short. Those that made it were mostly spent by the time they reached the enemy and bounced easily off the enemy's horn armour. In response, the tribal cavalry who had worked their way down the walls now responded to our attacks with their own horse archers, rushing the walls in relays, testing the resolve of our men with repeated flights of arrows- in the gathering night, fired to intimidate and threaten rather than with any real prospect of causing the defenders problems. At this, Constantius now ordered our ballistas and scorpions into action. Although the range was short and the weapons were lowered as far as possible, there was little to fear for these men as they spread out across the ground as they ran. However, the first boulder landing beyond the chiefs as they talked to Rassogos caused all to mount up behind one of the Roxolani and they made their way out of range and out of sight towards the woods in the distance where their lancers had formed up as they waited for a decision. The horse archers went with them.

As they retreated, Constantius turned to me. "So that accounts for Rassogos. But what of the rest of the Dacians? Where are they?"

I replied, having been thinking the same myself, "Rassogos likely opened that gate and was sent outside to wait for the enemy to give forewarning should their plan be discovered. I suspect the rest are still inside the walls. We will need to set a strong guard tonight in case they have further plans; and take the initiative by sending the Eleventh to search the city for them. We are unlikely to find them all: they know the area too well."

He looked back at me and said bluntly, "I think the one choice for them now will be escape. They know mercy will not be a possibility after this betrayal."

"True," I said. "Knowing Rassogos as I do, that action took much courage. He must have changed in the last year."

"Speaking of courage, it is an easy thing to come by when attacking vulnerable townspeople. It will be harder to find now that Naissus is so well defended. I think tonight will be the end of it and the Sarmatians will flee back across the river." Constantius turned to me, speaking ironically but with a definite pride. "Congratulations son. It would appear you have just saved a province."

Felix and Hosius were both beaming at me. "The favour of the gods, sir," I replied. "I know the town, and I know the people. It just did not feel right to me."

"Not just luck son. Sol smiles on you, and I know to remember that when you speak. Your suspicious mind helps also!"

Felix spoke up cynically, "Given Sol's lack of availability at night, I suspect the suspicious mind played more of a part sir."

Both my father and I glared at him for his lack of belief but said nothing. For there was little that could be said against this.

Hosius broke the tension with a weak attempt at humour that was enough to serve its purpose, "And what I would give for such a mind!"

As we descended from the ramparts, we saw that most of the townspeople were awake and filling the streets, keen to know what had happened. Felix organised the council to move among them describing the situation and sending them back home. It would have been foolhardy in the extreme for mounted cavalry of even the highest quality to attack town walls of this scale without the necessary equipment- they would be massacred. We were convinced that the Sarmatian force would realise with little argument that the plan had failed and they would go back to their side of the river before we could catch up with them. Some form of retribution would be taken at a later point; but that would be less of a concern for now.

CHAPTER 12: SALVATION

But assumption is ever a risk and the enemy of reality. We slept the sleep of men with little to fear that night, all precautions taken. The town was well-guarded, the Dacians' plans were in disarray and we knew the enemy must soon accept their failure and flee back across the river. The only remaining problem was our inability to find twenty traitors.

However, we were awoken at dawn the next morning by Felix thumping on the door of the mansio. As soon as we appeared he said to my father, "Sir. The men on the ramparts have reported that they found three ropes hanging down the other side of the south wall."

Constantius struck the doorframe with his fist in frustration. "By Sol! If only we had been swifter. They must have hidden and awaited their opportunity. Were the men asleep up there?"

"I do not believe so," Felix replied carefully. "They say not. Perhaps the traitors found a section unguarded? Or they had help... As Constantine said, they know the town far better than us."

Constantius chose to let the matter lie. The damage was done. He thought for a moment, then said, "Of course, the Roxolani will not leave their siege now. For the traitors will report the departure of a legion yesterday. They will know we are outnumbered. Dotos and his fellow Dacians now have nothing to lose, they are fully committed, and the Sarmatians have already taken the risk and passed between those two legions on the frontier- who sat there and did nothing. If they were even there at all!"

As the light strengthened over Naissus and the morning passed peacefully, Constantius and I walked the ramparts. Both of us were frustrated at inaction, at our inability to affect what would happen next. So we spent our time challenging each other with possible developments and what we could do in response. Hosius and Scipio would occasionally contribute their thoughts also.

As we passed a pair of legionaries sat down sharpening their swords, one whistling and another keeping a lookout over the wall in case anything of importance should occur, I spoke. "What if... one of our legions arrives? What do we do then?"

Constantius answered, "One of the situations that kept me awake last night. It depends on their reason for arriving."

Hosius jumped in, "It could only be to come as ordered, to make up for their previous unwillingness to fight. So they would, of course, be allies."

Scipio said, reluctantly, "But what if they are in league with the Roxolani? It is rare for a force this size to make its way across the frontier without anyone noticing or giving chase. And there will have been connections between the legion and the tribe- perhaps even men have been recruited from there. Even we had Sarmatian lancers with us at the Margus! Though they were of the Iazyges tribe."

Scipio had given voice to the fear we all shared. I thought carefully before answering. "We would have to assure ourselves of their loyalty."

"And how would we do that?" My father spoke more sharply than he likely intended, the unknown starting to affect him.

I felt he needed reassurance. "It would surely be clear as soon as they arrived. If they make camp in the face of the enemy but remain behind their palisade as soon as it is built, then we have nothing to fear."

Hosius spoke breathlessly, "And if the tribesmen attack them immediately, before the camp is built, we will know."

Scipio said gloomily, "And if they do not attack but allow the building of the camp, then the legion is unlikely to be our ally."

Constantius concluded with finality, "So we cannot possibly know until it happens."

We all lapsed into a resigned silence, the sound of whistling and whetstones offering an odd counterpoint to our difficult thoughts. This conclusion was too often how our suggestions would end.

Our deliberations were interrupted by a shout from a guardsman, "Sir! There is movement in the trees."

My father rushed over to the man. He was pointing north to where the Sarmatian army had gone the night before. "Over there. Can you see sir?"

He shaded his eyes and peered into the middle distance. "I can. A group of four. Wishing to speak."

One of those four started to move faster, and was soon in front of our main gate, shouting up for Constantius. My father made his way around the walls.

"I am here. And what do you wish to say?" He shouted back.

The man on the horse stared up at him, craning his neck back. "We wish for no men to die today. Will you talk?"

"I will." He turned to the three of us, saying quietly, "At least this will give us some indication of what the future holds: let's see what they want."

The messenger bellowed, "Then you must come to meet our commanders outside the walls. No weapons on either side."

Constantius responded again, saying "I will." Then he said to Scipio and me, "The two of you with me, and the prefect of the Eleventh, Marcus."

The three of us hastened down from the walls to mount our horses, readied for us by several legionaries led by Felix, and were joined by Marcus. The gates were opened, and we cantered out. The deputation had stopped halfway between the trees and the town, and we went to join them. I recognized the man to the right as soon as we were close enough to make out his features: Dotos. The middle man of the three was richly and heavily armoured, a sign of wealth and power- he had long hair and a thick beard. The final member of the group, as the messenger had returned to the woods, wore thick red robes and no protection. Likely an adviser, I thought to myself.

We confronted each other in the centre of what would be our battlefield if circumstances did not change, and introductions were made. Constantius spoke brusquely, "My son, Constantine. Prefect of the I Italica, Marcus. And Scipio, my right hand."

The man I assumed to be the adviser responded with far greater courtesy, bowing in return and saying in polished Latin, "We are much honoured by your presence. My name is Rasparagnus, counsellor to the king. And my lord here is Zanticus, King of the Roxolani. Dotos, you know."

My father sneered with disgust at the traitor, who glared back at him with equal hatred. The king cut through the hostility with strongly accented words, "You must surrender."

My father asked, politely but firmly, "Why must we surrender? Our supplies are adequate for a siege, you have only a small force of cavalry, and you are unable to surround our walls."

Rasparagnus started to reply, "Why, lord, you are isolated and there are no..."

But the king cut in, overriding his adviser's attempt to keep the peace and be more gracious, "Our infantry will join us by noon. You have no time. None of you will leave the city alive if you do not give it to us today. We will allow you to march out, but all of your possessions and weaponry must be left behind."

Rasparagnus looked taken aback at his king's abruptness and looked at Constantius apologetically as he followed up by saying, "I am afraid, sir, that he is correct. We need this place."

Dotos laughed harshly at Constantius' expression. "You Romans! The Emperor Carus is dead and the empire in chaos. You cannot rule yourselves, let alone anyone else."

My father looked him in the eyes. "And, as you know, traitor, the chaos is over. Diocletian rules as sole emperor and without opposition. You Roxolani take a risk even being here, for you know retribution will be swift and terrible. There will be a price to pay."

The king interrupted, bluntly and to the point. "This is what you say. But there have been four emperors in the last year. I do not fear for my tribe once we take Naissus. Your legions do not respond to your call quickly, and we do as we will."

My father cut him off. "We require a day to consider what you have said."

Rasparagnus replied, "You have until mid-afternoon. Then we must know your answer."

Considering this to be the end of the negotiation, each group returned to their respective sides, the gates of Naissus opening to readmit us. I was amazed when our gates closed, for my father was jubilant.

"They are on their way! I know it!"

"How can you tell?" I asked, doubting his words and not understanding what could have caused him to think this.

Scipio was the first to answer, as Constantius was already shouting for Felix. "A slip of the tongue by the king. He said they do not respond 'quickly'. And they have given us a very short time to decide, considering their infantry join them at noon."

Constantius turned back to me, "Zanticus will need the protection of our walls once the legions are in sight. His tribesmen are vulnerable out in the open, however many they have with them. They have made a great mistake. For the footsoldiers to be here so soon must mean they set off through the hills and forests long before the cavalry crossed the Danube and have been making their way here for many days. Regardless of Dotos and his Dacians, they were committed from the moment they left and the cavalry had no choice but to remain despite the east gate being closed last night. For the Fifth are marching from that direction and could have cut them off." He smacked his fist into his palm with delight, "We have them!"

As the Dacian faction had left their wives and children behind it did not take too long to get the full story out of the wives after threatening to torture their offspring. This was not a pleasant task, but once a burly, bearded legionary produced a wickedly sharp dagger and put it to the throat of Rassogos' younger brother, his mother was more than willing to cooperate. It was precisely as my father had suggested: with the empire in turmoil and feeling that his collaboration with the Romans had done nothing but turn him and his family into refugees, Dotos had decided to turn coat once again. He had arranged with the Roxolani to come over the river and take Naissus with the understanding that he would be their new 'king' of the province once the rest of it fell. This was no raid but a full expedition.

Constantius called for a council, commandeering an office in the forum in order to avoid having to include Lucius.

We met before noon. Gathered in the small space were my father, Scipio, Marcus, one of the town's magistrates, a cavalry commander and me. Constantius started the discussion.

"At least one legion cannot be far from us, or we would not be facing such urgency from the enemy. How far away do you think, Scipio?"

"Likely they will have arrived by sunset given the mid-afternoon limit we have been given."

Constantius said, "And what will they do if we have not surrendered?"

Marcus spoke this time, a heavily tanned prefect of North African descent, very experienced in warfare. "Very little," he said dryly. "Not much they can do. We are behind high walls and they have no siege machinery from what Scipio says."

Scipio hastily cut in, "None that we could see the tracks of with the cavalry. We knew nothing of the infantry on their way, however."

Marcus replied, "Not much to fear from that either, in my view. The Sarmatian tribes are horse-riders, so the only possible infantry they could have is Dacian in origin. And that infantry must have come by little-known routes through difficult ground if you did not see any signs of them- most unlikely that they will have transported heavy equipment with them. Especially as they thought to find the cavalry already holding the town."

Constantius nodded gratefully. "This is my view. I believe we have little to fear. Despite Zanticus' confidence, it is a bluff- there may be no infantry at all. Though there is a possibility that they have sufficient carpenters with them to start work on ladders. However, the priority is to make sure our legion does not march into a trap, for the Roxolani will be making preparations for their arrival. What steps can we take to support them?"

I had thought this one through, so I spoke up. "They must know by now that they are following a substantial army- the scouts will have seen their tracks."

The magistrate made his first contribution, saying, "It depends on which legion is on its way- it could be one or both. Either of them could be coming from the north rather than the east. If it is the Thirteenth, they will be marching from Oescus and could even be coming from the south if they have chosen to march on the Via Militaris."

The cavalry commander said, "We need someone to make contact with them before they arrive."

I leapt at the chance, saying eagerly, "I can do that! And Hosius could take another road so that we make sure we do not miss them. Nobody would look twice at us if we changed our appearance."

My father looked me up and down ironically, then said, "With your size? I could see Hosius doing it, but not you."

Scipio stifled a laugh, then said, "Sir, I must speak on his behalf. When we first met, he showed himself more than capable of looking like a peasant."

I was unsure whether to be grateful for his support or resentful of his bringing up that memory. My father was thinking, and the silence drew out.

Until eventually he said, "I do not see any other possibilities. And if there is one thing I have learnt recently, it is that you are capable of far more than I gave you credit for in Salona. But we must act quickly. Once- if- the Dacian infantry arrive, Zanticus will order the encirclement of the town and it will be very hard to get out. For now, they do not expect us to act until mid-afternoon. So we must take advantage… What shall we order the legion or legions to do, assuming one of the boys gets to them in time?"

I left them to their planning, going to let Hosius know and to prepare for our attempt to make contact. They would let us know what to say before we left.

◆◆◆

Hosius was standing above the east gate, waiting to see if the Dacian footsoldiers would arrive. As I joined him, having run most of the way from the council meeting, he pointed into the distance: "Good timing Con. There's the vanguard coming out of the valley now. It wasn't all a bluff."

We could see very little as yet, so I excitedly told him about our role. He was as enthusiastic at the prospect as I.

"How will we disguise ourselves?" he asked, focused on the practicalities as he looked down at the mail shirt he was wearing.

I answered, "We make ourselves as dirty and messy as possible. I have some experience with that! There's a pile of rubbish out the back of my grandfather's mansio that should provide us with what we need."

"And let's leave by the west gate!" he said, entering into the spirit of the adventure. "They won't be expecting that. If their reinforcements are coming from the east as they did, and our legions are most likely to arrive from the north or south, it's the best choice."

I joined in. "And if we go soon enough it's only a mile to that old run-down auxiliary fortress. That will give us cover while we work out which route each of us is going to take."

We grinned at each other with mutual delight, told Felix where we would be as he was responsible for ensuring we got out of the town safely, then ran down from the walls to Lucius' nearby villa. We found dirty tunics and yellowing trousers that someone had thrown away and cut additional holes in them with our daggers. We rubbed our faces in old vegetables that had been left to rot. A cook emerged from the kitchen with more scrapings, shook his head and went back inside with his leftovers. We looked at each other, startled, then bent double with laughter.

"No time to waste," I wheezed, straightening up. "Let's get to the west gate."

We ran across the town to the smaller exit where Felix was waiting. Nobody else was with him as we were aware that as little attention should be drawn to our departure as possible, in case spies remained in the town who were able to communicate with the enemy. There was a small door in the main gate itself, and he opened this briefly to look out.

"I have been watching closely," he said to us, closing the door, his voice quieter than usual, almost as if someone might hear. "They are sending out regular patrols to make sure nobody tries to break out. But they are more interested in groups of fighters, not in individual farmers or children. If you can avoid them that would be best. But I suspect, looking as you do," and here he looked at our dishevelled appearance with distaste, wrinkling his nose at the smell coming from us, "that you will be able to talk your way out of it. Something about farmhands trapped in the town and needing to get back to your crops should do it."

I was shaking with trepidation now, all of my former enthusiasm vanishing in the cold reality of what we needed to do next; and Hosius looked at me nervously. Felix then told us the message that we were to communicate to the prefect of any legion we made contact with. I shook my head in surprise at the simplicity of the strategy, and Felix said sharply, "The best plans are always the easiest. As you know, no matter how thorough the planning…"

I finished his sentence for him, "…it will go wrong within moments of the first blow."

"Correct," Felix replied. "May God go with you."

I barely noticed the lack of reference to Sol, my god, as he opened the door again. He handed us each a hoe, a package and a large engraved gem. We looked at him, confused as to the purpose of the last object.

He responded impatiently, "You will need some sort of authority when dealing with a prefect- that is the seal of a frumentarius working for Constantius. None will stand in your way with one of those. But perhaps more important is the package. It contains a mirror. Focus it on the west tower when you are ready: three flashes tells you we have seen it. Now go!" he hissed, pushing the two of us out on to the roadway.

We leapt to the side as soon as we were out, feeling very exposed against the bare wall. It was warm in the early afternoon sunshine; but there was no cover and we would be seen by any warrior riding past. This was not the same as my escape from a storeroom window so long ago, no crippled tutor attempting to stop me. This was war, and we knew the fate of Naissus, in some measure, depended on us.

We ran to the longer grass just metres away and lay down in it. We started to crawl, me taking the lead, intending to reach a field of crops that we could see in the distance. Although the hoes made movement more difficult, we knew they might save our lives and were worth the inconvenience. Halfway there, we paused to take a breath from our scrambling.

We heard hooves to our left, and then the sound of conversation. We lay in silence, imagining that we would be caught at any moment. The rustling of grass indicated further movement, and we saw eight pairs of horses' legs stride languidly across in front of us. The men riding the animals were engrossed in their own discussion and did not see us; and I realised that the colour of our choice of clothes was also giving us a form of disguise against the dusty ground and dry grass. We dared not lift our heads at all for fear of drawing attention. And then they were past.

I waited, then whispered to Hosius behind me, "Quickly!"

The horse-riders being well on their way, we crept a bit further. As soon as we reached the crops, we stood and tried to look like we fitted into the landscape around us, keeping our hoes out in front of us as if we were about to do some work on the crops.

Another patrol passed, the final warrior in the line looking at us disinterestedly as they moved on.

We kept walking and soon arrived at the fortress. It was a mound of stones rather than a fortress these days, as, once they had seen that it was no longer used, the locals had started stealing the stone from it to build their own homes and enclosures; but it would at least offer us some protection while we worked out what we would do. We had made it out, but our joy at this would be short-lived if we could not make use of the opportunity it afforded us. We climbed up to a higher point on the broken-down walls. From there, we had a view of the side of the town, and around to the north as well.

I said, "I'll go north." Then, pointing, I indicated the settlement to the south of the town that had been evacuated the night before. "If you take the Via Militaris and the south, then the shelter of those buildings will make it easy to get around to where you need to be, though you will have to avoid further patrols. Your problem will be making your way far enough down the road to be out of sight of the enemy- particularly once that infantry is sent out to surround Naissus- and yet able to see the legion before they arrive.

"I know," he said. "But I think it more likely they will come from the north. What will you do to ensure you get to them?"

"See there?" I said, pointing north. "That tree?"

"Yes," said Hosius, squinting.

"That marks the road."

"But that's really close!" replied Hosius. "You have the easier task! Not that I regret having the more difficult," he added hurriedly, not wanting to appear lacking in bravery.

"But as you have just said, the legions are more likely to come that way. And I do not choose that route lightly, but because the prefects should know of me as my acceptance by my father was the talk of the region a year ago. And they will be more likely to follow my instructions than yours."

Hosius said lightly, "And that is to be expected. I will play my part. Sol keep you."

And without further talk, he dropped down from our perch, waved one last time to me and strolled back into the fields, humming to himself and chopping his hoe down at a few crops as if cutting weeds out. I turned my attention back to my task.

From my vantage point, I could see that getting to the tree would be easy enough- but it would have to be done soon. Men on foot carrying spears were marching in columns from north of the town walls, wearing distinctive conical Dacian helmets and carrying their oval shields. The infantry had arrived and had been sent to surround the town.

I leapt down and copied Hosius' actions, leaving the comforting sanctuary of the fort's shadow and stepping out into the exposure of the bright sunshine. I wandered my way towards the tree, resisting the temptation to run as that would alert the enemy as the men drew nearer. They seemed to be relaxed, and none of them paid me any attention as I posed no threat. As I could see them more clearly, I realised it was not spears that they carried but the native falx, a curved blade on a long shaft, confirming that they were Dacian.

Reaching the tree I had been aiming for, I then started to walk up the road that I expected our reinforcing troops to come down. It paralleled the Via Militaris initially, but then turned a corner after about two miles and went around a hill. As I felt a weight fall off me due to now being out of sight of any observers, I thought about what was going on back in Naissus. I suspected my father would be on the eastern ramparts, focusing on what he would say when confronted by Zanticus' messenger for his answer at mid-afternoon. That would not be far away, I thought, looking up at the sun starting to descend from its midday height above me.

I made it to the bend in the road and entered a wood, the light disappearing in the gloom of the forest. At that point,

I threw away my hoe and started to run, for the entire plan depended on speed and timing if it were to work- and luck, given that I had no idea where the legion might be. And now I was out of sight of any potential suspicion. I cast a prayer to Mercury asking for speed and safety as I ran.

I saw movement amongst the trees to my right, up the hill's incline. Worried that I had drawn attention, I stopped still behind a trunk and tried to peer around it through the woods to identify where the movement had come from. It was not difficult to see as it drew nearer. There was a tribesman racing his horse through the undergrowth in the opposite direction, back towards Naissus, twisting around trees and jumping over fallen trunks, crashing noisily through the bushes. Intent on his own chase, he did not see me.

As soon as he was past I responded with renewed eagerness- a scout in such a rush would hopefully mean the legion was near. I ran once more, ensuring I did not exhaust myself as I did not know how much further I had to travel. About an hour later, though it was hard to judge due to my inability to see the sun through the forest canopy overhead, I heard shouts. I rapidly descended the side of the hill, turned a corner and stopped suddenly.

For there were two horsemen staring at me in the middle of the road.

Each of us looked warily at the other for a moment, taken aback, before one of the soldiers said slowly, "What have we here?"

"A peasant in a hurry. I wonder why," said the other, enjoying toying with me.

The first unsheathed his dagger, leaving his sword on his hip, and spoke again, "Come here, boy. Let's see what your rush is all about."

I was struggling to get my breath back due to the momentum I had gained coming down the hill. I tried to gasp out a few words, "Take me... to your... prefect. Urgent... Must see him."

The two of them were momentarily surprised as they made out what I was saying, but then frowns came over both of their faces at once. The second one said, "And what could you possibly want with our prefect? What makes you think he would even speak to you?"

The first laughed at my presumption, "A filthy peasant! Wanders along the road smelling and looking like a dung-heap and expects to be able to walk into the camp of a legion and do as he wishes. There is a lesson to be taught here my friend!"

He turned to the first horseman and their expressions took on an unpleasant cast as he took out his dagger too. They looked at me intently as they nudged their horses forwards. I hurriedly took out the gem that Felix had given me as his parting gift. "See this: the seal of a frumentarius. If you wish to delay my progress, then know that you will incur the wrath of the dux- and likely the new emperor also. I must see your prefect urgently."

Eyes suddenly staring, the two stopped their mounts where they were. Both sheathed their weapons and the first, who seemed to take more of a lead, beckoned. He said gruffly, "Let me see that." He took it from my outstretched hand, turned it over, examined it and passed it to his friend. "Never seen one of these before; but heard of them. Best be sure and take this lad to the commander. Then it's his problem."

Before I knew it, I was up behind the second cavalryman and we were galloping along the road. Neither man spoke to me. After about four miles, we came to an encampment built in a large glade, established in true Roman fashion with a ditch in front and a palisade. The banners of two legions flew over the front gate, both the black eagle of the Fifth and the golden lion of the Thirteenth were brightly embroidered on them- and I thanked Sol for his blessing yet again. Both legions! The plan would be sure to work now. Of course, I had yet to persuade the prefects to do as commanded when I was but a messy, dirty child with a spy's token.

The gates opened before us, the guards making way as they saw our speed, and the two horses hurtled straight down the central street to the commander's tent. I dismounted, and the two scouts did the same. We were immediately challenged by a pair of legionaries standing guard outside the tent entrance as my companions saluted.

"What do you want, Secundus? And who's the boy?"

"We need to see the prefect, sir, urgently."

Puffing my chest out, assuming as much dignity as I could, I announced, "I demand to see the commander immediately."

They chuckled at my presumption. So I took out the seal again.

But the prefect himself emerged from the doorway to his tent, having heard the noise. "What is this all about?" he asked, angry at the interruption.

"Sir, I come from the dux, Constantius. He asks for your immediate assistance with an invading force surrounding Naissus."

He looked at me in disbelief. "You expect me to take the word of a filthy scoundrel like you? This is a jest, surely!"

"It is not, sir," I said, irritated myself now. "I am the dux's son, Constantine. We have been with the emperor, Diocletian, defeating the false emperor. The Sarmatians have taken advantage of the confusion to make their way over the border."

I was careful to ensure I did not make reference to the failure of these two legions' either to come to Diocletian as ordered, or to at least guard the border adequately in the absence of law and order in the empire. I also made no mention of the instruction requiring them to come to Naissus. There must be no accusations made were we to gain their help at such a crucial point. The prefect's attitude changed at my words. He looked willing to listen, telling his guards to stand down and leading me into his tent.

Inside, he waved at another commander standing at a table studying a map- "Pollio Cornelius Crispus of the Fifth; and I am Valerius Resius Albanus, commanding the Thirteenth. Now explain the situation to me again."

I took the two of them through the events that had taken place so far as clearly and quickly as I could. Their expressions grew graver as I spoke, and they occasionally looked at each other to gauge reactions. Neither interrupted.

I finished by saying, "So my father needs your help. He has a plan; but it requires coordination of our forces. We only have a few hours to march to his aid, and we must leave as soon as the men can be ready."

The prefects looked at me doubtfully. Crispus responded first. "So he wants us to attack an established force of unknown size without scouting first to be able to make our own judgement?"

Albanus answered him placatingly, "But Crispus, we knew something of this already: our scouts have not been sat on their backsides for the last week, and we knew there was a large Sarmatian force somewhere in the hills. Had we not stopped at your request to await the supplies, we would have been at Naissus already- as had been ordered."

Shocked at the implicit suggestion that he had intentionally slowed down the legions' progress, Crispus protested defensively, "We needed them! And there was no suggestion of infantry accompanying this force. Finding Sarmatian cavalry in these hills with our legions would have been impossible, and we had been ordered to Naissus."

I spoke impatiently as there was no time for recriminations, "Have the supplies arrived?"

"Yesterday," said Albanus. "We have everything we need."

Crispus said to him, his brows furrowing with anxiety, "We need to talk- without this young man present." He turned to me. "Wait outside. We will make a decision and let you know what we will do."

I was astounded. "But you have no choice, sir! This is a direct order from the dux commanding the east with the authority of the emperor."

I presented the frumentarius gem in an attempt to reinforce my words.

Crispus just looked at me blankly, waiting for me to leave, the seal ignored.

Albanus said in a resigned voice, "Please do as he asks. We do only have your word for all of this and we will give it due consideration."

I walked out of the tent, astonished at the reluctance of these commanders to do as they had been instructed. They had no real doubts as to my authority, had expressed no genuine concerns as to the legitimacy of the orders I had brought- and yet still they hesitated. I could only conclude that their reluctance to join Diocletian's army was a deliberate decision; and that now they were equally unsure of committing to battle against an enemy of the empire. Was this justifiable caution or intentional mutiny? I could not let my father down. Or the many others now besieged in Naissus.

I waited for what felt like a long time, my head in my hands as I despaired of these cowards- maybe traitors- choosing the right course of action, my own powerlessness creating even greater frustration. And then the door flap lifted and Albanus emerged.

He spoke to the guards, "I wish to see all centurions and decurions right away- of both legions."

They ran to do his bidding.

And then he turned to me as I waited with great unease to hear his verdict. But I need not have feared.

"We march as soon as you have told us the plan." Taking me to one side and speaking in a lower voice, he said, "Forgive Crispus. He led the Fifth in their retreat from Dacia years ago. He is not the man he once was. He felt the abandoning of the province was a reflection on his ability to lead his legion. It is not cowardice; he just wishes to always be sure of success before he moves."

I looked at Albanus cynically, my expression saying more than words could.

He shook his head and said wearily, "I know. We have fought together for many years as he was at Potaissa while my legion was based in Apulum, a short distance away. We held Dacia together. And we left Dacia together."

I understood more now; but it was still no reason in my mind for not obeying imperial orders- particularly when my father's fate and reputation was at stake. Men started to arrive outside the prefect's tent until soon there were great numbers waiting to hear what needed to be said. Crispus did not come out. I was nervous, for I would be expected to speak to these highly experienced veterans and to do so in military terms which would make sense to them. The legions included several vexillations of auxiliaries who would come in very useful- particularly the archers and a rare specialist unit of mounted soldiers who fought with the full-sized legionary shield. Their cohorts of cataphracts would also make a difference against Roxolani lancers and Dacian infantry alike. I could not make a mistake in my judgement.

Albanus leapt up on to a barrel to speak first, saying, "Thank you, men, for coming so quickly. The dux is trapped in Naissus, and we have arrived at the right time. His son, Constantine, will now tell us the plan."

He gestured to me, leaping down and indicating that I should take his place. As I did so, my mouth dried up. I contemplated the array of faces in front of me, hardened soldiers with many years' experience of repelling border raiders. They were dressed erratically in a variety of informal clothing and half-armour which seemed to give them even more credibility in my eyes. I wanted to communicate that this was a chance to redeem themselves for not coming to the Margus when ordered; to let them know that there would be forgiveness and glory together if we could win this battle. But I could not say that, for it would cause resentment and no one would wish to fight.

Composing myself, I spoke spontaneously, saying, "Men! I thank you for your timely arrival. There is a legion relying on you a few miles away, a dux whose gratitude you will receive and an empire for you to protect and fight for. If we march fast, we will arrive as the enemy attacks the walls of the city. They will be vulnerable. We will be the hammer, and the walls of Naissus will be the anvil we crush them on. Now it is mid-afternoon…" I glanced upwards at the sun, and it would indeed be about now. "And the dux will be standing above the gate, telling the Roxolani King Zanticus that he will not surrender the town. The invading army will be drawn up around the walls as a threat: for they will either be expecting to march in, or to fight immediately as the king cannot accept defeat."

A voice at the back shouted, "So it should be easy."

Another shouted in reply, "It is never easy to stab men in the back."

I felt I had to speak before this continued, for I suspected that many of these men, based in Dacia for so long previously and then on the border, had friends amongst the enemy force, maybe even relatives. This reluctance from some to fight could turn to a refusal if I did not intervene.

"They are warriors, as are we! We all know what we do when we take up the sword of a legionary; and they know what it means to attack a Roman town. The Eleventh hold the city now, and they will fight hard. They will be waiting for their brothers to fight with them, to share the glory and receive the emperor's reward for loyal and faithful service."

The mood changed with that. Albanus leapt up beside me, teetering on the barrel but not wanting to lose the opportunity of the change in atmosphere.

"We march as soon as the men are formed up!" he bellowed. "Go now, leave everything but weapons and shields, for we can return once victory is won."

The men moved swiftly once the order had been given. I was given a horse to ride, and I led the men of both legions out of the camp gates alongside Albanus with only a few soldiers left behind to defend the camp and its remaining contents. There was still no Crispus nor was there any reference made to his absence. The cavalry came immediately behind us, five hundred of them, with the footsoldiers next. Supplies had been left along with all unnecessary possessions. And our six thousand men marched quickly as a result. Albanus told me as we left that he thought it should take us no more than two hours to reach Naissus using the road I had taken.

◆ ◆ ◆

And, despite my impatience and eagerness to get to the city, the journey did pass faster than I had anticipated: perhaps because a return with a fixed destination always seems swifter than a journey to an unknown destination on a road not travelled before. I do not recall much of the route, for my mind was focused on what could be happening outside the city- what could go wrong, what the enemy might do that was unpredictable, whether this plan was the right one. Not knowing what awaited us was the greatest difficulty for me; and I eventually resolved to stop considering what might happen and face the reality when we got there.

And we did.

Albanus ordered the marching column to stop as we approached the edge of the trees before the bend in the road to the north of Naissus. Our scouts had reported no enemy outposts, and I wondered if Crispus had been in Sarmatian pay- why else would the tribe be so sure that they had at least until the morning to take the city?

The two of us moved forward, accompanied by the two First Spear centurions of each legion and the decurion responsible for the cavalry, to see a section of the battlefield laid out before us. Horse archers working in squadrons were racing in to release flights of arrows at the ramparts of the city; while groups of infantry, having put together ladders using the wood from the surrounding hills, were running up to place them against the walls, clambering up one at a time. Ladders fell; but there was fighting on top of the walls in several places.

I turned to Albanus. "We must hurry!" I said urgently.

He looked at me and said calmly, "We will be no help if we do not do this in the right way. We must maintain some surprise. What does the dux wish us to do once we arrive?"

"I am to signal that we are in the woods. Then the Eleventh will open the gates of the city and come out to draw up on the plain, as if offering pitched battle to the enemy. Constantius says this will appear to be such a foolish move, leaving a fortified position that cannot be taken without siege towers, that they will be unable to resist the provocation. Once they are arrayed in battle order, we attack from behind. The Eleventh and their cavalry will hold firm and prevent any breakthrough; but they cannot hold for long. We must not wait."

"A highly risky strategy," replied the prefect. "But it could mean a resounding victory. I do not like it. But I am his to command and will attack as ordered. The risk is all his."

I looked at him, still surprised at his timidity. He had two legions behind him. Although there may be more of the Roxolani- five thousand cavalry and, from what I could estimate, perhaps four times the number of infantry- we were Romans! Invincible the world over, blessed by Sol Invictus.

Before he could see my expression I turned my head away, saying, "Let us wait until this wave of attacks stops. The dux suggests that he will open the west gate: the flattest plain and the area that suits our infantry best lies to that side of the town. From here, we would be able to come from the flank; but may I respectfully suggest that you send the light cavalry around behind the hills to follow up the river valley and approach directly from the south? We will break them first with our infantry atttacking from their flank- but the cavalry coming from there will cut off their flight and complete the victory."

Albanus nodded, considering, "Very well." He turned to the decurion and gave his orders. As we continued to watch, there was a lull in the fighting at the north gate. The ramparts had been cleared of tribesmen, the last few bodies being flung down to create more of an obstacle for other attackers; the horse archers were cantering back to the woods; and the infantry were running, limping and hobbling along the same path.

Albanus prompted me, "Time to send your signal."

I ran forward further into the light. On opening the package, the third of the items Felix had given me, I found the mirror as promised. My father had told me of the tactic used by a Roman general, Frontinus, two hundred years ago. So I took the small mirror and positioned it carefully to reflect the bright sunshine. The day was coming to an end, but the low sun made my task easier. I had had little time to practice before leaving the town due to the need to hurry; but as I moved the object around I was convinced I could see a circle of light falling on the upper wall above the north gate.

Hastily, I tilted the mirror to the side and back to raise it, concerned that Zanticus' hordes might see the light flashes and suspect something was amiss. Suddenly, there was a flicker back from the tower to the right of the north gate, and I could see movement up there. Three flashes was the indicator that my signal had been seen, and I waited impatiently. Two... three! They had seen it.

I ran back to where Albanus was standing and said eagerly, "They saw! We must ready ourselves Prefect."

CHAPTER 13: RETRIBUTION

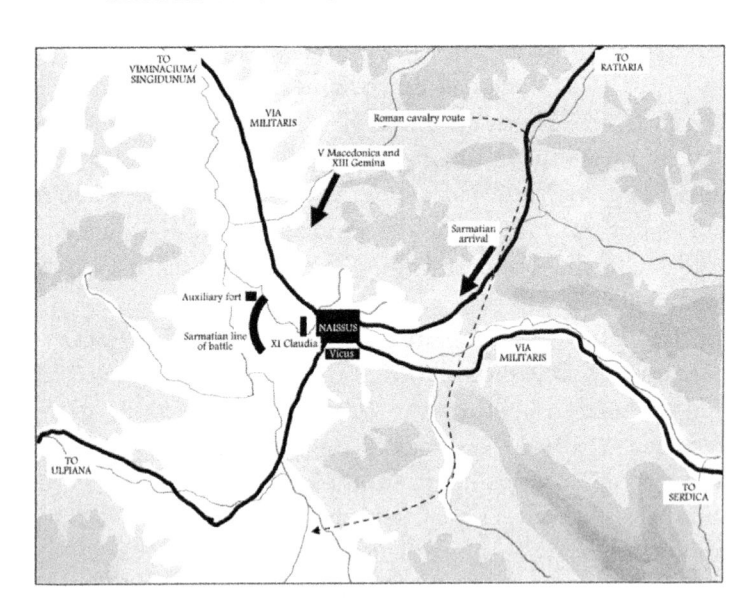

Albanus turned back and ordered the two First Spears behind him, "Prepare the men to advance ten deep. Do not give shouted orders until the battle in front commences- we have time to organize them well. Order the cataphracts to be the vanguard."

Due to the broken ground over the next mile, it would be difficult to maintain a consistent line. But by the time we reached the plain on which my father intended for us to fight, the men would have firmed up.

The army trapped in Naissus must have been waiting with great anticipation, for the gates began to open shortly after my signal had been seen. There was a great roar from the Sarmatians as they saw the gap grow, no doubt unable to believe an experienced commander could be so foolish. The tribes halted their attacks and pulled back to allow the Roman commanders the full opportunity to continue this mistake.

The gates opened to their widest extent and the legion began to march out. They made a great show of it, trumpeters blowing, legionaries beating their shields in a slow rhythm and cavalry emerging behind them with pennants flying from lanceheads held upright. In disciplined order, they formed up on the plain to the west as I continued to observe from the north.

There was a commotion to the north and east as Zanticus must have called in all of his infantry. Most had been sat around the walls doing very little as the previous attack failed. He would have been probing for a weak point, his men moving in from different points in waves to see if a section of the wall would give way, meaning a lot of men were uninvolved at any particular point in time. Soon, there were massed crowds of warriors moving quickly around the city to meet in front of the assembled Eleventh Claudia, waiting patiently before the west gate for the axe to fall. The Roxolani cavalry had arrived already, and now, for the first time, we could see the enemy in full. There were at least fifteen thousand tribesmen on foot, possibly more; while the horsemen continued to circle the battlefield making their exact numbers impossible to judge. I looked at Albanus, concerned that he might be hesitating. There was a frown on his face that may have been one of concentration, and I relaxed slightly- I could certainly see no paralyzing terror there.

Within an hour, both sides were ready. Nobody wished to lose the light, but dusk was not far distant. The Roman force looked small and vulnerable, the west gates closed behind them so that the town could continue to resist if they were defeated. The vast array of the Roxolani tribe was less ordered but had a broad structure to their shape, their size intimidating and ready to envelop and overwhelm the tiny army in their path. They had created a rough crescent shape despite the indiscipline of the cavalry, the riders forming dragon-bannered wings that moved out to the flanks in order to encircle the Roman square, solid and stalwart like a rock standing firm in the face of a fast-flowing river.

And then the Sarmatians began to move forward slowly, making a huge noise. At that point, I saw horses emerge from the river valley behind them, and I turned to Albanus, "Look sir, our cavalry! We must march fast if we are to hit their flank before they see or hear the cavalry behind them." He looked at me. He paused. And he thought. I grew impatient.

"We must go now, sir! Or they will escape. If we have not blocked their escape when they see our cavalry then their horsemen will flee back to the river!"

But the prefect just continued to look at me, his face blank. And it was then that I saw his natural caution assert itself. He spoke hesitantly, "We must wait… it is all about our timing… it is too soon."

His two First Spear centurions came forward and saluted, their transverse crests marking them out and an array of decorative discs attached to their chests proving their leadership by example. They had heard nothing of our words.

The centurion from the Thirteenth, Albanus' own legion, spoke first, "Sir. We are ready. Our cavalry have shown themselves and we must march now or we will miss the opportunity to crush the enemy. They will be ready if we do not move immediately."

Albanus said, "Not yet. See: the Eleventh have not made contact with the tribesmen. Wait."

The second centurion, from the Fifth, spoke up. He wore the rare civic crown on his harness, its oak leaves and acorns telling of his saving the life of a fellow Roman in battle. "Sir, if we do not move now we will not capture their cavalry. The victory will not be complete."

Albanus delayed more, arguing with the centurion as if he were an equal, "But our only real task is to relieve the city. That we will achieve. Anything more is an unexpected blessing."

I nearly felt sorry for the man, his uncertainty paralyzing him. I could see the centurions' frustration, and I decided I would take command- for it would only take one order for us to move. The Eleventh had taken a step back as the Sarmatians hit the front of their square; and the cavalry had nearly surrounded them.

Mustering all of the authority I could, I produced the dux's seal and announced to the two senior centurions, "In the name of the emperor, march!"

Albanus looked horrified at first, and I could see the protest rising to his lips. But then he quietened and I saw a look of relief pass over his face, hidden swiftly. For now it was no longer his responsibility and he had someone to blame should things not go as expected. The two centurions saluted me, gratitude in their every action, and ran to their men.

"Attack!" they bellowed, their vine sticks raised to point at the enemy.

And the line flooded past on either side of Albanus and me. I looked at him apologetically, but he heeled his horse forward, ignoring me. I followed behind our men feeling my task was done for the day. One of the prefect's slaves ran up with a horse. I gratefully climbed on to its back and cantered towards the city.

Our legionaries were still three hundred metres from the enemy's flank when the heavy cavalry struck. The Roxolani cavalry ran from them, splitting as the wedge formation approached at a steady canter; and the shock when they made contact with the infantry caused the Dacians to reel back, their men being pushed on to each other as the indomitable wall of armour hit them.

The panic this created due to the unexpected surprise of being hit from the side led, as we had predicted, to a movement of men pushed out from their right flank, as that was the only possible direction of movement. Our cataphracts bit deep, the two legions following up behind, and the enemy broke. The right wing of their army was now the only section that was not involved in the fighting. They could have supported their companions, reinforced them and enabled them to hold us off despite the surprise. But they chose not to.

Their cavalry had fled immediately, streaming away around the south of the city and through the huts and shacks of the vicus that stood on the bank of the river, aiming to escape into the mountains. The infantry right wing tried to follow- but our horsemen were there, blocking them off. The Roxolani lancers were allowed to flee, as, despite our cavalry having made their way to the rear of the Sarmatian army they had been too late to establish themselves fully. The tribesmen's horses, accustomed to fording rivers, swam across and made their way east and home.

The main battle turned into a disorganized rout as the enemy tried to recover. But they were now splitting up into many small forces of mainly Dacian infantry, isolated in their resistance and soon overwhelmed by our men. As I cantered towards the walls, there was a group gathered ahead of me assailed by men of the Eleventh who had taken the brunt of the initial fighting and now wished to gain their revenge.

Something seemed familiar to me about this group.

I urged my horse forward. There were about fifty men gathered on a small hillock, their shields presenting a wall as they hunkered down behind them for protection as the Eleventh called on their archers to fire. Several fell, screaming in agony as arrows bit into exposed flesh. I looked more closely and saw Dotos on the small height, giving orders to the men to drag the injured up and to close the gaps with those who were able to fight.

I shouted at the men, "Ceasefire!"

The Eleventh knew me well by now, and the firing stopped, the soldiers drawing back to create a space.

Staying on my horse, I moved further towards the incline and called up to the traitor, "Show yourself, Dotos."

He emerged from the shelter of a shield, and replied contemptuously, "What do you want?"

"To save your life. Surrender, and you may not be killed. Continue, and all of you will die."

"Never!" He shouted back. "I know well what Roman justice looks like. I cannot endure the shame again."

I said, "Is Rassogos with you? Could he be saved from your mistakes?"

There was an injured man seated halfway up the incline, his shield lying flat in front of him as he moaned with the agony of a heavily barbed arrow piercing his upper thigh, a sword cut in his upper right arm bleeding badly. A face appeared from behind him. The face was white and very afraid.

"I am here," Rassogos replied hesitantly.

"Are you injured?"

"No, I am not," he said defiantly.

"Do you surrender?"

To my surprise, he declared, "I do!"

And he started to make his way down through the huddled men, picking his way delicately between the dead and dying, the injured and the wounded.

His father reacted instantly.

Snarling, "You are no son of mine!" he leapt down to where the young man tenderly stepped. Raising his sword above his head he swept it down with all of his might. Rassogos did not see it coming, so focused was he on making his way out of this trap. The sword cleaved his head in two, blood and brains landing on those around him. They instinctively recoiled from the flying gore. His body dropped.

Disgusted and repulsed by what I had seen Dotos do, I waved my hand to the men surrounding the traitors: "Kill them all. That is what they wish for."

I turned away, not wishing to see the outcome of my order. The legionaries would stand off while the archers did their work, moving in for the final killing once there was less risk to them. I heard shouting, screaming and vicious blows behind me.

And then my father stood before me, his face covered in the blood of others, a demonic grin on his face. "Well done son! This is your victory." He took me in his arms to give me a great joyous hug. "You found the legions and brought them here." He looked at me quizzically, "But the cavalry cutting off their escape came late and many escaped."

I paused, unsure what to say as I did not wish for Albanus to be condemned without having the chance to defend his inaction.

The dux saw my reluctance. "No matter! There will be a tale to tell no doubt. For now, let us end this fight."

He sent his trumpeters around the small fights still raging, calling on the Dacians to surrender. This they did for the most part; and those who did not were swiftly dealt with. He personally interrogated the few remaining Roxolani tribal leaders who gave their swords up and was disappointed to find that Zanticus and Rasparagnus had both fled with the cavalry.

"Back in Dacia already given the speed of their cowardice," he grunted, irritably.

◆◆◆

Mere hours later, we were sitting drinking wine in Constantius' office as dusk turned to night. Hosius had just joined us, reproachfully saying to me, "I heard all of the noise from the tree I was hiding in over the southern road; but by the time I arrived it was all over."

I chuckled at his regret. "You didn't miss much. They took one look at the heavy cavalry on their flank, then at the two legions behind- and they were destroyed."

This was no comfort to my friend.

Felix reported first on the state of the army. "Lord. We have lost around two hundred legionaries from the Eleventh. A high price to pay, but we did fight alone for longer than expected due to the delay from the north. Another hundred injured."

He did not attribute blame for this so much as state the facts.

Constantius replied, "And what of the Fifth and Thirteenth?"

Felix spoke more carefully on this subject, framing his reply with tact. "About one hundred dead from each, sir, along with three hundred injured from the Fifth and four hundred from the Thirteenth. But one of the dead was the prefect of the Thirteenth, Albanus. And the prefect of the Fifth, Crispus, is missing. I have sent a man to their camp, as a centurion informed me he was not seen to leave his tent after Albanus gave the order to march. The centurion suspects he will not be at the camp."

My father took this information in without comment. Nor did any expression cross his face. He just looked at me and said bluntly, "Are either of these part of your tale?"

I looked him in the eye and said, "They are. But only Crispus is of concern- for I have a suspicion that he was well paid by Zanticus to keep the Fifth at Oescus and to persuade Albanus to stay close to home also. Though I believe he did so in good faith."

Felix said, "There was a strange story told to me by a legionary of the Eleventh. He said that the fighting was all but over when he saw a prefect charge at a group of Dacian tribesmen that was surrounded by our troops. He rode through our archers and past the legionaries. Didn't raise his sword or attempt to attack. They struck him down and he offered no defence."

I was not surprised by this account. In many ways, it was the best end for Albanus. He would have worked out Crispus' part in what had taken place over the last month, would have seen how his fellow prefect had taken advantage of him, of his caution and friendship. He would have known that his honour was at stake. His death meant there would be no enquiry, no recriminations and his reputation would remain intact.

Constantius understood and nothing more was said of Abanus. But he ordered Felix, "Let all know that any sighting of Crispus must be followed up immediately. I suspect we will not see him again. And what are the numbers for the tribesmen?"

Felix checked his notes, and said, "Three thousand dead, ten thousand prisoners. This will take the Roxolani king much time to recover from."

I added, "And the Dacian refugees are, I think, all dead."

I told them the story of what I had seen on the hillock.

My father shook his head, then smiled at me after hearing the sad end of the tale in Dotos' final words to Rassogos, saying, "On the other hand and for my part, I thank Sol every day for my son."

There was, naturally, a lengthy debate about the right course of action to take in the morning, despite the lateness of the hour. Felix and Scipio were present as the dux's principal advisers. Constantius, on my recommendation, called for the two First Spear centurions from the Thirteenth and the Fifth who had effectively been leading the legions in the absence of their prefects. I was there as a matter of course now, as was Marcus, prefect of the Eleventh.

"So, friends, your view on our next steps." My father opened the discussion bluntly.

"A retaliatory raid." Scipio spoke briskly, as if he assumed there would be little debate. "Quick in, quick out."

Felix nodded. "We have three legions with all of their supplies. They will be in fine mood for taking the fight across the river."

The two centurions were nodding eagerly. One of them spoke up, "And, as the Thirteenth will be the nearest legion to this part of the river, that would serve fair warning on the tribes as to what to expect of us. Sets the tone, so to speak."

I spoke carefully, aware of the enthusiasm for this idea but wanting to sound a note of caution. "Is there any such thing as a fast raid when it comes to Dacia?"

My father gave me his full attention. "What do you mean, son?"

"Well, I remember but little of what my tutor taught me so many months ago back in Salona. But did not Trajan invade Dacia?"

"And won!" Scipio responded quickly.

"He did. But at what cost? Nearly three years of war, half a million prisoners, who knows how many Roman dead...?"

Constantius said, "That was a full-blown war. I am not proposing that. I want a simple swift answer to their transgression into the empire."

Felix cut through our developing debate. "Sir, there is also the ahem... political perspective to consider. I assume you would be thinking about using the Eleventh to protect the borders and provide a way out if events did not go to plan?"

"Probably."

"What would our new emperor think of a provincial governor, recently promoted to dux, even one so loyal as you, setting himself up with three legions and an attempt at a victory over a talented and vicious barbarian tribe? A victory as well in the emperor's own region, so recently taken in battle from a usurper? And where the emperor Carus so recently took the title 'Sarmaticus' after defeating the Iazyges? We perhaps need to be careful here sir."

Constantius' chin was sunk on his chest as he slouched back in his chair, ruminating.

Felix followed up. "Aye. And what of the need for him to gain his own victories, win his own titles to consolidate his rule?"

My father suddenly sat decisively back up again. "The Thirteenth will return to Ratiaria- they need a commander, however. Scipio: you will be temporary prefect until the emperor appoints someone. The Fifth back to Oescus with you, Felix, in command." As an aside to the two First Spears, he said, "Not forgetting you: Scipio and Felix are temporary appointments and I will base future promotions on their recommendations." He turned back to the now-prefects. "Regular patrols on the roads between the two of you for the next six months; and a particular focus by fast-riding cavalry on any fords as far as Novae to the east and Viminacium to the west. The Eleventh can support you if needed as they will be back in Novae." He turned to Marcus. "My thanks to you for your loyalty and faithfulness to the empire- particularly in marching out of the gates from an easily defensible position in the face of an overwhelming enemy force." He grinned at Marcus as he recalled the bravery of the Eleventh. Returning to his main theme, he finished by saying, "That should be sufficient until the emperor returns this way."

"Sir." Felix snapped a salute, relief written all over his face. He was a cautious man, not given to take risks where they did not need to be taken; though quick-thinking and highly capable in the field. The two centurions left the room with glum faces. Scipio tried his best to hide his disappointment at the rejection of his course of action.

◆◆◆

This choice was proven to be the right one when word arrived by one of the imperial messengers two months later informing us that, due to a significant threat to the empire in Gaul and the size of the empire meaning that Diocletian could not manage the whole by himself, he had decided to raise Maximian to the status of Caesar- with himself as senior emperor, or Augustus. Maximian would now lead all of what had been Carinus' legions, near enough twelve thousand men. Based in Moguntiacum, his would be the task of defeating a rampaging tribe, the Bagaudae, which was ravaging the region in the absence of any legion presence- much as the Sarmatians had so nearly done themselves.

As we listened to the messenger recount this information, I watched my father's face closely. There was only the slightest and most momentary show of dissatisfaction, and one that could only have been noticed by someone who knew him very well. I could understand this fully- he had been nearly as much of a support for Diocletian, if not more at times, and yet he had received nothing for his efforts. He would soon be returning to Salona still merely a provincial governor, as he had been before and having even lost his command as dux, with little to show for the sacrifices he had made and the risks he had taken. I found myself becoming frustrated on his behalf.

But then he turned to the rest of us and said lightly, "Sol protect him. Twelve thousand disloyal snakes at my back is not what I would wish for. But he is just the man to win them: talented, courageous, loyal and fair. I would back him every time. And it should not take too much to beat these Bagaudae- victory creates its own faithfulness."

And so any discussion of what might have been was wisely ended before it began.

The same messenger also informed us that the emperor intended to take vengeance on the Roxolani. He would be with us in a month, the earliest he could come despite it being so near the end of the campaigning season.

◆◆◆

The three months between our defeat of the Roxolani/Dacian alliance and the emperor's vengeance were a very enjoyable time for me. Hosius and I would accompany occasional border patrols along the Danube, visiting Felix, Scipio and Marcus. We slept under the stars and skirmished with occasional, though increasingly rare, groups of bandits and raiders who had originally infested the border roads due to the lack of law and order. This was soon restored, however, and we became bored of the monotony of the journey. Instead, we would lord it in Naissus itself.

I had been well-known before I left with Antius; now, I was famous. And I knew that this was the stuff of legend: the bastard son, dreaming of his father and who he might be- proved right, and the father being the provincial governor no less, and now a dux and close friend of the new emperor. The stories about me grew, and I soon heard of my single-handedly fighting Carinus, striking his head from his shoulders and presenting it to Diocletian. That, and tales of my fighting off a band of elite praetorians without assistance from anyone else, protecting my father and the future of the empire. There were also rumours that were far less publicly told of my role in the defeat of the Sarmatian invaders. Those who heard such were even more in my favour as none wished to lose the prosperity and peace of Roman rule, exchanging it for the chaos of what many, despite some ancestry from across the river themselves, still chose to describe as 'barbarian disorder.'

So wherever we went, we were lauded by those who saw us. I thrived on it- and Hosius adored the reflection of this glory. We would ride our horses through the town centre acknowledging the greetings of all, accepting the tribute of the stallholders in the central market in the form of fruit or sweetmeats. Our destination was usually the baths, where we would be at the centre of our very own 'court' of likeminded young men, many of them older than ourselves. Others benefited too- not least, my grandfather, Lucius. He found that men who had avoided him as a foreign upstart engaged in trade were very willing, even eager, to meet with him, and he was fully accepted into the hierarchy of the local administration. He benefited a great deal as he was never loath to take bribes or do underhand deals where required, and his businesses prospered as a result. Soon, I suspected- though he would never admit it- he owned a significant proportion of Naissus itself. He was delighted when my father brought Helena to the city from Salona, as this gave him even greater leverage.

However, all of these activities were but biding our time as we waited for the main event- as if a great breath had been drawn in after the tribal invasion, and it had still not yet been released. It reminded me of the pause when we awaited

Diocletian's visit in Salona. As the early autumn approached, time seemed to slow further and even Constantius, occupying himself with the dull administrative work of governing a large province away from his base, became tense and began to snap at others. This was unusual for him, but all knew enough of the situation to allow him these moments.

Preparations for the emperor's arrival were very different to those when he came to us at Salona, however. Autumn was on us by now, and the focus was very much on ensuring the men would be ready to fight as soon as Diocletian arrived, despite the challenge a campaign at this time of year would bring. This led to much fretting from Felix as he worried over the emperor's lack of communication as to his intentions, trying to make provision for all eventualities. I laughed at him behind his back once as he finally admitted that here was something he could not control that he should be able to, if the universe would only run according to sensible rules.

Still, by the time Diocletian did arrive, the granaries were full, the armouries supplied and the men as trained as they could be.

◆◆◆

"I pray to Mithras I have not left this too late."

Diocletian shook out his cloak as he stepped in through the door of the basilica in the centre of town, rainwater flying across the chairs arranged before him. His arrival had been somewhat marred by the weather; but he had sent word that he had no desire for a formal welcome with the whole town turning out. However, the informality of my father's office in the forum would not be adequate, according to Felix, which was why we were in the high-domed echoing hall.

"I have defeated the Quadi to the north, so it was worth the delay. I have also made sure of the loyalty of the Rhine legions during the war, so it was doubly so. I have, however, brought with me the I and II Adiutrix in order to test their loyalty."

"Bit of a risk lord", my father spoke doubtfully. "Especially if you intend to use them in battle."

"Aye- it was impossible to tug them out of their shells during the civil war; but now their emperor is established they know where their fortunes lie."

The emperor walked around the seated circle of Constantius' advisers, grinning at me and ruffling my hair as he passed despite the fact that I was by now taller than him. He wore his purple cloak far more confidently than before the victory over Carinus, and the clasp holding it in place included several diamonds. His shoes were far more decorative also, and the glint of rubies made me suspect that wealth and power had begun to seduce him. My father had little time for such trappings and maintained himself as a common soldier might. The only exceptions were his weaponry and his horses, and this not so he would stand out so much as because he knew his life may depend on them. The guard surrounding the emperor, I noticed, no longer included any of the praetorians, and I wondered if their days were numbered. I had heard from Scipio that Aristobulus was lined up for the Senate, and so once he was gone...

Constantius interrupted my thoughts as he asked his old friend, "How were you received in Rome sir?"

The emperor frowned slightly, the worry-lines on his forehead deepening and narrowing. "As well as could realistically be hoped. I have left a number of my men in vital posts so that I can be sure of the Senate's loyalty. They are really quite irrelevant these days, but it is always worth paying lip service to the ancient traditions and expectations despite their lack of influence."

Formal introductions over, we moved to the council chamber in which our feast had taken place on that night so many months before. By this point, many others had joined us: First Spears, other senior centurions, and decurions from the many detachments the emperor had available. Marcus of the Eleventh had arrived early that morning, Scipio and Felix were there on behalf of the Fifth and Thirteenth, and there were two additional commanders who came in through the door, talking in the way of old friends: Pertinax of the I Adiutrix and Sergius of the Second.

There was little preamble as Diocletian was a confident decision maker and had had time to fully consider the action that was needed. The emperor summarized briefly what was to happen.

"We march tomorrow morning as the sun rises. The XI Claudia will form the vanguard, the I and II Adiutrix after them with the latter at the back along with as many cavalry as we can muster. I expect little opposition. We will be using the bridge at Oescus." He added for the benefit of the Pannonian commanders, "to the north of Serdica." And then went on to give more detail for all of those gathered in the chamber, "It is only a temporary wooden construction, built recently by the Fifth, so horses will be swum across and the supplies transported by barge. We will sweep through the area north of the Danube, scorching everything in our path. No force is to go far enough north to be in the foothills of the Carpathians- that would isolate them overmuch and we could not guarantee their return."

He nodded firmly, indicating that this was the end of our very swift orders.

My father asked at this point. "Who holds the border behind us sir?"
"The Thirteenth and Fifth have been doing well at this, you say, since you ordered them to patrol there after the invasion. Felix and Scipio will support us by holding the crossing and keeping our supply lines open. I would like you, dux, to oversee those lines. The Moesian fleet are sending ships and boats to aid you in this. To be completely clear," and here his voice deepened with a severity in his tone, "this is a war of retribution, not for territory. I have no desire to take Dacia back again- far more trouble than it was worth- but we do need to make it clear to these barbarians that trespassing on Roman territory will not be tolerated, and certainly not attacking an imperial city. Well done to all of you for not just holding them off but giving them a sound beating."
The men present either smiled in satisfaction at the praise; or nodded their agreement having not been present themselves.
But there was a sting in the tail: "I still question, though, how so many managed to escape when you had three legions at your disposal." He looked at my father, making no secret of his feelings on this; and I supposed that this may have been part of the reason for my father's delayed promotion, as well as for Diocletian's leaving him now with responsibility for the supplies.
"All the more for us to chase down now, lord!" I saw the First Spear from the Fifth wink at me after he called this out, breaking the tension between the emperor and his dux. The emperor slowly and warily joined in the laughing that followed this, then decided to finish the conference, saying, "Let us be ready to ravage Dacia in the morning. They will not soon recover from our visit!"

There was a muted cheer around the room at his words, and an excited atmosphere as everyone left, talking animatedly and eagerly, looking forward to passing the news on to their men. As I left, I heard the emperor say in a slightly more anxious tone than he had portrayed in front of everyone, "Constantius, tell me that Felix has the logistics all in hand?" And then my father's reassuring deep voice. "Of course, sir. We suspected you would take this course of action, and everything is prepared."

Naturally, my principal concern was far more intent on my own desire to go with the warriors of the three legions, and I addressed it with my father as soon as he returned to the mansio that night. I found him in the kitchens long after sundown, as he took some food from behind the counter.

"Father: I will be coming with you."

I had decided that the assertive route would be more effective than a request, so I tried to instil my words with as much assumed authority as I was able.

He spluttered through the bread in his mouth, and it was hard to tell if this was laughter, or shock at my boldness- though, knowing my father as I did, I suspected the former. After taking a draught of water to clear his throat and compose himself, he replied.

"You will be, son. I have asked Scipio to take responsibility for the two of you. Yes- Hosius can come too. But boy," and here a note of warning entered his voice. "This will not be a war as you may have imagined it in the past. No war is ever a good thing; but this" he spoke bitterly, "will be vengeance and deterrent combined. There is no glory in this. Although we are merely responsible for the baggage train", he spoke with a slight edge of offence to his voice, not that he would ever speak out his resentment. "You may see some sights you will regret seeing. And a side of the emperor that may shock you."

"As I would be shocked by torture, for example, sir?"

He looked at me out of the corner of his eye, aware that I was referring to my view of him after seeing the impact of his ordering of the destruction of his assassin.

"Worse than that son. We are talking of children and women. At least Quintus knew what he was doing and held his fate in his own hands: he made his choices. It is most likely that there will be no pitched battles, just villages either deserted or full of those unable to fight for themselves."

"But we know there are sufficient men- for they charged the walls of this town!"

"We do- but they will not sacrifice themselves needlessly. They will hang back, harass us with pin-pricks and by attacking our supplies. The destruction of their homes and families will mean something to them, but not enough to roll the dice on one battle."

◆◆◆

We marched the next day, taking a different road through the mountain to Oescus than that we had been so used to taking to Ratiaria during our patrols- but the scenery was similar and the only interest for me lay in there being so many of us this time. The Sarmatians must have known we were coming, but we crossed the river safely and without incident a few days later, overlooked by an emptied legionary fortress that nonetheless presented its own silent threat, and I watched as crowds of horses struggled across the fast-flowing river. Wide, but not particularly deep at this point, it was easier than it looked. The horses were well-trained, and, despite evident fear in their eyes and reluctance in their step, roped together in groups they would cross eventually. The barges that the fleet had provided did their task well, and the supplies came across even more easily. The army gathered on the far bank and were reorganised to scour the area. The I and II Adiutrix were to go east and west respectively, while the Eleventh would establish a northern perimeter and guard against unexpected attacks.

◆◆◆

I missed the worst of it. Fortunately.

For my father and I rode the length of the wagon trains and back again over the next month, on many occasions. We passed through burnt out villages and saw executed villagers wherever there had been resistance- and sometimes where there had not. We stood together, shame-faced, in the centre of one such village, staring at a pile of bodies surrounded by the ashes of what were once tribal huts. I heard my father mutter the words of the barbarian chieftain, Calgacus, as quoted by Tacitus: "To plunder, butcher, steal; they falsely call it empire."

I turned to him, miserable, and protested, "How do we prevent this, father?"

He replied quietly with another question, "What do you think caused it, son?"

I knew he was trying to teach me, even in the midst of the suffering we could see the remains of around us. I thought. "The chaos and disorder in the empire? For they would not have attacked had it not been for the civil war and deciding to seize the opportunity."

He nodded vigorously, saying, "So we caused this. And now answer your own question: how do we prevent it?"

"There is only one solution: strength. A single empire, a unified people and a sole- unchallenged- emperor."

Constantius tensed slightly at the last of these statements, looking around to see if anyone was near enough to hear. Then he chuckled, shame-faced at his own nerves, explaining by saying, "Maximian…" Then nodded, "Of course, you are right. None will challenge absolute power." We did not speak of sole emperors again- but the lesson taught had been remembered and learnt.

◆◆◆

A week later, we waited on the Moesian side of the bridge at Oescus as a long column of Roxolani captives, chained together and heads bowed, shuffled their way across.
Without looking at my father, I quoted a different line from Tacitus' Calgacus, "Where they make a desert, they call it peace."
He spoke carefully and gently in response to my not-so-veiled reference to our previous conversation; but his answer was not as sympathetic. "The chieftain was wrong, son. This desert is empire. That is the fact of it. What we do here is not pleasant or enjoyable. But we do it for a greater purpose: we do it to prevent the same things happening to our own people- regardless of the cause of their attack on Moesia. What do you imagine would have happened if the gates of Naissus had been open when the tribesmen arrived on that night three months ago? Would they have merely enslaved us? Or would they have publicly tortured us as Romans, ripped us apart slowly, then made an example of us throughout the lands that they control? We would have died long after, pleading for our own death while lying in our own shit and blood. Think of Rassogos, Dotos and the others who made a pact with the invaders- did they end well? It is about civilisation, Constantine, in that you are right. But it is about protecting our civilisation. We can only do this with terror. The fear of our retribution must be much greater than their desire for victory, or it will only be a matter of time before they invade again- and maybe with more fortune on their side. Or, at least," he smiled at me

proudly, "with no suspicious son of a dux to forewarn. Here ends my lecture."

I regarded him sadly. "You are right, father. But it makes me ashamed of my heritage. If only there were another way."

"There is no other way. We have tried mercy before: you have studied our history, so you will know that Trajan negotiated with the Dacians after two years of war. It meant that they would remain, in part, an independent people. He even offered them military and material support against their enemies. But within three years they were raiding across the Danube again, pillaging our colonies. That is what these tribes are like. I have experienced it myself when we fought the Palmyrenes- Aurelian would have willingly shown mercy to Zenobia, but she repeatedly took advantage of his goodwill. We cannot assume that these Sarmatians will act differently: there is too much risk involved. Overwhelming strength is all."

In the distance, columns of smoke hung sullenly in the air and there was great wailing from the women. A few remaining mounted Roxolani horsemen watched from a distance as their people were taken away from Dacia. Rain started as the final few crossed, matching the captives' mood; but amongst the Roman commanders there was satisfaction, if not elation.

Diocletian rode up behind us to see the final departure of his troops, legionaries from the Eleventh forming a rearguard behind the prisoners. He sat casually astride his horse, one hand resting on his knee as he watched, pleased with the sight behind us.

He smacked Constantius on the back jovially: "A good task completed, eh my friend? None will begrudge me the title

Sarmaticus Maximus now; just a word in the right place..."
He grinned.

"A necessary task sir, if not a pleasurable one. And my congratulations."

"I can now make my way back to the east without any worries about this area of my empire. You are a faithful servant, Constantius, and I know you have received little in the way of reward. Antius has been at his work and I am told you may have been protecting the reputations of two unwilling prefects- maybe worse. We have still not found Crispus..."

My father spoke stiffly. "I do not do this for reward sir, nor do I blame others. It is my duty to serve."

"I know that, my friend," the emperor replied in a placatory tone. "And no ruler could wish for a better servant. But your time will come. You will not be forgotten. Men of your sort are few and far between, which is why I must leave you in Salona for a little longer. Dalmatia is far too important to the empire to leave it in any lesser hands."

I saw the slight spasm cross my father's face as the emperor told him he must stay there. A minuscule creasing of the brow, a slight tensing of the muscles around the mouth. The emperor was oblivious, used already to men obeying his commands without question.

He had already turned away, speaking over his shoulder as he did so, "I will accompany you back to Naissus; but then I must hurry on to Nicomedia, so we will not stay. The East has been without me for nearly a year." He laughed suddenly. "I forget: last time I was truly there for any period of time, I was but an imperial bodyguard! So much has happened…"

"Aye, that it has," my father reflected quietly beside him.

And the two men, old before their time with the burdens placed on them by their own ambition and by the demands of an unforgiving empire, led the army of experienced legionaries and weeping women and children south towards the slave markets that awaited in Italy and across the Mediterranean in Africa. I stood to one side to let the column pass and give the emperor and Constantius some privacy, and considered how fortune had favoured me. I looked up in the direction of Sol, hidden behind the lowering clouds shedding their own load of tears on the assembled mass, and thanked him for his blessing.

CHAPTER 14: CHANGES

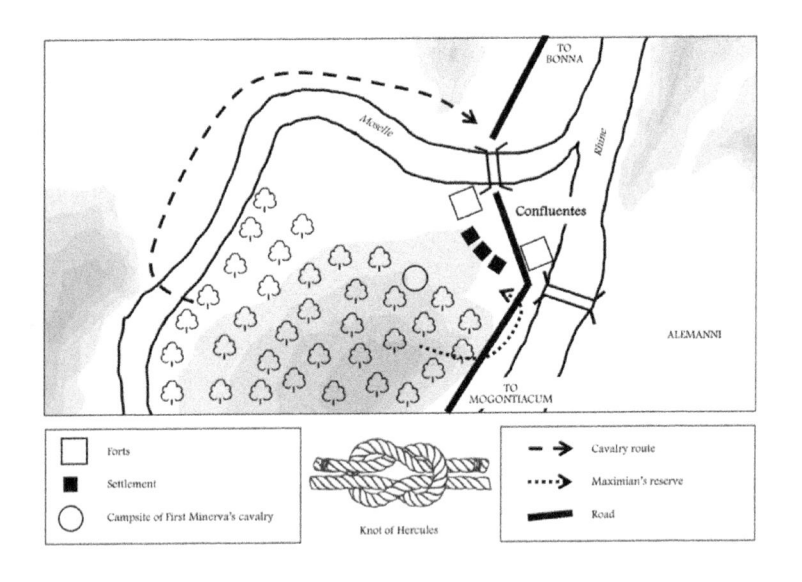

'A little longer' turned out to be nearly a year. And when it came, the prize was bittersweet.

It started with a rebellion in Britannia under a commander from northern Gaul called Carausius. His original successes had come when fighting the Bagaudae under Maximian. He was noticed and promoted, made commander of the Britannic fleet; and Maximian was promoted to Augustus alongside Diocletian as co-emperor at around the same time. The power, however, went to Carausius' head. He was corrupt and Maximian decided enough was enough, ordering his execution. Carausius fled to Britannia when he heard rumours of this and established himself as the new emperor in that province. In his conceit, he then claimed northern Gaul as well.

In the midst of these events, Maximian's right hand, the Praetorian Prefect Afranius Hannibalianus, who had been sent to arrest Carausius, was killed. He joined the Britannic fleet in Gesoriacum, and this may have been the reason the ship commanders were forced to make a decision. Choosing their loyalty to Carausius over their allegiance to Rome, the Praetorian Prefect was executed mid-Channel, his headless body thrown overboard, and the fleet went over to join the so-called 'emperor of the north'.

And so it was that my father replaced Afranius, uprooting all of us from our home in Salona in order to move far north and west to Mogontiacum in late summer. Leaving Salona seemed to me to be fulfilling the next step in our destiny; so it was no great hardship. I had become frustrated in this backwater after a year playing- as it seemed to me- such a crucial supporting role in the emperor's defeat of the usurper Carinus, and my mother had increased this sense of desire for something more. Ever since Constantius had accepted her on our arrival in the Dalmatian capital she had seen a bright destiny for the two of us. Sitting and waiting in Salona did not feature as a part of this plan. However, the wait meant that by the time my father moved his household north I was fifteen years old. I had grown even taller, my jaw had firmed up and my voice had strengthened, my shoulders broadening as they gained strength. I had become accustomed to barking orders and expecting instant obedience: a true son of Constantius in authority as well as birth.

As I was now accustomed to Scipio's presence and guidance by my side, I requested of my father that he be permitted to come north with us. Hosius, having grown but little in recent years, had become an even more committed companion and a lithe fighter, his technique reminding me in no small part of Antius. Fast, deadly with a blade and moving so easily he appeared to create his own time to deal with any close threat. So when we moved to Mogontiacum, he came also.

◆◆◆

Mogontiacum as a city served many purposes; principally, it was the base of XXII Primigenia. It guarded the Rhine frontier, close to several major Germanic tribes, and was heavily fortified as a result; it was also the launching point for any attacks on them. Early on in its existence as part of the empire, these purposes had meant that two legions were stationed here. But by the time we arrived from a fascinating and slow progress (due to the many people and items my father had chosen to bring with us: after all, a former governor, dux and current Praetorian Prefect must arrive in a certain style) through Pannonia, Noricum, Raetia and Germania, only the Twenty-Second was still in residence. My father had some slight connection with them, and had previously known several commanders. However, many men had moved on and those he knew were few.

At the back of my mind was ever the thought that this legion had supported Carinus; but the past had clearly been left behind as we were welcomed and soon felt at home. The town had built up around the legion's camp, with the main road leading through the forum and straight to the fortress's front gates, so the army dominated. In fact, the town had been enclosed by its own walls in recent years as it had been threatened a couple of decades before when the fortified forward frontier beyond the Rhine had collapsed and the army withdrew. The people of Mogontiacum had found themselves suddenly and unexpectedly on the front line.

Despite the challenge of this, the people were secure and comfortable: there was still an impressive aqueduct bringing water from further inland and we were well supplied due to the Germanican fleet being based upriver at Colonia Claudia Ara Agrippensium, so there was no sense that they would be abandoned in the face of a potential tribal invasion. This was despite the wrecks of several of our galleys still being visible in the harbour after an Alemanni raid five years before. Having lived in Naissus with a similar threat across the Danube, this was not new to me. There was the added defense of a small fortress on the opposite bank and an auxiliary fort just outside the town- so we were well protected from external threat.

However, one of the other reasons why Mogontiacum was such a significant place was that it was also where the cadet school of the protectores made its home. So Hosius and I were sent there, following in what my father saw as his footsteps despite his comparatively late entry into that elite guard unit. The following months saw me learning tactics, strategy and weapons in more and greater detail than ever before, and than I would have believed possible. Living in the barracks opened my eyes to the wider world and I established myself in a group of young men with all of the expanded experiences that that entailed. It was possibly my height, or maybe my bulk, perhaps even my previous hard-won familiarity with battle, but few seemed able to compete in the martial bouts with which we ended each day. The written work was of much less interest to me, but I persevered sufficiently to do well at it- and strategy came so naturally to me that battles on the maps laid in front of us were often easy victories. I felt older than my age and became even more acquainted with the habits and routines of command.

This idyll could not last, however. Soon after Saturnalia, as we moved towards the end of six months in our new home, we received a summons to the inauguration of the Augustus, Maximian, as consul. This was to take place in Colonia Augusta Treverorum, under a week's leisurely ride from Mogontiacum, and we set off in high spirits, grateful for the break from our routines.

Little remains to me as memories of the trip there, overshadowed by the events that followed- though one conversation did come back to me later. As we discussed the inauguration to come on the first day of travel, riding alongside the slow-moving Rhine on a cold but bright winter's day, it became apparent from Scipio's responses to our questioning that the post of consul was really nothing more than a ceremonial one- the inauguration itself consisting mainly of speeches. It was intended to be symbolic of respect for our Roman heritage; though it was in reality a recognition that the role had been taken over by the emperors.

Scipio rode on to join Constantius and Helena and I whispered to Hosius, "So then: perhaps it would have been better to stay at home. No excitement this week!"

It happened that this could not have been further from the truth.

◆◆◆

We rode into Augusta Treverorum one afternoon just in advance of the ceremony. We had been delayed after crossing the bridge at Bingium and leaving the Rhine, as, still being relatively new to the region, we had not realised that the well-worn Roman road became a less-used track until we reached Dumnissus. Having joined the Moselle further upstream at Noviomagus- and a better maintained road- we had followed the river to the massive gate to our destination called the Porta Nigra. An imposing and intimidating entrance, the galleries above contained many guards by way of both deterrent and as an exhibition of imperial might.

We rode underneath the edifice to find empty streets and an odd silence reigning across the town.

As we rode past a basilica on our left with a small but richly ornamented mansio beside it, I turned to Scipio, once again, to ask, "Is that where the ceremony will take place?"

He chuckled at my naivety and said, "Of course not! The city's people need to share in this celebration. It is to take place- maybe it has even started already given the lack of people around- in the forum where everyone can see. There will be a festival and games afterwards: the reason why everyone will be attending. Nobody wishes to miss such diversions."

Hosius grinned at me, as if to communicate that it may not be so dull after all.

Scipio continued, peering past me and narrowing his eyes, lifting himself from his saddle, "In fact, if you look to the left you should be able to see the walls of the circus- and is that the amphitheatre also? Should Mithras bless us, we will see some real entertainment if Maximian has spent enough on this."

The town was richly decorated for the ceremony, the people demonstrating their loyalty and love for their new emperor with visual proof- though the cynic in me wondered if the Emperor had his own 'Antius' to orchestrate these public demonstrations. Banners, flags and penants in profusion celebrated the recently elevated emperor and his new status as consul, while wreaths and garlands in purple hung from doors and balconies. We reached the forum and dismounted, slaves taking our horses from us. As we walked into the over-crowded space, we could hear Maximian's familiar loud voice.

My father turned around. "Just in time!" he said, smiling in anticipation, no doubt combined with relief.

He indicated to Lucipor to lead the way through the tight-packed forum to a temporary pavilion that had been erected in the centre near the front. This would be where we would take our seats, reserved for us due to Constantius' status as Praetorian Prefect. We managed to quietly find our places on the front row without disrupting proceedings, the Emperor acknowledging our arrival with the slightest of nods.

He was standing on a dais wearing a white toga with a purple border, the consular robe, and he began to declaim his oaths of office with great gravity. The forum was silent as everyone listened intently.

"I will obey the laws and traditions of Rome. I will not let personal interest or fear influence my actions, and I will put the welfare of the state above all."

"I will carry out my office justly and in accordance with the laws. I will not use my power for personal gain or act in a way that would harm the state."

The oaths were extensive and lasted a long time, Maximian's unfortunately monotonous voice adding little to the recitation. I became distracted and started to look around. To the far right of the forum, not far from the stage, there was a statue of Maximinus Thrax on a pedestal. The more I studied it, the more I considered the ironic, yet hopeful, nature of the memorial. Thrax had been made emperor when the Twenty Second (amongst others) had killed the Emperor Severus Alexander in Mogontiacum a half century ago. Though his rule had not lasted long due to the opposition of the Senate, it had been the start of the years of chaos. The accession of Diocletian, and now Maximian, should be the end of this- this was the substance of our prayers to Sol Invictus, my father's desire for order putting him at the forefront of these petitioners.

I also noticed, at the front of the crowd, a group of men standing, each also wearing a toga, though of a brown colour, wearing wreaths on their heads of red and white. Each also carried a set of large sticks with an axe in the centre.

I turned to whisper to Scipio, "What are those men doing there? And carrying battle-weapons in the presence of an Emperor!"

Hosius, short as he was, could see little and said, "What men? And what weapons?"

The last was said with incredulity.

I described briefly to him what I could see, as quietly as possible, and Scipio replied.

"They are the lictors. Twelve good men chosen to serve the consul. They walk before him wherever he may go, the bundle of rods- not sticks!- over their shoulder. They represent the authority of Rome: the rods to punish, the axe to kill."

At that point, the oaths finished and there was a huge roar of approval from the crowd. The senior magistrate of Augusta Treverorum, his status shown by the staff he carried, waited calmly for the people to quiet and then announced that the new consul would now go to make sacrifices to the gods, after which he would speak to us about his plans for the year to come. The lictors made their way up on to the stage to take position in front of Maximian, the crowd becoming talkative and restless as they prepared to move to the temple complex on the other side of the city.

At that moment, there was a commotion at the entrance to the forum and the crowd erupted in conversation about what was happening. They eventually parted and an exhausted imperial messenger on horseback rode into the forum- an action that would only ever take place in the most urgent of circumstances. A path to the dais emerged as people moved out of the way. The messenger made his way through. Maximian responded and the two met at the front of the staging.

The messenger spoke his piece to Maximian, answering the Emperor's questions with short responses, the consul-emperor nodding as he took it in.

Ignoring the messenger now, his message delivered, Maximian gathered his thoughts for a moment then turned to the crowd and shouted, "I have sad news my people! We have been invaded by the Alemanni! They have crossed the Rhine north of Mogontiacum, avoiding both the Twenty Second legion and the First Minerva to the north at Bonna. We must ride immediately and defend the empire. We will gather outside the east gate next to the amphitheatre in one hour."

Without a moment's hesitation, many of the men in the forum turned and started to make their way to the exit, impatiently beckoning to others and forcing their way through the crowd with loud expletives. Those giving the orders and doing the shouting were those that wore full ceremonial armour, including crests that marked them out above the town citizens, making it easy to track their progress across the forum; and those responding to their vigorous gestures were no normal civilians but were in fact the military aides. The latter went now to put their armour on, gathering their weapons as they did so, while those already prepared were going directly to the stables.

"They will be sending messages themselves immediately!" Hosius said excitedly beside me, knowing that their troops were currently leaderless and remained in their bases, reliant on the initiative of lesser centurions or decurions-depending on who had been left behind.

For our part, Constantius ordered Lucipor, accompanying us as ever, to escort my mother to an inn on the main street while we answered Maximian's call. My father was in his best armour: red horsetail crest, helmet decorated with sun symbols and facemask, full chainmail and his harness covered with gold and silver discs awarded for bravery. He looked down at it briefly, shrugged and then grunted at me, "No time to change. Let us go."

We were amongst the first to arrive at the gathering point, our late arrival at the inauguration meaning we still carried all we needed.

"Not quite how I wished to experience my entertainment this day", grumbled Scipio as he got my chainmail from my baggage and helped me into it.

"But how exciting!" responded Hosius enthusiastically, strapping greaves to his shins.

Maximian arrived not long after and rode over to us. Constantius would be his right hand so we would be the first to be informed of his plans. A scout, riding hard from the other direction, arrived at the same time, breathless with the speed of his travel.

"Lords, I have new information. I come from Bonna. The tribesmen crossed the river at Confluentes last night. You may recall the old forts there, one guarding the bridge over the Rhine and one doing the same on the Moselle. The enemy have occupied both. The First Minerva are already on their way as a passing merchant saw the Alemanni crossing. He reported it as soon as he arrived at Bonna so the legion set out at first light, led by the Principal Centurion and his second cohort."

Maximian was furious.

"This could, and should, have been foreseen! We left the bridge unguarded when troops were withdrawn to go East with the Emperor Valerian, thinking the defeat of the Franks had ended the problems there. Then Gallienus, once his father was captured by Persia, thought he could buy the loyalty of the tribes on the other side of the Rhine. A short-term measure that was never resolved due to the constant changes of imperial leadership."

My father replied more calmly, "The constant changes have ended at least. And the tribes are not raiding. They have made the easier choice. We have more than enough men- elite men at that- and time to throw them back to where they came from."

Scipio pointed out, deferentially, "Perhaps not as much time as we may hope, lords. They control access to the upper Rhine and the Moselle with those two forts. Not much trade will get past without some form of payment- and they will confiscate all military goods. They could last a long time and mount a stubborn defence with those re-supplies."

Maximian nodded his agreement with this assessment.

He spoke tersely, "We must act fast then."

By this point, most of the men had arrived from their preparations, and the emperor ordered us to set off. There was about a century altogether, and the Emperor left orders for any latecomers to follow. The ride could be completed in one day with hard riding, and so we intended to arrive the following afternoon. It would take the legion around two more days, despite their early start, though we expected to see their cavalry there already. Now the extent of the attack was known, the Emperor sent orders as we rode to the Twenty Second, as well as the local auxiliary cohorts, to return to their forts: a precaution in case the occupation at Confluentes were a distraction from a main thrust elsewhere. He also sent a messenger north to the Germanican fleet to set sail from Aggripensium. They could be of use if the Alemanni put up more resistance than expected- and would at least protect the river traffic. Maximian had also decided that the problem would be best resolved by infantry- which, according to one of our scouts, would not take long as the forts were in serious need of repair, the town wall at Confluentes itself being in ruins.

While this caused another explosion of frustration from Maximian due to the lack of foresight, the rest of us pragmatically regarded it as unexpected good fortune. Cavalry would not be much use, as the Alemanni would flee back across the river at the first sign of defeat.

◆◆◆

We arrived as we had hoped, four turmae of the First Minerva's cavalry wing already having stopped short of Confluentes, their lances stabbed into the ground beside them while their horses peacefully cropped grass nearby. The men were playing dice, drying out after fording the Moselle downstream- the bridge being inaccessible due to the Alemanni having taken the western fort that overlooked it- and awaiting orders.

Maximian left them there while we rode on to assess what we faced. Riding over the remains of the wall, all but levelled with brick and stone scattered in the deep grass, that effectively extended across the base of what amounted to a very rough triangle, the two rivers forming the other sides, we approached the forts opposite each other across the apex. The settlement- not even a village really- had emptied the morning after the attack and all that remained were a few scattered thatched houses of timber lying on the short road joining the two forts. As we emerged on to the road itself, we could see that the forts had been fully repaired, standing tall, strong and apparently impregnable. Tall, bearded, long-haired tribesmen shouted abuse from within, spitting at us over the ramparts of their sturdy defenses and shaking their longbows and spears in defiance. A few fired their arrows, no doubt hoping to catch us in a crossfire, and we retreated once more amongst the huts.

Maximian gathered his main commanders around him once far enough from the threat and swore long and hard in renewed frustration, even to the extent of throwing his shield to the floor in his anger.

"Why was this not reported? These tribes must have been rebuilding the forts for several weeks! Yet we heard nothing."

My father nodded sympathetically. "We cannot take the forts with the few men we have. They are too well defended. We will need to await the legion and then attack."

"But we need siege weaponry that we do not have!" Maximian continued to rage. "And no expertise in the making of such weapons. It would take a month to bring them here! We would lose many men in a frontal attack without the necessary equipment. But we must act now! I have an empire to rule! I do not wish to remain here longer than I have to. Worlds have been lost due to unwarranted caution."

The assorted commanders mumbled their agreement, none daring to voice an opinion in the face of their leader's fury.

With what in hindsight can only have been the audacity of youth, I stepped into the circle. "Lord, I have an idea."

The Emperor stared at me. "You, a beardless boy? When none of my seasoned warriors can answer me?"

My father spoke up. "Lord, I must speak for him. He has often been found to be right. He saved me from Quintus' men when we travelled through the mountains- and the Emperor Diocletian's life too."

Maximian replied grudgingly, "Tell me then lad. But make it quick. Do not be offended should we laugh overmuch."

◆◆◆

In the absence of any alternative ideas, Maximian decided to adopt my suggestion- with adaptations that would make it even more effective. The key to success was to be bringing the Alemanni out of the forts, our apparent vulnerability tempting them into an attack that would appear to be an easy enough victory to warrant their leaving the safety and security of the walls protecting them.

As a result, we made a great show of riding away down the Moselle valley, the First Minerva's dismounted men starting on their evening rations as we left them behind, their hobbled horses grazing amongst the trees alongside the road. Except for occasional shouts from west and east as the tribesmen reminded us that they were there with imaginative insults, it became a serene and tranquil setting as we departed. We wished to give the impression that the dismounted cavalry were complacently settling in for a siege, feeling no threat from the forts and awaiting reinforcements. The assumption should be that we were fetching these men.

However, as soon as had entered the treeline on the slight incline just short of Confluentes' peninsula, and the cover of its darkness, we stopped. Maximian ordered sixty of the experienced men we had brought from Augusta Treverorum, to ride to the ford that the First Minerva had found and cross to the opposite bank. Their task would be to re-take the two forts. The rest of us were told to get some sleep.

The night was overcast and warmer than might have been expected. Given we would be sleeping amongst the dense oaks and beeches, the ground cover from old leaves would also provide us with some comfort. The campsite of the First's cavalry was just visible through the foliage that still clung to some branches, and, as we tried to rest as ordered, we listened as they made a great show of ransacking the settlement's houses.

There were shouts of delight accompanying what appeared to be finds of strong beer and wine. We watched while darkness fell as they had a raucous time, attempting to outdo one another in their performances as they reeled around the campsite. The bravest even approached the forts to drunkenly and mockingly offer a drink to the warriors inside, moving into arrow-range to do so. Sleep gradually overcame even the most hard-headed, and men staggered back to their equipment or just lay where they had fallen around the fire at the centre, snoring loudly in their contentment.

◆◆◆

I was woken an hour before dawn. Maximian beckoned to me to join him and my father, and we stepped carefully out of the treeline for a better view. The embers in the middle of the First's campsite glowed brightly in the early morning. There was a sudden burst of sparks as a half-asleep legionary swayed his way to the fire and added more logs (a nice touch, I thought). A light mist had built across the Rhine and now drifted across. The outlines of the men lying on the ground, wrapped in their cloaks, could be dimly seen through the pale darkness. The sight was one of peace. In a few moments the sleepers would awake, unwrap themselves from their cloaks, stretch and shake off the dawn cold, staggering to their feet.

The scene was set.

However, the camp was by now a carefully crafted appearance. Most of those appearing to be asleep on the ground were empty cloaks under which lay the baggage rolls that each cavalryman carried behind his saddle, the legionaries having cautiously crept their way during the night to join us in the woods. A few had remained voluntarily to present a more reliable appearance through occasional movement and sound. The Emperor raised his hand and we saw distant eyes glinting in what little remained of the firelight as vague shapes turned cautiously in our direction.

He dropped his hand.

The men returned to their feigned slumber. They were ready. Now to wait.

We stepped back into the trees, thanking the Unconquered Sun that all looked as my plan had indicated it should.

Moments later a sentry approached and spoke, having waited for his moment: "Lord, several of the enemy have left the forts. They conferred on the road; and there are now men low in the long grass nearing the camp." He focused on a point beyond the First Minerva, "There, lord."

"You have far better eyes than I, Cassius," Maximian chuckled softly. "I will believe you!"

Watching carefully for some time, the sentry eventually spoke. "They are returning to the forts lord. None went close enough to see the true nature of the sleepers- they will have been wary of waking them."

The darkness was starting to ease and the murk was clearing slightly. This combination, I thought as I watched the soldier silently make his way back to the men hidden in the depths of the wood to warn them of imminent action, would make the campsite a perfect killing-ground. The same thought should be occurring to the tribesmen as well- they must attack at any moment if they were to take advantage of apparent vulnerability.

A scout came towards us. A skilled tracker of Alemanni heritage himself, he had been set to watch the forts from as close to them as he could get. He was very damp as the mist had started to settle on the grass and he had had to crawl away from the forts before entering the trees.

"Speak, man," said Maximian impatiently.

"Lord. There is a force leaving each fort and making for the campsite."

"Horsed or on foot?" asked Constantius.

"Horsed sir. These invaders, despite the time taken to repair the forts, will be seeking to test Roman resolve. They will be wanting to avoid sacrificing the lives of their tribesmen. The Alemanni avoid direct confrontation if possible. It is possible that this is a single warchief seeking to make a name for himself, to boast of his feats in the great hall."

Maximian rubbed his hands in gleeful anticipation. "I am looking forward to this! How many?"

"They have left guards on the walls of the forts- but it would appear the entire raiding party other than these few: perhaps a century altogether. Alemanni warriors would not pass up a chance for such easy glory lord!"

We could now see the outlines of the men through the lightening mist, their spears and throwing axes glinting occasionally as shards of sparse sunlight struck them. Constantius, as Praetorian Prefect, sent a quick message back to the men in the woods warning them about keeping weaponry covered to avoid any hint of an ambush.

The tribesmen started to organise themselves into what our tracker told us was known as the 'boar's head'- the chief at the front and centre, with his men arranging themselves in order of importance behind him. We knew we had done all we could to prepare and now we must trust our men to perform their roles. As we watched through the half-light and from the darkness of the trees hiding us, the Alemanni brought their spears parallel to the ground. They were about to charge, intending to lance the men on the ground as they passed and be through the camp before any could rub the sleep out of their eyes.

And they charged, their light horses seeming to float over the ground due to the remaining haze, the dragon banner of their warchief flying above them, the serpent on it undulating out of the twilight towards the camp. They raced in silence, waiting until the last second to unleash the awful howl that had so often brought them victory by terror as the bowels of those opposing them turned to water. Even experienced Roman warriors had been known to turn and flee at the sound. I could only imagine the impact this would have had, had our men truly been asleep and unaware.

The scene appeared somehow unreal to me even as it took place before my eyes. A sudden strike of remaining moonlight on extended spear caught my eye, and I gasped with the beauty of the scene. Never before having been a mere observer of battle, it fixed in my mind for a moment, more striking than any imperial artist's best work. The deep blue of the night, the black of the horses and their riders, the lighter blue of the river behind. The only colour was the red-orange of the coals forming a bright if trifling counterpoint to the darkness as the enemy attacked.

But dreaming had no place at this time, and I shook my head in rebuke, glancing sidelong at Maximian and Constantius to check that they had not noticed my inattention. The warrior-riders came on fast, hooves thundering into soft turf, clods of grass thrown back from the sprinting horses- their teeth bared in the joy of it- the Alemanni screamed that feared war-cry at the very last moment and struck hard. The outer lines of sleepers were lanced where they lay, confused tribesmen finding their spears held in bundles of clothing. They lifted these aloft to examine as they galloped on through the camp, battle-joy turning swiftly to puzzlement and confusion as they slowed their headlong rush.

Some of the men left under cloaks in the centre of the camp were stabbed, rolling in agony away from the questing points looking for further blood. They had a task to do and they knew the risks, I told myself. They had volunteered for this. Sufficient remained for the role they had to play.

The raiders milled around the centre of the camp, bewildered at this turn of events, comparing the various objects caught on their weapons.

Maximian brought his arm down sharply. His trumpeter had appeared behind the Emperor and he blew a sharp, piercing note. The war-band stopped still as one, complete and total shock staying them where they were. The undiscovered Romans left in the camp threw off their cloaks and leapt up from where they lay. They roared at the horses around them, coming at the animals from the side to scare them, hitting out with the flats of their blades. The horses were as taken by surprise as the men riding them. They reared and several threw their riders. The soldiers' task was to hamstring as many as they could while avoiding the flailing hooves. The enemy warriors dropped their spears swiftly to free their hands for close-in fighting, disentangling themselves from the clothing they had swept up in their attack.

But the Romans, many of them former legionaries and as nimble on their feet as on horseback, were too fast. They cut at the horses' legs, slicing tendons before swords could be drawn or any defence offered.

The air was filled with the sharp screams of injured horses and the heavy grunts of men struggling for their lives. The occasional war-cry rang out, as if to propel forward whichever soldier it was more urgently to his task. Horses were falling all around the central fire. Tribesmen fell with them. They were stabbed where they lay, or tried to fight from the ground, often despairingly from beneath their mount- a battle always won by the standing Roman.

One fell from his horse into the embers at the centre of the camp and the fire flared vividly, the man screaming and staggering out of the flames, beating at his clothes. The legionaries in the trees with us, having gathered light javelins from everyone else, now stepped out from their hiding place and threw them. They aimed high to avoid the unprotected volunteers. One warrior, marked clearly by his long hair and heavy beard outlined in the firelight, rode his horse into the melee to try to turn the tide. He was targeted by my father's swiftly shouted order, knocked hard back off his horse and on to the ground as three spears hit him at once. I saw him gazing down at his stomach from which two sharp points stood out, watching in wonderment as his life ebbed away. His head fell forward, blood suddenly gushing from his mouth.

Attacked from above and below by a camp full of men that had appeared to be soundly dreaming in the land of Morpheus but moments before, even the bravest of soldiers would have broken.

Maximian had meanwhile prepared for the final act in this piece of theatre. All that had happened so far had taken place in the space of a few breaths. Covered by the noise of the battle, the remaining soldiers had, under his personal command while Constantius managed the battle at the campsite, already moved further back into the woods to where their well-trained horses stood quietly, most of the First's hobbled mounts having been gathered as soon as night had fallen. There was, however, no need for silence now given the noise of both men and animals coming from the site of the battle. The Emperor's soldiers climbed astride and made their way calmly to the right flank, parallel with the Rhine and the Alemanni homeland on the other side. I hurried to join them, determined that I would not miss out on this final fight. When the enemy broke, as they would in the next few moments, it was only to be expected that they would flee back where they had come from. Safety lay in the forts or across the Rhine and they had the strength and speed of their horses to rely on.

It happened just as we had hoped. As the tribesmen turned to flee the camp, the sun broke clear of the horizon. The mist swiftly and suddenly turned transparent and cleared. I saw from the height of my horse that the Alemanni had left at least half of their men, and several of their horses, on the ground. Some warriors were running, and such was the skill of those still on horseback that they were swept up to ride with their compatriots, two to a horse. It would be a shame to have to kill such men, I thought; for they had fought well against an overwhelming ambush.

And these remaining few, looking over their shoulders for any indication of pursuit, would not realise the threat in front of them until it was too late. They would now know it was an ambush, but would not have been allowed time to fully consider the implications of this.

The Emperor ordered, "Walk!"

His trumpeter signalled the same. His cavalry moved at once, in a long line consisting of two rows, towards the tribesmen riding fast towards the forts. The intention was to take them from the side. I looked up at Sol Invictus and thanked him. For I had just seen several banners appear above the forts to east and west, the Emperor's symbol, a purple Knot of Hercules, clearly visible on them. The cavalry we had sent across the Moselle the night before had been ordered to make their way across the bridge from the north as soon as the Alemanni attack started. Splitting into two groups, they were to make their way to each fort and take advantage of the sentries' attention being entirely on the massacre at the First Minerva's campsite. We had gambled on the tribesmen being either so sure of their success- or, far less likely, needing to guarantee a swift return- that they would have left the gates open. It had worked! The gates were now closed and there would be no refuge there for the men we faced.

I turned my attention back to the warriors ahead, now only a hundred metres away. The men, their attention fixed on the forts, had also seen the banners appear and they swerved with their warchief's change of direction as he realised his only chance now was to swim the Rhine- but bringing him into direct conflict with the force on his flank that he had sought to avoid. The raiders' horses missed a step as if they too were re-considering the course they were taking.

"Our turn now", bellowed the Emperor, enjoying the moment of the full plan being revealed. "Lower spears!"

As one, we lowered our lances and prepared for the shock of the fleeing men hitting the line. And they came on as fast as before. I found myself focusing on a large warrior near the front of the wedge that formed, more by accident than by conscious decision. This was no boar's head. Being at a disadvantage, the braver fighters naturally moved to the front of the charge while those more eager to keep their lives slowed their horses so that they would not have to face the first sweep of the Roman swords. The warrior charging at me had a long moustache, styled, I saw in a moment of frozen serenity, like two blonde wings sweeping back from a strong-jawed face. He was large, even for a tribesman, and very powerfully built. The warrior's sword, as he drew it and pointed it at me, seemed twice the size of my own. I rarely regretted my choice of weapon, as I found the sword much more flexible and effective than the unwieldy spear, but the thought did occur to me now due to the length of his reach. Every detail of the man's face impressed itself upon him: the teeth bared in a taut grimace of rage and focus, eyes ferocious and sparking with fury and frustration at being outwitted. I drew back my arm as my opponent drew near and timed my blow much more accurately than the tribesman. Whether he was still in shock from the ambush or blinded by the sun which had risen behind us, his strike was too slow. My stabbed sword penetrated under the raider's armpit as he tried to bring his weapon down in a great arc on my head. But by the time it was a foot away the blow had already faded in time with his own life, the swing having taken too long compared with my simple thrust. For my strike, perfectly aimed, honed now after several years of training and experience, had gone deep into the warrior's side, cutting under his ribcage. His sword finished its arc, all energy behind it lost as it diverted to my right, striking my shoulder a light blow and then falling from the warrior's hand as his strength left him. The horse's momentum carried it on through the centre of our lines and away, the big warrior slumped loosely over its mane. Blood sheeted the animal's side with crimson from the fatal wound. The same momentum pulled my sword clear.

I looked over my shoulder as my horse continued through the very slowest of the enemy. They posed little threat, as the disorganised flight had petered out on the solid barricade of our disciplined troops. In individual combat such as this had become, the disciplined Roman cavalrymen almost without fail won their own fights, destroying the rest of the warband. The fact that the raiders were so heavily outnumbered and had lost so many men already no doubt played its part. Maximian's voice sounded once more over the battle.

"Let the rest run lads! We need someone to report back that this raid has failed. It will serve as a warning to the rest that this border is no longer undefended." He paused for effect, finishing with, "Order has returned to the empire!"

Those who were not still fighting cheered his words with gusto as five tribesmen plunged into the water. Swimming frantically with their horses across the river, one or two of our men who had not heard the Emperor's words fired arrows at their exposed backs and heads, only three making it to the safety of the right bank.

Maximian grinned, "That will do nicely!"

I cantered over to Hosius. He had leapt off his horse and was cleaning it on a tribesman's tunic. He greeted me, sounding slightly disappointed.

"Well, that was simpler even than I had expected! Killed my man when my spear caught his horse and it threw him."

"Any injuries?" I asked.

"Only to my pride. I underestimated him and he gave me this for my trouble." He showed me a sword-cut on his forearm that would heal quickly.

"That does not even need stitching! What are you complaining about? Best get some vinegar on it though."

Hosius laughed and the two of us made our way back to the First Minerva's campsite to join my father. He had a very serious look on his face as we approached.

Urgently taking me to one side, he spoke very softly, "Son, listen carefully. Though I believe I know the Emperor well enough by now, it would be wise to keep quiet as to your part in the planning. No emperor wishes for glory to go elsewhere, and few will say this was your idea. For my part, I am proud of your stepping forward and of your strategy.

It worked better than could ever have been expected and you deserve much praise and glory. But do not expect anything of Maximian."

As we set off to return to Augusta Treverorum, our few casualties resting in a commandeered cart at the back of the column, Maximian rode past me on his way to the head.

He grunted and said, almost inaudibly, "Good idea boy."

My father was to my right. Having heard, he raised one eyebrow at me to indicate surprise. And that was all.

◆◆◆

Despite our victory, when we returned to Mogontiacum, having collected my mother and Constantius having spent some time closeted with Maximian in discussions as to his plans for the future, my father was downcast. He refused to share the reasons for this mood. I struggled to understand why he would not speak to me, and I visited my parents' home more frequently in the hope that he would volunteer the reason why he felt as he did. I knew that eventually there must be an invasion of Britannia and a reckoning with Carausius; so I assumed at first that this must be the reason why. He enjoyed Mogontiacum, and Helena seemed to be very happy here; so perhaps it was merely the thought of leaving the city and facing possible death and loss as a result. But this did not really make sense to me: he had dealt with such things many times before, so why now would his face be so sad whenever I spoke to him? He rarely smiled, even when my mother entered the room as we spoke; if anything, his disposition would worsen even further when she joined us, and arguments between them were more common. These were usually initiated by him, my mother's tranquil responses provoking him to further excess of anger.

After two months of this, I began to avoid my home. I had no desire to be in such a place and found no peace there as

I had done previously. I spoke less and less to my parents, avoiding them even when I saw them in the forum.

Hosius eventually spoke to me one day as he had seen the distance grow, and I knew there must be a resolution. So when my father sent a request asking me to come I visited my parents once more, determined to find out what had caused such a change.

◆◆◆

I confronted my father in his study. It was early summer yet the air was unseasonably hot, still and sultry, moisture forming on your body as soon as you moved. The window that gave on to the Rhine was wide open yet had no effect on the heat in the room. As I sat facing him, the tension grew and neither of us spoke. Until my father picked up a tablet lying in front of him, a slight frown on his face drawing down his eyebrows and causing a droplet of sweat to appear. "Son. I have here a complaint from the commander of the school stating that you beat another cadet severely with a blunted sword in a mock battle two days ago. This is not how you usually behave. Is there a reason for it?"

I sighed, a perverse gratitude filling me that at least this challenge meant I could address the issue at the centre of things.

"Father, I find an anger in me that I struggle to control. For circumstances have changed around me, but I am unable to say how or why. Your behaviour is unusual, yet you refuse to acknowledge anything."

His frown deepened, his voice strengthening. "And you assume you have the right to question me on this? What if it is something that affects the entire future of the empire? That I am unable to speak of?"

"Then surely that means it is something that affects me!" I knew I spoke impatiently, even petulantly. "And I have a right to know as a result…"

He changed the subject, his voice becoming harder and more terse. "But we do not talk of such events. We are speaking of you. Of your harming a fellow cadet in a mock fight. What is your explanation?"

Frustrated at his avoidance of my query, I spoke impulsively and too hastily, "My explanation, then, father, is that it is your fault."

"Mine? How dare you!"

He started to rise in his anger, and I foresaw, were I not to explain quickly, his calling for Lucipor and my imminent ejection from the house. Or, even worse, his four guards to appear from the front door and their escorting me back to the barracks. Either way, humiliation. So I spoke fast to forestall this.

"Father, I know something has happened. I know that it is not good. You have been angered more easily than ever in the three years I have known you. The sight of me seems to upset you; the sight of my mother, even more so. And it has been so since our return from Augusta Treverorum. What has changed?"

I spoke as forcefully as I could while attempting to keep a balance of respect in my tone.

He slowly sat back down, his taut eyebrows and pursed lips relaxing and his anger turning swiftly to something else, something indefinable but with a sense of sorrow in his movement. As he took his seat, his shoulders slumped and it was his turn to sigh with a note of resignation in the sound.

"I must speak of it at some point. I hoped to do it at a time of my own choosing; but it may be that I would never have had the courage had you not pushed me." He looked at me strangely. "Please, Constantine, do not judge me for what I am about to tell you. Remember that all I do, I do for the good of this empire that I love and give my life to serve."

I sat forward, eyes wide, anticipating the worst; he slumped back in his seat as I did so, closing his own eyes as if to avoid seeing my reaction to what he was about to say.

"The Emperor Maximian has asked me to take command of the war against the Franks."

I leapt from my seat in excitement. This was the opposite of what I had expected given his words. "At last! Father, no man has deserved his opportunity more. How could this possibly be bad news? I am delighted for you…"

My protestations of pleasure slowly faded as I realised he was not responding; in fact, he still had his own eyes closed. He spoke slowly and with shame into the ensuing silence.

"There are, though, conditions attached. To gain this promotion, I must marry."

"But you are married father! That is no problem!"

He flapped at me with his hand to sit back down, his eyes finally opening. "I must marry into his family. I must divorce your mother and send her away." He spoke quickly to explain. "Maximian needs me to secure the Rhine in preparation for the invasion of Britain. He himself will be building the fleet."

But my mouth had opened in shock and I spoke over his words, not hearing the explanation but reeling off every expletive I had ever heard through being around the army and its rough crew of soldiers.

"They cannot ask that father! They cannot! You love her!" And then, as the secondary thought occurred to me. "And who must you marry?"

"That, son", he sat up sharply, "is the true heart of the matter." Having told me the worst, his spine appeared to stiffen and his voice grew stronger. "Theodora is to be my new wife."

"Who is Theodora?" I snarled back at him.

"Theodora is Maximian's stepdaughter."

My blank expression must have said it all, and he explained to me patiently. "To command a war of this sort, leading legions, auxiliaries and federated tribes, the Emperor believes I must be tied by marriage in order to guarantee my trustworthiness given the usurpations over the last decades. Besides which, though she is supposedly his stepdaughter, my sources tell me that she is his actual daughter. So the Augustus would become my father-in-law."

It was my turn to collapse back in my seat. After a few moments of consideration, I said sharply: "Does my mother know?"

He nodded guiltily. "She does. She understands. She leaves soon."

I leapt to my feet, whirled and ran from his room as would a child. As ever with my mother, she was ready for me and spoke first when I found her in the kitchens.

"Not here my boy. Come with me."

She spoke gently but firmly and led me out into the garden at the back of their villa. She sat me down on a bench and took my hand in hers. Her hand was cool on my palm.

"Constantine, this has to happen. It is the only wise and sensible course, and I suppose I always knew that what I had was too good to last."

This final comment would have sounded bitter from anyone else, but from my mother it just sounded accepting. Nonetheless, shaking her head as if realising how it could have come across, she changed her words, "No, not too good to last. More that I have been so blessed to have found what I have. I never expected to. And we have had three years. That is more than many imperial servants. I know that my God will bring good out of this, though I cannot see how just now." She spoke as if persuading herself. "For he is God; I am but me."

"But where will you go? What will you do?" I burst out. "How could Constantius do this to you? To us?"

"Oh my boy," she said as she stroked my face. "Never to you! His greatest fear about all of this is losing you. He could endure the loss of one of his family; but never both of us."

"If he can keep me", I said darkly, implying a threat I knew would never become a reality.

She smiled at me, knowing this as she knew me. "As for me, I have always wanted to go home."

"To Naissus? How would you suffer the complaints and whining of Lucius?"

"No," she shook her head. "Not to Naissus. To Bithynia, where we came from when I was a child." Her eyes glazed over, a wistful look on her face. "I remember it so well. The warmth of the coast and the cool of the mountains and forests. The fruit, especially the scent of the ripening oranges…" Her eyes came back into focus. "I should very much like to spend my days there. It would be a comfort."

I felt the trickle of what I knew to be a self-pitying tear making its slow way down my face. "But what would I do without you?"

She laughed out loud at that, a delightful tinkle of glee. "You would do very well Constantine! I have heard from your father of your successes, though you speak but little of them when you come to visit."

I turned as I heard the crunch of a distant footstep on gravel. My father had entered the courtyard and was making his way through the flowering bushes to join us. His walk was hesitant, and he stared at the ground as he stepped through the garden. He stopped several paces away and then looked up tentatively, the guilt written transparently on his face. Unsure of our reaction, he waited. My world had been turned on its head in the course of such a short space of time and I did not know how to respond, my foundations shaken.

My mother, as usual, made the first move.

"Come and join us, husband." She spoke quietly.

The final word could so easily have been meant ironically but she spoke it as if tasting the meaning for the first time; and drawing pleasure from the sensation.

"Constantine", he started and broke off. Then his words came out in a rush. "Constantine, I have been speaking to Maximian about you. I meant to tell you earlier before you left. As you are so close to your mother, he has suggested that, due to your rapid progress amongst the cadets, you are ready to take up some imperial duties. The obvious place to do so would be at the court of the Emperor Diocletian himself."

I spoke dully, resigned to my loss. "And how would that help my mother or me?"

He said, "Because the emperor has his headquarters in Nicomedia, as you know- and your mother wishes to live in Drepanum, less than a day's journey on a good horse along the coast." He looked at me, pleased, as if waiting for congratulations on this piece of information.

"I will consider it. I need time."

A slight frown came over his face at my response; but my tone had not changed, so he turned and left us.

We watched him go, and then my mother turned to me and spoke carefully.

"You really should consider it. I think it is the best that can be done. Your father could even be an emperor one day my son: this is the future we have been waiting for. Not in the way we wanted it, nor how we expected it- but that is often how my God works. Imagine what this could mean for you. And I would be so proud if my son were emperor after him, though I would not be able to share the joy of it with my husband."

I looked at her steadily, her dreams written on her face. I whispered in reply, "It would seem like a betrayal of all you have done for me, mother. Not the reward you deserve for your faithfulness to me and your loyalty to… him."

I struggled to say his name, the anger still burning within.

"But this is normal life within the imperial family. Connections and relations are what bring power within reach. It is not usual to marry for love, to live a happy but private life, to choose your future for yourself. We have been fortunate."

I just looked at her. It did not feel that way on that day in that garden.

◆◆◆

It took longer to organise my mother's departure than we had anticipated. I was grateful for the opportunity to think and to decide. It was early autumn by the time we gathered the caravan that was to accompany Helena on her journey south outside the villa that she and Constantius had occupied for what now seemed to me to be too short a time. My men formed up on me as a guard for her as she climbed gracefully into her litter.

I had eventually decided that my father had orchestrated us all as well as he possibly could, and Nicomedia would be the best place for me. Maximian had given me my first independent command with the order to accompany my mother, ensuring her safety and that of her household. There were sixteen cavalrymen in my command, Hosius acting as my optio; while my mother in fact took very few people with her. She was naturally a modest person and had never fully taken to the entourage expected of a governor's wife when we lived in Salona. Lucipor accompanied us as the closest thing to a dowry that Helena had brought with her into her marriage to Constantius. He reverted to her as part of the divorce. But, other than her litter bearers and three maids, she took little else.

She turned to me as the slaves lifted her: "I brought nothing, I leave with nothing." She chuckled a little at that and added, "Other than the two remaining men in my life."

I grinned at her, reconciled to the situation and determined to make the best of it. The worst part for my mother had been her repudiation by my father in front of witnesses. Despite the humiliation of that, borne by her with head held high, she had continued to be grateful and to look forward. Without a backward glance at the villa, I ordered eight men to ride in front of the litters carrying the women and eight to the back. The men mounted their horses and moved into position while Hosius and I made our way to the front. My father was nowhere to be seen. While my parents had spent as much time as they could together over the winter, given the circumstances and the offence that could potentially be caused to his new wife should this be too obvious, I had found his choices very hard to forgive and avoided him.

The long, dry road beckoned to us and I shouted at the top of my voice, "March!"

We left Mogontiacum behind us and I felt a freedom I had never felt before as we did so, as well as a sense of exhilaration at what the future held. The fraught issues of the last few months were now resolved and there was little purpose in dwelling on them. I looked up at Sol Invictus, blazing in the sky as we rode over the first hill beyond the city's boundary, and swore to him: my mother and father had given me the opportunities- I would make the most of them. Like my god, nothing would conquer me.

Historical Note

I thought it would be worthwhile adding some small detail to describe the extent of the accuracy of this novel.

The third century before the accession of Diocletian was a time of great turbulence with many emperors dying unnatural deaths. In fact, for a number it remains uncertain as to how they died- including, for example, Carus and his son Numerian. The same applies to their precise origins. As a result, this version of Constantine's origins is partly based on Eusebius' 'Life of Constantine', though he does not go into any detail.

Constantine's father was Constantius, and Constantius was governor of Dalmatia when Diocletian assumed power in 284AD. Events surrounding the Emperor's accession are accurate based on the sources; and the death of Lucius Aper is similar to that described here.

Of course, Constantius' involvement in planning for the showdown with Carinus, his men's journey to the River Margus and the flight down it are all figments of my imagination. However, there really was a Battle of the

Margus between Diocletian and Carinus in 285AD, and the latter was unexpectedly killed by a Praetorian Prefect called Aristobulus. I do find it hard to see how Constantius could not have been involved in this given his proximity.

The following raid by the Roxolani on Naissus is, again, a product of my creativity with the facts; however, raids across the Danube were not unusual- and Diocletian's responding with a raid into Dacia is supported by the evidence.

Finally, Maximian's inauguration in 287AD was famously interrupted by an invasion across the river- though we do not know any details regarding what this looked like. And Constantius was ordered to marry Maximian's daughter, with Constantine and Helena leaving to join Diocletian's court in Nicomedia.

The evidence for this period is hard to come by due to the chaos of the period, with many of the more 'traditional' elements of the Roman Empire having disappeared altogether or being in flux. This makes the story-teller's job easier in some ways; but far harder in the sense that complete accuracy is impossible. No doubt this is always the case for the writer of historical fiction; but I feel I must add this caveat!

Note, finally, that I have reduced some distances and changed some timings to ensure that the tale fits together well.

Cast Of Characters

Most of the Republican Roman naming conventions relating to praenomen, nomen and cognomen had become irrelevant, confused or (effectively) meaningless by the late imperial period. As a result, I have used only a single name to identify individuals in almost all cases.

Aemilius- temporary bodyguard of Constantine.
Albanus- prefect of the XIII Gemina.
Antonius- father of Hosius and commander of a wing of the Dalmatian Horse.
Aristobulus- Praetorian Prefect and consul under the Emperor Carinus.
Aldis- Dacian immigrant.
Antius- centurion and frumentarius.
Carausius- self-styled Emperor of the North, led a rebellion in Britannia.
Carinus- Co-Emperor, responsible for the western Empire with, first, his father Carus; and then his brother, Numerian.

Carus- Emperor and then Co-Emperor with his son, Carinus.
Crispus- prefect of the V Macedonica.
Constantine- son of Helena and grandson of Lucius.
Constantius- Governor of Dalmatia.
Diocletian- cavalry commander in the army of the Emperor Carus.
Dotos- Dacian immigrant and magistrate of Naissus, spokesperson for the Dacian immigrant population.
Felix- Constantius' chief of staff.
Galerius- cavalry commander in the army of Carus and supporter of Diocletian.
Gratian- prefect of the I Parthica.
Helena- mother of Constantine and daughter of Lucius.
Hosius- friend of Constantine, son of Antonius.
Julian- governor of Pannonia.
Julian- prefect of the IV Flavia Felix.
Lucipor- Helena's Nubian slave.
Lucius- Owner of a Naissus road-station on the Via Militaris, father of Helena and grandfather of Constantine.
Lucius Aper- father-in-law of the Emperor Numerian and Praetorian Prefect.
Marcus- prefect of the XI Claudia.
Marsallus- commander of an irregular troop of scouts.
Maximian- prefect of the VII Claudia; formerly commander in the army of the Emperor Carus and supporter of Diocletian.
Numerian- Son of the Emperor Carus and Co-Emperor with him, and then with his brother Carinus.
Quintus- Praetorian centurion under the Emperor Carinus.
Rasparagnus- councillor to the Roxolani king, Zanticus.
Rassogos- Dacian immigrant, son of Dotos.
Romulus- frumentarius.

Remus- frumentarius.
Scipio- frumentarius and mentor to Constantine.
Titus- temporary bodyguard of Hosius.
Zanticus- king of the Roxolani, a tribe within the Sarmatian confederation.

Printed in Great Britain
by Amazon